Alfred Owen Legge

The Unpopular King

The Life and Times of Richard III. Volume 1

Alfred Owen Legge

The Unpopular King
The Life and Times of Richard III. Volume 1

ISBN/EAN: 9783744675291

Printed in Europe, USA, Canada, Australia, Japan

Cover: Foto ©Raphael Reischuk / pixelio.de

More available books at **www.hansebooks.com**

King Richard the III.

The Original in the Royal Collection.

Sign Manual of K. Richard the 3.

From an Original Letter in the Possession of

John Thane

THE UNPOPULAR KING:

The Life and Times of Richard III.

BY

ALFRED O. LEGGE, F.C.H.S.,

AUTHOR OF "THE LIFE OF PIUS IX.," "THE TEMPORAL POWER OF THE PAPACY,"
"A LIFE OF CONSECRATION," ETC.

"And if by chaunce thou light of some speache that seemeth dark, consider of
it with judgment, before thou condemne the worke; for in many places he is
driven both to praise and blame with one breath, which in readinge will seeme
hard, and in action appeare plaine."—*Promos and Cassandra.*

IN TWO VOLUMES

VOL. I.

LONDON:

WARD AND DOWNEY

12, YORK STREET, COVENT GARDEN, W.C.

1885.

I inscribe these Volumes to

MARY,

TO WHOSE FILIAL LOVE AND UNTIRING DEVOTION,

IN A SEASON OF DARKNESS AND SUFFERING AND OF THE SHADOW
OF DEATH,

THEY OWE THEIR EXISTENCE.

PREFACE.

THE justification of another life of "The Unpopular King" lies in the fact that no portion of our history has been more disfigured by passion, prejudice, inaccuracy, and wilful perversion, than the brief reign of the sovereign whom Mr. Sharon Turner has described as "this almost proscribed King." It is true that none of these blemishes disfigure the work of the latest and distinguished historian of this period. At the same time it is precisely because Mr. Gairdner's conclusions do not appear warranted, even by the valuable material which he has rendered available to the historical student, that I have attempted this slight contribution towards the elucidation of a period of our history, and the formation of a true estimate of its principal actor, which the paucity of impartial records has beset with difficulty.

The indefatigable labours of Mr. Sharon Turner, and the pungent criticisms of Horace Walpole, have laid the student of history under obligations which it would be impossible to exaggerate. But in their day the Public Records—the issue of which, during the past half-century, has shown how very defective were our ancient historians—were inaccessible, by reason of their marvellous abundance. In the first "Report of the Commissioners on the Public Records," it was stated that so voluminous were the State documents contained in the

Tower, that the timbers which supported the roof of the room adjoining the chapel were, some of them, so decayed and sunk by the weight of the records as to require immediate repair. In the Rolls Chapel these documents were deposited in presses round the walls, so constructed as not to excite the notice and divert the attention of worshippers. Every available place—not excepting the pulpit and the seats in the pews, which had been converted into boxes—was put in requisition for their storage. It is impossible to doubt that many of the conclusions of Mr. Sharon Turner would have been modified, had these uniquely rich and comprehensive archives been accessible to him. Horace Walpole was too much occupied with the task of exposing fallacies to produce a constructive history, or to give a living distinctness to the portraiture of the King, whose character he has done so much to redeem alike from the slanders of prejudice and ignorance, and the mists of exaggeration and legend.

The virtues and vices of Richard III.. were strangely mingled, and Walpole leaves no impression upon his readers of that very wantonness of intellectual wealth, that greatness of soul, and generosity—boundless, and incapable of exhaustion because of his instinctive scorn of meanness—which characterised the King. Nor has he shown how Richard's better nature was gradually warped and dwarfed by the ingratitude, the faithlessness, and selfishness of the men and women who had experienced most of his bounty and generous confidence.

The hidden stores of knowledge which Mr. Gairdner alone has brought to light, destroy all reliance on the finality of previous inquiries in relation to any period of our country's history. Hence the disingenuous suppression of facts by earlier writers on the later Plantagenet period, encourages us to go back to the old materials for new facts, with a reasonable expectation that the light thus derived will enable us to form juster views of a much misunderstood epoch of history.

Allegiance to truth requires us to weigh impartially the evidences upon which history is based, to eschew paradox, to discard every ascertained gloss or myth, however long and closely it may have been associated with our beliefs. The earliest printed chronicles relating to the time of Richard III. were not published until after the accession of the Tudor dynasty. They contain a mass of fable and misstatement, and, with the exception of the "Croyland Chronicle," their authors are basely subservient to that dynasty. The difficult duty of the historian is patiently to explore, collate, and analyse them, gratefully accepting their help in arriving at facts, but not allowing them to influence his historical judgment. Where we cannot have certainty, there are degrees of probability in the narratives of the early chroniclers, upon which careful and comprehensive inquiry may enable us to bring such collateral evidence to bear as shall determine the measures of their value as legitimate sources of history. One writer—as the Croyland chronicler—may be a good authority for the facts of an epoch; another—as Dr. Warkworth—for the acts of an individual; and a third—as Fabyan—for what passed before his eyes; yet all may be wholly untrustworthy in other directions.

It is unnecessary to discuss here the relative value of the authorities upon which I have relied. Their mere enumeration would more than occupy a page, and the more important of them are referred to in the foot-notes. I thankfully acknowledge much kind assistance received from Dr. Garnett, and the assistant librarians in the British Museum, in the consultation of the Harleian and other manuscripts, unknown to earlier, and so strangely ignored in their most essential points, by later writers. The Rolls of Parliament, the Public Records, and the manuscript known as the "Fleetwood Chronicle," are authentic sources of history to which I have constantly referred; and I have found especially valuable the volumes of letters and papers illustrating the reigns of Richard III. and Henry VII., ably edited by Mr. James Gairdner. Differing as I do from Mr. Gairdner in the estimate I have formed of "The Unpopular King," his "Life of Richard III." has also been laid under contribution.

By the kind permission of the Marquis of Hartington, I have also been enabled to consult a contemporary MS. of great interest in the library at Hardwick Hall, to which no former writer has referred. This unique and important document is entitled "The Encomium of Richard ye Third," by William Cornewaleys. Suggested in all probability by the tergiversations of Rous, it is wholly free from that servile adulation or scurrilous abuse which destroy the historic value alike of the original and of the amended version of the Warwick Roll. It aims at recording impartially facts within the knowledge of the writer and his contemporaries. "Historians," he justly complains, "are corrupted. The most part of their records are forged." Whilst other sovereigns "have been injuriously dealt with," one, "not less wise than the wisest, valiant, just, temperate, yet hath the corrupted breath of the vulgar polluted and defaced his virtues, scandalized his memory, and turned all in to vices . . . . that worthy Richard ye 3^d, whome though both the tradicion of ^{l}ewde tonges and lewder writings hath sought to defame," yet truth has so prevailed that they have exhibited their malice rather than their power. Others, he says, have equal knowledge, but "have refrained to publish it, and, for himself, he looks for no reward save calumny."* He had no personal object to serve. The King to whom he sought to render justice was dead, and the path to royal or popular favour was open only to those who would cringe, and flatter, and fawn upon the victor at Bosworth Field. "The Encomium" is a manly protest against this sycophancy, written at the

---

* "Encomium of Richard III.," Preface.

author's peril, dictated by conscientious motives, and by the
conviction that in their judgment of contemporary events men
were "apt to erre infected by this folley." *

It has been said that "the youth of England take their
religion from Milton and their history from Shakspeare."
Both Lord Chatham and Southey have acknowledged the
truth of this observation as regards themselves, and it is
undoubtedly true of multitudes. For each single student who
investigates original documents there are at least a million
readers of our immortal bard upon whose minds his dismal,
but powerful portraiture of Richard III., unrelieved by one
redeeming feature, is imperishably engraven. The fault is not
Shakspeare's, but that of the authorities from which he drew
his history. Foremost among them are Sir Thomas More,
Hall, and Holinshed.

If the work attributed to Sir Thomas More were really the
product of his pen, it would be entitled to the highest possible
respect. If—as appears far more probable—it was originally
the work of Bishop Morton, we know that the pen which
wrote it was steeped in venom. It is now a generally received
opinion that the materials of the history were supplied by
Morton, "the ornamental and classical varnish" by More.
Dr. Laing indeed regards this as an ascertained fact. This
"*discovery*," he says, "may exculpate More from the imputation of propagating deliberate falsehood."† Mr. Gairdner
considers it "a translation of a work of Morton;"‡ and
this opinion is shared by Horace Walpole, and supported by
internal evidence which is only, if at all, short of being conclusive. The author speaks as though he had been present at
the last illness of Edward IV., which Morton almost certainly
was, whilst More would then be just three years old. The
narrative abounds in touches such as only a spectator or a

---

* "Encomium of Richard III.," Preface, p. 1.

† Laing's "Appendix to Henry," vol. xii., p. 414.

‡ "Letters, etc., of Richard III.," vol. ii., p. 18, *note.*

romancist would give. Thus, in describing the King's dying appeal to Hastings, Dorset, and others to lay aside their mutual jealousies, the writer says, "*lifting up himself and underset with pillows,*" Edward addressed them.* Morton was also present at the arrest and execution of Hastings, which is introduced into the history with dreams and omens, and related in a way impossible to More, or at least wholly inconsistent with the chaste dignity of his style. Again the writer of the history speaks of the attainder of Sir Richard Hawte as More could hardly have done, since his attainder was reversed by Henry VII. when Sir Thomas More was yet a boy.

A comparison of dates tends to confirm the opinion that More simply edited a work of Morton's. Grafton says that More was Under-Sheriff of London when he "composed" this work. He was appointed to that office in 1508, at the age of twenty-eight. But Morton died in 1500, when More was still in his teens; and though the pupil may have conversed with his master of the events in which he had been a prominent actor, "if so raw a youth can be supposed to have been admitted to familiarity with a prelate of that rank, and Prime Minister," † it is improbable that he would gather from him more than an outline of the history which is related with such minute detail. Yet the work attributed to More is either a pure romance—possible on the intellectual, as it is impossible on the ethical side of the author of the "Utopia"—or it is the work of one who, however he perverted the truth, was intimately acquainted with the history of the last two decades of the fifteenth century. But again, no man had less reason for extolling the Tudors than More, whilst it is impossible to suppose that a man of his high integrity could prostitute his refined intellect for the gratification of the Tudor Court.

---

* More's Works, p. 38. † Horace Walpole.

The fact is not peculiar to the Tudor period that men do not take the trouble to search after truth, if anything in its guise is ready to their hands. The high reputation of the Chancellor invested a work attributed to him with a weight and interest, which the chroniclers turned to account without any nice regard to truth. Surreptitiously printed as a history, it is a romance injurious to More's reputation as a historian, and to his veracity as a man. The piracy was early exposed, and the account of the matter given by Buck—of whom Horace Walpole said that "he gains new credit" the deeper the history of this period is fathomed—has commended itself to most unprejudiced minds. King Richard's adversaries, he writes, "not only, as the proverb says, *cum larvis lactare*, contend with his immortal parts, but raked his dust to find and aggravate exceptions in his grave .. . . . and find it as well guerdonable as grateful to publish their libels and scandalous pamphlets. . . . They gave their pens more gall and freedom, *having a copy set out by Dr. Morton, who had taken his revenge that way, and written a book in Latin against King Richard, which came afterwards to the hands of Mr. More* (sometime his servant). . . . Dr. Morton made the book, and Master More set it forth, amplifying it and glossing it with a purpose to have writ the full story of Richard III. (as he intimateth in the title of his book); but it should seem he found he work so melancholy and uncharitable as dull'd his disposition to it, for he began it in 1513, when he was Under-Sheriff . . . and had the intermission of twenty-two years . . . to finish it before he died, which was in 1535, but did not." *

It is at least certain that the book was left by More in an unfinished state, and the inference drawn by Sir George Buck is more than plausible. Reverence for his master would dictate a purpose—even though the task were not imposed upon him

---

* Buck, in Kennett, p. 517.

—which greater reverence for conscience constrained him to leave unfulfilled. Hence the work, which bears traces of his elegant style, and of Morton's reckless attempts to blacken the character of Richard, was never published by More. His brother-in-law, Rastall, when he made the collection of his works in 1557, pointed out the incorrectness of Grafton's un-authorised impression of the history published under the sanc-tion of More's illustrious name. And it is from that version, full of interpolations and omissions, that writers, from Shakspeare to Hume, have derived their materials for narratives flagitiously untrue. Upon these the traditional estimate of the character of Richard III. has been formed, and is still cherished by countless multitudes, who erroneously believe that in accepting the fables of Hall, Holinshed, and Grafton, they honour the great Chancellor and the greater Bard.

It is not intended to suggest that the history attributed to Sir Thomas More is valueless. On the contrary, if due allow-ance is made for the strong bias of the writer, its value is enhanced by regarding it as the work of a contemporary and actual participator in the scenes described. In either case it is the work of one whose judgment was blinded by party hatred, and who possessed neither the judicial faculty proper to a Lord Chancellor, nor the honesty and charity which would not misbeseem a Bishop. We read it with interest; we may even accept it as an authority upon many matters of detail; but in its main features, it is a historical romance to which the illustrious Chancellor never lent, but was much too honest to lend the sanction of his name. It is time that this fact was generally recognised, and I have discussed the question of authorship here, rather than relegate it to an appendix, in the hope of directing attention to it afresh.

GORTON, NEAR MANCHESTER,
   10th September, 1885.

TABLE OF CONTENTS.

CHAPTER I.

Four Hundred Years Ago—Death-roll of Plantagenet Kings—Development of Constitutional Freedom arrested by the long Minority of Henry VI.—Humphrey, Duke of Gloucester—Henry Beaufort—Richard, Duke of York—His Claims to the Throne—Character of Henry VI.—Margaret of Anjou affianced to the King—The Marriage opposed by the Duke of Gloucester — Favoured by the Beauforts — Dishonourable Conditions — Marriage and Coronation — Margaret's Influence over the King — Her Obligations to Cardinal Beaufort—Alienation of the Yorkists—Murder of the Duke of Gloucester—Death of Cardinal Beaufort—Suffolk succeeds him in the Queen's Favour—Foundation of Eton College and of Queen's College, Cambridge—The Loss of Normandy—The Earls of Salisbury and Warwick join the Yorkists—Death of the Duke of Suffolk—Jack Cade's Rebellion—His Death—Edward Beaufort, Duke of Somerset—Precipitates Civil War—Return of the Duke of York—Vacillation of the King—The King's Illness—Fall of Somerset—Birth of Edward, Prince of Wales—Origin of Margaret's Aversion to the Earl of Warwick—The Duke of York becomes Protector—First Battle of St. Alban's—York's second Protectorate—Margaret retires to Greenwich—The King's Health restored—Henry Beaufort, Prime Minister — Intrigues of Queen Margaret — Plots the assassination of the Duke of York and the Earls of Salisbury and Warwick—Reconciliation of the Rival Factions—Royal Progress through the Midland Counties—Margaret's Love of Hunting—The Yorkists again take up Arms — "Margaret's Safe Harbour" — Flight of the Duke of York—The Duchess of York and her Infant Sons taken Prisoners—Pride and Arrogance of Queen Margaret—The Earl of Warwick commands the Yorkist Army—Battle of Northampton—Flight of the King and Queen—The Duke of York returns from Ireland—Lays claim to the Throne—Declared Heir to the Throne, Prince of Wales, and Protector of the Realm—Queen Margaret in Scotland—Crosses the Border—Battle of Wakefield — Death of the Duke of York — Margaret's Brutality — The

Battle of Mortimer's Cross—Second Battle of St. Alban's—London closed against Margaret—The Earl of March enters London—Is proclaimed King—Battle of Towton—Escape of the King and Queen—Edward IV. at York—Margaret's Negotiations with Louis XI.—Her Last Effort at Hexham —Her Encounter with Robbers—Adventures in the Forest—Takes refuge with King René—"The Rose of Raby"—The Younger Sons of the Duke of York find an Asylum in Burgundy.   .   .   .   .   .   *pp.* 1—40

CHAPTER II.

Edward IV. fails to curb the Power of the Feudal Barons—The Country overrun with Marauders—Extension of the Power of the Crown—The "King-Maker"—Edward's Rule Absolute—The Hold of the Feudal System upon Society—The Duchess of York—Early Training of her son Richard— English Life in the Fifteenth Century—Hindrances to the Growth of a Middle Class—The Code of Chivalry—Condition of Society in which Richard (afterwards Richard III.) entered on his Chivalric Training— Authentic Sources of History—The Decay of Parliamentary Influence— The Political Training of Prince Richard—His Return from Utrecht— Created Duke of Gloucester—Committed to the Guardianship of the Earl of Warwick—His Devotion to Edward IV.—His Intellectual Gifts— Marriage of Edward IV.—Violation of his Contract to espouse Bona— Warwick's Mission to France—His Policy reversed by the King's Secret Marriage—The Woodville Family—Elizabeth Woodville—Expostulation of the Duchess of York—Infatuation of the King—His Admission of Bigamy —A Royal Marriage in a Forest Lodge—Promotion of the Woodvilles— Alienation of the Old Nobility—The Burgundian Marriage—It aggravates the Alienation between Warwick and the King—Warwick withdraws from the Court—He meditates Rebellion—Grounds of Edward's Jealousy of the Duke of Clarence—The Duke of Gloucester employed to convey the Remains of his Father to Fotheringay—The King's Partiality to Richard, Duke of Gloucester—Margaret of Anjou meets Louis XI. at Tours—Im- prisonment of George Neville, Archbishop of York—Margaret consents to ally herself with Warwick—Their Aims Divergent—The Grounds of Warwick's Defection from Edward IV.—Testimony of the Chevalier Baudier—Warwick is Ambitious to be the Progenitor of Kings—He is Present at the Marriage of the Princess Margaret—Wins the Duke of Clarence to his Party—Accepts the Governorship of Calais—Dangerous Triumph of the Woodvilles—Warwick's Popularity in the Country—The Duke of Gloucester's Counsels to the King—Richard with the Army on the Scottish Border—Warwick suppresses the Rebellion in Lincolnshire —Edward forbids the Marriage of the Duke of Clarence with Warwick's Daughter—He alienates the whole Family of Neville—Their Enormous Wealth—Clarence and Isabel Neville are married at Calais—The Rebellion of Warwick and Clarence—Edward IV. is their Prisoner—His

Escape—Suppresses a Second Rebellion in Lincolnshire—Warwick and Clarence seek Asylum in France—The Lancastrians distrust Warwick—His Reconciliation with Queen Margaret—Prince Edward contracted in Marriage to Anne Neville—Warwick and Clarence land in England—Hasty Flight of Edward IV.—Restoration of Henry VI.—The Duke of Gloucester shares Edward's Exile—His Character contrasted with that of Clarence. . . . . *pp.* 41—80

CHAPTER III.

The alleged Physical Deformity of Richard—Evidence from Portraits—The Testimony of Contemporaries—Of Sir Thomas More and Others—It was the Fabrication of a Later Age—Circumstances amid which Richard's Character was developed—Early Display of Great Powers—The Duchess of York strives to reconcile her Sons—Edward IV. attempts to land at Cromer—Lands at Ravenspur—Occupies York—Richard effects a Reconciliation between the King and Clarence—Warwick rejects Overtures for Peace—Edward welcomed in London—Treachery of George Neville—Imbecility of Henry VI.—Edward at Whitehall—Battle of Barnet—Death of Warwick and Montague—The Yorkists reunited—The Countess of Warwick at Beaulieu—Landing of Queen Margaret—She determines to take the Field—Battle of Tewkesbury—Death of Prince Edward—Of the Duke of Somerset—The Victory that of Richard, Duke of Gloucester—His Rewards — The Tradition that he assassinated Prince Edward—Opposed to all Contemporary Narratives—A Fiction of the Chroniclers—Adopted by Shakspeare—Queen Margaret committed to the Tower—Desperate Enterprise of the Bastard Falconbridge—The King's Reliance upon the Duke of Gloucester—Death of Henry VI.—Attributed to Violence—He is buried at Chertsey—Grief the Probable Cause of Death—Richard charged with Regicide—Incredulity of Habington—The Crime Objectless and Physically Impossible—The Charges of the Tudor Chroniclers Inconsistent—Based upon no Evidence—Margaret hears of the King's Death—Her Subsequent History—And Unlamented Death. . . . *pp.* 81—118

CHAPTER IV.

Fraternal Affection of Edward IV. and the Duke of Gloucester—Grants and Offices conferred on Richard—He receives the Thanks of Parliament—Takes the Oath of Allegiance to the Infant Prince of Wales—Receives the forfeited Estates of the Earl of Warwick—His Loyalty—Early Attachment to Anne Neville—His Want of Money—Jealousy of Clarence, who opposes

his desired Marriage with Anne Neville—Shakspeırian Fictions—Anne
Neville not married to Pri..ıce Edward—Clarence conceals Anne—She is
discovered by Richard—Clarence seizes her Lands—Violent Dissension
between Clarence and Gloucester—Edward's Harsh Treatment of the
Countess of Warwick—Marriage of Richard and Anne Neville—He is
appointed to the Command of the Army of the North — At Home at
Middleham—Pontefract Castle—Execution of Falconbridge—Seized upon
by the Tudor Chroniclers to asperse the Character of Richard—Falconbridge suffered at Southampton—Richard Ignorant of his Arrest—His
Wise Administration of the North—Offers the Countess of Warwick an
Asylum at Middleham—Sir James Tyrell conveys her thither—The War
with France in 1475—Dishonourable Peace—Richard alone refuses to be
bought with French Gold — Treaty of Pecquigny — Wine and Money
Edward's Spoils — Queen Margaret ransomed — Growing Popularity of
the Duke of Gloucester—Disastrous Consequences of the disbanding of
Edward's Army—Edward's System of "Benevolences"—Complaints of
the Clergy—Position of the Duke of Clarence—His Harsh Treatment by
the King—Quarrels fomented by the King—A Pretext found for his
Arrest—Attainted of High Treason—His Trial before the House of Lords
—Richard "resists openly" the King's Vindictiveness—The Murder of
Clarence—Indecent Levity at Court—Richard said to be in the North—
Edward IV. the Sole Pleader against Clarence—More's Insinuations—
"Divining upon Conjectures"—Richard's Protest against the Death Sentence—Edward's Remorse—Clarence a Victim to the Hatred of the Woodvilles—No Evidence to implicate Richard—He founds Religious Establishments at Barnard Castle and Middleham—Repairs Churches, expres-
sive of a Native Religious Sentiment—Entertained before the Impeachment
of Clarence—Birth of Richard's Son—Despotism of Edward IV.—His Dissolute Habits—Richard's Exalted Position—He purchases Crosby Place
                                                        pp. 119—159

CHAPTER V.

Richard Lieutenant-General of the Kingdom—Commander-in-Chief of
the Army—Objects of the Scotch War—Richard acquires New Renown—
Recovery of Berwick—Parliament acknowledges Richard's Services—His
Hostility to the Woodvilles—Earl Rivers Governor of the Prince's
Household—The Prince's Residence at Ludlow—Louis XI. cancels the
Marriage Treaty—Edward resents the Insult—Appeals to the Barons—
Who clamour for War—The King claims the Tithes then falling due—
Public Enthusiasm—Preparations for War—Death of Edward IV.—His
Last Attempt to unite the Rival Factions—A Brilliant Promise unfulfilled
—The Penalty of a Life of Dissolution—Edward appoints Richard Pro-
tector of the Kingdom and Guardian of his Son—The Overthrow of the

Woodvilles determined on—The King's Death attributed to Poison—
Archbishop Bourchier—His Rapid Promotion—Popular with the Chiefs
of both Factions—Advanced to the See of Canterbury—Shares the
Practical Infidelity of the Clergy—His Persecution of Pecock—Became
Chancellor in 1455—Sacrificed to the Jealousy of Queen Margaret—Effects
a Reconciliation between the Yorkists and Lancastrians—Is driven to ally
himself with the Yorkists—Seeks to prevent fighting at Northampton—
Opposes the Duke of York in the House of Lords, and suppresses a
Revolution—Officiates at the Coronation of Edward IV.—His Moderation
—Receives a Cardinal's Hat—The Cardinal's Interest in the Revival of
Learning—He prevails on the Citizens of London to welcome Edward IV.
on his Return from Exile—An Arbitrator in the Settlement of Peace with
France—His Retirement to Knowle—Declines to officiate at the Funeral
of Edward IV. .   .   .   . *pp.* 160—185

CHAPTER VI.

Hastings summons the Duke of Gloucester to undertake the Government
—The Duke determines to assert his Rights—His Letter to the Queen—Per-
forms a Funeral Service for his Brother at York—Exacts an Oath of Fealty
to Edward V.—The Queen's Anxiety to remove her Son to London—Disputes
concerning the Royal Retinue—Preparations for the Coronation—Richard's
Chief Purpose was to subvert the Power of the Woodvilles—Edward V.
arrives at Northampton—Is hurried thence to Stony Stratford—Richard
at Northampton—His Interview with Earl Rivers and Lord Richard Gray
—Arrival of the Duke of Buckingham—Richard holds a Council at Northampton—Seizure of Royal Treasure by the Marquis of Dorset—The Protectorate, and not the Throne, the Object of Richard's Ambition—Rivers
and Gray arrested—The Young King's Attendants dismissed—The Plans
of the Woodvilles defeated by Richard's Prescience—Arrest of Sir Thomas
Vaughan—Painful Scene between the Protector and the Young King—
Richard's Considerate Treatment of the Prisoners—Flight of the Marquis
of Dorset—Queen Elizabeth takes Sanctuary at Westminster—The Great
Seal delivered to her by Rotheram — Hastings assures the Lords of
Richard's Fidelity — Excitement in London — Allayed by further As-
surances from Hastings—Richard foresees Personal Rivalries—Stanley
and Hastings averse to a Protectorate—Edward V. and Richard enter
London—The Lords Spiritual and Temporal take the Oath of Fealty—
Disturbances—Dean Hook's Testimony to Richard's Moderation—Hastings
allies Himself with the Queen's Party—Richard surrounded by Men
whose Aims were Irreconcilable—Proofs afforded of the Treasonable
Purposes of the Queen's Party—Lord Howard unjustly censured—The
Claims of Hastings unrecognised by the Protector—Instance of Richard's
Consideration for his Nephew—The Council confirms his Protectorate—

Coronation fixed for the 22nd of June—The Choice of a Royal Residence
—The Tower a Royal Palace—Effects of the Queen's Conspiracies—The
Time favourable for usurping the Crown—Richard did not seek his own
Aggrandisement—Edward V. not closely confined to the Tower—Gentle-
men summoned to receive the Order of Knighthood at the Coronation—
Richard's Knowledge of Secret Conspiracies—He summons Troops from
York—Issues Warrants for the Execution of Rivers, Gray, and Vaughan
—Arrival of the Duchess of York in London—Corresponds with a Change
in Richard's Purposes and Actions—He aspires to the Throne—Divisions
in the Council—Catesby a Spy in Hastings' Service—His Faithlessness—
The Duke of Buckingham wavers in his Allegiance to Richard—False
Friends and Open Enemies—Apprehensions raised by the Postponement
of the Coronation—Stanley objects to the Divided Councils—Hastings'
Reliance on Catesby—Hastings an Impediment to Richard's Plans—His
Removal decided on—The Council at the Tower—The Protector's Accusa-
tion—Arrest and Death of Hastings—Not Assignable to any Single Cause—
Hastings forewarned by Stanley—His Meeting with a Pursuivant bearing
his own Name—The Protector feigns Alarm at his Conspiracy—Issues a
Proclamation to the Citizens—Assuagement of Popular Indignation _pp._187—234

CHAPTER VII.

Execution of Rivers, Gray, and Vaughan—A Retribution for the Murder
of Clarence—Will of Earl Rivers—Queen Elizabeth in Sanctuary—The
Protector demands the Surrender of the Duke of York—Opposition of
Archbishop Rotheram—Russell succeeds him as Chancellor—The Pro-
tector's Address to the Council—Protest of the Archbishops against the
Violation of Sanctuary—Speech of Buckingham—Submission of the
Archbishops—Their Interview with the Queen—She defies the Protector—
Cardinal Bourchier guarantees the Safety of the Duke of York—The
Queen consents to his Surrender—He is received by the Protector at the
Star Chamber—Character of the Prince of Wales—Position of Richard—
Chancellor Russell's Speech—Preparations for the Coronation—Its Post-
ponement—Richard's Ambition—Condoned by Public Opinion—The Pro-
tector's Relations with the Duke of Buckingham—Dr. Shaw's Sermon at
Paul's Cross—More's Misrepresentations—Shaw's Slander of the Duchess
of York—Provokes the Indignation of the Citizens—And of Richard—
Perversions of Later Writers—Richard's Claim to the Throne based on the
Illegitimacy of Edward's Children—Buckingham's Address at the Guild-
hall—His Advocacy of Richard's Claims Unsuccessful—The Recorder also
fails to move the Citizens—Buckingham again addresses them—The
Crown offered to Richard at Baynard's Castle—And accepted by him—
Perversions of Tudor Historians—Thomas Penketh—The alleged Previous
Marriage of Edward IV.—Evidence of Dr. Stillington—His Treatment by

Edward IV.—The Duchess of York privy to the Marriage—Evidence of Sir Thomas More and others—And of the Rolls of Parliament—An Informal Parliament—Purpose for which it was summoned—Buckingham elected Speaker—His Address to the Protector—Richard's Reply—The Lords refuse to acknowledge Edward's Children—Richard accepts the Crown —Popular Rejoicing—The Duchess of York at Baynard's Castle *pp.* 235—273

CHAPTER VIII.

Motives for Richard's hesitancy in accepting the Crown—He is proclaimed King—The Young Princes Confined to the Tower—Archbishop Bourchier sanctions the "Usurpations"—His reasons—Richard's clemency—Sir John Fogge—Bishop Morton committed to the Custody of Buckingham—Preparations for the Coronation—Richard's Assumption of the Crown had the Unanimous Consent of Lords and Commons—A Royal Progress through the City—The Duke of Buckingham's Place in the Pageant—The Coronation Sanctioned by the Church—The great Officers of State and the Positions assigned them in the Coronation Procession— The King and Queen—Ceremony of Anointing—Crowned by Cardinal Bourchier—The Banquet at Westminster Hall—Challenge of the King's Champion—Richard's Assumption of the Crown not a Usurpation—Some grounds of the Validity of his Title—Civil War averted—The Garrisons of Calais and Guisnes—Their Loyalty secured—The Brewer of Beaumaris— His Son marries Queen Katherine—Margaret Beaufort—Marries Edmund Tudor—Her posthumous Son Henry—His Early Training—Becomes Earl of Richmond—Presented to Henry VI.—For Twelve Years a Prisoner in Brittany—His Mother marries Lord Stanley—Her Maternal Affection— Her Character—Richard demands the Surrender of the Earl of Richmond —Mission of De Mainbier—Affairs in Brittany—Richard III. firmly seated on the Throne—His Rule of Government—Proclamation for the Preservation of Peace—Spurious Loyalty—The King desires the Love of his Subjects—His Administration of Justice—Earl of Kildare appointed Lord Lieutenant of Ireland—Royal Progress to York—The King is entertained at Oxford—Visits Gloucester—Is joined by the Queen at Warwick —Receives Ambassadors from Spain, France, and Burgundy—Arrives at York—Independence of the Burgesses—Their Loyalty to Richard—Letters of the King's Secretary—Preparations of the Corporation—Enthusiasm of the Citizens—The Prince of Wales invested with the Insignia of his Office—Richard's Second Coronation a Historical Myth—Not recorded by Contemporaries—The Splendour of Richard's Apparel—His Illegitimate Son knighted—Continuance of Festivities—Results of the Royal Visit— The Character of Richard III. contrasted with that of Edward IV.—First Symptoms of Disaffection—The Gathering Storm—Queen Anne retires to Middleham .   .   .   .   *pp.* 274—313

LIST OF ILLUSTRATIONS.

PORTRAIT OF RICHARD III. (*Etching*) . . . . *Frontispiece.*

PORTRAIT OF MARGARET OF ANJOU . . . *To face p.* 33

MIDDLEHAM CASTLE . . . „ 65

PORTRAIT OF ANNE NEVILLE „ 113

PONTEFRACT CASTLE . . „ 129

BARNARD CASTLE . . . „ 153

CROSBY HALL . „ 161

PORTRAIT OF EDWARD V. . . „ 209

WARWICK CASTLE „ 305

THE UNPOPULAR KING.

CHAPTER I.

On the 22nd of August, 1485, King Richard III. fell at the battle of Bosworth Field. Three months later Caxton gave to the world his *magnum opus*, the Golden Legend. The royal line of Plantagenet came to an untimely end; the Printing Press was fairly launched upon its beneficent mission. Two such events distinctly mark a new point of departure in the annals of our country, and suggest contrasts between the England of to-day and that of four hundred years ago, upon which it may be instructive to dwell.

Upon the battle-field on which the last of a dynasty of soldiers fell, the first of a dynasty of statesmen was crowned. The reign of brute force which had stifled the intellectual life of England ended with the Plantagenets. The printing-press heralded the dawn following that night of England's darkness which I propose to investigate. It was a period stained with many crimes, but also adorned with many virtues. It demands to be studied calmly, dispassionately, patiently; and so approached it will yield instruction and interest, whilst, perchance, some rays of the light of truth, concentrated upon its darkest spots,

like richest alchymy,
Will change to virtue and to worthiness.

For near four hundred years one dynasty had occupied the throne of England. During the four hundred years following the battle of Bosworth Field four dynasties in succession have reigned. But not on that account was the former period less free than the latter from civil strife, domestic feuds, foreign war, and all the evils attending the unbridled exercise of personal ambition. The annals of no royal line in Europe present a darker picture than those of the House of Plantagenet.* Fourteen sovereigns of this line occupied the throne of England. Of these, three only, Henry III., Edward I., and Edward III. lived to old age. Henry IV. Henry V., Edward IV., and Edward V. died in early life; Henry II., John, Richard II., and Henry VI. had their days shortened by violence; and the remaining three, Richard I., Edward II., and Richard III. were slain. Throughout the one epoch and the other, and in spite of such periods of retrogression as the Wars of the Roses, and Tudor and Stuart despotism, the principles of constitutional freedom were progressively developed. To each may be

---

* The progenitor of this blood-stained house, Geoffrey Plantagenet, in his pilgrimage to Jerusalem, was said to have adopted the name and habit of a Broom-man, wearing the plant or stalk of a broom (*Planta genista*), whether because the broom is a symbol of humility, or for the use made of the twigs with which he was scourged at Jerusalem, cannot now be determined. (See Buck, in Kennett, vol. i., p. 515.)

applied the words of De Comines : "Among all the world's lordships of which I have knowledge, England is that where the public weal is best ordered, and where the least violence reigns over the people." Even when acts of violence were most prevalent, as under the Plantagenets, sparks of liberty were struck out in the encroachments which kings and nobles made on each other, and every such spark was indestructible.

But the principles of constitutional freedom were equally obnoxious to kings of Plantagenet, Tudor, or Stuart dynasty, since they involved the transference of the destiny of nations from monarchs and statesmen to the people composing the nation. From first to last the struggle for freedom was the people's battle. It assumed the most varied forms, and moulded the most discordant characters. Constantly driven back, it was never suppressed, for it was the sigh of humanity. However manifold and seemingly inconsistent were the forms which this struggle assumed, its main object was never wholly lost sight of. Constitutional retrogression might arrest and threaten its destruction; it overleaped every barrier, and transformed it into an instrument of progress. Its leaders might prove traitors, its sincere but timid friends might utter warning cries of danger from the spread of "the restless and ignorant movement of a democratic principle;" its strength lay not in them, nor in any theory, but in the eternal and fundamental law of justice, in defence of which the people were ready to suffer persecution or to wield sovereignty.

The accession of an infant to the throne in 1422 was the indirect cause of plunging the nation again into the horrors of civil war, and of arresting for three decades the struggle for constitutional freedom which had promised to place England in the van of political, commercial, and social progress. Henry V. bequeathed the regency of the realm to his younger brother, Humphrey, Duke of Gloucester. His qualities of mind and heart, sullied though they were by sensual excesses, had acquired for him the popular title of "the Good Duke." One of the most cultured men of his age, he was the founder of the Bodleian Library, to which he made the munificent bequest of one hundred and thirty books. His appreciation of literature and of literary conversation fitted him to be the patron of men like William of Worcester and Lydgate, who have enriched our literature, whilst his high position enabled him to secure the promotion of the learned or deserving clergy. He was thus rapidly rising in the estimation of all classes. But in that rude age it was his martial reputation and his stern and equal justice that endeared the heir-presumptive to the throne to the common people. The popular estimate of the Duke may be gathered from a ballad, preserved in manuscript in the British Museum, of which the following stanzas are a specimen :

> Duc off Gloucestre men this prince calle,
> And notwithstanding his stoat and dignyte,
> His corage never doth appalle
> To studie in booke of Antiquite ;
> Therein he hath so gret felecite
> Vertuousli hymself to occupie,
> Off vinous slouth to have the maistrie.
>
> And with his prudence, and wit his manhood
> Trouthe to susteyne, he favour set aside,
> And hooli churche menteynyng in deede
> As verrai support, upholdere, and eek guyde,
> Spareth non, but maketh hymselff strong
> To punisshe alle tho that do the church wrong.

The writer of the above records that the Duke "had considered the book of Boccasion on the Fall of Princes," and adds, "he gave me commandment that I should after my coming this book translate, him to do pleasance."*

Parliament set aside the nomination of the late King in favour of Duke Humphrey's uncle, Henry Beaufort, Bishop of Winchester, son of John of Gaunt. It thus prepared the way for the eventual accession of the Tudor dynasty. For the present the Beauforts were the mainstay of the House of Lancaster, and in this capacity they found a more formidable opponent than "the Good Duke," in Richard, Duke of York. John Beaufort, Duke of Somerset, was the grandson of John of Gaunt; but the Duke of York, as we shall see, stood nearer to the throne. As Regent of France, Richard, Duke of York, had displayed ability both as a statesman and a general. His success excited the jealousy of the Beauforts, who disguised their schemes of self-aggrandisement by placing William de la Pole, Earl of Suffolk, at the head of the Council of Regency. The title of the Duke of York to the throne might be disputed by the Beauforts. It was at least superior to that of the King *de facto*, who was descended from the fourth son of Edward III., whilst York claimed an unquestionable hereditary title through his great-grandmother, Philippa, sole daughter of Lionel Plantagenet, Duke of Clarence, who was the third son of that monarch.† As the descendant of Edward III.'s fifth son, the Duke of York had an additional claim, his father's assertion of which had cost him his head. It was to traverse

---

* See Sharon Turner, vol. iii., p. 155.   † Buck, in Kennett, vol. i., p. 515.

these claims that Henry, now Cardinal Beaufort, the great-
uncle of Henry VI. and the Earl of Suffolk, urged the
marriage of the young King. Henry was now twenty-three
years old, of a highly-cultivated and refined mind, but wholly
destitute of those qualities which had distinguished his father
and grandfather. Virtuous and devout, he displayed already
that indecision of character which soon developed into imbecility. It was these characteristics, as well as the desire
to conclude a peace with France, which led Cardinal Beaufort
to desire his union with Margaret, daughter of René, Duke
of Anjou and King of Sicily, Naples, and Jerusalem.* The
Princess was renowned for her beauty and wit no less than
for the energy and intrepidity of her character.

Margaret of Anjou occupies so prominent a place in the
history of the country—her life being conterminous with five
of its sovereigns—that, although we do not propose to follow
in detail the history of the civil war which preceded the accession of Edward IV., it is necessary to form an accurate conception of her position and character. From her mother,
Isabella of Lorraine, the contemporary of Joan of Arc, whose
courage was on a level with her commanding talents, Margaret
inherited a proud and domineering temper, a resolute will,
and a courage which, after unprecedented vicissitudes, remained untempered by adversity. It needed little prevision
to perceive that the plastic mind of the young King would
leave him a helpless tool in the hands of a young and
fascinating Queen of such character, allied with a vigorous

---

* These pretentious titles were no indication of actual sovereignty. René
did not possess a foot of ground in either country of which he was titular
king.

mind and versatile talents. Those who could win her confidence might reasonably hope to find in her an instrument for turning the constitutional defects of Henry VI. to their own aggrandisement. At the age of fifteen Margaret was affianced to the King, and she formed no exception to the unbroken story of the unhappy effects of all English alliances with French princesses.

The influence of the Duke of Gloucester in the King's Council was overborne by the Beauforts; but he opposed the marriage "with reasons drawn as well from conscience as policy." * In May, 1444, a truce with France for two years was signed, as a preliminary to the most unfortunate marriage ever contracted by an English sovereign. At the instance of the French plenipotentiaries, René, whose provinces of Anjou and Maine were then occupied by the troops of the fiery young Earl of Warwick, had the courage to demand these provinces as an appanage of his brother, Charles of Anjou, who was Prime Minister of France. The English Ministers offered little, if any opposition, and René, whose daughter was dowerless, had no difficulty in making this surrender the price of his consent to the bestowal of her hand. The Cardinal, and the Earl of Suffolk—who received a marquisate for his services—were nothing loth to make a sacrifice which should appeal to Margaret's gratitude, and secure for themselves an ascendency in her confidence. The honour and welfare of the nation were thus trafficked away for the attainment of their own selfish ends. Margaret was a niece of the Queen of France, and this fact deprived her

* "Calamities of Margaret of Anjou," by the Chevalier Michel Baudier.

father of the right to dispose of her without the assent of
the King, who could not be expected to signify his approbation without such concession on the part of England as
would further his views, and put an end to a war so destruc-
tive to his kingdom.* A beginning was thus made of
the surrender of French territory, of which, in a few years,
nothing remained but the town and fort of Calais. " O peers
of England ! " exclaims Gloucester in *Henry VI.* :

> " O peers of England, shameful is this league ;
> Fatal this marriage—cancelling your fame ;
> Blotting your names from books of memory ;
> Razing the characters of your renown ;
> Defacing monuments of conquered France ;
> Undoing all, as all had never been ! "

The marriage by proxy took place at Nancy in November,
1444, in the presence of the King and Queen, and all the
chivalry of France, the King taking leave of Margaret
with many tears.† At Titchfield Abbey, on the 22nd of
April following, the royal wedding took place. The youth
and beauty of the Princess secured her an enthusiastic
reception, notwithstanding the unpopularity of the alliance
with France, and the dissatisfaction of the nation at her
want of dower. The coronation took place at Westminster
on the 30th of May, and the novel spectacle of a Queen-
Consort appealed to a sentiment which, for that day at least,
inspired genuine rejoicing.

By the energy of her character, Margaret acquired at
once a powerful influence over the mind of her Consort,

---

* " Life of Margaret of Anjou," by Mary Anne Hookham, vol. i., p. 236.
† Monstrelet's " Chronicles," vol. iv., p. 385.

and a baneful ascendency in his court. "This woman," says Polydore Vergil,* "when she perceived the King her husband to do nothing of his own head, but to rule wholly by the Duke of Gloucester's advice, and that himself took no great heed nor thought as concerning the government, determined to take upon her that charge, and by little and little to deprive the duke of that great authority which he had." †

The first step in her public career as Queen of England was calculated to neutralise the good impression made by her personal charms, and to estrange her subjects. To Cardinal Beaufort, Margaret owed her elevation from abject poverty to the highest throne of Christendom. The most strenuous opponent of that elevation had been the Duke of Gloucester. Gratitude to the former blinded her to the great qualities of the latter, and the child-Queen manifested a violent partisanship. The Duke of York was involved with Gloucester in the Queen's aversion, from the fact that they were equally opposed to her influence. The elevation of Somerset, Cardinal Beaufort's nephew, to the office of Regent of France, from which the Duke of York had been removed, completed the alienation of the Yorkist party, of whom Gloucester was the recognised head. The King was childless, and should the Duke of Gloucester ascend the throne, the partisans of Margaret trembled for their liberty and their

---

* Polydore Vergil, a native of Urbino, was sent to this country by Alexander VI. as sub-collector of Peter's Pence. He enjoyed the friendship of Erasmus, and was recommended to Henry VII. by those who had been acquainted with him in his exile. It was at the request of that monarch that he wrote his history, which is tinged with a strong Lancastrian bias.

† Polydore Vergil, Cam. Society, Book xxiii., p. 71.

lives. By his death alone could their policy triumph, or their safety be assured.

In February, 1447, Parliament met at Bury St. Edmund's, probably because the Duke of Gloucester's supporters were less numerous there than in London.* The Duke was arrested on a charge of high treason, and as all men knew the deadly hatred entertained towards him by the Cardinal and Suffolk, his death a few days later caused little surprise. "The conspirators," says Polydore Vergil, "were afraid lest it should cause some uproar amongst the people if a man so well beloved of the commonalty should be put to death openly, and therefore determined to execute him unawares."† He was found dead in his bed, and Margaret was universally believed to have instigated or sanctioned his murder. In the absence of any proof of her criminality, justice forbids that the Duke's death should be laid to her charge; but the absence of any investigation into its cause leaves no room to doubt that a murder was perpetrated. Cardinal Beaufort and Suffolk had encountered a storm of indignation when their secret surrender of Anjou and Maine became known. The Cardinal died shortly after their victim had perished at Bury, and Suffolk now became odious to the nation from the belief that he had been a party to the death of Gloucester.‡ He was shortly afterwards made Duke, "who was increased with that dignity because (as after was manifest) he had been

---

* "Whiche parlement was maad only for to sle the noble duke of Gloucestre, whose deth the fals of Suffolk, William de la Pole, and ser James Fynes, lord Say, and others, of their assent hadde longe tyme conspired and ymagyned." —*English Chronicle*, written before 1471, p. 62.

† Book xxxiii., p. 72.

‡ "Calamities of Margaret of Anjou," p. 31.

the principal contriver of that devilish device to kill the said Duke of Gloucester." * *Quem Deus vult perdere prius dementat.* The unhappy Queen took Suffolk into greater favour the more he was detested by the nation.

The King's thoughts were not of this world, certainly not of affairs of state. Absorbed in schemes of piety, his new college of Eton and the duties of religion divided his attention.† His youthful Queen, unfamiliar with English institutions and with the manners and customs of the people, and barely eighteen years of age, had the executive power of the crown at her sole command. She allied herself, indeed, with the Duke of Suffolk; but whereas Beaufort had controlled the Queen, who profited by his great experience, Suffolk was her tool. The period for which a truce had been arranged with France was expiring, and Margaret's relationship to Charles VII. exposed her to suspicion at home whilst it demanded from her prudence, firmness, and a knowledge of the temper and resources of the people which she did not possess. In this year (1448) Margaret founded and endowed, slenderly indeed, but probably as liberally as her means permitted, Queen's College, Cambridge.

The truce with France expired, and the war was renewed. The great warriors who had

> Received deep scars in France and Normandy,

Bedford, Gloucester, York, Salisbury, Warwick, were dead

---

* Polydore Vergil, Book xxiii., p. 74.

† Emulating the example of William of Wykeham, Henry VI. founded Eton School in 1441. He was fortunate in having Lyndwood for his counsellor —a man who, having the wit to perceive that the monastic system was nearly effete, placed the college in the hands of the secular clergy.

or in disgrace, and Charles VII. had been too sagacious
to extend the truce. The renewal of the war was fatal to
Suffolk. The English were driven from Rouen, and by the
surrender of Cherbourg in August, 1450, every inch of
territory in Normandy was lost. The Duke of York was
absent in Ireland; but he had drawn over many of the
nobility to his party, and notably the Earl of Salisbury and
his son the Earl of Warwick. They attacked the Queen
through her favourite Minister, charging him with treasonable
practices, whilst they declared that the King was "fitter
for a cloister than a throne, and had in a manner deposed
himself by leaving the affairs of his kingdom in the hands
of a woman who used his name to conceal her usurpation,
since, according to the laws of England, a queen-consort had
no power but title only." *

The Duke of Suffolk fell a victim to the hatred of "the
French woman," as Margaret was now called. His tragic
death, a blunder and a crime, animated the Queen with
a hatred, amounting to frenzy, towards all who had opposed
her favourite's policy. At the same time it emboldened the
discontented to seek new victims; and the rebellion under
Jack Cade revealed the fact that it was no mere party
in the state who were ready to take up arms against the
French woman. The insurgent body had very much the
character of a regular army. The musters, levied by the
constables in many of the hundreds, included the Abbot
of Battle, the Prior of Lewes, with other ecclesiastics,
knights, and yeomen of Kent, Surrey, and Sussex.† The

---

* Miss Strickland's " Margaret of Anjou."
† See "Illustrations of Jack Cade's Rebellion," by B. B. Orridge, p. 6.

royal troops refused to fight against the Kentish men, and the citizens of London secretly favoured the rebels. When Cade cut the ropes of the drawbridge with his sword, no opposition was offered to his entering the city. It was only when his undisciplined troops began to pillage that the citizens were stung into resistance.* Margaret attributed the rebellion to the influence of the Duke of York, to whom, since the death of Gloucester, attached the odium of being the next heir to the throne so long as the Queen was childless.† Her conduct, so inconsistent with the dauntless courage and ferocity afterwards shown in war, when her presence on the battle-field counted for more than a battalion, was doubtless prompted by her supreme anxiety for the safety of the King. But it was both pusillanimous and treacherous. She persuaded Henry to flee with her to Kenilworth. Having thus practically acknowledged his inability to subdue the Kentishmen by force, the King, yielding to the advice of the Archbishop of Canterbury, appealed to them to lay down their arms, and offered pardon to all, their leader, Jack Cade, alone excepted. "Whereupon the people, as having that which they desired, hasted home immediately with the spoil they had gotten, leaving their captain, who was taken soon after."‡ Cade attempted to effect his escape into Sussex, but was taken and put to death by the Sheriff of Kent. The rebellion quelled,

---

* "Calamities of Margaret of Anjou," p. 38.

† Through his mother Anne, the heiress of the Mortimers and of their claims as representatives of Lionel of Clarence, third son of Edward III. See Green's "History of the English People," vol. i., p. 559.

‡ Polydore Vergil, Book xxiii., p. 86.

Margaret violated the conditions of the truce on the faith of which the insurgents had sacrificed their leader.*

Edmund Beaufort, Duke of Somerset, now occupied the place in the Queen's confidence which his uncle had formerly enjoyed. Murmurs of disaffection, which presently swelled into an outbreak of national wrath, served only to inspire Margaret with new dreams for the aggrandisement of her favourite, and the utter extinction of the rival faction. Possessing the pride and chivalry without the self-control of Suffolk, or the administrative ability of his uncle the Cardinal, the impetuous young noble was only too anxious to test the power of that faction, and to stake the crown upon a struggle which should once for all destroy or be destroyed by it. He thus precipitated a condition of chronic civil war, which distracted the country for two years. The main object of the insurgents was to secure the dismissal of the Queen's favourites, and the recall of the Duke of York from his honourable banishment in Ireland. Meanwhile, of all the English possessions in France, Calais alone remained, and Calais was threatened. Parliament met in November, 1451, and endorsed the national demand for a change of Ministers. But although the King yielded, or made a show of yielding, to this claim by ordering the arrest of Somerset, the Queen's influence secured his immediate release and promotion to the captaincy of Calais.

In the spring of the following year the Duke of York, who had only escaped arrest by secretly quitting Ireland,

---

* The particulars of Margaret's faithlessness are related by Miss Strickland, "Queens of England," vol. i., new edition.

marched on London, declaring at once his loyalty to Henry, and his determination to enforce the will of Parliament. The feeble King was persuaded by Margaret to resist all changes in the Government, and to take the field against the remonstrants headed by the Duke, whom she now regarded as the rival of her Consort rather than of his Minister. But Henry's gentle heart could not endure the thought of shedding his subjects' blood. All his mind was "bent to holiness":

> To number Ave-Maries on his beads ;
> His champions are the Apostles and the Prophets ;
> His weapons holy saws of sacred writ ;
> His study is the tilt-yard, and his loves
> Are brazen images of canonised saints.

The haughty Queen and no less irascible noble were compelled to negotiate with the foe whom they were burning to exterminate.* Somerset and York were alternately arrested, and the crisis was terminated by the latter taking an oath of fealty to the King, at St. Paul's. But a truce, which left both parties with new wrongs to avenge, could not be of long duration. The Duke of York retired to his castle at Ludlow, and, "when he was in a sort exiled," Somerset, we are told, "got greater authority, and with Margaret, the Queen, ruled all things."†

The King's mind was ill fitted to bear the strain of ceaseless conflict between the occupations of the cloister and the state, and the distractions arising from conscious incapacity and conflicting counsels. In the spring of 1453, he was seized with the first attack of that painful malady which

---

* Polydore Vergil, Book xxiii., pp. 88–90.   † Ibid., p. 90.

overshadowed all his future life. The Ministers were compelled to call a Council of Peers to consider the claim imprudently advanced by Margaret, to be invested with full regal authority. The Duke of York was authorised to summon a Parliament in the King's name; and Somerset, to whose incapacity the loss of Normandy was attributed, was committed to the Tower.

On the 13th of October the Queen was delivered of a Prince. It was St. Edward's Day, and it was all too readily regarded as an indication of a desire to propitiate the people that Margaret bestowed a name so dear to England on her son. With the birth of an heir to the throne the rivalry of York and the Beauforts for the right of succession was removed. The fact that this event occurred after nine years of barren wedlock, may have justified some suspicion that a supposititious child had been introduced to defraud the Duke of York of his rights. But the stories circulated to the disparagement of the Queen were self-contradictory, and the lords spiritual and temporal accepted the fact that the prince was legitimate. Margaret bitterly resented the imputations upon her chastity, and frantically sought to win from the clouded mind of her royal Consort some recognition of the heir to whose birth he had looked forward with transports of delight. It was a cruel provocation of the sorrows of the worse than widowed Queen to represent that the holy King *would* not recognise a child that was either supposititious or illegitimate. Such, however, was declared to be the fact by the Earl of Warwick, who had violently espoused the cause of the Duke of York.

However malignant was Margaret's subsequent hatred

of the King-maker, which was never softened—even when in her son's interest it was suppressed—it must be admitted that in its origin it was abundantly justified. Her knowledge of her husband's imperfect title to the crown inspired her with an ardent zeal to overthrow pretenders to the throne, and to protect the birthright of her infant son. From the day of his birth this became the one absorbing passion of her life, and explains the invincible hatred which she conceived alike towards Warwick and the Duke of York, to which she lost no opportunity of giving expression.

The apparent hopelessness of the King's malady necessarily raised the question of a Regency. On the 27th of March, 1454, the Duke of York was appointed Protector, and the preposterous claims of Margaret to the Regency were set aside. The Queen attributed this rebuff to the absence of Somerset from the Council Board, and another link was forged in that chain of events which rendered her hatred of York implacable. In November the King began to amend, and shortly after Christmas he resumed the reins of government. In this the Duke of York would have acquiesced, but for the release and restoration to office of the Duke of Somerset, which he attributed to "nothing els but the fraude and fury of a woman, meaning the queene." * Hence he was led to appear in arms against his sovereign. He knew the King's aversion to war; and he knew also the hopelessness of effectually opposing Margaret, save at the head of strong battalions. His marriage with Cecily Neville, the sister of the Earl of Salisbury (and

---

* Polydore Vergil, Book xxiii., p. 102.

the twenty-second child of the Earl of Westmoreland),
had bound that powerful baron, no less than his equally
powerful son, to his cause. Accompanied by these two Earls
he now marched upon London. On the 22nd of May he was
intercepted by the royal forces at St. Alban's. The King
refused his demand for the surrender of Somerset. In the
short but decisive battle on the following day, the Duke of
Somerset was slain, the King wounded and taken prisoner,
and the royal army routed. Kneeling before his royal
captive, York besought the King to take him for his true
liegeman, and rode by his side to London. The King's
wound was not serious, but the excitement and distress
brought on a renewal of his malady. Parliament was at
once summoned, and gave its sanction to the extreme
measures which the Duke had adopted. On the 4th of July
1455, he was reinstated in the Protectorate. The Earl of
Salisbury was made Lord Chancellor, and the Earl of
Warwick appointed to the captaincy of Calais, from which
York had been recently recalled.

There is no reason to suppose that the Duke of York was
at this time insincere in his expressions of loyalty. He acted
with commendable moderation at a moment when he might
have seized the crown, had his courage been as unscrupulous
as his ambition was legitimate. Margaret retired to Greenwich, where, apparently absorbed in the education of her son
and in ministering to her afflicted Consort, she carried on
intrigues with the survivors of St. Alban's, who, with the fury
of despair, were eager for any enterprise which promised
them an opportunity of avenging the blood of their fallen
comrades. It was probably a result of these Greenwich con-

ferences that Richard's second Protectorate proved of short duration. The King had shown symptoms of returning sanity, and Margaret, keeping her purpose a profound secret, waited only a propitious moment for the overthrow of the Protector. In February, 1456, during the temporary absence of the Duke of York, she induced the King suddenly and unexpectedly to enter the House of Lords. Seating himself on the throne Henry declared that, since by the blessing of God he was now in good health, the kingdom was no longer in need of a Protector. Delighted at seeing their King amongst them the Lords acceded to his desire, and issued an order for the Duke to resign the Protectorate. The triumph of Margaret was complete. The Duke again descended from his high position, and Margaret selected as Prime Minister Henry Beaufort, the heir of the Duke of Somerset.

Margaret, who was always irritated by obstacles and impulsive in her efforts to remove them, had twice succeeded in depriving her hated foe of the Protectorate of the realm. Her object now was to avert the danger to her child of his being again called to fill that office. To this end two things were necessary: the King's health must be preserved; the Duke, with his numerous and powerful partisans, must be discredited. Her efforts in the former direction were as pathetic as, for a time, they were successful. For the accomplishment of the latter she resorted to intrigues which, but for the patriotic forbearance of the Duke of York, would have resulted in civil war. With the view, probably, of ascertaining how far the country gentlemen had committed themselves to the cause of York, perhaps also of winning them back to loyalty to the throne by her commanding beauty and persuasiveness, Margaret visited Bristol, Chester, Coventry, and other towns. The loyalty of Coventry was assured, and it was not without design that the ancient city was made the goal of the royal progress through the Midland counties. The burgesses received the Court with enthusiasm, of which there is too much reason to believe that Margaret designed to avail herself for the perpetration of a crime even more atrocious than that which had been enacted at Bury. Letters under the Privy Seal were sent to the Duke of York, the Earl of Salisbury, and the Earl of Warwick, summoning them to attend a Royal Council. They readily came, notwithstanding that some suspicion was caused by the fact that neither of the Earls was a member of the Council. "But being advertised by secret friends of what was intended against them," they suddenly left the Court, "and so escaped the danger."* York retired to his castle at Ludlow, Salisbury to Middleham, and Warwick to Calais. There can be no doubt that Margaret had sanctioned, if she did not organise a plot for the assassination of the three lords. Its timely discovery created widespread alarm, and induced Archbishop Bourchier to attempt a reconciliation of the two parties. He was zealously supported by the King, whilst his known probity, moderation, and piety, eminently qualified him for the office of mediator.† The Archbishop persuaded the heads of the rival factions to agree to a public solemn ceremony of reconciliation. Henry VI. took his station before the high altar in St. Paul's

---

* "Calamities of Margaret of Anjou," p. 58.

† Bourchier, Archbishop of Canterbury, was the grandson of Edward III. and the brother of Henry Bourchier, the Earl of Essex. "As great a man as ever sat in that archiepiscopal seat."—Habington, in Kennet, vol. i., p. 410.

Cathedral, and thither the rival barons walked, two and two in procession—one of each faction hand in hand; the beautiful and high-spirited Margaret taking the hand of Richard, Duke of York; "the news whereof made all men so glad, as that all sorts of men, everywhere, gave by mutual congratulations apparent testimony of rejoicing without measure." * The truce thus effected, in January, 1458, could only be temporary, and so it was regarded by both parties.

The success which had attended Margaret's experiment of stumping the country induced her, in the following summer, to make another royal progress through the counties of Cheshire and Stafford. The reason assigned was benefit to the King's health by gratifying his favourite pastime of hunting, from the enjoyment of which he had been long debarred. The real object was to win the personal attachment of the country gentlemen by condescending and familiar intercourse, by her surpassing beauty, and by the interest which she hoped to awaken in her princely son, a handsome boy of six years, who accompanied her. It is not intended to suggest that Margaret was indifferent to the chase. She shared with the King, the Archbishop, bishops, and nobles the love of the "noble science" which was made the ostensible ground of the second royal progress. The following is one of many letters printed by the Camden Society, which show the jealousy with which she resented any attempt at encroachment upon her forest rights:

"By the Queene. To the Keeper of O^r Park of Apechild † or his Depute there. Wel beloved, we wol and expressly

* Polydore Vergil, Book xxiii., p. 101.

† In the parish of Great Waltham, Essex.

charge you that, for certain considerations moving us, our game within our parc of Apechild, whereof ye have the saufe garde and keping, ye do with all diligence to be cherished, favered, and kept, without suffryng eny personne, of what degre, estat, or condicion that he be, to hunte there, or have course, shot, or other disporte, in amentising our game above said, to th' extent that, at what tyme it shall please us to resorte thedor, yor trew acquital may be founden for the good keping and replenishing thereof, to th' accompissement of O^r intencion in this partie. And that in no wise ye obeie ne serve eny other warrant, but if hit be under our signet, and signed with O^r owne hande. And if eny personne presume t' attempte to the contrarie of the premisses, ye do certiffie us of their names; and that ye faill not hereof, as ye will eschew our displeasure, at yor perill, and upon forfeiture of the kepyng of O^r said park."

In the following year hostilities broke out. The Earl of Salisbury, at the head of 5,000 Yorkists, marched towards Coleshill, in Warwickshire, where Henry was lying ill. With that stern vindictiveness which ever afterwards characterised her, Margaret ordered Audley to bring the Earl before her, dead or alive. From the tower of Muccleston Church she herself witnessed Audley's brave attempt to carry out her behest, saw his banner fall, and himself, with 3,000 of his followers, slain. She fled to Coventry, "Margaret's safe harbour," as the citizens chivalrously called it. Not in panic did she make good her escape from that fatal affray, but with a fierce resolve to avenge herself upon her enemies; to animate her nobles with her own courage; to shrink from no effort, no sacrifice, in the assertion of the rights of her husband and her son, and to give battle again to the Yorkists on the first opportunity. Many adherents had been won in the Midlands by Margaret's charms, her brilliant hunting-parties, her lavish promises, her pathetic appeals; and above all by her young and beautiful son, for whose rights she had quitted the palace for the battle-field. "She was amiable, artful, and insinuating," says Baudier; "nobody knew better how to flatter the hopes and engage the affections of the people."* The King's health improved, and Margaret roused him to head his forces and advance upon Ludlow.

It was midsummer, 1459. The partisans of the Red and the White Rose were roused to fury, from want of faith on the one side and on the other a determination to rid the country, or at least the Government, of "that French woman." In October the two armies met near Ludlow, bent on mutual destruction; but a contest which threatened to be obstinate and bloody was prevented by treachery. Many of the Yorkist soldiers deserted to Henry when they read the royal proclamation offering pardon. Their leaders sought safety in flight, and the royal army won an almost bloodless victory. The Duke of York, with his young son the Earl of Rutland, found an asylum in Ireland, where his former mild and just administration had secured the love of a grateful and warm-hearted people. His eldest son, Edward, Earl of March, escaped with Salisbury and Warwick to Calais, there to concert plans for renewing the civil war. Ludlow Castle

---

* " Calamities of Margaret of Anjou."

was plundered; every article of value that could not be
carried off was destroyed. Within a secret apartment the
despoilers found the Lady Cecily and her infant sons, George
and Richard. By command of the King they were made
prisoners of state, and consigned to the custody of the Lady
Cecily's elder sister Anne, the nineteenth child of the Earl
of Westmoreland, who was contracted in marriage to Walter
Blount (Lord Mountjoy), a firm supporter of the House of
Lancaster.

Margaret now believed the Yorkists to be entirely crushed.
Yet there were precautions to be taken which prudence
would dictate, even though vindictiveness were quiescent.
She knew that the legitimacy of her son would be called
in question, and she met the danger by securing the attainder
of the Duke of York and his sons. But Margaret did not
enjoy a monopoly either of prudence or courage. Arbitrary,
insolent, and cruel, she presented to the eyes of the nation
a foil to the loftier character of the Duchess of York, who,
undismayed by her misfortunes, bore them with resignation,
and acted with consummate prudence. The powerful influence and vast wealth of her numerous kindred were pledged
to maintain the pretensions of her husband. They had a
right to arm in self-defence, for their castles and manors
would otherwise be in danger. The sympathy of the nation
was only wanting to render their power irresistible, and
Margaret was fighting *their* battle.

In 1460 the Earl of Warwick assumed the command of
the Yorkist army, which sprang into being at his summons.
The Duke of York's eldest son, Edward, Earl of March, had
returned with Warwick from Calais, and, though still a youth,

his handsome figure and martial bearing won favour to his father's cause and to himself, of whom some even now dared to speak as their future King. The Queen's party were not taken unawares. In July an important battle was fought at Northampton, in which Margaret—who met the crisis like a heroine *—resolved that her son, then but seven years old, should undergo his "baptism of fire;" or at least that he should take his first lesson in the art of war. The fond and intrepid mother, accompanied by the young Prince, after haranguing the troops, took a station whence the action could be advantageously watched. Warwick sought a parley with the King, either in the hope of avoiding bloodshed or to gain time, for the Duke of York had not yet arrived from Ireland. But it was Margaret, and not the peace-loving Henry, who directed the campaign, and Warwick's overtures were disregarded. A second and a third herald were dispatched from Warwick's camp, and with the third a message that the Earl would speak with the King by two o'clock, or die in the attempt. But the Queen was averse to all parleying, and "was as much intent on fighting as the King was on his devotions." † The issue of the battle disappointed the hopes she had too confidently cherished. The royal forces, formidable from the superiority of their artillery, fled before the gallant charge of Edward, Earl of March. The Duke of Buckingham and the Earl of Shrewsbury were slain; the Queen and Prince escaped with difficulty, leaving the King, who was found sitting in his tent, a prisoner in the hands of Warwick. But although the

* She was "of herselfe for diligence, circumspection, and speedie execution of causes comparable to a man."—POLYDORE VERGIL.

† Baudier, pp. 88–90.

Queen had fled with her son, first to Durham—where her haughty temper had so estranged the inhabitants that it offered her no secure asylum—then to Wales, and eventually to Scotland, she had no intention of accepting accomplished facts.

Summoned from exile by his triumphant party, the Duke of York arrived in London on the 10th of October. The Lady Cecily had, probably by the connivance of her sister, found an asylum in the chambers of Sir J. Paston; * and the long-separated branches of the family of York enjoyed a brief reunion at Baynard's Castle. The Duke now boldly advanced his claims to the throne, protesting his willingness to submit them to Parliament and to accept its decision. Reflecting probably the sentiment of the country towards the son of the hero of Agincourt, Parliament decided in favour of the King; but the barons agreed to a compromise, which, however wise or necessary, and due to the hereditary heir to the throne who had shown so much deference to their constitutional rights, was the immediate cause of the civil war. Whilst stoutly refusing to decree the deposition of Henry VI., Parliament set aside the claims of his son, and declared the Duke of York heir to the throne with an indisputable title. It was further enacted that henceforth, " to encompass the Duke of York's death should be considered high treason," and he was created Prince of Wales, Earl of Chester, and Protector of the realm. In thus adding a Parliamentary title to that of heredity, Richard—always moderate and cautious—was probably content. He was in the position of a man who could afford to

---

* " Paston Letters," vol. i., p. 199.

wait, the more so that the King, his prisoner, acquiesced in the decision of Parliament. In this he but yielded to the necessities of his position, and Margaret was not at hand to inspire him with the courage of resistance.

Intelligence of these proceedings reached Margaret in Scotland. A fugitive, without money and without an army, the energy of her character commands our admiration, although the mother alone proclaims her womanhood. She lived only for her son, and the pusillanimity of the King in signing away the boy's birthright aroused her indignation and nerved her for instant action. The King of Scotland—himself the son of a Lancastrian princess—had recently died; but his widow received the fugitive Queen with effusive courtesy, and supplied her with money. She could count upon the loyalty of the men of the northern counties, and trusted that elsewhere the open display of the Duke of York's pretensions would goad her partisans to resistance. In mid-winter she boldly crossed the border. Within a few weeks 20,000 men rallied to the banner of the Red Rose. Richard was hastily summoned to oppose the Queen. Leaving his younger children with the Duchess of York, he hastened with his second son, the young Earl of Rutland, to his fortress at Sendal, near Wakefield. The Earl of March remained in Wales, where Henry Beaufort, the son and successor of the Duke of Somerset who had fallen at St. Alban's, was gathering an army for Margaret. The Duke of York was wholly unprepared for her remarkable success, even in the county which had always been faithful to his house. Confident that his presence in Yorkshire would rally to the White Rose many whose chivalry had

been touched by the beauty and misfortune of the young
Queen, he marched into that county with a small army.
The Queen was now at Wakefield, and when the Duke offered
her battle, his army barely numbered 6,000 men. The
Nevilles remonstrated with him for thus rushing on destruction, urging that his son Edward was coming to his support
with a powerful force.* But Richard disdained to retreat
before "a scolding woman," and resolved to risk a battle,
as he had often successfully done in France, against enormous
odds. His army was utterly routed, and he himself slain.
The Earl of Rutland, a boy of twelve, was captured by
Lord Clifford whilst fleeing with his tutor. On his knees
the boy cried for mercy. But Clifford's father had fallen at
St. Alban's, and he ruthlessly answered: "As your father
killed mine, so will I kill you!" and plunged his dagger
into the young Earl's breast.† Then, having found the dead
body of the Duke, he cut off his head, affixed it to his
lance, and presented it to the Queen, encircled by a paper
crown, in derision of his claims.‡ Margaret received it with
unseemly exultation. With the vindictiveness characteristic
of the times, she gloated over [the executions which
followed her victory, some of which were no doubt directed
by herself. The death of the Duke of York has even been
assigned to her own hand. Every one will recall the powerful scene in which Shakspeare gathers up the traditions
of his time.§ It is needless to say that they have no historical

---

* Polydore Vergil, Book xxiii., p. 108.   † See Appendix A.
‡ "His head, during life busied with expectations of sovereignty, was
mock'd with a paper crown after his death."—HABINGTON. I find no evidence
to warrant the gratuitous assumption that this indignity to the Duke's remains
was offered by Margaret herself.   § *Henry VI.*, Part III., Act i., Scene 4.

foundation, and the character of the Queen who, when urged to "look upon this King without a kingdom," who had endeavoured to usurp her husband's rights, laughed long and loud at the gory trophy wearing a paper crown, requires no accretion of myth to blacken it. She served most effectually the cause of her enemies by the undying animosity which she inspired in the minds of those who, in the complications of the near future, would probably have sought her alliance. By her order the Duke's head was affixed to the gates of York. It was fitting, she said, that he should overlook his own city. The Earl of Salisbury was amongst those who fell by the axe, and his head was placed beside that of the Duke. "Leave room for the heads of March and Warwick," said the Queen, "for they shall soon follow," little suspecting that she spoke of the future King and "King-maker." With both she had soon to reckon.

The Earl of March, now Duke of York, was marching from Wales to avenge the death of his father with the force which he had hoped to bring to his assistance at Wakefield. On the 2nd of February, 1461, he encountered the Lancastrians at Mortimer's Cross, near Ludlow. The royal army, commanded by Sir Jasper Tudor, Earl of Pembroke, was signally defeated, and Sir Owen Tudor, the Earl's father, was taken prisoner and beheaded, in reprisal for the murders at Wakefield. Margaret, meanwhile, was hastening to London at the head of a considerable army, with the intention of rescuing the King. The Earl of Warwick intercepted her march at St. Alban's, but was defeated, leaving the King in her hands. Again the ferocity and treachery of her character were displayed in the execution, in her presence, of Lord Bonville and Sir Thomas Kyriel, who had accompanied and protected Henry in his retirement from St. Alban's, relying upon the royal promise that their lives should be spared.*

Margaret, believing her enemies vanquished, hastened to London with the King and the young Prince Edward. But the citizens, who knew that if Henry reigned Margaret would rule, stoutly refused to receive her. She had exasperated them by threats, and had actually ordered her army to plunder the country up to the very gates of London. What clemency, what justice could be expected from this revengeful Amazon? Who might not be the victim of her unreasoning rage? Her pride and ferocity were exclusive of hope, and sealed the fate of her family.

The reunited armies of Warwick and his young cousin, now Duke of York, bent on avenging the defeat at St. Alban's and undismayed by their great losses, had followed the Lancastrian army to London. Margaret, equally determined not to yield to misfortune, resolved to turn to the North to raise new forces, and Edward, Duke of York, entered London amidst the loud acclamations of the populace. In his person and bearing he was "every inch a king," and he brought with him a brilliant reputation as a warrior. The lords spiritual and temporal, who had so recently rejected the claims of his father, met at Baynard's Castle to discuss those of the son. Their choice lay between an

---

* "The lord Bonnevil that came to King Henry would have withdrawn, as other lords did, and saved himself from his enemies ; but the king assured him that he should have no bodily harm." In spite of this pledge he was put to death at the instance of the Queen, and "with him a worthy knight of Kent, called Sir Thomas Kiriel."—*English Chronicle written before the year* 1471 (Cam. Soc.).

infirm and idiotic King, the helpless tool of a malignant and ambitious French woman, all whose advisers were as implacable as herself, and the youthful and energetic heir of York, already the idol of the nation, and surrounded by wise and powerful counsellors, some of whom had been staunch Lancastrians.* They unanimously declared that Henry VI., having broken faith with them by the execution of the late Duke of York, and other crimes, had forfeited that title to sovereignty which he derived from Parliament *alone*.† They had already recognised the *hereditary* right of Richard, Duke of York, and they now declared the hereditary and Parliamentary right of his son Edward. The Parliamentary election was confirmed by an enthusiastic meeting of the citizens in Westminster Hall. Within fifteen days of the second battle of St. Alban's, and barely two months after the cruel death of his father at Wakefield, Edward, Duke of York, was proclaimed, though not yet crowned and anointed, King of England.

The worst passions of the two factions were now inflamed. By her personal charms, her vicissitudes, borne with Spartan heroism, and her jealous custody of England's discrowned King, Margaret appealed to all that was chivalrous in an age when chivalry was esteemed the noblest virtue. Roused by her misfortunes to greater energy of action, she was soon at the head of an army of 60,000 men, a force greatly in

---

* "Edward was much desired of the Londoners, in favour with the common people, in the mouth and speech of every man, of highest and lowest he had the good will. He was for his liberality, clemency, integrity, and fortitude praised generally of all men above the skies. Wherefore there was concourse to him of all ages and degrees of men with wonderful affection."—POLYDORE VERGIL, xxiii. 110.   † Ibid., 109.

excess of that which the popularity of Edward and the renown of Warwick had attracted to the White Rose of York.* Yet it was impossible that Edward IV. could consolidate his power until a crushing blow had been inflicted upon Margaret. Like his father, he resolved to accomplish this, or die in the attempt. His pursuit of the Queen was rapid, and on the 29th of March, the two armies met at Towton, in Yorkshire. Even the lion-hearted Earl of Warwick was dismayed at sight of the superior forces he was called to encounter. But he shared Edward's resolution to strike an immediate blow, the issue of which should be the termination of the civil war. It was Palm Sunday, and the pious King would fain have postponed the conflict until the morrow; but the troops on either side were eager for the fray. At break of day the Yorkists advanced through a heavy snow-fall. The battle was long and furious. On either side were arrayed equal daring, equal valour, equal hatred; and on either side the prize contended for was a crown. The prowess of Warwick was more than counterbalanced by the inspiriting presence of Margaret. Victory alternately seemed to favour both.

> Now sways it this way, like a mighty sea,
> Forced by the tide to combat with the wind;
> Now sways it that way, like the self-same sea,
> Forced to retire by fury of the wind;
> Now one the better; then another best;
> Both tugging to be victors, breast to breast,
> Yet neither conqueror, nor conquerèd;
> So is the equal poise of this fell war.

---

* There is much reason to believe that the numbers reported by the chroniclers to have been engaged in the battles of the Roses are frequently exaggerated. But the late Mr. Green, who always errs on the side of moderation, says: "The two armies together numbered nearly 120,000 men." —*History of the English People*, vol. i., p. 575.

MARGARET OF ANJOU.

In one critical moment, to inspire his yielding troops with his own courage, Warwick is said to have leaped from his charger and stabbed the noble animal to the heart, swearing on the cross of his sword that he would share the perils of the common soldiers, and that if they fled he alone would defy the whole army of the Red Rose. The field was thickly strewn with dead and dying, and the Yorkists were again giving way before a foe equal in every respect but in numbers, and in that greatly excelling, when the Duke of Norfolk brought up his levies from the eastern counties. The tall men of Norfolk sustained the shock of the brave Northumbrians, repulsed it, and for the honour of their Duke and the White Rose attacked and broke the line of their advancing foe. Cries of "A Warwick!" "A Edward!" rent the air; the whole Lancastrian army fled, hopelessly vanquished. Edward's herald counted 20,000 Lancastrian corpses on the battle-field, and his own loss was estimated at from 15,000 to 18,000 men. "It was," says Baudier, "the bloodiest battle fought in these intestine wars, above 37,000 men being left dead on the plain."[*] "The prisoners and wounded numbered 10,000."[†] Margaret escaped to Newcastle, and afterwards to Berwick, accompanied by the King, the Prince, and only six followers. Eventually she received a generous welcome to Edinburgh by the widow of James III., who had before succoured her in adversity. Here, as the price of asylum, she proposed to the Queen-mother the surrender of Berwick when the King should have his own again,[‡] and concluded a matrimonial alliance between

---

[*] "Calamities of Margaret of Anjou," p. 105.

[†] Polydore Vergil.   [‡] Baudier, p. 107.

her son and the Princess Margaret, sister of James III.;
whilst Henry at Kirkcudbright entangled himself in an alliance
with the powerful Scottish noble the Earl of Angus.

Edward had meanwhile hurried on to York, where he
removed from the gates the heads of his own and the Earl of
Warwick's father, setting up in their places those of the Earls
of Devon and Northumberland, symbolising his conquests
from south to north.   Not yet had he learned to estimate
aright the indomitable courage and energy of Queen Margaret.
Whilst he abandoned himself to soft delights or to impolitic
quarrels with his nobles, confiscating their estates and attain-
ting their persons, Margaret, forsaken and alone, turned in
despair to Louis XI.   The hospitality of the Scottish Queen
was not equal to the continued entertainment of a guest who
might compromise her with other parties.   It was in vain that
Margaret looked for more disinterested kindness from her
own and her husband's cousin, the King of France.   The wily
Louis was willing to give her aid—for a consideration.   In
vain she prostrated herself at his feet, and frantically appealed
to him to redress her wrongs and to vindicate the rights of
her son.   She was outcast, proscribed, and attainted.   What
could she offer in exchange for the succour she demanded,
and which, if granted, would make him an enemy in the
popular young English King?   The faithless Margaret knew
well the price that was expected of her; and, as she had
already truculently bargained with the Scottish Queen for the
surrender of Berwick, so now she accepted the paltry sum of
15,000 livres, pledging Calais for its repayment within twelve
months.   Having obtained this parsimonious subsidy, Margaret
sailed for England in October, 1461, and once more took the

field. Pierre de Brezé, the Seneschal of Normandy, accompanied her, with 2,000 men arrayed at his own charges. The dread name of Warwick, who was reported to be approaching with 4,000 men, struck terror into the craven hearts of these mercenaries, who fled to their ships. Margaret and De Brezé, with Prince Edward, were left alone at or near Tynemouth. She was fighting not a losing, but a lost cause, and her partisans made a meagre response to her pathetic appeals to their fidelity. She obtained some help, however, from Scotland, and Henry VI. brought some recruits from his hiding-place at Haerlech Castle.

With varying success the Lancastrians struggled against misfortune until the spring of 1464, when they suffered an overwhelming defeat at Hexham. Separated from her husband, who, says Hall, was the best horseman of his company that day, for he fled so fast that none could overtake him, Margaret escaped with Prince Edward, and such jewels and treasures as they could lay hands on, into a neighbouring forest. Here she fell into the hands of a band of robbers, who stripped her of her jewels and costly attire. They dragged her, she says,* with violence and threats before their leader, and threatened her with insult and death. Flinging herself upon her knees, with clasped hands, the unhappy Queen implored their pity, telling them that she was the daughter and wife of a King, and their own rightful Queen. Her captors' attention was turned to the spoil as Margaret, preparing for death, commended her soul to God. The unsuspected richness of their booty

---

* Chastellain's "Chronicles of the Dukes of Burgundy," quoted by Miss Strickland, "Queens of England," new edition, vol. i., p. 599.

excited the cupidity of the leaders of the gang, who objected to an equal distribution. High words were followed by blows and even slaughter. Amidst this scene of confusion Margaret, favoured by the darkness of the night, addressed herself to one who stood near her, conjuring him "by the passion of our Lord and Saviour Jesus Christ, to have pity on her, and do what he could to assist her to make good her escape." Touched with compassion, the man bade the Queen mount a horse behind him, and taking the young Prince in front, they galloped off unobserved by the ruffians, who were butchering one another. Pointing out to the terror-stricken Queen the direction best adapted for concealment, the brave guide left the wanderers, who plunged into the interior of Hexham Forest.

The night was chill; both were deprived of half their clothing, and exhausted by fatigue, excitement, and want of food, whilst the now risen moon quickened their apprehension of pursuit. The sense of danger nerved them to new effort. They directed their flight to a denser part of the forest, when suddenly they were confronted with a forest outlaw of large stature and stern aspect, holding a drawn sword in his hand. Never were Queen Margaret's courage and readiness of resource more admirably displayed. She realised her danger, and she knew her power of exciting those chivalrous instincts which exist in every man, and redeem the most depraved from brutal barbarity. She appealed to all that was generous in the man's nature by reposing in him an absolute confidence, revealing her station, and thus putting it in his power to reap a rich reward in betraying her. If he were in want of booty, she said, she and her little son had already been robbed of all they possessed. She was sure he would have pity on her when she told him that it was the unfortunate Queen of England who had, in her dire distress, fallen into his hands. But, she continued, "if you slay me, spare at least my little one, for he is the only son of thy King, and if it please God, the true heir of this realm. Save him then, I pray thee, and make thine arms his sanctuary. He is thy future King, and it will be a glorious deed to preserve him—one that shall efface the memory of all thy crimes and witness for thee when thou shalt stand hereafter before Almighty God. Oh man! win God's grace to-day by succouring an afflicted mother and giving life to the dead."* On his knees the fierce robber, now melted into tears, vowed fealty to his sovereign, declaring that he would die a thousand deaths and endure any torment rather than abandon, much less betray, the noble boy.† Carrying the young prince in his arms he conducted his intrepid mother to his lair, where his wife attended on them and supplied every comfort it was theirs to bestow. Tradition still points to the robber's den, at the foot of Black

---

* "Chronique des Ducs de Bourgoyne," Part II., chap. xxi. It is impossible to doubt that in her relation of this narrative to Chastellain, Margaret must have drawn considerably upon her imagination. I have quoted a small portion only of Miss Strickland's translation of this narrative from the almost untranslatable Burgundian French of the fifteenth century.

† "A ces mots, on aucques près en substance, la povre royne arraissonna le brigant ; le quel voiant ses larmes et se desconforté semblant, ensemble et qu'elle estoit royne du pays, print une amère pitié en ly ; et suscité du Sainct Esperit qui l'amolist en cuer, prist meisures à plourer avenaques elle et de soy ruer à ses pieds, disant : qu'ains morroit de mille morts, et d'autant de tourmens, premier qu'il abandonnast le noble fils et ne le menast au port de salut, maugré tous hommes."—CHASTELLAIN'S *Chronique des Ducs de Bourgoyne* Part II., chap. xxii.

Hill, which bears the name of "Queen Margaret's Cave."
The outlaw proved entirely trustworthy and rendered the
royal fugitives many services, eventually assisting their retreat
to the coast, whence, accompanied by their faithful friend
De Brezé, they crossed over to Flanders.

For the romantic narrative of Margaret's visit to the
Burgundian court, the reader is referred to Miss Strickland's
biography, in which the Queen's adventures are related
in her own words, probably somewhat embellished by the
chivalrous and eloquent historian of Burgundy. She took
refuge with her father, King René. In penury and grief,
augmented by the intelligence of the betrayal of her royal
consort, and the indignities heaped upon him by Edward IV.,
she continued for some years to superintend the education
of her son, in the lonely castle near the town of St. Michiel,
near Verdun, placed at her disposal by René.

Without further following the vicissitudes of Henry VI.,
his committal to the Tower, his restoration by Warwick in the
counter revolution of 1470, and his miserable end, enough has
been said to illustrate the character and the evil influence
upon English politics of the beautiful, talented, and unprincipled French Princess who became his Consort. It stands
in striking contrast with that of the widow of the Duke of
York, who, whilst rivalling the Queen in ambition, excelled her
in prudence, and exhibited those domestic and Christian
virtues which endeared her to the north-country people, to
whom she was familiarly known as " The Rose of Raby."
This lady was the daughter of Sir Ralph Neville, Earl of
Westmoreland, by his wife, Joan de Beaufort, natural daughter
of John of Gaunt, third son of Edward III. She lived to see

two of her sons occupy the throne of England. Unhappily for them and for their country, they were early removed from the pious influences which surrounded them in their infancy, of which a curious glimpse is afforded in the "Ordinances for the Government of the Royal Household." If the manner of life of a great English lady of the fifteenth century here described savours of the ascetic, it is a very oasis of repose and virtue amidst the wilderness of strife and passion which the dark history of her time presents.

"She useth to arise at seven of the clock, and hath ready her chaplain to say with her matins of the day and matins of Our Lady; and when she is full ready she hath a low mass in her chamber; and after mass she taketh something to recreate nature, and so goeth to the chapel hearing the divine service and two low masses. From thence to dinner, during the time whereof she hath a lecture of holy matter. After dinner she giveth audience to all such as have any matter to show unto her by the space of one hour, and then sleepeth one quarter of an hour, and after she hath slept she continueth in prayer unto the first peal of even-song, then she drinketh wine or ale at her pleasure. Forthwith her chaplain is ready to say with her both even-songs, and after the last peal she goeth to the chapel and heareth even-song by note. From thence to supper, and in the time of supper she reciteth the lecture that was had at dinner to those that be in her presence. After supper she disposeth herself to be familiar with her gentlewomen, to the season of honest mirth. And one hour before her going to bed she taketh a cup of wine, and after that goeth to her privy closet and taketh her leave of God for all

night, making end of her prayers for that day, and by
eight of the clock is in bed."

After the fatal battle of Wakefield, this Arcadian life
which had been enjoyed at Middleham and Fotheringay, the
patrimonial residences of the Duke of York, came to an
end. Not even London, which was held by the Earl of
March, could afford a safe asylum for the Duchess and her
younger children. The Earl of Warwick, who was their
uncle, as Admiral of the Channel was master of the sea,
and favoured their escape. George and Richard, then aged
respectively eleven and nine years, with their sister Margaret,
were sent to the Low Countries, where they received a
generous welcome at the court of Philip, Duke of Burgundy,
whose consort, Margaret, was their mother's sister.

CHAPTER II.

Had Edward IV. been content to consolidate his power at home, to curb the rapacity of the nobles, to restrain his self-indulgence, and to withdraw from foreign entanglements, his reign might have been long and glorious. But Edward, with all his great qualities, found himself almost powerless to break the brutal power of the feudal barons, or to unite in one homogeneous whole the discordant elements into which society was broken up. Especially was this the case north of the Trent, where his power was for some years scarcely felt. Honest industry could hardly be looked for where it provided only booty for the miscreants who roamed over the country, pillaging farms and sacking towns, regardless of laws which, however excellent, there was no power to enforce. As Margaret's army had claimed the right of plundering all places south of the Trent, so the southerners now retaliated upon their northern neighbours. Farmyards were plundered, homesteads burnt, and murders committed with impunity.*

---

* " Croyland Chronicle."

The lawlessness of the barons was felt especially in those counties where the peasant proprietors were growing in wealth and numbers; and nothing more demonstrates the decadence of Parliament than the universal craving for protection at the hands of the monarchy.* But neither the peasantry nor the mercantile classes were deluded by false hopes. To both, the greed and the lawlessness of the dissolute and ferocious nobles had been a greater curse than foreign war. The people had bitterly resented the incompetence and failure which had signalised the foreign wars of Henry VI.; but had now discarded that craving for foreign aggrandisement which had proved fatal to national prosperity, and, under a strong government, they desired to pursue the arts of peace and industry.† The wealthier classes, the merchants and agriculturists who had not yet suffered excessive and arbitrary taxation, were willing to connive at the extension of the power of the crown if only it were powerful enough to secure to them peace and protection. They looked to Edward as their saviour from social anarchy and foreign war.

Their disenchantment was speedy and complete. Desirous of peace Edward undoubtedly was; but from the first year of his reign to the last his actions were provocative of war, and involved the country in complications with most of the European powers. At home the diminution in the

---

* See Green's "History of the English People," vol. ii., p. 17.

† "The Warkworth Chronicle." Dr. Warkworth, master of St. Peter's College, Cambridge, was a violent Lancastrian. But, allowing for that party zeal which led him minutely to "enumerate every evil trait that could in any degree sully the fame of the enemies of his own faction," his chronicle is valuable as that of an intelligent contemporary. It is often chronologically incorrect, but in other respects is worthy of credit.

number and power of the great houses rendered the task of government comparatively easy. After the battle of Towton alone, twelve barons and many powerful knights had been attainted. But Edward inflamed the greed of his favourites by accumulating in their hands the vast estates, with all the power they conferred, of those who had suffered attainder and perished on the field or on the scaffold. Thus the Earl of Warwick already overshadowed the throne which he had erected. His enormous wealth and the many thousands who wore his livery enabled him to shake, to destroy, and to rebuild that throne at pleasure, and acquired for him the sobriquet of " the King-maker."

At the same time the very forms of constitutional government were set at naught. Money was illegally levied, estates illegally seized, and their owners illegally imprisoned. Verily the times were out of joint. Edward IV. was the heir of great opportunities, which he sacrificed to sensual indulgence ; and the brilliant promise of the morning of his reign was soon effaced. The darkest hour of England's history had begun, and a night of agony must precede the dawn.

King and people, moved by different impulses, were at one in their desire for the overthrow of the feudal nobility. But whilst in the minds of the multitude the baronage was associated with memories of turbulence and cruelty, a conservative instinct—hostile to all change—endeared it to not a few who viewed with apprehension that growth of a middle class, which was properly regarded as the inevitable result of its decadence. The greatest achievements in English history had been the work of the barons. Around them centred the military glory of four centuries. The minstrel who sang their

praises was always sure of an applauding audience, and
Warwick, though a ruthless warrior, was popular in the
country and the theme of every martial ballad. The
character of Edward IV., his motives, and the methods employed, were all ill adapted to the successful uprooting of a
system ingrained in the structure of society, and whose
bulwarks were the Church and the baronage.

In the Middle Ages such education as high-born youths
enjoyed was generally derived from their mothers, or at any
rate under maternal supervision. It was almost necessarily so
in an age when, between feudal obligations and that ever
wakeful jealousy which armed noble against noble, their
fathers were more familiar with the camp than with their
hereditary estates.

One of the most gifted and accomplished ladies of the
fifteenth century was the Lady Cecily, wife of Richard, Duke
of York—the "Rose of Raby"—whose personal and domestic
virtues we have already observed. Like many other eminent
men, her sons owed their success in life to the care of a
mother who trained their intellect and educated their
affections, subjecting them to a severe discipline, and
imbuing their infant minds with sentiments of religion.
But we have seen only one side of the Lady Cecily's character.
In her veins flowed the proud blood of the Nevilles, whilst
her alliance with the House of York—with a prince of that
house whose ancestral right to the crown Parliament had
recognised — inflamed and gave direction to her haughty
ambition.* And when the hope of wearing the queenly

---

* In the neighbourhood of her baronial residence of Fotheringay the
common people called her not the Rose of Raby, but "Proud Cis," from her

diadem herself was lost at Wakefield, she all the more tenaciously educated her sons, by example and tuition, to regard the throne as their lawful inheritance. So long as the powerful Neville interest, and especially the influence of the mighty Earl, her brother—the King-maker of the coming days—was loyal in its adhesion to the House of York, there was little to endanger their succession. The King was a fugitive, and weak both in mind and body. Only the sun of York could convert the long winter of discontent into glorious summer.

Such were the ideas in which her fourth and youngest son, Richard, was nurtured, for his elder brothers had been associated with their father or uncles in those turbulent scenes which culminated in the disaster of Wakefield.* The seeds of that fatal ambition which in after life involved Richard in crime and disaster, and has covered his memory with unmerited infamy, were sown in the nursery of Middleham. The atmosphere which surrounded his very cradle was that in which religion, morality, and the domestic virtues were highly esteemed, but were all made subservient to that fatal ambition which he drank in with his mother's milk, which never could be and never was eradicated from his mind. Of his childhood we know next to nothing. Family papers had small chance of preservation in that turbulent

---

indomitable pride. In the castle she had a throne-room where she assumed the state of a queen.

* The Nevilles were remarkably prolific. The Lady Cecily, herself the twenty-second child of the Earl of Westmoreland, had no less than nine brothers who were either by descent, marriage, or creation, peers of the realm, whilst several sisters were also united by marriage to the nobles. Such a fact throws some light upon the enormous influence wielded by this powerful family.

age, and all that Hutton, writing a century after his death, can tell us, is that "his infancy was spent in his father's house, where he cuckt his ball and shot his taw with the same delight as other lads." *

It is not easy to place ourselves in a condition of things differing widely, and both outwardly and inwardly, even from that of the days, which some of us recollect, before steam and electricity had revolutionised modern society. Yet, unless we resist the general tendency to invest these mediæval ages with the attributes of our own time, we can form no true conception of the men whose characters were moulded by them. No portraiture of Richard III.—the Unpopular King—that is even approximately true has yet been presented, precisely owing to this fatal habit of investing the past with the characteristics of later times. From a foundation of sentiment, a superstructure of fable has naturally arisen.

The feudal system was in full activity; but though it had worked efficiently and well, and neither peasant nor peer desired relief from its ties, it was moribund. The imagination is struck with the deeds of daring courage, the reciprocal obligations, the self-sacrifice which it fostered, and we are compelled to recognise the fact that "we have lost something in exchanging these ties for the harsher connecting links of mutual self-interest." † But that daring courage in which the feudal lord was trained from childhood was not always, nor generally, directed to noble ends. There were no Sir Galahads in England in

---

* Hutton's "Bosworth," p. 17.   † Froude, vol. i., p. 18.

the fifteenth century. The restless, mercenary, and vindictive violence of the nobles diffused calamity everywhere, and destroyed the prosperity and the happiness of the helpless victims of "reciprocal obligations." Commerce and agricultural industry periodically revived only to be anew depressed by the drafting of the operative classes into obligatory military service, and by that excessive taxation resulting from incessant civil war. The towns were everywhere falling into decay. The population, which to-day increases at the rate of nine hundred per day, was, at the best, stationary; the normal increase being wholly swept away by war and the vindictive strife of mercenary barons. Serfdom, it is true, was rapidly merging into free servitude. But it was not illegal, and on the royal domains the aspiration for freedom was hopeless.

The feudal system perished because it was inimical to that constitutional freedom in which a growing, industrious, and energetic middle class saw a panacea for the intolerable evils by which they were afflicted. With that remarkable grasp of the tendencies of his age which characterises Richard III., he addressed himself to the abolition of an institution already effete, and incongruous with the existence of that middle class in whom he recognised the very nerve and sinew of a great and powerful nation. The state of that society in which he was brought up, with its vices and redeeming qualities, demands, therefore, the most careful and continuous attention. The subject is too wide for exhaustive treatment in this place. An occasional digression may, perhaps, enable us to bring a faint ray of light from that far-off domestic, social, and political life of

England that may serve to relieve the monotonous darkness of the lines in which the portraiture of Richard III.
has been drawn, even by historians of the nineteenth
century.

In the fifteenth century the young noble, when he was
fortunate enough not to be an orphan, was under maternal
care until the completion of his seventh year. The principles
of religion and some elementary knowledge of letters were
supposed to be imbibed by his infant mind, and often
enough his religious and intellectual training was carried
no further. On the completion of his seventh year he was
admitted into the family of some renowned feudal lord, whose
duty it was to ensure a healthy physical development, and to
initiate the young candidate for knighthood into the mysteries
and hardships of a military career.* He was now a page, and
in that capacity, irrespective of rank, another probationary
period of seven years was passed. At fourteen he was
invested with his first degree, that of squire. He now exchanged the short dagger of the page for the sword allotted
to this second grade of chivalry, and was qualified to follow
his gallant leader to the joust and tournament, or to the field
of battle; to lead his war-steed; to buckle on his armour;
and, in addition to the various and sometimes arduous services
due to his leader, it was now possible to him, by bravery or
by favour, to win the spurs of knighthood. The squire of
royal blood, or belonging to a powerful house, often received
the honour of knighthood whilst still a boy. For others the
second grade of chivalry, like the first, unless owing to cir-

---

* Appendix B.

cumstances quite exceptional, had seven years' duration. At the age of twenty-one his chivalric training was complete, and the honour of knighthood was conferred. The initiation no longer possessed that picturesqueness and solemnity which in earlier days the mystic services of the Church, with her pompous ecclesiastic processions, had thrown around it. But it was still associated with religion, with impressive rites and ceremonies, and with festivities; it still appealed to the imagination, the ambition, and the vanity of aspirants, and embodied a noble idea; and it appropriately paled before that "gentlemanly perjury" which was the fashion in the later years of the reign of Edward IV.

It would be impossible to paint in too strong colours the disorganisation of the times when Richard, the fourth son of Richard, Duke of York, attained the age proper to his entrance upon the first grade of a chivalric training. True, the old order was changing, but the feudal conception of society was ingrained in the minds and social habits of the nation. The indigent and the outlaw, as well as the feudal retainers, sought bread and protection in the train of the great barons, whose lawlessness the crown had lost the power of restraining. Laws were set at defiance by a noble who could command a following of thousands of armed and disciplined men. Sheriffs and judges were overawed, juries bribed or bullied, and the administration of the law had become a farce.

All this may be gathered from the old chroniclers, whose confused and strongly biassed stories reflect the growing confusion of the State. Authentic materials for a history of the fifteenth century are scanty. It has been plausibly

suggested that the discovery of the art of printing is a cause
of this defect, which it would seem so well calculated to
remove. One of its first effects was the decay of the art
of writing. Men ceased to multiply their manuscripts, and
they have perished; whilst those who wrote for the printing-
press overlooked contemporary history in their laudable
anxiety to preserve that of the past. But in the Rolls of
Parliament, the Harleian and Cottonian Collections, in the
British Museum, the Public Records, and the publications of
the Camden and other learned societies, we have valuable
resources which have been so much neglected, that what has
passed for history the careful reader discovers to be
but fable—the product of ignorance, prejudice, and mis-
representation.

The dislocation of society was attributable to various
causes, but all find their explanation in the decay of
Parliamentary life. Vast estates of confiscated lands had
accumulated in the hands of men to whom honour, loyalty,
and good faith were unknown virtues. In their savage
natures no emotions of pity or justice were stirred for the
dispossessed nobles and knights driven into exile or penury
when they escaped the block. Herein we see the causes
of the decay of Parliamentary life. Under the forms of
constitutional government, intestine strife and anarchy everywhere prevailed; therefore it was said its forms were
valueless. For hope of better things, the King was regarded
as the embodiment of the Constitution, Parliament was
discredited, whilst assassination, rapine, war, spread terror
through the land.

The political training of the Princes of the Blood was full

of evil omen for the time to come. The King's younger
brothers, George and Richard, who had been sent by their
mother to Utrecht after the fatal battle of Wakefield, were
wisely entrusted to the charge of the most magnificent Prince
in Europe. Had they been permitted to grow to manhood
in the polished Court where constitutional law was respected,
literature and the fine arts cultivated, and the expiring
customs of chivalry cherished, their characters would have
been formed upon a higher model than was possible in war-
distracted England, and the name of Richard III. handed
down as the greatest of mediæval Princes. At the ages of
twelve and ten years respectively, they were recalled from
Utrecht. George, who was created Duke of Clarence, was
an amiable, sunny, light-hearted boy, contrasting strongly
with Richard, whom the King created Duke of Gloucester,
and whose pale face, reserved but courteous manners and
love of reading, commanded respect, rather than affection.

There is reason to believe that on his return from Utrecht,
Richard was entrusted to the care of his natural guardian,
the Earl of Warwick. In the fifth year of the reign of
Edward IV. an entry appears on the Issue Roll of the
Exchequer, showing that money was paid "to Richard, Earl
of Warwick, for costs and expenses incurred by him in behalf
of the Duke of Gloucester, the king's brother."* This was
in 1465, when Richard would be fourteen years old, and the
natural inference is that he had then passed through the
prescribed probation for noble youths destined to be trained
in the chivalrous accomplishments of the age. Warwick's

---

* Miss Halford's "Richard III.," vol. i., p. 120.

father, the Earl of Salisbury, who fell with the late Duke of
York at Wakefield, had been the principal ·instigator of
York's pretensions to the throne. His son, already renowned
throughout Europe, was the most fitting person to whom
the King could entrust his young brothers, his purpose being,
as Sir George Buck informs us, "to season their forwardnesse
and honour of knighthood which he had bestowed upon them."*
It does not appear, however, that the Duke of Clarence
shared that honour with Richard of Gloucester.   On the
contrary, his irresolute and restless spirit would seem thus
early to have inspired that distrust in Edward's mind which
was never removed.   Richard, on the other hand, was reserved, cautious, firm of will, endowed with discretion beyond
his years.   In him we may well believe that the sagacious King
detected the dawn of a fearless and subtle genius.   Edward's
contempt for learning may have led him to under-estimate
his young brother's indebtedness to the scholars of Utrecht.
He certainly took a greater pride in his skill in the tilt-yard,
acquired under the training of Warwick, than in that intellectual culture which he deemed appropriate only to clerics
and necromancers.   The Duke of Gloucester was entirely
devoted to the King, who, being ten years his senior, exacted
a deference which, perhaps, Clarence may have failed to
render.   Whatever the cause, Edward henceforward regarded
Clarence with distrust and Richard with a degree of affection
and confidence which his loyalty, his princely deportment,
and his promising intellectual power were fitted to inspire.†

---

* "History of Richard III.," by Sir G. Buck, p. 8.

† A parchment, preserved in the Cottonian Collection, bears the auto-
graph of Richard, with the motto which so well became him.   It is signed:
"*Loyaulte me lie*, RICHARD GLOUCESTRE."

Perhaps it was the King's purpose to detach Richard from the influence of the great Earl to whom he owed his throne, and whose hostility as well as that of his whole baronage he was about to provoke. That Edward was a libertine we know. This would be no discredit to him in the eyes of most of the barons; but that the King of England should presume to fall in love and contract a marriage of affection was intolerable. This offence Edward committed. At the supreme moment of Warwick's power, when the "King-maker" had crushed Margaret's last effort at the battle of Hexham in 1464, had taken Henry prisoner and firmly established the House of York upon the throne which he aspired to dominate, this un-kingly act of Edward IV. undermined his power, "broke the bonds of amity," and foiled his most cherished purposes.*

It was the Earl's policy to secure a settled peace by means of a triple alliance between England, France, and Burgundy. The preliminaries were arranged, including a marriage treaty by which Edward contracted to espouse Bona, sister of the Queen of France. Modern historians have affected to treat as altogether mythical a fact which appears to be as well authenticated, and in itself as probable, as any event in Edward's life. The positive assertion of Dr. Warkworth proves at least that it is not the "groundless fable" which they have characterised it.† Polydore Vergil was a boy at the time, but his opportunities for ascertaining the facts were

---

* " Encomium of Richard III.," by William Cornewaleys, p. 2.

† " The Warkworth Chronicle," p. 3. See also Buck's " Richard III.," p. 116. Gavin, in his " Chronicles of France," writes : " The earl was received by King Louis XI. at Rouen with great pomp, had secret conferences with him for twelve days consecutively, and was loaded with presents when he took his departure."

unapproached by any writer of his age.   He says that Edward
"sent Richard, Earle of Warwicke, ambassador into France
to demand in marriage a young lady caulyd Bone, syster of
Carlot, Queene of France, and doughter of Lewys, Duke of
Savoy." *   Too much importance has been attached to the
silence of Monstrelet.   It would not have been in harmony
with his method to record an affront offered to and tamely
accepted by his master.   Moreover, he is equally silent respecting the espousals of Prince Edward and Anne Neville, in
the arrangement of which Louis was so much interested.
The historian Habington relates the fact of the proposed
marriage in substantial harmony with his contemporaries.
Amongst all the Princesses, he says, "which that time
gloried in, and of whom several were proposed to the king's
choice, viz., Margaret, daughter of the King of Scots, and
Isabel, sister of Henry IV., King of Castile, Bona was then
thought worthiest of his bed. in respect of the excellence of
her beauty, greatness of birth (as being daughter of Lewis,
Duke of Savoy), and the mighty marriage of her other sister
Charlotte with Louis XI., King of France, with whom she
then was.   This last consideration being a main inducement."
The Earl of Warwick, he continues, was deputed to negotiate
this marriage, for the consummation of which the two Kings
were equally solicitous : " Edward, that he might without fear of
more danger enjoy the glory of a late-recovered kingdom; Louis,
that he might be freed from the dangers of an English invasion
and the importunities of Queen Margaret for assistance." †

---

* Polydore Vergil, Book xxiv., p. 116.   Cornwallis also states that Warwick.
had been "sent into ffraunce to treate for a marriage with a neece of ye ffrench
king's."—*The Encomium of Richard III.*, p. 2.

† Habington, in Kennett, vol. i., p. 437.

This was indeed by far the most important article of the treaty, its object being to deprive Margaret once for all of that assistance from Louis XI. which constituted the only remaining hope of the House of Lancaster. In the autumn of 1464, Warwick prepared to cross over to St. Omer for a final conference with the French king.* As early as the previous year the marriage treaty had been communicated to the Duke of Burgundy. In that month Edward privately married Elizabeth Woodville. The marriage was kept secret, and was communicated to his Council only six days before the date fixed for Warwick's embassy.† The Council were dumb with dismay. Warwick alone, probably, realised all that this announcement involved; the advancement of the Woodvilles at his expense, the overthrow of his most cherished plans, and especially of the sway which till now he had wielded in the royal Council.‡ The reversal of his policy, his rebellion, his triumph, and his fall were events yet hidden in the womb of time. But every member of the Council shared his indignation at that act of "as high exception as improvident" which the King had perpetrated, "For his barony thought it a most unworthy and unequal match, distrusting it the more as done without their consent, which they assever'd the king ought to have by their ancient privileges; and were the more exasperated considering the great inequality between her condition and the

* Hall's statement, in which he is followed by later historians, that Warwick was at this time in France, is clearly inaccurate.

† "King Edward having changed his purpose of taking to wife the lady Bona, daughter of the Duke of Savoy, married Elizabeth, the widow of Sir John Gray, concealing upon account of the meanness of her birth what he had done."—POLYDORE VERGIL.

‡ See Green's "History of the English People," vol. ii., p. 32.

Imperial Majestie of England, being the relict but of a poor knight, his mortal enemy too." *

But the gravamen of Edward's offence was that he had married one whose husband had been "a very vehement Lancastrian, revolting from the House of York, and therefore the more hateful to those of that family, and the well-wishers thereof." This was John Gray of Grooby, who was knighted by Henry VI. at the second battle of St. Alban's, where he fell whilst commanding Margaret's cavalry. His widow Elizabeth, who had been in the service of Queen Margaret, had been a no less ardent partisan of the House of Lancaster. Sir John Gray had been one of the numerous victims of Edward's cupidity. After the overthrow of Margaret, his manor of Bradgate, which had been in his family since the Norman Conquest, was seized by the King, and his widow and two children were reduced to poverty. Her father, Sir John Woodville, had married Jacquetta, Duchess of Bedford, and Elizabeth, with her two children, had returned to her maternal home. After a day's hunting in Wychwood Forest, the King—so runs the tradition—called upon the Duchess and was waylaid by Elizabeth, who, leading a fatherless boy in either hand, solicited the restoration of their patrimony. The King, we are told, could not but yield to any request made by so conquering a beauty, and presently himself grew as earnest in soliciting her, though in a more unlawful suit.† That Edward contemplated an honourable

---

* Buck, p. 110. "The nobylytie treuly chafyd and cast owt open speaches that the king had not doone according to his dignitie."—POLYDORE VERGIL, Book xxiv., p. 117.

Habington, in Kennett, vol. i., p. 437.

marriage with this lady at the very moment when the
marriage treaty with France was arranged cannot be
supposed. She was ten years his senior. In conversation her eyes were always averted from the individual to
whom she spoke, or by furtive glances she conveyed the impression of an artful and crafty mind. And though described
by most authorities as beautiful, and wearing still the bloom
of youth, her features are said to have been relieved from
insipidity only by an expression of cunning, which we must
suppose to have been the King's ideal of female beauty. For,
says Sir George Buck, "He was so deeply and obstinately
surprised with her beauty," that neither the despised state of
widowhood, nor the meanness of her condition, neither the
earnest dissuasions of his mother, nor the counsels of his
best friends* could induce him to give her up. But "she was
of so pregnant and reserved a wit (seconded by the caution
and counsel of the duchess her mother) that his highest
temptations and sweetest batteries could not win upon her,
protesting never to yield to any dishonourable parley or
unchaste motion, although it might warrant the safety of
her life." †

We shall have to speak hereafter of an impediment in
the way of Edward's marriage from the fact of a pre-contract,
if not an actual marriage, with the Lady Eleanor Butler.
Of this Elizabeth was certainly ignorant. But she knew
the King's moral weakness, and made it the instrument of
her own ambition. Notwithstanding the insinuations of

---

* It does not appear that Edward communicated his intentions to any of
his friends except the Duchess of York, his mother.

† Buck, in Kennett, p. 563.

De Comines, there is no reason to doubt her chaste intentions, but, in the light of the character which she subsequently developed, we must receive with caution Sir George Buck's testimony to her artless humility. She humbly implored his grace, he tells us, "not to think her so exorbitantly and vainly ambitious to wish herself a queen, or to have the hope and presumption to be anything higher than what she was—his poor and humble vassal; nor was she of so low and lost a mind as to violate her chastity, or be a concubine to the greatest king." *   In a word, Elizabeth Woodville insisted upon an honourable marriage, and Edward, finding that "he must shift his sail to that scantling of the winde," protested that such was his desire, notwithstanding her inequality, for, in his esteem, her love, her beauty, and her virtue made her dowry great and high enough for any King.

The Duchess of York, foreseeing the calamitous consequences of this marriage, alike from the umbrage it would inevitably create in the Court of France, the offence to the English nobility, and, more than all, from the taint of bigamy, earnestly dissuaded her son from so impolitic an act. The arguments she employed are thus summarised by Sir Thomas More.†   .

"My liege lord, and my dear son,—It is very commonly reported you are purposed to marry the Lady Gray, a widow and a mean gentlewoman, which you cannot but conceive will redound to your disparagement and dishonour; all the wise, great, and noble persons of your kingdom thinking

---

* Yet even Buck admits that it was Edward's faithlessness to Elizabeth Lucy which induced "the subtil widow" to insist upon a marriage.

† Quoted by Sir George Buck, in Kennett, vol. i., p. 564.

it' far more to the advantage of your honour, profit, and
safety to seek the alliance of a noble progeny, and rather
in a foreign country than your own. . . . Also you may
not safely marry any other than the Lady Bona, the Earl
of Warwick having proceeded so far in the current of
that march already, that 'tis likely he will not sit down
contented if his troublesome and costly negotiation should
be so slightly blown off and frustrated. Besides, sir, consider it is not princely for a king to marry his own subject
. . . but will be less tolerable to all opinion than if
a rich man should marry his maid. . . . Yet there must
needs be more honesty in such a marriage than can
be honour in this which you affect. For the difference
is not so great betwixt a rich merchant and his servant, as
you must think between the king and the widow Gray; in
whose person (albeit there be nothing to be misliked) there is
nothing so excellent, but it may be found in divers other
women much more noble and many ways exceeding her, and
more comparatively to your estate (those also virgins, who
must be thought of a much more honourable estimation than
widows), wherefore the widowhood only of Elizabeth Gray
(though in all other things she were convenient for you) were
enough to restrain you, being a king, and so great a king.
*And it must stick a foul disparagement to the sacred majesty of
a prince (who ought as nearly to approach the priesthood in
pureness and cleanness as he doth in dignity) to be defiled with
bigamy in his first marriage."*

Edward lightly repelled these arguments, and reasonably
asserted his own prerogative. As for marrying a subject, he
believed it would win the affection of his people, when they

saw that their Prince disdained not affinity with them.* And
as for the lady herself, "he found her in the treasures of her
mind most abundant, and in the perfections of her body
excellent to please him."† Nor could he doubt that his cousin
Warwick's love was true and reasonable; he could not expect
his prince to be ruled by his eye rather than his own; "that
were to make me a ward, and bind me to marry by the
appointment of a guardian, with which servile and hard conditions I would not be a king." And, finally, he admits the
bigamy, which he probably purposed but failed to purge by
divorce. "Let the bishop," he says, "lay it hardly in my
way when I come to take orders of priesthood, for I confess I
understand bigamy is forbidden to a priest, but I never wist
it yet forbidden to a prince. Therefore, I pray you, good
madam, trouble yourself and me no further in this matter." ‡
Nor did he defer his marriage longer than was necessary;
"but marry her he did, and with such dispatch that he stayed
not for the advice of any, either counsellor, kinsman, or other
whatsoever. Nay, his speed admitted not the approved ceremony of banns asking. And such was the want of reverend
bishops then that he was fain to take an ordinary priest to
marry them, in a chamber too instead of a church, and that
in a lodge or forest house, nobody being present but the
duchess and some few of her company." §

As Warwick had foreseen, the King proceeded to raise
his wife's family to a greatness designed to balance his own,
and especially to neutralise his influence at the Council Board.

---

* Habington, in Kennett, p. 437.   † Ibid.   ‡ Buck, in Kennett, p. 564.
§ Ibid., 563.   Buck's statement, however, as we shall hereafter see, is not
borne out by Dr. Stillington, Bishop of Bath and Wells.

Her father, Lord Rivers, was made Treasurer and Constable. Her brother Anthony married the daughter of the late Lord Scales, whose title and estates—a portion of the latter forming the seat of the Prince of Wales at Sandringham—were conferred upon him. Her brother John, then in his twentieth year, married the opulent Dowager Duchess of Norfolk, aged eighty. Her eldest daughter was married to the Duke of Buckingham, and four others to members of the old nobility, whilst Edward's niece, the heiress of the Duke of Exeter, whose hand Warwick had sought for his brother's son, was betrothed to Elizabeth's son by her former marriage.* But whilst Edward thus checkmated his powerful subject, he alienated many old supporters of the family of York who emulated the Lancastrians in their hatred of the Woodvilles.† Warwick took note of the fact. The advancement of the Woodvilles involved the reversal of his foreign policy, and in nothing was this more apparent than in the marriage of Edward's sister Margaret to Charles, Count of Charolois, and afterwards Duke of Burgundy.

With purblind infatuation, egged on, it cannot be doubted, by the Queen and her brothers—whose hatred of Warwick knew no bounds — Edward repeated the dangerous affront which he had offered the Earl in the matter of his own marriage. Disappointed in securing the hand of Margaret for his brother, Lord Montague, Warwick obtained the King's consent to her marriage with a Prince of the royal family of France. In 1467 he was sent to France to conclude an

---

* See Green's "History of the English People," vol. ii., p. 34.

† "The queen's blood daily so rose without desert, but that they were of her blood."—CORNWALLIS, *Encomium of Richard III.*, p. 3.

alliance with Louis XI., of which the marriage treaty was again the most important article. The Woodvilles embraced the opportunity furnished by his absence from Court to persuade the King to an act of perfidy, the result, and probably the purpose of which was to create an open breach between Edward and his great baron. The bastard brother of Count Charles of Charolois was received at Court, and a marriage arranged between Charles and Margaret.* Warwick's embassy was thus dishonoured in the face of the world, and the affront was aggravated by the personal enmity towards the Earl of the bridegroom whom Edward had preferred. Lord Lytton correctly describes this as the first *open* dissension between the King and the Earl. On the former occasion, when Edward repudiated the negotiation for the hand of the Princess Bona, Warwick's indignation was as great, but he had more to gain than lose by restraining his anger. Now it was not so much the King as the Queen and her family who had thwarted and dishonoured him, and the outrage was not to be condoned. He withdrew in disgust to his castle at Middleham, where he was even more formidable than at Court. Hitherto he had been regarded as the head of the Yorkist party. If he was now discredited with his party, the King was not less so. If his policy with regard to France was reversed, he succeeded in moulding the policy of

---

* With that fine appreciation of the real character of the Duke of Gloucester, which even prejudice could not wholly obscure, Lord Lytton represents the King as paralysed with fear at the sudden return of Warwick, whilst he was amusing himself with a bevy of ladies at the Palace of Shene. Turning to Hastings, he despatches him in hot haste to Baynard's Castle, with these instructions : "Bring back Gloucester. In these difficult matters, that boy's head is better than a counsel."—*The Last of the Barons.*

Louis XI., in breaking up the triple alliance, and disappointing Edward's hopes of French conquest. Nor was this all. Aware of the disaffection of the Yorkists towards the King, he formed the design of rallying them round the Duke of Clarence, whose undisguised jealousy of the Woodvilles was his best title to their regard.

We have already seen that Edward regarded the fickle and pleasure-loving Clarence with distrust. The fact that he was the next heir to the throne was not calculated to lessen that distrust, whilst it gave the Duke an importance in Warwick's eyes which outweighed all defects of character. Immediately after his victory at Towton, Edward had caused the head of his father to be removed from the walls of York and interred with the body, and that of the young Earl of Rutland, at Pontefract. He now determined to transfer their remains to the magnificent collegiate church at Fotheringay, founded by his ancestor, Edward Plantagenet, one of the heroes of Agincourt. The funeral, as described by Sandford,* was of regal magnificence, and designed to impress the people with the kingly estate of the deceased Duke. The black velvet which covered the bier was overlaid with cloth of gold, and at its foot stood a white angel bearing a crown of gold to signify that of right he was a King. Bishops and abbots went in advance, to prepare the churches for the reception of the royal Duke's remains; and many nobles accompanied the imposing procession from Pontefract, through Doncaster, Newark, Grantham, and Stamford to Fotheringay, which was reached on the seventh

* Book v., p. 373.

day, Monday, 29th of July, 1466. The remarkable feature of this imposing ceremony is the absence of the Duke of Clarence. To Richard, Duke of Gloucester, was assigned the office which filial love would regard as the post of honour. As chief mourner he followed next after the hearse which conveyed his father's remains in that seven days' journey. The King, accompanied by several Dukes, Earls, and Barons, met the cavalcade "at the entry of the churchyard." The Queen and her two daughters were within the church. The absence of Clarence is unaccountable. Perhaps the reason, suggested rather than stated by Habington, is the most probable: "He was too open-breasted for the court, where suspicion looks through a man, and discovers his resolutions though in the dark, and locked up in secrecy." He was heir-presumptive to the throne. His unquiet and restless spirit may have led him already into those indiscretions which culminated in rebellion. It is at least obvious from the position assigned to Richard in the obsequies of his father, that Edward was in some degree alienated from Clarence.

Every year the estrangement increased. Whilst we find the name of the Duke of Gloucester constantly associated with that of the King, we hear little of the Duke of Clarence, and that little to his disadvantage. In 1468, Sir John Paston informs his mother of the King's visit to London, and adds: "There came with him and rode again in company with him, the Duke of Gloucester." The following year the King visited Norwich, and Sir John writes: "We find the Duke of Gloucester accompanied the king, but we hear nothing of the Duke of Clarence." Between

MIDDLEHAM CASTLE.

these dates the marriage of the King's sister, Margaret, with Charles, son of the Duke of Burgundy, had taken place, and the common love of an only sister once again united the brothers, who, accompanied by the Earl of Warwick, escorted her to Margate. Thence she embarked for that home which was destined, ere long, to be the asylum of two of her three brothers.

Queen Margaret had been no uninterested spectator of the divisions in the royal family, and the alienation of their great champion, the Earl of Warwick. In December, 1469, she proceeded with her son to meet Louis XI. at Tours, for the purpose of conference as to the means of turning these dissensions to her own advantage.

The opposition of Edward IV. to the proposal of Clarence to marry his cousin Isabel, Warwick's eldest daughter, incensed his brother and galled the pride of the great Earl. For Edward carried his opposition so far as to petition the Pope to refuse his sanction to the marriage on the ground of kinship. Uneasy as long as a Neville was in power, the King also secured the person of Warwick's brother, the Archbishop of York, robbed and imprisoned him, first in England, and afterwards at Guisnes.* All this Margaret heard with undisguised satisfaction, and, in spite of her strong antipathy to Warwick, she was ready to ally herself with the subverter of her husband's throne, and to employ her influence in reconciling the Lancastrian nobles to their most hated foe. When, however, the hour for action came, the sense of her irremediable wrongs and cruel sufferings—

---

* Lingard, vol. iv., p. 195.

of all the calamity to the King and her son, of which Warwick had been the author—rendered her less compliant. Warwick was equally unwilling to commit himself whilst the attitude of the Duke of Clarence was doubtful. His personal interests and private aims did not harmonise with the ideas of the exiled Queen. If the phlegmatic and inconstant Clarence failed him, all those interests would be jeopardised. He held the affronts received from his sovereign sufficient justification for the transfer of his allegiance, provided that it placed no hindrance in the way of his interest and ambition. For Warwick's conception of national morality, of the obligations of party faith or public honour, of consistency and disinterestedness, were not in advance of his age. The Duke of Clarence fell an easy prey to the Earl's intrigues, not the less so that they embraced the offer of the hand of his eldest daughter and wealthy co-heiress.

The much-controverted ground of the Earl of Warwick's defection demands a brief examination. The earliest, and in some respects the best-informed, writer attributes it to the removal from the Chancellorship of the Earl's brother, the Archbishop of York, in favour of Dr. Stillington, Bishop of Bath and Wells; and he adds: "thei nevere loffyd togedere aftere." * It is unnecessary to examine the various suggestions of later writers. If we would discover the true explanation we must distinguish between the *cause* and the *motive* of that defection, a distinction which appears to have been very seldom drawn. With the deference due to so cautious and trustworthy a guide as the continuator of the " Croyland

---

* "The Warkworth Chronicle," p. 4.

Chronicle," * I venture to think that this confounding of
cause and motive has led him to form an erroneous judgment.
He attributes Warwick's defection to the marriage treaty by
which the Princess Margaret was affianced to Charles, Count
of Burgundy. But, however the Earl may have dissembled
his discontent, and maintained an outwardly peaceable de-
meanour towards the Queen, even to the extent of standing
godfather to the infant Princess, it is impossible to doubt that
his rebellion was planned before the treaty with Burgundy
was proposed. There is but one incident which, both from its
importance and the date of its occurrence, can furnish the
required solution. By his marriage with Elizabeth Gray,
Edward IV. had set his proud noble and kinsman at defiance;
had defeated his elaborate diplomacy, disappointed his ambition, introduced an innovation by elevating a subject of low
rank to share his throne—and that subject the widow of an
attainted rebel—alienated the old nobility, and practically
deposed Warwick from that position of proud pre-eminence
and almost absolute power of which the King may well have
grown weary. From the moment when the fact of the King's
secret marriage was communicated to his Council, Warwick
realised that his power was gone, unless he recovered it by
the sword. From that moment he was a rebel in heart
and purpose. The Chevalier Baudier, a councillor of Louis XI.,
writes : "Richard, Earl of Warwick, returned into England

---

* The continuator of the "Croyland Chronicle" was a member of Edward's
Council. He was, therefore, well informed, and his narrative, though frag-
mentary, and primarily concerned with ecclesiastical affairs, is generally un-
biassed. "Whenever his assertions are positive," says Horace Walpole, "and
not mere flying reports, he ought to be admitted as fair evidence, since we
have no better."

full of confusion by the ridiculous part he had been made to
act in his embassy.   He was a man of judgment and temper,
well versed in all the arts of a court, and took care to let
nothing escape from him, either in word or action, that might
discover the least resentment at his treatment.   But in his
soul he meditated vengeance." *   Of yet greater weight is the
testimony of Dr. Warkworth, who says that when the Earl
returned home and heard of the royal marriage, "then was he
greatly displeased with the king, and after that rose great
dissention ever more and more between the king and him." †

The doubt which modern historians have endeavoured to
throw upon the fact of Warwick's embassy, and the proposed
marriage with the Lady Bona, is singular in the face of so
much independent contemporary evidence.   Equally opposed
to the testimony of history is the attempt to find in the
Burgundian marriage a first and principal cause of Warwick's
alienation.   "After the earl had intelligence from his friends
of the king's secret marriage, and that his dealings with the
ambassage of King Louis as touching the contracting of this
new affinity fell out in vain and to no purpose, he so highly
began to be angry thereat, that forthwith he adjudged King
Edward as a man unworthy of the royal sceptre, meet to be
expelled by all means possible; yet there is a common
rumour at this day that the cause of their variance should
have been this : because the earl dissuaded the king not to
place his sister Margaret in marriage with this son to Philip
Duke of Burgundy, whom the earl hated worse than any man
living, and for that King Edward would not hear his advice,

---

* " The Calamities of Margaret of Anjou," p. 126.
† " Warkworth Chronicle," pp. 3–4.

therefore this grudge to have grown between them, . . . and this is a mere fable of the common people." *

The question of *motive* is more complex. But it may be summed up in the word AMBITION. The King-maker would be the progenitor of kings. His pride was humbled by a double disappointment. Not only had Edward chosen a wife for himself instead of marrying Warwick's eldest daughter, but he had objected to her union with his brother Clarence. No female sovereign had ever yet ruled in England. Clarence was therefore still Edward's heir. The friends of Margaret were raising an army in the North with the purpose of rallying the old nobility to the support of the hereditary rights of her son Prince Edward, and Warwick resolved to marry his two daughters to George, Duke of Clarence, and Edward, titular Prince of Wales. Thus allied to the Houses of York and Lancaster, it was only necessary to secure the deposition of Edward IV. to raise one or other of his daughters to the throne. The cause and the motive of his rebellion are thus explained in perfect harmony with the chronology of events.

The Earl had obeyed the King's summons to be present at the marriage of the Princess Margaret. But he appeared, not as the Woodvilles believed, humbled by disgrace, but resolved upon a counter demonstration which should attach the wavering Yorkists to himself through the Duke of Clarence. The French alliance was unpopular in the country, and Warwick had been suspected by the Yorkists of coquetting with the Lancastrians at Rouen. The apparent reconciliation

---

* Polydore Vergil, Book xxiv., p. 118.

between the King and his recalcitrant noble did not survive
the embarcation of the Lady Margaret. No man knew so
well as Warwick the wily character of the French King,
or that whilst Margaret of Anjou could look to him for aid, no
member of the House of York could sit securely upon the
throne of England. His attachment to the House of York was
sincere, and it was unfortunate that Edward, who could not
expect the mere name of King to have much sanctity in
Warwick's estimation, proceeded to offer new affronts to his
pride at the very moment when policy was drawing him into
an alliance with Margaret. Whether, as Sandford suggests,
the Earl sought to seduce the Duke of Gloucester from his
loyalty may be doubtful. His success with the inconstant
and discontented Duke of Clarence was complete.

Warwick was constant to his desire to maintain at least
amity with France, and thus afforded his old enemies the
opportunity of renewing their accusations of treasonable
intercourse with Louis. Edward impoliticly declared war
with France, and snapped the brittle thread which bound the
stout Earl to his service. It was hardly possible, surrounded
by the harpies who ever whispered suspicion into his too
willing ears, that Edward could cling to the man who had
defied his power and menaced the throne which his own
hands had built. The noble whom he dare not defy he got
rid of by appointing him Governor of Calais—one of the
richest and most coveted preferments in the gift of the
crown. But Warwick was not deceived as to the King's
purpose. Meanwhile Louis XI. had patched up a peace with
Burgundy and Brittany, and Edward found the alliances which
he had made to thwart the Earl as durable as a rope of sand.

The loss of the masculine vigour which had so long guided the counsels of the indolent and luxurious King involved a weakening of the royal authority. For Edward, daring, energetic, and skilful in war, always surrendered himself to the guidance of others in times of peace, which for him were times of guilty indulgence. The Woodvilles had triumphed over the great Earl whom they had openly laboured to supplant; they were powerless to secure for the King's government the popularity and respect accorded to the name of Warwick; and while Edward was feasting at Shene * the Duchess of Bedford and her family swayed the royal counsels, and "encroached on all the good things power could bestow and avarice seize." The people suffered all the abuses for protection from which they had been accustomed to look to the strong arm of the Earl, and all men in England, we are told, "longed daily more and more to see him again, as men who thought themselves bereft of the sun in this world." † The King, seeing the Earl's faction growing daily stronger, became apprehensive of his return, and invoked the good offices of Louis XI. and Charles of Burgundy to prevent it. But Edward forgot that he had to reckon with the people.

Whilst the way was thus prepared for a popular rebellion, the youthful Duke of Gloucester alone had the courage to warn Edward of the danger of driving his great vassal to extremities. The King was too much absorbed in pleasures,

* Edward III. built the Palace of Shene, the extensive park attached to which was a favourite resort of Henry VI. and Queen Margaret for hunting, and of Edward IV. for indolent and effeminate pleasure. Henry VII. conferred upon it his own name of "Richmond."

† Polydore Vergil, Book xxiv., p. 120.

too glad to be rid of the imperious Earl who overshadowed his throne, and too thankful to have prevented, as he believed, the marriage of his brother Clarence with Warwick's daughter, to heed the counsel of the beardless youth, much as he loved his brother Richard, whose cool head and penetrating intellect rendered him wise in counsel as he was shortly to become valiant in war. But the time was at hand when Richard's prudent counsel was recalled, and the King is said to have exclaimed : " Would that the Duke of Gloucester were here ! " Richard was with the army on the Scottish border when the rebellion under Robin of Redesdale broke out in Lincolnshire. It was only when the insurgents had defeated the royal forces at Edgecote, pursued them into the Forest of Dean, slaughtered 5,000 men, and beheaded the father and brother of the Queen, that Edward listened to the angry demand for the recall of Warwick. Instant was the stout Earl's response. Neither past ingratitude and betrayal, nor the distrust thence engendered, could keep him from his post at the King's side in the hour of peril. His guerdon was the inflamed suspicion and ingratitude of Edward. For Warwick, the sight of whose banners sufficed to disband the insurgents against whom the whole royal army had been powerless, still patriotically insisted upon the removal of all the Woodvilles, the Queen alone excepted.

Warwick and Clarence continued their importunities to the King to give his consent to the marriage of the latter with Isabel Neville. The King's hesitation is intelligible, for the alliance between Clarence and Warwick was as distasteful to himself as to the Woodville faction, since it was perilous to the throne. But Edward suffered their importunity to be made a Court jest, and thus aroused against himself the enmity of the whole Neville family. George Neville, Archbishop of York, encouraged Warwick in his determination that the marriage should take place; and their brother Lord Montague, the courtier and time-server, "worldly, subtle, and designing," secretly acquiesced. It is difficult to account for the infatuation which could thus alienate the entire family of Neville, whose wealth and power Edward too well knew. In a society where the whole atmosphere was redolent with magical and astrological notions, with which the King himself was known to be infected,* it is not surprising that the populace believed him to be bewitched by Jacquetta, the Queen's mother, and her necromancer, Friar Bungay.† In illustration of the enormous wealth of the Nevilles, Lord Lytton‡ mentions the fact that no less than 30,000 persons were daily feasted at the open tables with which Warwick allured to his countless castles the strong hands and grateful hearts of a martial and unsettled population. At the installation of his brother, George Neville, as Archbishop of York, in 1460, 104 oxen, 1,000 sheep, 2,000 pigs, 500 stags, bucks, and roes, 22,512 fowls of different sorts, 204 cranes, 400 heron-shaws, 12 porpoises and seals, 300 tuns of ale, 100 tuns of wine, and 1 pipe of ipocrasse constituted the bill of fare !

The Duke of Clarence—a lad of nineteen—was induced

---

* Whilst the mathematician and astronomer, Boliubroke, had been hanged and quartered as a wizard, the impudent impostor, Friar Bungay, received honour and patronage from the King's household.

† This man, who acquired such influence with the Duchess of Bedford, was, in his youth, an itinerant mountebank. He became a clever juggler, and appears to have possessed some knowledge of animal magnetism. Hence his great reputation in a superstitious age.

‡ Preface to "The Last of the Barons."

to visit Warwick at Calais.   There the Earl's brother, the
Archbishop of York, awaited his arrival, and solemnised
his marriage with the Lady Isabel Neville on the 12th of
July, 1469.   It was for this act that the King deprived him
of the Chancellorship.   The Archbishop and the Marquis
of Montague now openly joined Warwick's conspiracy.   From
this time also the jealousy with which the King had regarded
the Duke of Clarence developed into bitter hatred.*   Within
six months he was a prisoner in that hated brother's hands,
and it was not in human nature to forgive the indignity
which eventually cost the unhappy Clarence his life.   The
fact of the King's imprisonment is involved in some obscurity.
The historian and the novelist have alike surrounded it with
an atmosphere of romance which this history is not concerned to dissipate.

Warwick had defeated the insurgents at Edgecote, but the
increased prestige which this victory brought him intensified
the King's distrust and the jealousy of the Woodvilles.
Whatever the cause of the Earl's final desertion of the King,
there is no doubt that Edward was now practically if not
actually his prisoner.   Hume indeed argues that the records
in Rymer allow of no interval for his alleged detention at
Middleham and elsewhere.   But Hume makes the singular
mistake of placing it in the year 1470, whereas it was in
1469, after the overthrow of Redesdale, that Warwick is said to

* In justice to the unstable Clarence, it should be borne in mind that he
had real ground of complaint in the extravagant favour shown to the Queen's
family.   Whilst still resisting Warwick's overtures, he is said in a conference
with the Earl to have exclaimed : " By St. George, if my brother of Gloucester
would join me, I would make Edward know we were all one man's sons, which
should be nearer to him than strangers of his wife's blood."—HALL's *Chronicle*,
p. 271.

have "approached the King's camp as secretly as he could in the night, and having killed the watch and ward, took the King at unawares, whom he brought with him to Warwick."* The question, however, is set at rest by Edward IV. himself, who, in the subsequent attainder of Clarence, enumerates it amongst his offences, "in jupartyng the king's royall estate, persone, and life, in straite warde, putting him thereby from all his libertie." † The confederated nobles found their illustrious prisoner a source of embarrassment. By detaining him they offended the Yorkists without conciliating the Lancastrians, who would be satisfied with nothing less than the restoration of Henry VI., whilst they alienated the great majority of the people with whom the King was popular. The essential thing for Warwick was to retain his influence with the warrior barons, and he soon found that they almost unanimously demanded the King's release.‡ Upon this then he decided. After transferring him from Warwick Castle to Middleham, and finally to York, where he was committed to the custody of the Archbishop, his freedom appears to have been granted with the consent both of Warwick and the Duke of Clarence, although Dr. Warkworth says that "by fair·speech and promise, the king escaped out of the bishop's hands, and came unto London and did what him liked." §

After some futile attempts to effect a reconciliation, a formidable rebellion broke out in Lincolnshire in the spring of 1470. It was headed by Sir Robert Welles, a partisan of Warwick's, and its avowed object was to place Clarence on the throne. The insurgents were routed and the King wreaked

---

* Polydore Vergil, Book xxiv., p. 124.   † "Rot. Parl.," vol. vi., p. 193.
‡ Sharon Turner, vol. iii., p. 321.   § "The Warkworth Chronicle," p. 7.

his vengeance upon their leaders. Warwick and Clarence, disappointed of the support on which the Earl had relied, sought an asylum in France. They were cordially received at Amboise by Louis XI., who had summoned Margaret of Anjou and her son to his Court. Warwick's brothers had again changed sides. The King, assured of their loyalty and realising the folly of having driven the Earl to extremities, invited him and Clarence to return and confide in his clemency. It was too late. Warwick distrusted the King's sincerity, and had now openly espoused the cause of Henry VI., and persuaded Clarence, who had so recently all but grasped the sceptre for himself, to join him in an invasion of the country on behalf of the rival House of Lancaster.

But although the Earl had espoused the Lancastrian cause he was regarded by the party with suspicion, jealousy, and aversion, and after the failure of Clarence his hope of Yorkist aid was at zero. It was his ambition to be the founder of a race of kings, and the great whirligig of time offered as the instrument of that ambition his most hated and inveterate foe, the ex-Queen Margaret. But Warwick had misjudged his ability to persuade Margaret to repose confidence in one at whose hands she had suffered beyond forgiveness. Her haughty spirit was as little humbled as her angry passions were softened by affliction. Nothing short of the countenance of Margaret could shield Warwick from the danger of Lancastrian vengeance, and he was importunate in his pleading for a reconciliation. She spurned the humble suppliant from her feet, and for a fortnight remained deaf to the entreaties of her son and the French

King. Louis agreed to be surety for all the Earl's promises, and prayed the Queen that "at his request she would pardon the said Earl of Warwick, shewing the great love he had unto him, and that he was bounden to the said earl more than to any other man, and therefore ho would do as much and more for him than for any man living." *

To this appeal Margaret at length yielded. Her hatred to Warwick was great, but her passion of revenge against Edward "absorbed all lesser and more trivial causes of resentment." When, however, Louis proposed to consummate this reconciliation by a marriage contract between Prince Edward and Anne Neville, the queen's indignation knew no bounds. "What!" she exclaimed, "will he give his daughter to my son whom he has so often branded as the offspring of adultery or fraud?" She saw no honour in such an alliance, either for herself or her son, and she refused to listen either to Warwick or her father's counsellors. The antiquary Stow explains the secret of Margaret's obduracy where the interests of her son appeared to be so seriously jeopardised. He says that she showed the King of France a letter, recently received from England, offering the hand of the Princess Elizabeth (then four and a half years old) to her son, and "so the queen persevered fifteen days" before she would assent to Warwick's proposal.

---

* Ellis's "Original Letters," 2nd Series, vol. i., p. 133. The same letter lends some countenance to the idea that Richard had an emissary at Amboise, whose business was to deafen Margaret's ears to all overtures from Warwick. It would, she argued, be a thing greatly prejudicial to King Henry, herself, and her son to take part with Warwick. There were *certain parties and friends* whom they might perchance lose by this means, "and that would be a thing that greatly might grieve them" and do them more harm and hindrance than the said Earl and his allies "might advantage them."—*Ibid.*, p. 132.

At length, to win a kingdom for her son, the proud Margaret gave a reluctant consent to an alliance, to the details of which we shall presently recur. The Earl also had received despatches from England which may have quickened Margaret's decision. They signified that "the people universally throughout the realm, did so much look, hope, and long for his return into England that they were already everywhere in arms awaiting his arrival; * willing him therefore to make haste, yea, though it were without any army, for as soon as he should set foot a-land many thousands of men would repair to him thither forthwith . . . . that the commons were wholly thus affected; yea moreover that many noble men also were right ready to minister money, etc., to that war, and with hand and heart to help the same." †

On the 13th of September, 1470, Warwick and Clarence landed at Dartmouth. Edward was pursuing Lord Fitzhugh and Robin of Redesdale in Lincolnshire. Having been privately assured that his brother would return to his allegiance, he hastened back towards London, anxious to encounter Warwick. But Fitzhugh pursued him. Clarence made no . overtures. Montague seized the opportunity of avenging himself upon the King for which he had long watched. A year had passed since Edward had released Henry Percy from the Tower, and conferred upon him the title and estates of his father which Montague had enjoyed as his share of the Yorkist spoil. He now declared for his brother, his troops shouting: "A Warwick! A Warwick!

---

* "Warwick showed the French king letters out of England, promising that he should have 50,000 fighters at his commandment."—ELLIS' *Original Letters,* 2nd Series, Letter 42.   † Polydore Vergil, Book xxiv., p. 132.

Long live Henry VI. ! " In this dilemma, and conscious that he had forfeited the respect and confidence of all the old nobility, Edward declined to strike a blow for his crown. He was at Castle Rising, near Lynn Regis, when the tidings of Warwick's invasion reached him. Accompanied by his brother Richard, he hastily took ship at Lynn, and sought an asylum with his sister Margaret, now Duchess of Burgundy. "His flight was so hasty," says Habington, "that not only his apparel and other furniture were lost or left behind, but even his treasure, so that to defray the charge of his transportation he was necessitated to give the master of the ship a gown furred with martens," and to land in his waistcoat.

Warwick entered London in triumph, for the Lancastrians held the city and had organised a welcome to the once hated Queen. Her misfortunes, and still more her policy in overcoming her just indignation, thus uniting the three great Houses of York, Lancaster, and Neville, appealed to the sympathy and won the gratitude of the citizens.

Henry VI. was restored amid the acclamations of the citizens, but his incapacity rendered it necessary to appoint a regency. Parliament was summoned in the name of the restored King. It met on the 26th of November. An Act of Settlement entailed the crown on the male issue of Henry VI., and, in default of such issue, on the Duke of Clarence, and Edward's humiliation was completed by the nomination of Warwick and Clarence as Protectors of the Realm during the minority of Prince Edward.

I have thus far followed the fortunes of Edward IV., in order to make clear his relations with his two brothers— the duped and disloyal Clarence, and the ever-faithful and

strong-minded Gloucester. In sharing his brother's exile
we may learn from De Comines * how real were the privations
to which he was exposed, for the Flemish historian relates
that he had seen the Duke of Exeter, who had married
a sister of Edward IV.'s, "barefoot and ragged, begging
his meat from door to door in the Low Countries. Yet,"
writes Miss Halsted, "did Gloucester voluntarily share
Edward's privations in Burgundy, and serve him in adversity
with as much cheerfulness and fidelity as when he had
accepted with grateful feelings, in days of prosperity, the
high honours and wealthy endowments which that monarch
so early bestowed upon him. A comparison cannot fail to
be here drawn between the unworthy feelings that influenced
Clarence to accelerate the downfall of so near a relative,
one who had distinguished him in his youth by kindness
little less than paternal, and that of the much-defamed
Gloucester, who, traditionally reported to be void of every
kind and generous sentiment, was, nevertheless, the willing
companion and friend in his adverse fortune of that brother
who had so tenderly fostered him in childhood; and who . . .
scrupled not to sacrifice all wealth, honours, independence,
to become a houseless wanderer . . . to participate in the
attainder that deprived King Edward, and himself as his
partisan, of every possession whether hereditary or acquired." †

---

* The history of Philip de Comines has a special value, both from the
opportunities he enjoyed of learning the history of these dark years, and from
the fact that, as a foreigner, writing for the information of his Government, he
was free from bias, and wrote without fear or favour. M. Guizot speaks of
him as "one of the most eminent Flemish politicians who, after having taken
a chief part in the affairs of their country and their epoch, have dedicated
themselves to the work of narrating them in a spirit of liberal and admirable
comprehension."

† "Richard III.," by Caroline A. Halsted, vol. i., p. 165.

CHAPTER III.

Much that is undeserving the name of history has been written concerning the physical and moral deformity of the Duke of Gloucester, afterwards Richard III., and our great dramatist has rendered it impossible that, in the popular conception, the truth concerning "the Unpopular King" should ever supersede portraitures of Lancastrian origin—the expression of political and personal animosity. Mankind are generally agreed as to what constitutes physical deformity, and it may not be uninstructive to consider the evidence for and against this popular and traditional conception.

The evidence afforded by several contemporary portraits is valuable, though not conclusive. Artists in all ages, especially such as have been entrusted with the delineation of princes, have shown a disposition to flatter their originals by dissembling natural defects. Few men, and perhaps fewer princes, have emulated the sturdy honesty of Cromwell, who insisted that the unwilling artist should depict the wart upon his nose. Still a contemporary portrait possesses a value as evidence of physical characteristics, second only to the testimony of contemporary writers. The most authentic

portrait of Richard III. is, by common consent, admitted
to be that at Windsor Castle by an unknown artist. There
are several copies, probably by the same hand. Another
undoubtedly contemporary portrait is in the possession of
the Society of Antiquaries. There are also two original
likenesses by the contemporary chronicler Rous, in the
later only of which the critical eye may detect a slight
want of symmetry in the shoulders. In none of these is
there the slightest trace of that deformity which Rous
describes in his "Warwick Roll," written, be it remembered,
under the patronage of Henry VII.* Their general
characteristics are the same; the face sad rather than cruel,
thoughtful rather than crafty, and suggesting that firmness
which we know to have been characteristic of Richard,
whether as Duke of Gloucester or King of England. The
figure (half-length) is erect, well-proportioned, and suggestive
of low stature, but without a trace of deformity.

Of greater importance is the testimony of contemporary
chroniclers. With a single exception, none of these make
the most distant allusion to a fact which, of all others, we
should have expected them to notice. Especially in those
lampoons which were designed to bring Richard into contempt, and of which many were circulated, would a circumstance so favourable to their avowed object be pressed
into service. The continuator of the "Croyland Chronicle," as

---

* As a writer, Rous is wholly unworthy of credit. He "raked together
monkish stories and reproduced them to flatter Henry VII." A servile
flatterer, he prostituted his pen to ignoble purposes. When nothing more was
to be had from a patron, or when it became dangerous to stand by him, he
turned against him. Thus, notwithstanding his great obligations to
Richard III., he returned his kindness in wormwood and gall.

a member of Edward IV.'s Council, must have been well
acquainted with Richard. We shall hereafter see that he
had the temerity at least to insinuate that the Duke or his
brother Edward was guilty of the murder of Henry VI. He
was therefore unlikely to be deterred by any tenderness to
Richard, or by the scruples of a courtier, from reference
to his deformity. Yet we search the Chronicle in vain for one
word of comment. William of Worcester was a contemporary
historian, Sir John Paston and the Fleetwood Chronicler had
personal relations with Richard, yet neither of them makes
any allusion to his deformity. Fabyan,* who was Lancastrian
in his sympathies, and strongly repugnant to Richard, knows
nothing of it. De Comines, an historian of undoubted veracity,
whilst he extols the personal bearing of Edward IV., is equally
silent as to any defect in that of his brother; whilst Dr. Shaw,
of whom we shall hear presently, appealed to the people
whether Richard was not the express image of his father's
person. "Not all the preacher's power could have kept the
muscles of the mob in awe, and prevented their laughing
at so ridiculous an apostrophe had Richard been a little,
crooked, withered, hump-backed monster as later historians
would have us believe." †

Rous alone, and that after Richard's death, says that *his
shoulders were uneven,* and his features small—"*curtam habens
faciem.*" He has sketched him, as we have seen, with the
pencil as well as the pen in the "Warwick Rolls," where the

---

* Fabyan was a merchant, and had been Sheriff of London. He wrote in
1490, and is well informed in matters relating to London and the neighbourhood. Considering that he wrote under the jealous eye of Henry VII., his
testimony in favour of Richard possesses a peculiar interest and value.

† Horace Walpole's "Historic Doubts," p. 103.

uneven shoulders are barely perceptible, whilst the face is
gentle almost to effeminacy. Thirty years later, Sir Thomas
More notices a similar deformity ; but whilst Rous says that
the left shoulder was lower than the right, More tells us that
the right was lower than the left, and seems to treat the
current stories of deformity as idle and malicious reports.
In 1484 the Scottish Commissioners, when treating for peace,
in their address to Richard notice the fact that he was
small of stature, but of his personal appearance they say :
" In your face (is) a princely majesty and authority royal,
sparkling with the illustrious beams of all moral and heroical
virtues." This is the language of extravagant adulation ;
but it is impossible to regard it as mere burlesque. Fifty
years later the antiquary Stow says that in his investigations
he had "spoken with some ancient men who from their own
sight and knowledge affirmed he was of goodly shape, comely
enough, only of low stature." *   Unreliable as Rous is—a
mere collector of monkish stories, and a fawning flatterer
of royalty—we cannot wholly discredit the testimony of one
who had often *seen* Richard. It is probable, indeed, that
he has preserved for us the small modicum of truth which
has been the foundation of the most extravagant fables. In
the original edition of his " Historic Doubts," Horace Walpole
introduces a print of a drawing which had come into his
possession, and which confirms Rous's statement, except that
it is the *left* shoulder which is here the highest, and Richard
has "a sort of tippet of ermine doubled about his neck,
which seems calculated to disguise some want of symmetry
thereabouts." †

---

* See Buck, in Kennett, p. 548.   † " Historic Doubts," p. 104.

Evidence then of the first class there is none. The utmost that can be deduced from authorities so prejudiced as Rous and More is that Richard's shoulders were so slightly uneven that they contradict one another, and Rous contradicts himself in describing the deformity. But against this equivocal evidence must be weighed the strong indirect testimony afforded by the silence of Richard's enemies. This, as we remember the bitter hatred that was borne to him, is almost equivalent to evidence of the first class, and leaves us in doubt whether even the minor deformity existed in fact. For the testimony of Stow's authorities that Richard "was of bodily shape comely enough," is confirmed by the Countess of Desmond, who had danced with him in King Edward's court, and declared him "the handsomest man in the room, his brother excepted." *

It must then be allowed that the popular conception of Richard as a "hunchback" finds no support in history, and is not so much as hinted at by the most malicious of his contemporaries. It was the fabrication of a later age; but the idle tradition holds its ground, and will doubtless continue to do so for all time, in virtue of the malignant slanders which Shakspeare, by their adoption, has made imperishable :

> I that am rudely shaped, and want love's majesty.
>   *   *   *   *   *
> Cheated of feature by dissembling nature,
> Deformed, unfinished, sent before my time
> Into this breathing world, scarce half made up,
> And that so lamely and unfashionable
> That dogs bark at me as I halt by them.

With the chroniclers the calumny probably originated in

---

* Hutton's " Richard III.," p. 159.

the recognised necessity of representing some physical expression of that *moral* deformity which they attributed to Richard.

> There's no art
> To find the mind's construction in the face.

The hand of genius had depicted upon canvas a face in which posterity could not recognise a moral monster; but the pen, dipped in venom, takes its revenge in describing its original as a hunchback, with savage teeth and withered arm! An idle calumny passes into the region of historical fact, and a late historian has not hesitated to disgrace his pages with the following elegant description of Richard III.: "Of body he was but low, crooked-backed, hook-shouldered, splay-footed, and goggle-eyed; his face little and round, his complexion swarthy, his left arm from his birth dry and withered; born a monster in nature, with all his teeth, with hair on his head, and nails on his fingers and toes; and just such were the qualities of his mind." [*]

That Richard was stern and occasionally cruel need not be questioned. In the formation of character the surroundings of childhood and its early impressions exercise a potent influence. Sickly, if not deformed, he was in his infancy familiarised with scenes of anarchy. In his third year the civil war broke out; in his fourth his father fell a victim to the ferocious cruelty of Margaret. He returned from Utrecht to have his precocious intelligence ripened amid scenes of horror which unhealthily stimulated the natural firmness of his character. Before he was out of his teens,

---

[*] Baker's "Chronicles of the Kings of England," p. 234.

in 1469, he was made Constable of England, and the following year Warden of the West Marches of Scotland. Thus, says Hutton, "he was early taught to rise who in a few years was able to teach himself." Thus also was responsibility, with all that it involved in those lawless days, prematurely thrust upon the boy who should have been learning the art of governing in the school of obedience. Thus he became infected with the cruel and relentless spirit of his age, which, if his power of self-control had not infinitely transcended that of his brother Edward, must have developed a character such as the hostile chroniclers of the succeeding reign portrayed, and which succeeding historians—with a logic more rigorous than discriminating—have accepted. He very early displayed that "leading capacity" which explains the confidence reposed in him by the King, and which, amid the turmoil of political strife, of discord, treachery, and domestic feud, in which he was now to be a principal actor, marked him out as an object of fear, and jealousy, and execration. At the age of twenty he was a military commander, thirsting to revenge his father's cruel death, as his brother Edward had done at the sanguinary battle of Towton, where 35,000 men, including the flower of the Lancastrian nobility, were slain.

Richard was a fugitive with his brother Edward at the court of the Duke of Burgundy. The Fleetwood Chronicler *

---

* "History of the Arrival of Edward IV. in England," found in the library of Fleetwood, the well-known Recorder of London in the time of Elizabeth. It is remarkable how little use has been made of this important MS. (Stow's Transcripts, 543), the very existence of which is unknown to many scholars. It is the earliest, and indeed the only authorised record from a Yorkshire source, and by a writer enjoying exceptional opportunities for gathering information. The MS. was edited by Mr. Bruce for the Camden Society. "The

informs us that the Lady Cecily, Duchess of York, used the great influence she possessed over her sons to bring about a reconciliation, and that in this effort she was warmly supported by her daughter, the Duchess of Burgundy.* The nobler feelings of both had been outraged by Clarence's treachery, and when, by their representations, he was led to realise his true position and that of his brothers, to perceive that he had been used to serve the purposes of others, and that "himself was had in great suspicion," he promised his support to Edward so soon as he should be able to effect a landing in England. The Duke of Burgundy secretly favoured Edward's enterprise, and extended a real though carefully disguised hospitality to his friends. But Charles the Bold was indisposed to incur the animosity of Louis IX., by giving his brother-in-law overt assistance. He therefore forbad his subjects to enlist in Edward's service, or in any way to aid his enterprise, whilst he privately assisted him with money and ships for the transport of his army from Flushing to the English coast.

On the 2nd of March, 1471, Edward had collected 2,000 brave and resolute Englishmen at the Dutch port. A violent storm prevented their sailing that night; but Edward, having gone on board, refused to leave his ships. "The wind fell not good for him," and it was not until the 11th that his little fleet sailed direct to the coast of Norfolk. On the evening of

---

author," observes Mr. Bruce, "says he was a servant of Edward IV., and that he presently saw in effect a great part of his exploits, and the residue knew by true relation of them that were present at every time."

* "By right covert wayes and meanes were good mediators and mediatricis, and highe and myghty princis my lady theyr mother; my lady of Exeter, my lady of Southfolke, theyre systers . . . . and other well disposyd parsouns."
—*Fleetwood Chronicle*, p. 10.

the 12th it was before Cromer, and a boat was sent ashore. The people were not unfriendly, but on learning that " those parts were right sore beset by the Earl of Warwick," and that the Earl of Oxford was vigilantly watching the coast, Edward declined to court annihilation and sailed northward.* Again a tempestuous storm threatened his destruction; but every man was animated by the same spirit of determination and courage which inspired their leader. On the 14th he disembarked near Ravenspur, in Yorkshire, with Hastings and 500 well-chosen men; the Duke of Gloucester, Lord Rivers, and the rest landed at various points within a few miles, "where they might but get land."

Having ascertained that the people stood too much in fear of Warwick, and were too indifferent to the rival claims of the Red and the White Rose to espouse his cause, Edward hastened to York, nothing doubting a welcome in his own city.† The very name of "Yorkshireman" to-day is a synonym for good faith, sincerity, urbanity, and warmheartedness. It was otherwise four hundred years ago, and Edward discovered that the city was as disloyal to his house as the county had proved. He artfully appealed to their sympathy by professing that his object was simply to claim his inheritance as Duke of York. The ruse was successful, but the citizens still refused to open their gates until they had exacted an oath from Edward " thenceforth

---

* "The Fleetwood Chronicle," p. 2.

† "As to the folke of the countrya there came but right few to hym, or almost none, for by the scuringe of suche persons as for that cawse were, by his said rebells, sent afore into thos partes for to move them to be again his highness, the people were sore endwaed to be contrary to hym, and not to receyve ne accepe hym as for theyr kynge."—*Ibid.*, p. 3.

to be obedient and faithful to King Henry." * With sixteen or seventeen attendants he entered the city, "and came to the worshipful folks which were assembled a little within the gates, and shewed them the intent and purpose of his coming in such form and with such manner language that the people contented them therewith." † Once in possession of the city, Edward little heeded his oath, but after placing a strong garrison in possession he marched with extraordinary rapidity by Wakefield, Sendall, and Leicester, to Coventry, passing Montague who lay motionless at Pontefract. He had now been joined by "ryght-a-fayre felowshipe of men" to the number of 7,000, and for the purpose of putting Clarence's sincerity to the proof — before the Lancastrians were strengthened by the arrival of the Dukes of Exeter and Somerset—he hastened to Banbury.

Warwick was wholly unprepared for the treachery of Clarence. With 4,000 men he would have cut off Edward's approach to Leicester, "and there the Earl of Warwick had fought with him but that he received a letter from the Duke of Clarence that he should not fight until he came." ‡ It is interesting to note that the Duke of Gloucester was the intermediary between the brothers, whose reconcilia-

---

* Polydore Vergil, Book xxiv., p. 189.

† " Fleetwood Chronicle," p. 5.

‡ Leland's "Collectanea," vol. iv., p. 504. So also Dr. Warkworth. Stow, in his Chronicle, says that the Duke of Clarence's letter was addressed " to the Marquis Montacute." But however unintelligible the supineness of Montague and Northumberland in allowing Edward to pass them unchallenged, it is impossible that the latter, and very improbable that the former would be influenced by any order of the Duke of Clarence. The authority of Dr. Warkworth is certainly preferable to that of Stow.

tion was effected in presence of the two armies in the neighbourhood of Banbury. The contemporary Chronicler, who probably witnessed the scene, writes: "Then spake together the two Dukes of Clarence and Gloucester, and, after, the other noblemen being there with them, whereof all the people there that loved them and owed them their true service were right glad and joyous, and thanked God highly of that joyous meeting, unity, and accord. . . . . And then the trumpets and minstrels blew up, and with that the king brought his brother Clarence and such as were with him to his fellowship, whom *the said Duke welcomed into the land in the best manner.*" * This Yorkist writer is confirmed by Polydore Vergil, who says: "Richard, Duke of Gloucester, as though he had been appointed arbiter of all controversy, first conferred secretly with the duke; then he returned to King Edward and did the very same with him."† All authorities agree as to Richard's solicitude for his brother the Duke of Clarence. The historian, Habington, so unfriendly to Richard, tells us that "the Duke of Gloucester and other lords, seeming to abhor the inhuman nature of the proposed battle, passed often formally between the brothers, and urged them by all respects, both religious and political, to prevent a quarrel so ruinous and so scandalous to both, wherein the triumph could not be but almost the destruction of the conqueror." ‡ One more authority may be quoted. "In the night," says the Chevalier Baudier, "the Duke of Gloucester went to speak with his brother the Duke of Clarence, and after some private discourse

* "Fleetwood Chronicle," p. 11.
† Polydore Vergil, Book xxiv., p. 141.   ‡ Habington, p. 448.

together the latter went over with 12,000 followers to King Edward." *

To Richard, then, belongs the credit of the peace-maker; whilst Clarence—"false, fleeting, perjured Clarence"— removed further from the throne by the birth of a prince during Edward's exile, consulted his own safety by changing sides after securing a pledge for the condonement of his rebellion, "Wherewith the other lords were somdeale abashed." † Clarence, however, must be credited with an attempt to prevail on Warwick to treat with Edward; but the Earl had, as Clarence knew, too deeply pledged him- self to Margaret to be able to abandon her cause without provoking the hostility of Louis and covering himself with dishonour.‡ The sword was now the only arbiter he would admit between himself and Edward, and that fatal point was reached when neither could ever again trust the other. Clarence's compunction was probably as sincere as that of most men, who, having perpetrated irretrievable injustice with the intoxication of complacency, calmly watch its effects upon their victims. When Warwick received his message, we are told, "first he accursed and cried out upon him that, contrary to his faith and promise given, he had in such shameful manner fled unto King Edward." § Then he turned to the Duke's messenger and indignantly exclaimed: "Go and tell your master that Warwick, true to his word, is a better man than the false and perjured Clarence." ||

The rapid march of Edward's army, the defection of

---

* "The Calamities of Margaret of Anjou," p. 177.   † Fabyan, p. 660.
‡ "Fleetwood Chronicle," p. 12.   § Polydore Vergil, Book xxiv., p. 142.
|| Lingard, vol. iv., p. 185.

Clarence, the reception accorded to the Yorkists in London—more hearty, and perhaps less insincere than that so recently given to Warwick—might well have filled the Earl's mind with dismay. He had appointed his brother, the Archbishop of York, to maintain his cause in the metropolis. The Archbishop had 6,000 men under his command, and had he acted with zeal and good faith, London might have been saved to Warwick. The Earl wrote to him, as also to the Mayor, urging them "to provoke the city" against Edward, and keep him out for two or three days, when he would not fail to come with great force.*

The populace admired "the handsomest man in England," the merchants were grateful for the prosperity which nine years of almost unbroken peace had secured to them. But a King driven into exile by a subject! Did not the fact absolve them from further allegiance? The question could not be answered by reference to vague abstractions without a close study of facts. And then, the good King Henry, the son of the hero of Agincourt, was his incapacity as great as had been represented? He had recovered from more than one attack of imbecility. Perhaps he was now in full possession of his faculties. At least his long exclusion from public view was suspicious. Availing himself of this wave of public sentiment, George Neville, whose only concern was to ally himself with the successful party, thought to convert it into an enthusiasm for the afflicted King by parading him through the streets of London.† In this he overreached himself, and played into the

---

* "Fleetwood Chronicle," p. 15.

† "The whiche rather withdrewe manes hertes than otherwyse."—Fabyan, p. 660.

hands of the more astute Archbishop of Canterbury, who, across the marshes of Westminster, was watching his proceedings from Lambeth Palace. When the citizens, prepared to receive their ill-used King with rapturous applause, looked upon a guileless, hopeless puppet, in whose vacant countenance and unmeaning smile less than mere animal] intelligence was expressed, the kingly robes that were piled upon him seemed a cruel mockery. The reaction in public feeling was sudden and complete. The populace who lined the long bush-grown passage of the Strand were moved, not to enthusiasm, but to a sympathetic sadness; the rulers of the City discovered that the King had but a feeble following.* He had no wrongs to avenge, no capacity for discharging the duties of a King. If nominally restored to that office he would be ruled by an ambitious Queen, that "outlandish woman" whose cause Warwick had espoused, but whose sway neither London nor the country would accept.

Archbishop Bourchier, meanwhile, was in correspondence with Edward IV., and profiting by the mistake of his brother of York, arranged a *coup de théâtre*, of which we shall speak more particularly when we come to review the Primate's career. Edward received the ovation which George Neville had laboured to evoke on behalf of Henry VI.† After invoking the Cardinal Archbishop's benediction at St. Paul's, he hastened to Westminster, where, during Warwick's occu-

---

* "Fleetwood Chronicle," p. 16.

† Fabyan says that Edward "found King Henry almost alone, for all such lords and others as in the morning were about him, when they heard of King Edward's coming, anon they fled, and every man was fain and glad to save himself." P. 660. Archbishop Neville took the lead in this treachery, and secured his own safety by a promise of submission secretly conveyed to Edward. See "Fleetwood Chronicle," p. 17.

pation of the City, Queen Elizabeth had taken sanctuary. There she presented him with her infant son, born during his exile. The royal family took up their residence at Whitehall, the palace of the Archbishop of York. It was Holy Week; but the churchman permitted his guests to convert it into a festival, and, we are told, "they refreshed themselves all the Thursday and Good Friday." *

On Easter eve the King, accompanied by the Duke of Gloucester, marched out of London with 7,000 men "to keep a bloody Easter-day at Barnet," a village midway between London and St. Alban's. It was quite dark when Edward arrived, and now a curious mistake happened, attributable perhaps to the anxiety on both sides to observe the strictest silence in order that the adversary might be uninformed of their movements. It was Edward's intention to encamp directly in Warwick's front, but owing to the darkness he threw out his line far beyond the Earl's left, and leaving his right entirely unopposed.† Enjoining absolute silence upon his army, he waited the dawn to commence the attack. Both armies "had goons and ordinaunce," but Warwick is believed to have been much stronger in artillery than the King; fortunately for the latter, he had placed it on his right wing. Leland says "they shotte Gunnes al Night one at the other." ‡ But it appears certain that it was Warwick alone who kept up this night cannonade, whilst the King had the satisfaction of seeing him expend his gunpowder in firing into the air.§ "Edward,"

---

* Dean Hook, "Lives of the Archbishops," vol. v., p. 351.
† "Fleetwood Chronicle," p. 17.   ‡ "Collectanea," vol. iv., p. 504.
§ "On the nyght, weninge gretly to have anoyed the Kinge and his

says Mr. Sharon Turner, "as the flashes of the guns illumined by fits the gloom of midnight saw the advantage of his unintentional error, and to prevent Warwick from discovering it reiterated his orders for the most profound silence."* On the morning of Easter Sunday, the 14th of April, the two armies advanced to battle, but owing to a dense mist they were invisible to each other. Edward was in the field arranging his troops soon after four o'clock. It is no slight proof of his confidence in his younger brother that he assigned the post of honour and of danger to the Duke of Gloucester, who commanded the van of the Yorkist army. The battle commenced at five o'clock. It is said, though on questionable authority, that Edward placed the helpless, imbecile King in his front ranks that he might fall at the hands of Warwick's soldiers.

For three hours the fearful struggle continued. A dense mist, "by reason of the incantations of Friar Bungay,"† enveloped both armies, whilst the fear of mutual betrayal beneath its veil demoralised the Lancastrians. The confusion and alarm, as sudden as they were groundless, would be increased, and the superstitious fear of Friar Bungay's incantations intensified by the unfamiliar sight of the smoke from the artillery, lying dense and almost motionless upon the heavy atmosphere of that still April morning.‡ At

---

hoeste with shot of gonnes, th' Erle's fielde shotte gunes almoste all the nyght. But, thanked be God! it so fortuned that they alway overshote the Kyngs hoste and hurtyd them nothinge, and the cawse was the Kyngs hoste lay muche nerrar them than they demyd."—*The Fleetwood Chronicle,* p. 18.

* Sharon Turner, vol. iii., p. 355.   † Fabyan, p. 661.

‡ This is the first battle, on English soil, of which we have any certain evidence of the use of artillery, though it is said to have been employed both at Wakefield and Towton.

eight o'clock a ray of sunlight struggled through the mist, showing the Duke of Gloucester in the thickest of the fight, seeking combat with the valiant Earl, the hero of a hundred battles, with a courage which should for ever have silenced the stories of his deformity and withered arm! He bore down all before him, says Sir George Buck, "and entered so farre and boldly into the ennemies army that two of his esquires . . . were slain, yet by his own valour he quit himselfe, and put most parte of the ennemies to flight." The panic continued. Lord Fitzhugh mistook the shining star of Oxford for the cognisance of Edward.* His error was shared by others. Instantly 2,000 arrows from Warwick's troops dealt death to their own comrades. A cry of "Treason!" threw Montague's contingent into confusion. But, in view of the contradictory statements of the Lancastrians themselves, it is impossible to say whether treason, or panic, or an error caused by the darkness was the real cause of an act which ended the strife.†

Four thousand men lay dead upon the field, and the Duke of Exeter was left for dead among the slain, when

---

* Oxford's badge was a star with rays, Edward's a sun with rays. At, or before, the battle of Mortimer's Cross a parhelion appeared, and Edward, assuring his affrighted army that it betokened the Trinity in whose name they would vanquish their enemies, there and then adopted the white rose *en soleil* as his personal cognisance—*Croy. Chron.*, p. 444. In the "English Chronicle" written before the year 1471, p. 110, the phenomenon is thus described : "The Monday before the daye of batayle aboute X atte clocke before none, were seen iij sonnys in the fyrmament shynyng fulle clere whereof the peple had grete marvayle, and thereof were agast."

† "The Earl of Warwick's men by reason of the mist not well discerning the badges, so like, shot at the Earl of Oxford's men that were of their own party. And then the Earl of Oxford and his men cried 'Treason!' and fled from the field with 800 men."—LELAND.

Hastings brought up the reserve under Clarence, fresh, and eager to win the confidence of Edward. But the battle which had been a succession of partial actions, was over. In vain Warwick sought to dispel the belief that Oxford's men had deserted to the foe, and to rally his demoralised troops. When all seemed lost, he ordered Montague to retreat to the wood, in which a company of archers were posted; and supported by only fifty knights, he covered his retreat. Valiant as his brother, Montague was quickly at his side again. Urged to flee, the Earl refused to desert one common soldier whom he had drawn into the strife. With the courage of despair he faced an army, repelled charge upon charge, rushed into the midst of the enemy, and, killing many with his own hand, fell at last with his brother Montague, covered with wounds—"a death truly worthy of so great a man." * The honour of that "wonderful, glorious, and unhoped-for victory," which wrought the final overthrow of the Nevilles, belongs to Richard, Duke of Gloucester.

Warwick's vacillations were little calculated to inspire that enthusiasm which impels men to stake life and fortune in their fidelity to a leader. His death, whilst it reunited the friends of the House of York, did not greatly weaken the Lancastrian cause. Few of the nobles whose hopes centred in Margaret had extended their confidence to the King-maker. It was known that Margaret and her son were upon the sea,

---

* Baudier, p. 180. Polydore Vergil writes : "Beating down and killing the enemy, far from his own forces, him also was thrust through and slain manfully fighting, together with the Marquis his brother who followed him."—Book xxiv., p. 146. This disposes of the absurd story that Warwick met his death at the hands of a common soldier whilst fleeing from the field of battle.

and her party, more united than it had been during her seven years' exile, only awaited her arrival to strike, as they believed, a decisive blow at Edward's throne.

The fleet which conveyed Margaret and her adherents was kept sixteen days at sea. The Countess of Warwick "had a ship of advantage," and landed before the Queen, at Portsmouth. Purposing to meet Margaret at Weymouth, she proceeded to Southampton. Here she learned her husband's fate, and secretly crossing Southampton Water, hurried into the New Forest, where she took sanctuary in the Abbey of Beaulieu.* On the 13th of April, Margaret, with her son and Anne Neville, landed at Weymouth. On the following day, whilst the cause of the Red Rose was being overthrown at Barnet, she kept her Easter festival at the Abbey of Cerne, and returned thanks for the restoration of her Consort! This intelligence had reached her in Paris, where it was received with great enthusiasm. A few hours later she received tidings of the disaster at Barnet. Her first thought was for her Consort, and as she realised his danger and the utter collapse of all her hopes, she wrung her hands in anguish and swooned.† When consciousness was restored, hope in some measure revived in the breast of the iron-hearted Queen. Her son was yet safe, and with him she followed the Countess to Beaulieu. "Then," says Polydore Vergil, "might Queen Margaret have called to mind that

---

* "Fleetwood Chronicle," p. 22.

† "When she harde all these miserable chaunces and misfortunes, so sudainly, one in another's necke, to have taken effecto, she, like a woman all dismaied for feare, fell to the ground, her harte was perced with sorowe, her speache was in a manner passed, all her spirits were tormented with maloncholy."—HALL, p. 297.

these mischiefs had chanced principally for the death of Humphrey, Duke of Gloucester, for surely if that one man ad lived and ruled the realm, King Henry had never come in so many hazards of his life." But the thirst for vengeance was strong within Margaret. She lent a willing ear to the assurances of her counsellors that a defeat which seemed so overwhelming was no real disadvantage.* She claimed the allegiance of the survivors of Barnet, and of the Lancastrians generally who were represented by Jasper Tudor and other leaders who had held aloof from Warwick.

The men of the western counties flocked to the standard of the Duke of Somerset, whilst Lancashire and Cheshire, already prepared for another trial of strength, were ready to follow their example as soon as Margaret should cross the Severn. But the Welsh, who had armed at the call of Jasper Tudor, discouraged and perplexed by the inaction of their English allies, wavered and retreated. Under these circumstances, Margaret was anxious to avoid a battle. Her forces outnumbered those of Edward, but they were ill-disciplined and deficient in artillery, in which the Yorkists were strong, Edward having provided "artilary, and ordinaunce, gonnes and other for the filde, gret plentye."† On both sides passion was stimulated to frenzy, as Margaret and Edward harangued their troops. The King, anxious to fight without delay, left

---

* The Duke of Somerset, Thomas Courtenay, and others persuaded Margaret that "they should have right good speed, and that they doubted nothing but that they should assemble so great puisaunce of people in divers parts of England truly assured unto their party that it should no more lie in the king's power to resist them, and that in that county they would begin."—*Fleetwood Chronicle*, p. 22.

† "Fleetwood Chronicle," p. 24.

Windsor on the 23rd April, but in vain he offered battle whilst Margaret was separated from her Welsh supporters. Her purpose was to make her way by Bristol, Gloucester, and Chester, to Lancashire.* On the 3rd of May she demanded admission to the city of Gloucester; but the governor, Richard Beauchamp, being apprised of Edward's approach, and ordered to keep the town and castle for the King, refused to open the gates. The only unobstructed passage over the Severn was at Tewkesbury. There she arrived at four o'clock on the afternoon of the 3rd of May, and encamped upon a site which is described as "a right evil place to approach as could well have been devised."† At daylight, on the 4th, the two armies confronted each other. Margaret rode about the field animating her soldiers and promising the most lavish rewards; ‡ whilst Edward, as at Barnet, was busy arranging his army before sunrise. His opinion of the courage and ability of his brother, Richard, was again shown in assigning him the post of danger. He then displayed his banners, the trumpets sounded an advance, and he marched straight upon the Duke of Somerset's entrenched camp.§ Gloucester led the attack; his banners were first seen within those entrenchments, "right evil to approach," and to him the honour of that day belongs. The Lancastrians broke in every part, and fled for shelter to the "foul lanes," "deep dykes," and woods. Many, weighed down by their heavy

---

* "Croyland Chronicle," Bohn's ed., p. 465.

† "Fleetwood Chronicle," p. 28.

‡ Sharon Turner, vol. iii., p. 367. From the authentic narrative in the "Fleetwood Chronicle," however, it appears that Margaret withdrew for safety to a neighbouring religious house before the battle commenced.

§ "Which was strongly in a marvaylows strong grownd pyght, full difficult to be assayled."—*Fleetwood Chronicle*, p. 29.

armour, were drowned in a mill-stream in a meadow, where the Avon and the Severn had both overflowed their banks; many sought refuge in the church, the abbey, and the town. The contest was short and decisive. Margaret, with the Lady Anne Neville, had already taken refuge in a small religious house in the neighbourhood, where she was presently discovered and made prisoner. Her only son, Prince Edward, the last hope of the House of Lancaster, perished in or after the battle, whilst three thousand of her followers fell before their foes. The Earl of Pembroke contrived to escape into Brittany with his nephew Henry, the young Earl of Richmond, whilst Somerset was ruthlessly put to death by the King. In the interest of historical truth, nothing is more deplorable than the eagerness with which every foolish and demonstrably fictitious story of the chroniclers has been seized upon to disparage Richard III., whilst acts of cruel treachery, such as the murder of the Duke of Somerset, are wholly ignored. The Duke took refuge after the battle in the abbey church of Tewkesbury, whence he withdrew on the King's solemn promise of a free pardon. Two days afterwards he was beheaded—a fate from which gratitude for his preservation of Edward's wife and children when in sanctuary should have protected him.*

Edward was once more firmly seated on the throne. The Lancastrians in the direct line were extinct, and those

---

* The charge of violating the right of sanctuary which has been made against Edward IV. is unwarranted. The abbey was not a sanctuary church. "There neither was, nor had at any time been granted any franchise to that place for any offenders against their prince having recourse thither."—*Fleetwood Chronicle*, p. 31.

Yorkists who had been seduced from their allegiance by "the last of the barons," hastened to make their peace with the King. Whatever opinion might have been entertained of Edward's title to the crown whilst the son of Henry VI. lived, it now admitted of no question at all. His claim by birth, by Parliamentary title, and by conquest was indisputable. His two brothers, George and Richard, had already been endowed with numerous manors from the large estates of Henry de Beaufort, Duke of Somerset, who commanded the Lancastrians at Hexham. Richard's great services were yet further rewarded. The Letters Patent conferring the great estates, to which reference will be made in the next chapter, were not issued until December, and his reputation has suffered from the unwarrantable assumption that they were the reward, not of honourable service, but of flagitious crime. No greater perversion of fact has been recorded on the page of history. They were the just and honourable recognition of distinguished military service. There is probably no other instance on record of a military character rising to fame with such rapidity. "Though in law an infant," says Mr. Hutton, he was "in the field an hero. . . . This gave him consequence in Edward's court, and, what was more to his honour, he possessed that confidence without its airs."

The final blow inflicted on that memorable 4th of May, upon the hopes of the House of Lancaster, was due to the singular valour and able generalship of the Duke of Gloucester, in view of all the chivalry of England. It is not improbable that Anne Neville was an actual spectator of the battle of Tewkesbury, and that Richard's knowledge of the fact may have contributed to inspire the valour which commanded even Edward's admiration.* The issue of this battle must decide whether Anne should be the bride of the young Prince to whom she was affianced, or whether Richard should realise the consummation of hopes which had their roots in the happy days of childhood, passed with Anne Neville in the stately halls of Middleham.

The tradition that Richard imbrued his hands in the blood of the young Prince Edward after the battle of Tewkesbury is justified by no contemporary authority. As, however, it is almost universally accepted as an historical fact, it is necessary to examine the evidence upon which it rests. It was certainly not obtained from eye-witnesses, whilst the silence of Sir Thomas More and Lord Bacon compels us to believe that it was either unknown to or discredited by them. The earliest authorities distinctly assert that Prince Edward fell on the field of battle. We naturally turn first of all to the contemporary Croyland Chronicler, the least biassed, the best informed, and the most accurate writer of his day. He tells us that the Prince was slain " either in the field or after the battle by the avenging hands of certain persons." † This has been held to give countenance to the stories invented twenty years later. But when it is remembered how brief the struggle was, and that after Richard's gallant charge upon the strong position chosen by the Duke of Somerset, approached only " by ugly lanes and deep dykes," the whole Lancastrian army fled in disorder, it is obvious that the slaughter not of the

---

* Habington, in Kennett, vol. i., p. 456.
† " Croyland Chronicle," p. 466. Cornwallis, however, suggests that it may have been by command of the king (" Encomium of Richard III.," p. 2).

Prince only, but of the great majority of those who fell, was "after the battle." The record of the Croyland Chronicler simply affirms the uncertainty of the time or manner of the Prince's death; he was slain in the field or after the battle.

Of no less weight as an authority is the contemporary writer of the "Warkworth Chronicle," and his statement divests the words of the Croyland Chronicler of all ambiguity. A zealous Lancastrian, he would assuredly not have spared the King and his brothers, had they rested under suspicion of the crime first imputed to them after all were dead. These are his words, and they are corroborated by the Fleetwood Chronicler:* "Edmund, Duke of Somerset, and Sir Hugh Courtenay, went out of the field, by the which the field was broken; and the most part of the people fled away from the prince, by the which the field was lost to his party; and there *was slain in the field* Prince Edward, who cried for succour to his brother-in-law the Duke of Clarence. Also there was slain Courtenay, the Earl of Devonshire." † These latter words appear designed to convey the idea that the Prince, the Earl, and others met a common death. If historical evidence is worth anything at all, the literal agreement of contemporary writers so violently opposed to each other as Dr. Warkworth and the writer of the "Fleetwood Chronicle," settles the question that the Prince "was slain in the field." The latter writer was, in all probability an actual spectator of the event which he thus reports: "Edward,

---

* Horace Walpole observes that the "Fleetwood Chronicle" appears to have been written with the express view of making known to foreign countries the incidents of Edward's restoration.

† "Warkworth Chronicle," p. 18.

called Prince, was taken fleeing to the townwards *and slain in the field.*" * And the testimony of these writers is yet further confirmed by a manuscript in the Harleian Collection.† It is important to remark, says Mr. Sharon Turner, that "this authentic manuscript not only gives no sanction to the popular tale of Edward's calling the prince before him, rebuking him for his opposition, and striking him for his answer, and of Gloucester and Clarence stabbing him, but declares that he was slain in the field. Another writer, still in MS., Bernard Andreas, who wrote the life of Henry VII. in 1509, about 38 years after this battle, and in the highest style of compliment to this Lancastrian king, speaking of the death of this young prince, though he abuses Richard most zealously for his other crimes, yet does not hint that Richard had stabbed the son of Margaret. On the contrary, his words imply like the present author's that he fell in the battle." ‡

Evidence, then, of the first class, that Gloucester and Clarence murdered the Prince in cold blood there is none. We next come to the chroniclers of the Tudor period, and the mythical origin of their stories acquires the stronger probability that successive writers relate the circumstances with a constant accession of details and increasing incon- sistency. The King, it is said, offered a reward of £100 a year to any who should yield up the Prince's body dead or alive, "with protestations not to offer any violence to his person, if alive." § The Prince was brought to the King by Sir Richard Crofts, and Edward questioned him to ascertain "whether his spirit would stoop to acknowledge a superior."

---

* "Fleetwood Chronicle," p. 30.   † Harleian MSS., 545, f. 102.
‡ Sharon Turner, vol. iii., p. 369.   § Habington, p. 452.

To the angry inquiry why he had entered his kingdom in arms, the Prince—so runs the legend*—boldly replied : "To recover his father, miserably oppressed, and the crown violently usurped he had taken arms. Neither could he be reputed to make any unjust claim who desired no more than what had been possessed by Henry VI., Henry V., and Henry IV., his father, grandfather, and great-grandfather, Kings of England, and acknowledged by the approbation not of the kingdom only but the world, and even by the progenitors of King Edward." Exasperated with this speech the King is said to have thrust him disdainfully away with his gauntlet, "Which so mighty rage observed, and his so distempered parting out of the room, the Dukes of Clarence. and Gloucester, the Marquis of Dorset, and the Lord Hastings seized suddenly upon the prince and with their poniards most barbarously murdered him."† It is unnecessary to follow these writers in detail. Fabyan, the earliest and the most entitled to respect, says that Edward struck the Prince with his gauntlet in the face, "after which stroke, so by him received, he was *by the kynges servants* incontinently slaine." The Tudor historians copied from Fabyan, but maliciously substituted *brothers* for "servants." ‡

Amongst modern historians Lingard aims at reconciling these various statements by one yet more equivocal. The Prince, he says, was slain "by Clarence and Gloucester, *or perhaps* the knights in their retinue." Hume simply adopts the opinions of the later chroniclers, whilst Sharon Turner, relying upon contemporary and unprejudiced

---

* This story rests on the doubtful authority of Hall.
† Habington, p. 455. ‡ Stow.

authorities, such as De Comines and the continuator of the
"Croyland Chronicle," says that the Prince "was taken as
flying towards the town, and was slain in the field." Carte,
whom Horace Walpole describes as "one of the few modern
historians who seem not to have swallowed implicitly all the
vulgar tales propagated by the Lancastrians to blacken the
House of York," distinctly says that the murder was perpetrated by Dorset and Hastings.* If the fact of the murder
could be established they were certainly the most likely agents.
What appears least likely is that Richard, the youngest of the
four implicated, a lad of eighteen, described as good-natured
and obsequious, would in the presence of his elders, to whom
he had always shown deference, execute the royal vengeance,
and in so doing claim precedence over them. And this is confirmed by Buck, who says he had seen "in a faithful manuscript chronicle of those times that the Duke of Gloucester
only of all the great persons stood still and drew not his
sword."† Such an attitude is precisely what we should
expect from the young, chivalrous knight, who, however willing to strike down a foe in fair fight, would not sully his
honour by slaying in cold blood a prostrate enemy.

This story then, like so many others related to disparage
Richard, was born of ignorance or malice, and vanishes like
other spectres of the darkness before the growing light of

---

* Carte, "History of England," vol. ii., p. 190.

† "Richard III.," by Sir George Buck, p. 549. Buck writes with the
avowed purpose of vindicating Richard, but without the violent partisanship of
his predecessors, whilst he shows a penetration in which they are deficient.
There is justice in Hutton's remark that he wrote many things that were weak
and foolish, but more that were true. Later discoveries endorse the view of
Horace Walpole, who says "he gains new credit the deeper this dark scene is
fathomed."

knowledge and patient investigation. Yet the self-accusation which Shakspeare has put into the mouth of Richard still avails to settle the question of his infamy in the public mind.

Leaving his brother Richard and the Duke of Norfolk to try the prisoners taken at Tewkesbury, Edward IV. hastened to London. At Coventry Sir William Stanley met him with the ex-Queen Margaret, who, with the Lady Anne Neville, was sent to the Tower. Stanley was the bearer of serious tidings. A new assailant had started up. During the period of Edward's exile the Earl of Warwick had appointed as Admiral of the English Channel the illegitimate son of his uncle, Lord Falconbridge, thenceforth known as the Bastard Falconbridge. After the fall of Warwick this man had turned freebooter. He is said to have had at his disposal forty-seven ships and an army of 16,000 or 17,000 men.* Edward IV. now learned that he had formed the desperate purpose of attacking London, ostensibly for the purpose of rescuing the King, hoping for aid from the apprentices and desperadoes always ready for plunder. On the 13th of May the Bastard had "gathered a riotous and evil disposed company of ship-mates and other," with whom he expected to overawe and pillage the City. Finding himself opposed by the stout-hearted citizens, he attacked the City at Algate, Bishop's Gate, and London Bridge, "shot guns and arrows, and fired the gates with cruel malice." The neighbouring mansions, "which had been built at a vast expense," took fire, but the assailants were driven off by Anthony Lord Rivers, who then commanded the Tower.†

---

* "Fleetwood Chronicle," p. 33.
† "Croyland Chronicle," p. 467. Fabyan, 662.

On the receipt of these tidings, Edward summoned the
Duke of Gloucester to his assistance, thus affording new proof
of his confidence in the judgment, the loyalty, and the ability
of his brother.* For Elizabeth with her daughters and infant
son were in the Tower "in the greatest jeopardy that ever
was."† Falconbridge and his shipmates were chased to
Blackheath.‡ In the following night they stole out of the
river and retired to Sandwich. On the 21st May Edward IV.
and the Duke of Gloucester entered London in triumph. That
night Henry VI. died in the Tower.

In an age when political expediency was held a justification for the darkest deeds of which men were capable, it
was inevitable that the King's death should be attributed
to violence. The rebellion of Falconbridge was formidable
only because its avowed object was the release of Henry VI.
It is perhaps hardly too much to say that his desperate attempt sealed the fate of the King. It may well have been
that Edward IV, "began to consider how dangerous his life
was to the State, and that his death would disarm even the
hope of his faction." § This conjecture acquires force from the
fact—if fact it be — that, at the recent battle of Barnet,
Edward had dragged the miserable King from the Tower
and placed him in the front ranks of his army "to be shot at."
But that the historian was "divining upon conjecture," appears tolerably certain from the words which follow: "It
was therefore resolved in King Edward's Cabinet Council,

---

* "The Encomium of Richard III.," by W. Cornewaleys, p. 3.
† "Fleetwood Chronicle," p. 34.
‡ "Where for awhile he entrenched."—HABINGTON, p. 455.
§ Habington, p. 103.

that, to take away all title from future insurrections, King Henry should be sacrificed." *   Here we have demonstrably an accretion of myth, for the continuator of the "Croyland Chronicle," *a member of King Edward's Council,* thus writes:

"I would pass over in silence the fact that at this period the body of King Henry was found in the Tower of London, lifeless. May God spare and grant time for repentance to the person, whoever he was, who thus dared to lay sacrilegious hands on the Lord's anointed. Hence it is that he who perpetrated this has justly earned the title of a tyrant, while he who thus suffered has gained that of a glorious martyr." †

This language is designedly vague, but there can be no reasonable doubt that it expresses the conviction of the writer, that the King had suffered a violent death at the hands of Edward IV. But it is the language of suspicion only, and wholly exclusive of belief that the death of the King had received the sanction of the Council. The conjecture that he points the finger of suspicion at the Duke of Gloucester is unwarranted, as, rightly understood, is that of the credulous and staunchly Lancastrian master of ~~St.~~ Exeter College, Cambridge. His statement is important from the singular minuteness of his description, and from the evidence it has

---

* A significant illustration is here afforded of the recklessness of statement in which the Tudor historians habitually indulged. In the very next page Habington says: "The death of King Henry was acted in the dark, so that it cannot be affirmed who was the executioner; only *it is probable* it was a resolution of the State, the care of the King's safety and the public quiet in some sort making it, however cruel, yet necessary."—HABINGTON, p. 104.

† "Croyland Chronicle," p. 468.

been held to furnish that the populace were clamorous to see
proofs of violence on the body of the royal victim, and that
the Duke of Gloucester was the murderer.   These are his
words :

"And, the same night that King Edward came to London,
King Henry being in ward in prison in the Tower of London,
was put to death the 21st day of May, on a Tuesday night,
between eleven and twelve of the clock, being then at the
Tower the Duke of Gloucester, brother to King Edward, and
many other ; and on the morrow he was chested and brought
to St. Paul's, and his face was open that every man might see
him.   And in his lying he bled on the pavement there, and
afterwards at the Blackfriars was brought, and there he bled
new and fresh ; and from thence he was carried to Chertsey
Abbey in a boat, and buried there in Our Lady's Chapel."

If, as has been asserted, the public were inconveniently
anxious to view the body and ascertain the real cause of death,
such marvels as are here described could only have intensified
that anxiety and rendered resistance impossible.   There is,
however, no evidence of any doubt in the public mind that
Henry had died from the effects of grief.   The MS. " London
Chronicle "* expressly says that *how* the King " was dede
nobody knewe, but thedir (to St. Paul's) he was brought dead ;
and in the church the corps stode all nyght, and on the morne
he was conveyed to Chertsey, where he was buryed."

The Fleetwood Chronicler, who, not writing for English
readers, was more free from bias than any of his confraternity,
gives expression to this belief, and probably preserves for us

---

* See Mr. Halliwell's Introduction to the "Warkworth Chronicle."

ANNE NEVILLE, QUEEN OF RICHARD III.

the real facts of the King's death. After relating the defeat of the Lancastrians at Tewkesbury, the death of the Prince of Wales, and the imprisonment of Queen Margaret, he continues : "The certainty of all which came to the knowledge of the said Henry, late called king, being in the Tower of London ; not having afore that knowledge of the said matters, he took it to so great despite, ire, and indignation, that of pure displeasure and melancholy he died, the 23rd day of the month of May." *

But the fact that Dr. Warkworth mentioned Richard's presence in the Tower on the night of Henry's death, was seized upon by his enemies for attaching to him personally the crime of regicide. Habington, who was contemporary with Sir Thomas More, and unfriendly to the Duke of Gloucester, controverts the views of the Tudor historians. " For however some," he writes, " either to clear the memory of the king, or by after cruelties, guessing at precedents, will have this murder to be the sole act of the Duke of Gloucester, I cannot believe a man so cunning in declining envy, and winning honour to his name, would have taken such a business of his own counsel and executed it with his own hands ; neither did this concern Gloucester so particularly as to engage him alone in the cruelty, nor was the king so scrupulous, having commanded more unnecessary slaughters, and from his youth been never any stranger to such executions." †

It is improbable, as Sir J. Hamilton has observed, that those who had spared Henry VI. through so many scenes

---

* " Fleetwood Chronicle," p. 38. † Habington p. 103.

of blood, should at last incur the odium of destroying him.
Popular ballads and prophecies—of which the following, by
John Audley, a blind poet, is a specimen—had familiarised
the people with the belief that the King would die a violent
death.   This expectation was so universal that probably
under no circumstances would his death have been attributed
to natural causes.*   The ballad was written in the Monastery
of Haghmond, as early as 1426.

> Now graunt him hit so he may—
> Pray we that Lord is Lord of Alle,
> To save our Kyng, his reine ryalle,
> And let never myschip uppon him falle,
> Ne false traytoure him to betray.
> I praye youe, seris, of your gentre,
> Syng this carol reverently :
> For hit is mad of Kyng Herre,
> Gret ned fore him we have to pray !
> Gif he fare well, well schul we be,
> Or ellis we may be ful sore :
> Fore him schul wepe moue an e,
> Thus prophecies the Blynd Awdley.

But why should Henry die?   Above all, why should
Richard be his murderer?   Childless, as he now was, he
would hardly have been formidable if at large.   But he was
a safe prisoner in the Tower.   Queen Margaret was far the
more formidable foe of the Yorkists, hating and hated by
them.   She also was a prisoner in their power, and had the
Duke of Gloucester been minded to perpetrate a murder,

---

† It was believed that two attempts to assassinate Henry VI. had already
been made, in one case, at least, when both Edward and Richard were in exile.
In this last attempt the King is said to have been wounded in the neck by a
dagger, from the effects of which wound he was still suffering.—SHARON TURNER,
vol. iii., p. 377.   This circumstance may not improbably account for the
report that he had been murdered.

whether on personal or political grounds, Margaret was far more likely than Henry VI. to have been his victim.

One very important fact seems to have been ignored as if by common consent; viz., that at the time of the death of Henry VI., *Earl Rivers was Governor of the Tower*, and of the two esquires in attendance upon the unhappy King, *one was Richard Ratcliffe.* Here, then, were two of the "many others" present, and their names are full of suggestiveness. With Rivers in military command of the Tower it is perfectly certain that Richard could have had no free access to the royal prisoner, whilst on the impossible supposition of the connivance of the governor, no opportunity for the perpetration of the crime can be discovered. He arrived in London with his brother Edward on Tuesday, the 21st of May. As the day of the week is mentioned, there can be no mistake as to the date.* He was at Canterbury on the 25th. If, therefore, we were without the independent evidence afforded by the "Fleetwood Chronicle," that the brothers were in London *for one night only,* we might conclude that, since the journey from Coventry had occupied five days, that from London to Canterbury, a distance of seventy miles, would, with his increased military impedimenta, occupy not less than three. He must, therefore, have left London, as we know that he did, on the 22nd.† Edward was received in London with demonstrations of delight, such as two great

---

* "Fleetwood Chronicle," p. 38. Fabyan also says that the King's corpse was conveyed to St. Paul's on the 22nd.

† Falconbridge and his followers surrendered to the King at Sandwich. "Whereupon the king sent thither his brother Richard, Duke of Gloucester, to receive them in his name, and all of the ships, *as he did on the 26th day of the same month.*"—*Fleetwood Chronicle*, p. 39.

and decisive victories, and the final overthrow and capture of Margaret, "the outlandish Frenchwoman," were certain to call forth. In these victories Richard had, though still a mere boy, so distinguished himself as to divide with his brother the popular admiration.* With him also he shared the extraordinary fatigues of that one day in London. The congratulations of the citizens and of the nobility, the conferences with his Council, the arrangements for the immediate despatch of an expedition against the rebel Falconbridge, the banquet, and the happy reunion with his family; "in all these deeds and preparations of state, council, festivity, and war, Richard was a principal person, and must have been as much employed as the king the only day that both were in London."† For him there was no escape from the onerous duties which brooked no delay, nor from the pomp so congenial to his disposition, nor from the public eye of soldiers, statesmen, and applauding multitude. And for him we may confidently say there was no opportunity for the perpetration of the cowardly murder with which tradition has aspersed his memory. For the banquet which closed that busy day released neither of the brothers from their exhausting labours. Affairs of state had yet to be long and gravely discussed at the Council-board, from which we are asked to believe that Richard—a lad of eighteen—brave, courteous, "whom all men were praising and applauding," stole away to do the work of a cowardly assassin, his victim being the idiotic King whom Parliament had deposed, and the only effect of

---

* "A high-spirited youth whom all men were praising and applauding for his leading share of the triumphs."—SHARON TURNER, vol. iii., p. 376.
† *Ibid.*

whose death would be the raising up of a new pretender to the throne! Whether Henry VI. died a natural death, accelerated by the ruin of all his hopes, or by the hand of violence, cannot now be ascertained; but the fact of Richard's presence in the Tower on the night of his decease will not bear the sinister interpretation which has been put upon it.

The chroniclers, who wrote from twenty to thirty years after the alleged tragedy, relate it with inconsistent details. More says that Richard "slew with his own hands King Henry VI."; De Comines that he *"caused the king to be murdered* in his presence"; Rous that "he killed by others, or, as many believe, with his own hand, that most holy man King Henry VI."; and all, with the single exception of Dr. Warkworth, avowedly base their statements upon mere rumour, guarding them with such expressions as "divers tales were told"; "as men constantly say"; "the continual report is," &c. Fabyan says that the King "was stykked with a dagger"; Polydore Vergil that he was "killed with a sword"; whilst others simply say that he was murdered.

If we credit Richard, at this early period of his life, with that grasping and unscrupulous ambition which "the mob-stories and Lancastrian forgeries" attribute to him, it is difficult to believe that he would have perpetrated so great an act of folly as the murder of Henry VI. The deposed, captive, and childless King did not stand in *his* way. By the great majority of the people, who recognised his incapacity to rule, he was still beloved; a reputed saint, the odium attaching to whose murderer an ambitious Prince would not willingly incur. The supposition that Richard had already formed designs on the crown is the last resource of those who would find a motive

for a cowardly act of regicide.   Edward IV. was in early
manhood—just thirty—in robust health, with an increasing
family, between whom and Richard was the Duke of Clarence,
who was already a father.   The ambition and subtlety of the
late Duke of York lived again in his son, but there is no
particle of evidence that the Duke of Gloucester aspired to any
other than that high position in the State to which his birth
and his great qualities entitled him.   The attempt to find in
his vaulting ambition a motive for a diabolical crime has
resulted in strengthening the evidence of his innocency of the
imputed villainy.

Margaret had been brought a prisoner to the Tower, where
within a few hours of her arrival she received the tidings of
her widowhood.   Bereft within a fortnight of husband and
son, she abandoned herself to grief.   The objects and instru-
ments of her ambition removed, life had neither charm nor
purpose for one who had lived in an atmosphere of intrigue.
After passing four years in different fortresses in England she
was ransomed, as we shall see hereafter, by Louis XI., and
returned to France, where she died some years later.   Conspicuous as was the part she had played on the world's
stage, the world soon forgot one who had done nothing worthy
of remembrance.   The date of her death is uncertain ; it was
probably about 1506.   "In addition to her other miseries,"
says Habington, "she was punished with a long life, which
she spun out sadly and ingloriously. . . . Her death was so
obscure that it is not left certainly in story when she died." *

---

* Habington, p. 454.

EDWARD IV. had been reconciled to the Duke of Clarence; but the recollection of his rebellion, which could never have been effaced from the memory even of a generous brother, rankled in that of the vindictive King. The fraternal affection which united Edward and the Duke of Gloucester was as marked as the distrust between Edward and Clarence. Richard had been chief mourner at the obsequies of their father; he afterwards represented the King in their sister's state progress before her marriage, and he alone of all the royal family or the old nobility had acquiesced in Edward's marriage, though approving it perhaps less than all.

The grants of offices and lands which Richard now formally received from the Crown, though, as we have seen, they were actually conferred before the death of Henry VI., have been regarded by his detractors as evidence of his participation in the double murder which extinguished the direct line of the House of Lancaster, and entitled him to these munificent rewards. It is only just, however, to remember that Richard had been constant in his loyalty to Edward when Clarence was seduced into rebellion, that he had shared his exile and poverty, and suffered outlawry for his fidelity. Such services, followed by his brilliant achievements on the fields of Barnet and Tewkesbury, were only fittingly rewarded.

But if we assume that Edward IV. was willing to condone, if not to reward the crimes which have been laid to the charge of Richard, it is wholly inconceivable that the thanks of Parliament would be given to an acknowledged regicide. Yet we find that within two months of Henry's death, Richard, Duke of Gloucester, in presence of "his most royal majesty, having before him his lords spiritual and temporal," received the thanks of the House of Commons through their Speaker, William Allington, for his "knightly demeaning," and "for his constant faith," with divers other nobles and yeomen being with the King beyond the sea.*

On the 4th of December following, the King, by letters patent, thus gave expression to his estimate of the upright conduct and firm allegiance of his brother: "The king, especially considering the gratuitous, laudable, and honourable services in many wise rendered to him by his most dear brother Richard, Duke of Gloucester, his propinquity in blood, his innate probity, and other deserts of manners and virtues, and willing therefore to provide him a competent reward and remuneration, to the end that he might the better maintain his rank, and the burthens incumbent thereupon, granted to him the forfeited estates of Sir Thomas Dymoke, Sir Thomas de la Laund, John Truthall, and John Davy," all of whom had been convicted of treason.

By another patent Richard was nominated to succeed the

---

* "Journal of Lord Grantham," quoted by Miss Halsted.

Earl of Warwick as Great Chamberlain of England; he was also appointed Steward of the Duchy of Lancaster beyond Trent, and the estates of the attainted Earl of Oxford were added to his already great rewards.* Owing to the unsettled condition of the North of England, these great estates had probably only a prospective value, and such rewards were fully justified by precedent.

By the singular discovery, a century since, of Richard III.'s seal, which was purchased with a lot of old brass and iron, it appears that he was also invested with the earldoms of Dorset and Somerset, no doubt the rewards of his brilliant exploits at Tewkesbury. The inscription round the rim of the seal runs thus: "Sigillum Ricardi Ducis Gloucestriæ Admiralli Anglice et Comitis Dorset et Somerset."

On the 3rd of July, 1471, Richard subscribed the oath of allegiance to the infant Prince of Wales. It is interesting, as showing the confidence and gratitude of Edward IV., who lost no opportunity of bestowing rewards for his brother's undeviating fidelity, to note that eleven days later he conferred upon him by patent the forfeited estates of the Earl of Warwick. These consisted of the castles, manors, and lordships of Middleham and Sheriff Hutton in Yorkshire, and of Penrith in Cumberland.

The loyalty of the Duke of Gloucester to his brother, in spite of his antipathy to the Queen and her family, is noticed by all writers. Sir George Buck observes that it bore a constant expression "in this motto, *Loualto me lie* (Loyalty bindeth me) which I have seen written by his own hand and

---

* Gairdner's "Richard III.," pp. 21–22.

subscribed Richard Gloucester." * But it was a loyalty wholly free from the cringing spirit of the flatterer and tuft-hunter. One of many evidences of this is furnished in the firmness with which, in opposition to Edward's inclinations, he pressed his suit to be allowed to marry Anne Neville. Reference has already been made to the attachment formed between the cousins in their childhood at Middleham. That they were intimately associated in childhood is no mere matter of conjecture. At the costly feast on the occasion of the installation of their uncle, George Neville, as Archbishop of York, both were present. Leland quotes "out of an old roll" a minute description of the ceremony, in which the following passage occurs: "Upon the days . . . . was seated the Duke of Gloucester, the king's brother; on his right the Duchess of Suffolk, on his left hand the Countess of Westmoreland . . . . and *two of the lord of Warwick's daughters.*" † Each eventually married their first cousins, in spite of the danger of their marriages being annulled by the Pope; and each experienced that legacy of domestic sorrow which such unnatural marriages frequently entail. The only son of Isabel was little better than an idiot; the only son of Anne, delicate from his birth, died in early childhood.

The Duke of Clarence, as we know, had married Warwick's eldest daughter, thus vastly increasing his wealth and influence. Already he had a son. Edward had failed to move the Pope to annul the marriage, and an increase in the number of those

---

* Buck, in Kennett, p. 550.

† Leland's "Collectanea," vol. vi., p. 2. They were probably thus placed as companions of his own age, since their mother sat at the second table, a place of less dignity.

whose title to the Crown would take precedence of that of Richard was naturally to be expected. In spite of his great estates the Duke of Gloucester was poor, and at this precise time was driven to borrow money.* A letter soliciting the loan of one hundred pounds, to defray the expenses of his journey to the north, is preserved in the Cottonian MSS. It is addressed to an unknown correspondent and dated the 23rd of June.

"Right trusty and well-beloved, we greet you well. And forasmuch as the king's good grace hath appointed me to attend upon his highness into the north parts of his land, which will be to me great cost and charge, whereunto I am so suddenly called that I am not so well provided of money, therefore," he solicits the loan until the following Easter. But the significant part of the letter is a postscript, which is entirely in the Duke's handwriting :—"Sir I pray you that ye fayle me not at this tyme in my greto neede, as ye weele that I schewe yow my goode lordshype in that matter that ye labure to me for." †

Thus we see that the distrust of Clarence which Richard shared with the King, was inflamed by several personal grounds of jealousy. Edward had only one son, and the chance of Richard's succession to the throne was rendered improbable only by the prior right of his brother Clarence. Clarence was wealthy, and courted popularity by the lavish

---

* In the fifteenth century great estates did not secure a heavy rent-roll. The foresters' accounts show that they often produced no profit to their owners beyond a few hawks' nests, " honey, nuts, and hips, hares, cats, and badgers, and vermin of that kind."—See Elton's "Origins of English History," p. 224.

† Sir Henry Ellis, " Original Letters," 2nd Series, vol. i., p. 144.

exercise of patronage which this letter shows us that Richard
had not the means to dispense. And Clarence, in possession
of Isabel's fortune, claimed a right to the disposal of that
of Anne Neville, and violently opposed his brother's suit
for the hand of Warwick's co-heiress. But Richard was not
to be diverted from his purpose, to the accomplishment of
which he was equally impelled by affection and policy. Yet
surely, even in that age, such a purpose was hardly possible
to the murderer of the affianced husband of Anne Neville, and
of his father, Henry VI.! At all events his success should,
after the fullest allowance for mercenary and political motives,
clear Richard from the least suspicion of guilt on the part of
Anne Neville.

The halo of romance and ideality which, in the interests of
dramatic art, Shakspeare has thrown around this lady, is
fatal to any true historical conception of her position and
character. At the very time that he represents the unnatural
wooing to have taken place in presence of the corpse of the
late King, the Duke of Gloucester was marching against
Falconbridge with his brother Edward, and we know that
Anne was a close prisoner with Queen Margaret in the Tower.
There is absolutely no evidence that she was wedded to Prince
Edward. As a matter of fact she was but sixteen years of age
at the time of his tragic death.

Warwick had indeed so far succeeded in his ambitious
project as, with the help of Louis XI., to effect a reconciliation
with Margaret of Anjou and to secure her reluctant consent to
a marriage treaty; but her consent was made contingent upon
two conditions, neither of which was complied with. Anne
Neville was to remain "in the hands and keeping" of

Margaret, and the marriage should be *perfected* only when the
Earl had recovered the kingdom of England for the House of
Lancaster.* When, therefore, the continuator of the "Croyland Chronicle" says that the Lady Anne had been *married* to
the son of Henry VI., he can only refer to the marriage *contract* into which Margaret inserted this clause which effectually
prevented its consummation. We thus see, as in the case of
Edward IV., the degree of importance which in that age was
attached to betrothments. Opposed as Margaret reasonably
was to the union of her only son with the daughter of the man
whom she hated and scorned, it is quite certain that she would
suffer no closer union than betrothment until Warwick had
fulfilled his solemn pledge "on the gospels" to restore her
royal Consort. We have seen that one reason of Margaret's
objection to the marriage was that a proposal had been made
to her which contemplated the union of the Houses of York
and Lancaster. Edward's infant daughter was too young for
Margaret to be willing wholly to reject Warwick's suit, and
she determined so to act as eventually to select one or the
other bride for her son as should be most expedient.

Anne Neville was taken prisoner with Margaret after the
battle of Tewkesbury, and, in accordance with the custom of
the times, after a brief confinement in the Tower she would
naturally be entrusted to the charge of her sister Isabel,
Duchess of Clarence, as twelve years earlier the mother of
Edward IV. had been committed to the custody of her
sister, the Duchess of Buckingham. It is certain that
Clarence was aware of his brother's inclinations, and he at

* Ellis, "Original Letters," 2nd Series, vol. i., p. 132.

once adopted measures to thwart them.   The betrayer in turn
of his brother and his father-in-law had no higher motives[*]
of justice than the rest of the Plantagenets.   In right of
his wife he inherited the half of the princely domains of
the "King-maker," and had seized Anne's moiety, which owing
to her attainder was now at the disposal of the King, and had
in fact been already in part bestowed on Richard.   He knew
the temper of his brother Edward too well to doubt that if
Richard married Anne her dower must be surrendered.   He
therefore conveyed the lady away and concealed her so
effectively that by many her fate was considered doubtful.
"But," says Hutton, "the gallant Richard, with the eyes of
Argus, the diligence of Jason, and the assistance of love,
like a faithful knight and true to his injured mistress, neither
gave himself nor others rest in the pursuit."   Success at length
crowned his efforts.   The heiress of the Nevilles and of the
Beauchamps, the late affianced bride of a Prince, was found
in an obscure place in London, "disguised in the habit of a
cook-maid." [*]   The suggestion that she may have concurred
in Clarence's plan for her concealment, either believing
Richard guilty of the blood of her affianced husband, or from
the fact that she was included in the attainder of Margaret,
finds no warrant even in the writings of Lancastrians, and
is opposed to all probability.   Richard carried her off in
triumph and apparently with her own good-will.   For temporary security he placed her in the sanctuary at St. Martin's-
le-Grand, whence she was conveyed to the custody of her
uncle, George Neville, Archbishop of York.

---

* "Croyland Chronicle," p. 470.

A violent dissension now arose between the two brothers, who argued their dispute before the King with so much ability, and with such equal show of reason, as to excite the surprise and envy of the lawyers and others present in the Council Chamber. The Croyland Chronicler, himself a doctor of the canon law, remarks : "These three brothers, the King, and the two Dukes, were possessed of such surpassing talents, that if they had been able to live without dissensions, such a threefold cord could never have been broken."* At last the King determined to act as mediator. His ultimate decision was that Richard should marry Anne Neville, and have so much of the late Earl's lands as should be agreed upon by arbitrators, the rest remaining in the possession of the Duke of Clarence.†

The Countess of Warwick was ruthlessly despoiled of her estates, which were divided between her two daughters. Edward's harshness to a lady, cultured, high-minded, and as indisposed to, as she was incapable of, mischief, whose only fault was that she had been the wife of Warwick, contrasts unfavourably with Richard's subsequent treatment of the unfortunate Countess, and also of the widow of the Duke of Buckingham, and the Countess of Oxford.‡ The Countess was robbed to settle the pecuniary disputes of the King's brothers, and in 1474 an Act was passed partitioning between the two brothers "in the right of their said wives, all honours, lordships, castles, etc., which were or be, belonging

---

* "Croyland Chronicle," p. 470.   † *Ibid.*
‡ Harl. MSS., 433, f. 193. "Commandment to suffer Dame Alice Neville peaceably to occupy the third part of several lordships, as in the right of her dower. Given at Tutbury, 25th October, 1484."

to the said Countess of Warwick . . . . to have and to hold to the said Dukes and their said wives, as if the said Countess were now naturally dead . . . . and that the said Countess be barred and excluded as well of all manner jointures, dower . . . . title and interest of, in, and for all the honours, lordships, etc., that at any time were the said Earl's late her husband." * Provision seems to be made in the following clause against the canonical invalidity of Richard's marriage, or, as Clarence had similarly married within the prohibited degrees, there may have been some unrecorded irregularity in the marriage of Richard. " It is ordained by the same authority that if the said Richard, Duke of Gloucester, and Anne, be hereafter divorced, and after the same be lawfully married, that yet this present Act be to them as good and vaillable as if no such divorce had been had, but as if the same Anne had continued wife to the said Duke of Gloucester." And if, after such divorce, he " be lawfully married to the said Anne the daughter, and during the life of the said Anne be not wedded nor married to any other woman ; that yet the said Duke of Gloucester shall have and enjoy as much of the premisses as shall appertain to the said Anne during the life of the said Duke of Gloucester."

Immediately after his marriage Richard, who had been appointed to the command of the army in the north, withdrew with his bride to his lordship of Middleham in Yorkshire, full of resentment towards his brother Clarence, whose determined opposition had well-nigh prevented their union. Cordial relations between the two brothers were probably never restored.

---

* " Rotuli Parliamentorum," vol. vi., p. 100.

PONTEFRACT CASTLE.
(*Demolished in 1648.*)

And this family quarrel has been gravely set forth as the motive for a cruel act of fratricide! The absurdity of the charge was too glaring even for Hall and Holinshed, who, far from hinting at Richard's guilt, affirm that he openly opposed his brother's murder.

The Duke of Gloucester's engagements in the north admitted of the enjoyment of a season of comparative tranquillity in his northern homes, which, after four years of ceaseless vicissitudes, of war, and diplomacy conducted at the sword's point, he had well earned. And he was not yet twenty years old. He had been a second time appointed High Constable of England, and the almost regal powers conferred by this high office and that of Chief Seneschal of the Duchy of Lancashire were worthily wielded by great York's greater son. His time appears to have been passed in the Castles of Middleham and Pontefract, the former endeared by the associations of childhood both to himself and his youthful Consort, the latter destined to be associated with the darkest stain upon his life. The celebrated fortress of Pontefract, frowning over the town in which Richard's father and brother had found temporary sepulture, had a weird and terrible history. Thomas, Earl of Lancaster, and Richard II. had here both suffered execution; and the castle, which was the ancestral home of the royal House of Lancaster, had several times passed to the Crown. "Rearing its embattled towers amongst scenes fraught with the most stirring national associations, built on a rock whose rugged surface seemed fully in keeping with the impregnable stronghold that crowned its summit, the Castle of Pontefract . . . soared high above the surrounding lands, a fitting abode for the princely seneschals and hereditary high stewards of England."*

In September of this year the bastard Falconbridge is said to have been executed by Richard in the north, it does not appear upon what charge.† The statement rests upon the authority of Dr. Warkworth, but is demonstrably erroneous. It has of course been cited as evidence of the cruelty and perjury of the Duke of Gloucester. After his retreat to Sandwich in May, the freebooter had surrendered on condition of pardon, which had not only been granted, but, probably with the view of converting so dangerous a rebel into an ally, he was reinstated in his office and received the honour of knighthood. The Duke of Gloucester had received Falconbridge's submission and given the king's pledge of pardon and favour.‡ Four months later, it has been alleged, he gave the order for his execution. "And anon after, by the Duke of Gloucester *in Yorkshire* the said bastard was beheaded, notwithstanding he had a charter of pardon." § If this were so, the natural inference would be that something had occurred in the interval, some violation, of the conditions of pardon, or some new act of rebellion, rather than that Richard was cruel and perfidious. And there is some evidence that he had thus anew incurred the penalty of death, which he suffered, not in Yorkshire, but at Southampton, and which Richard was not even instrumental in inflicting. Polydore Vergil writes that Falconbridge "*arrived unadvisedly* at Southamptom, and was taken and

---

* Miss Halsted.   † " Paston Letters," vol. iii., p. 75.
‡ Habington, p. 456.   § " Warkworth Chronicle," p. 20.

beheaded."* The King, meanwhile, had gone to Canterbury "where many that were at Blackheath with the bastard were arrested and brought before him. . . . After that the king rode unto Sandwich. . . . and took the prisoners with him, and returned again to London." † It is obvious that Falconbridge was again in arms, and threatening the south coast, and that with his usual celerity Edward had pounced upon him and quashed the rebellion. Polydore Vergil is confirmed by Fabyan, who writes that the bastard "was taken about Southampton, and *there put to execution*, whose head was sent to London and put upon London Bridge among others." ‡ And finally Sir John Paston says that his head was placed upon London Bridge, looking towards Kent. § It is unfortunate that those who seize with avidity upon any story disparaging to Richard, should be able in this case to appeal to so good an authority as Dr. Warkworth; but his error is not open to question, and the whole case against Richard falls to the ground.

For three years, in comparative tranquillity, Richard administered the affairs of his northern province. Two features of that administration claim a passing notice, as they indicate the existence, at a time when he could have no personal interest to serve, of principles which, when consistently carried out as King, were attributed by his adversaries to sinister motives. These were his regard for religion, and his energetic endeavours to heal the dissensions

---

* Polydore Vergil, Book xxiv., p. 154. So also Habington: "Coming into Southampton he was apprehended and put to death," p. 456.
† "Warkworth Chronicle," p. 21. ‡ Fabyan, p. 662.
§ "Paston Letters," vol. ii., p. 82.

and jealousies of the great nobles. Whittaker relates that
the county of Richmondshire furnishes abundant evidence of
his bounty to charities and religious houses. " He bestowed
liberally," he says, "on the monks of Coverham and the parish
of Skipton for the repair of their respective churches." *
Whilst gratifying his taste for building at Penrith, Marston,
and elsewhere,† he was always liberal in his response to claims
for the building or restoration of religious houses. We possess
evidence of this in the terms of the patent by which, amongst
others, the manor of Skipton was granted. "The king, in
consideration of the laudable and commendable services of his
dear brother, Richard, Duke of Gloucester, as for the encourage-
ment of piety and virtue in the said Duke, did give and grant
him . . . . the castle, manor, and demesne of Skipton with
the manor of Marston."

The turbulent nobles who had supported Queen Margaret's
invasion were under Richard's jurisdiction. The Percys and
the Cliffords hated the Yorkist domination even more than
they hated one another. For a youth, who, according to the
strict laws of chivalry, still only occupied the status of an
esquire, to attempt to control these lawless spirits might seem
quixotic. By the exercise of patience, adroitness, and firm
decision, and still more by the example of self-control, Richard
succeeded in softening asperities, quelling revengeful feelings,
and freeing the country from the distraction under which it
had so long groaned. Well might it be said that Richard,
represented as a monster of mankind after his death,
" was not so esteemed in his lifetime in these northern

---

* Harl. MSS., cod. 433, art. 1517.
† "History of Richmondshire," vol. i., p. 335.

parts."* By his intercession, the Marquis Montague escaped attainder. On the 23rd of February, 1475, an Act was passed reciting the King's purpose, "which to do, he, at the humble request and prayer of his right dear brother, Richard, Duke of Gloucester, and other lords, of his blood, . . . spareth, and will no further proceed in that behalf." Such was Richard, Duke of Gloucester, whom our great dramatist represents as a self-calumniating bloodthirsty tyrant.

> Sword, hold thy temper ; heart, be watchful still ;
> Priests pray for enemies, but princes kill.

One other incident in connection with Richard's administration of the north has been frequently cited against him. The Countess of Warwick, tired of her long detention in sanctuary, "was willing to confide herself to Richard's protection." † Despoiled of her great estates by Act of Parliament, "as if she were naturally dead," nothing was more natural than that she should seek an asylum in her native county, perhaps even in her daughter's home at Middleham; but that Richard "imprisoned her for life" is a reckless fabrication of the priestly antiquary of Guy's Cliff. Even he does not venture to name the fortress in which she was detained, nor is there the slightest authority for his malicious charge. Whether she left sanctuary voluntarily or not, it is clear that Richard had nothing whatever to do with it.‡ Sir John Paston thus states the fact: "The Countess of Warwick is now out of Beaulieu sanctuary, and Sir James Tyrell conveyeth her northward, men say by the

---

* Drake's " York."   † Gairdner's "Richard III.," p. 29.

‡ Dugdale favours the views of a voluntary migration, "She thence *privately* got into the north."—*Antiquities of Warwickshire*, p. 334.

King's assent; whereto some men say that the Duke of Clarence is not agreed." * It does not follow from this that Tyrell was the King's agent. Mr. Gairdner says that he was not, but "was probably known to be the Duke of Gloucester's." † On the other hand, Miss Halsted quotes an accepted authority ‡ for the statement that "Sir James Tyrrel, though associated in after years with Richard, was at this time in the service of Edward IV., being Master of the Horse, and a considerable officer of the Crown." The probability is, that as Edward was about to embark upon a war with France, he was unwilling to leave in Hampshire one who, although he had cruelly stripped her of all her possessions, he did not regard as powerless for mischief, and whom he preferred to confide to the gentle custody of her daughter, as a few months before that daughter had been committed to the custody of the Duchess of Clarence. The statement of Mr. Gairdner that the son-in-law whom the Countess "was most disposed to trust, shut her up in prison," is certainly without authority. §

---

* Paston Letters," vol. ii., p. 145.   † "Richard III.," p. 29.

‡ Horace Walpole in the "Archæologia" for 1770.

§ Harl. MSS. cod. 433., arts. 1986–7. The fact is beyond dispute that Richard not only secured to her the third part of several lordships as in the right of her dower, he also commanded the officials of the lordships of Umby and Righton in the bishopric of Durham to pay to her such rents and duties as they ought to pay by reason of their tenures. As an illustration of the irony of history it is instructive to contrast the treatment of this unhappy lady by the much-belauded Henry VII. with that of Richard, whose actions were as much misconstrued as his motives were calumniated. As far as can be ascertained Henry found her in actual occupation of Barnard Castle, where in all probability Richard had accorded her protection. For otherwise it would have been his rightful possession by conquest. Not satisfied with his title to the coveted possession, he caused an Act to be passed restoring to the Countess of Warwick all the estates which had come to her as sole heiress of the Beauchamps, *that she might convey the fee to himself.* This was done by a special feoffment in December of the same year, thus making

The abortive war with France in 1475 need not detain us here. It was discreditable to all concerned, with the single exception of the Duke of Gloucester. The subtlety of the French King was displayed in his appeal to the cupidity of his English enemies.* His offer of an immediate payment of 75,000 crowns, and an annual tribute of 50,000, which the wily monarch never designed to pay, induced Edward to withdraw his army. To insure a continuance of peace between the two countries it was also arranged that the Dauphin of France should marry the Princess Royal of England as soon as the parties were of age to fulfil this part of the contract. On these terms a seven years' truce was concluded.† But Louis XI. had also to reckon with the chivalrous warriors who accompanied Edward, one only of whom refused to barter his own and his sovereign's honour for French gold. The Duke of Gloucester, loyal to England's ally, Charles, Duke of Burgundy, jealous of his country's fame, and above the reach of avarice, absented himself from the interview between the two kings at Pecquigny,‡ objected altogether to the peace, and refused to accept the pension which even the members of Edward's Council did not scruple to receive.§ The Lord Chancellor,

---

his title indisputable, and leaving her to die in poverty."—See Dugdale's "Antiquities of Warwickshire," p. 334.

* " Yet had he many virtues, whereof largesse was one."—FABYAN, p. 665.

† Rymer, xii., pp. 14, 19, 20.

‡ "On the English side the Duke of Gloucester was absent, in regard his presence should not approve what his opinions and sense of honour had heretofore disallowed."—HABINGTON, p. 468.

§ It was only when Edward arrived at Calais that he learned that the Duke of Burgundy, who had incited him to attack France, was unable to provide the promised assistance. But he was not dependent upon the Duke's alliance. He well knew that Louis was unprepared for war, and his conduct showed that *the spoils of war*, and not the re-conquest of France, was the real object

Morton, (afterwards Cardinal) Lord Hastings, the Marquis of
Dorset, Lord Howard, and others thus bartered their con-
sciences.   Hastings indeed declined a pension; if he accepted
a gift he would not sully his fine sense of honour by giving a
receipt, not even by touching the gold, but, if the French
King was urgent, he told his envoy, Peter Cleret, that he
might put the money in the pocket of his sleeve!* Nobly
does the conduct of Richard Duke of Gloucester contrast with
such meanness and cupidity.   "We have gained nòthing,"
he indignantly exclaimed, "for all our labour and suspense,
but shame!"   And so thought the English people.   Pensions
to the King and his warriors might satisfy *them*, but the
immediate payment of 75,000 crowns did not go far to meet
the expenses of transporting an army of 17,000 men to France
and bringing them home again.   The heavily taxed people
murmured, and "received condign punishment for their presumption."

Some modern historians have sought to justify this ignominious peace, apparently for the purpose of impugning the
judgment and conduct of the Duke of Gloucester.   It is
interesting, therefore, to inquire how it was regarded in
France.   De Comines says that some people would think
Louis' proposals "too great a condescention in our King;
but the wiser sort may see . . . . *that his kingdom was in
great danger.*   We had besides many private intrigues and

---

of this expedition.   "The Duke refused to have any further dealings with the
King, who thus proposed to make peace with their adversary."—*Croyland
Chronicle*, p. 472.

   * "Camden's Remains," p. 352.   Hastings is said by some authorities to
have accepted a pension from Louis; "denying absolutely that ever his hand
should be seen among the King's accounts at Paris, but welcomed still the
pension which without that formality was continued."—HABINGTON, p. 469.

secret cabals among us."* So astonished were French statesmen and soldiers at the eagerness with which Edward came to terms, that "some were of opinion all this was but a trick and falacy in the English; but the King was of another mind. .... Besides, our King was perfectly acquainted with Edward's humour, and that he loved to indulge himself in ease and pleasures." These are the words of a member of the Council of Louis XI. Speaking of the condition of the French army, he admits that it was unable to contend with Edward's veterans. "To speak impartially, his (Louis's) troops seemed but raw and unfit for action in the field, for they were in very ill order, and observed no manner of discipline."† He relates a conversation he held with a Gascon gentleman in Edward's service: "I asked him how many battles the King of England had fought? He told me nine, and that he had been in every one of them in person. I demanded next how many he had lost? He replied, never but one, and that was this in which we had outwitted him now, for he was of opinion that the ignominy of his returning so soon after such vast preparations, would be a greater disgrace and stain to his arms than all the honour his majesty had gained in the nine former victories."‡ Louis, who appears to have been present at this conversation, was in great alarm lest this gentleman should drop some word which might suggest to the English that he imposed upon and laughed at them.

Elsewhere, De Comines remarks that the three hundred

---

* De Comines, p. 214. The Flemish historian and statesman had now transferred his services to the French King, and is the best authority upon this period of history.   † De Comines, p. 219.   ‡ De Comines, p. 227.

cart-loads of the best wines in France, which Louis sent as
a present to Edward, made as great an appearance as the
whole French army.   Wine and money were the spoils of
Edward's bloodless campaign, and the Duke of Gloucester
alone raised his voice in energetic protest against the dishonour brought upon the English army and the English
name.

There was, however, one result of this miserable enterprise that might be regarded with general satisfaction ; but
that also was attributable to Edward's sordid love of money.
Margaret of Anjou was still a prisoner in England. Louis XI.
was himself very largely responsible for all her troubles, and
ought long since to have ransomed her.   There is no reason
to suppose that she had been treated with severity by
Edward IV., who had entrusted her to the charge of her
old favourite, Anne Chaucer, Duchess of Suffolk, the grand-
daughter of the poet, at Wallingford Castle.   But there was
certainly an unkingly smallness in depriving her even of the
retrospective title of Queen, in the deed by which he required
her to resign all the rights which her marriage had given her
in England.   Louis was willing to ransom her, but, as on a
former occasion, his help could be given only *for a consideration*.   And so the puissant Kings of France and England
agreed to rob the indigent old King René, that Margaret,
his beloved daughter, might go free.   " The King of Sicily
entered into engagements with the king, that the country
of Provence, after his decease, should revert, with all its
rights and privileges, to the king to be united for ever to
the crown.   In return for this, Queen Margaret . . . was
released from her imprisonment by the King of France, who

paid King Edward 50,000 golden crowns for her ransom." *
On the 30th August, 1475, thirty years after she had landed,
as Henry's bride, in the flush, and pride, and beauty of youth,
Queen Margaret left the shores which it had been well for
her had she never seen, and returned to her father's home a
pensioner of France.

The inglorious issue of the invasion of France overwhelmed
Edward IV. and his advisers with discredit in the eyes of
the people, whilst the popularity of Richard, hitherto confined
to the north, increased, to the disadvantage of the King.
He alone had refused to tarnish his honour, "drawing the
eyes of all, especially the nobles and soldiers, upon himself." † The suffering of the people was aggravated by the
sudden discharge of thousands of soldiers who, being without
means of sustenance, betook themselves to the profession of
highwaymen, " to theft and rapine, so that no road throughout
England was left in a state of safety for either merchants or
pilgrims." ‡ The inland trade of the country was paralysed
by these brigands, too often supported by profligate young
nobles who, sometimes as a mere freak, but more often
with a view of sharing the spoils, joined in their acts of
aggression.

Individuals were enriched with French gold and pensions;
but the treasury was empty. Edward was in urgent need of
money, but a loan could be only legally contracted by the
authority of Parliament, and to face Parliament at such a
juncture was the last thing that he was disposed to do. In
this extremity he had recourse to the iniquitous system of

---

* Monstrelet's "Chronicles," vol. iv., p. 368.
† Bacon's "Henry VII.," p. 3.   ‡ "Croy. Chron.," p. 473.

"Benevolences" — a singular misnomer for *forced gifts.*
There can be little doubt that Morton, who was now high in
the King's favour, was the real author of these oppressive ex-
tortions, since, ten years later, when Henry VII. revived the
system, we find that it received the designation of "Morton's
forks." The people bitterly resented the exaction, and would
probably have resisted it but for the tact and condescension
with which the King, still popular with the middle classes, to
whom he was always affable, requested their help in his great
need.* Holinshed gives us a specimen of the manner of
Edward IV. in extracting these gifts. He sent, among others,
for an old rich widow, before the French invasion. With an
insinuating smile the King inquired what she would give
towards the prosecution of the war? The lady, struck with
his beauty, replied, "For thy lovely face thou shalt have
twenty pounds." This, being twice as much as the King
expected, he gave her thanks and a kiss. With kisses of any
sort she had long been unfamiliar, but she was so delighted
with a royal one that she doubled her offer and gave him forty
pounds.

But, after the return from France, frowns were as often
employed as smiles and kisses, for the classes with whom
the King had been most popular were alienated by exactions
which had reduced to poverty all those who possessed ought
of which they could be despoiled. The clergy were loud in
their complaints. Since it was not lawful for them to bear
arms, they had been specially assessed for the maintenance

---

* " He rode about the more part of the land, and used the people in such
fair manner, that he raised thereby notable sums of money."—FABYAN,
p. 664.

of the French war.* Their disaffection was becoming general, and it was contagious. Nor was it checked by the vindictiveness with which it was remembered that Edward had punished with death even a jest at his right divine. In allusion to the sign of "The Crown" over his shop, a grocer had said that he "would make his son heir to the Crown." The joke was reported to the King, and the grocer was hung. Now men openly spoke of the Duke of Clarence as the Parliamentary heir of Henry VI.

The reconciliation of Clarence with the King had not restored him to his brother's confidence. There can be no doubt that he was regarded both by Edward IV. and by the Duke of Gloucester as a dangerous rival. The King, we know, was superstitious. His mind was said to be disturbed by a soothsayer's prophecy that the name of his successor should begin with a "G." This he applied to George, Duke of Clarence. The Queen's family, and especially her mother, the Duchess of Bedford, inflamed the King's jealousy and superstitious apprehensions, and Clarence's disgrace was decided on. Pressed for money, and knowing that his subjects would not submit to further taxation, Edward persuaded Parliament to pass an Act of Resumption, whereby all royal estates, without regard to whom they had been granted, except those specially reserved, were resumed by the King. In the list of special exemptions the name of the Duke of Gloucester appeared; that of Clarence was absent. The Duke was naturally indignant, since he was thus deprived, by his brother's arbitrary and ill-natured decision, of the Manor

---

* Polydore Vergil, Book xxiv., p. 170.

of Tutbury and many other lands. This was only one of several injuries, real or imagined, which increased the alienation between the brothers, and induced Clarence, who was beloved by the people, to use his influence in fomenting sedition. Every day their relations became more strained. The Duke absented himself from the King's table, was silent in council, and professed to attribute to necromancy or poison the death of his wife, which occurred shortly after the birth of her third child. The Duke, however, was not inconsolable for the loss of his wife. It happened about this time that the Duke of Burgundy fell at the siege of Nanci. His only daughter, Mary, was sole heiress to his immense possessions, and the animosity of the King was accentuated by the proposal of Clarence for her hand. Edward may well have felt that so great an exaltation would make his brother more dangerous than ever, and as he favoured the suit of Maximilian, the son of the Emperor, he threw every impediment in the way of Clarence.* Here again he yielded to the Queen's remonstrances, though she had another candidate in view for the hand of the wealthy heiress. It was no secret that Elizabeth desired this eligible match for her brother, Earl Rivers.

Clarence, it must be remembered, had a Parliamentary title to the Crown, on the failure of Henry's issue, confirmed after his restoration by Henry VI. and the Earl of Warwick.† He was therefore a rival whom neither Edward IV. nor the Duke of Gloucester could afford to despise.

His arrest was decided on, and it was not difficult to find a pretext. A certain astrologer—one Master John Stacy—

---

* "Croyland Chronicle," p. 478.　　† See "Rot. Parl.," vol. vi., p. 191.

had been arrested for necromancy. His confession had implicated Thomas Burdett, an esquire in the household of the Duke of Clarence. Both were condemned to death, Burdett protesting his innocence. On the following day Clarence appeared at the Council Chamber, accompanied by a famous doctor of the universities, who read Burdett's declaration of innocence, when both withdrew, no word apparently being added to this formal protest.* The indiscretion furnished the King with the opportunity of arresting his brother with a show of legality. He summoned the Duke to appear before him at the palace at Westminster, when he formulated charges so easy to the irresponsible tyrant, whether on the throne, in the counting-house, or the shop, the most complete answer to which is less than nothing to the man who has freed himself from the trammels of morality. The Duke was placed under arrest, and never tasted liberty again. Whilst there is no proof of that overt rebellion with which he was charged in his subsequent impeachment, there can be as little doubt that the King regarded him as a traitor, the more dangerous that he was a popular idol, and his tragic end is sufficiently explained by the cruel and vindictive character of Edward IV.†

The Duke was committed to the Tower, and in the ensuing Parliament was attainted of high treason. His trial was conducted by the highest tribunal of the realm, the King himself pleading against him in the House of Lords. The Croyland Chronicler relates the incident with brevity and

* " Croyland Chronicle," p. 479.
† Dr. Warkworth says that Clarence had compromised himself further than is generally supposed, instigating the country people to disloyalty by imposing upon their fears of the King's vengeance.

evident reluctance. His mind, he says, "shudders to enlarge upon the circumstances; for there was to be witnessed a sad strife carried on between these two brethren of such high estate. For not a single person uttered a word against the Duke, except the King; not one individual made answer to the King except the Duke." *

The royal indictment set forth that of all the acts of treason, from the commencement of his reign, that of the arraigned Duke was the most malicious, unnatural, and loathsome; contrived "by the person that of all earthly creatures, besides the duty of allegiance, by nature, by benefits, by gratitude, and by gifts and grants, of goods and possessions, hath been most bounden and beholden, whom to name it greatly grieveth the heart of our said sovereign lord." † His riches ranked next to the King's.

By his treason the King had been driven from his realm, "which all, the King moved by nature and love, utterly forgave, intending to have put all in perpetual oblivion." But the Duke, unmoved by such affection, had "conspired new treasons, more heinous and lothesome than ever before," aiming at the destruction of the King; for which purpose "he cast and compassed the means to induce the King's natural subjects to withdraw their hearts, loves, and affections from the King" by many subtle ways. Especially had he persuaded the people "that Thomas Burdett, his servant, who was lawfully and truly attainted of treason, was wrongfully put to death; to some of his servants of such like disposition he gave large sums of money and venison, therewith to assemble the King's

---

* "Croyland Chronicle," p. 479.   † "Rolls of Parl.," vol. vi., p. 193.

subjects, to feast them and cheer them, and by their policies and reasoning induce them to believe that the said Burdett was wrongfully executed." He also caused his servants to report that the King had wrought by necromancy, was therefore unfit to govern a Christian people, and that he "had used craft to poison his subjects, such as him pleased." "And over this the said Duke being in full purpose to exalt himself and his heirs to the Crown of England, and clearly in opinion to put aside for ever the said Crown from the King and his heirs, upon one of the falsest and most unnatural coloured pretexts that man might imagine, falsely and untruly noised, published, and said that the King our Sovereign Lord was a bastard, and not begotten to reign upon us."

The witnesses by whom these charges were to be substantiated, "filled," says a reluctant deponent, "the office of *accusers* rather;"* and the King was fain to fall back upon one of those errors which he professed to have condoned. The Duke had obtained the recognition of Henry VI. to his title to the throne after Prince Edward, "which the said Duke had kept with himself secret, not doing the King to have any knowledge thereof . . . . and also the same Duke, purposing to accomplish his said false and untrue interest, and to inquiet and trouble the King. . . . now of late willed and desired the Abbot of Tweybury, Master John Tapton, Clerk, and Roger Harewell, Esquire, to cause a strange child to have been brought into his castle of Warwick, and there to have been put and kept in likeness of his son and heir, and that they should have conveyed and sent his said son and heir

---

* "Croyland Chronicle," p. 479.

into Ireland, or into Flanders, out of this land, whereby he might have gotten him assistance and favour against our said sovereign lord." *

An obsequious Parliament passed sentence of condemnation; but, from what cause does not appear, the execution was delayed for some time. It is not improbable that the Lady Cecily may have used her influence, personally, or through the Duke of Gloucester, to move her son from his vindictive purpose. More tells us that Richard "resisted openly" his brother's purpose. It is, then, simply incredible that he should have been the instrument of carrying the sentence of the House of Lords into effect. "Is it credible," asks Horace Walpole, "that in a proceeding so public, and so solemn for that age, the brother of the offended monarch and of the royal criminal should have been deputed, or would have stooped, to so vile an office?"

On the 18th of February, 1478, George, Duke of Clarence, was secretly put to death. The story, with which every schoolboy is familiar, of his having been drowned in a butt of Malmsey wine, is unauthentic, and was probably a picturesque accretion attributable to the vinose propensities of the alderman who first gave it currency.† The assassination was secret, and the means unknown to contemporary chroniclers, not excepting Fabyan, who, twenty years later, gave expression to unfounded rumour. All that can be said in support of this tradition is that there is no inherent impossibility in the suggestion of Shakspeare that the murderers, unnerved by conscience, faltered in their butchery,

---

* "Rolls of Parliament," vol. vi., pp. 193–4. See also Lingard, vol. v., p. 228.
† Fabyan, p. 666.

and completed their bloody crime by availing themselves of the butt which stood conveniently by.

> "Take that, and that! If all this will not do,
> I'll drown you in the Malmsey-butt within."

But the story is altogether improbable, and entirely un-authenticated. It may have originated in the belief that poison was conveyed to Clarence in a glass of his favourite beverage.

We learn from the contemporary historian of the reign of Edward IV. that, whilst all this mischief was "secretly in contriving against Clarence, in the Court appeared no face but those of jollity and magnificence." * Lost to natural feeling, Edward gloated over the perpetration of a crime which left him free to indulge his effeminate love of ease and pleasure, but has left the darkest stain upon his memory, and which, when seized with remorse, he vainly and disingenuously sought to transfer to others.

But what was the Duke of Gloucester's share in this inhuman tragedy? If Miss Halsted may be credited, he was away in the north of England, discharging the duties of his office as Keeper of the Northern Marches. The evidence adduced in support of this theory is, like all that this accomplished lady has written, deserving of careful consideration, and none more so than the statement that many documents relative to the repair of fortresses, etc., dated from Sheriff Hutton, "are valuable as establishing Richard's absence from the scene of strife."† Unfortunately, the dates of these documents are not stated; and these are

---

* Habington, p. 475.   † Miss Halsted's "Richard III.," vol. i., p. 331.

essential to give them any value when mistakes might so readily arise by confusing the old and new computation of time. The whole argument is, as a matter of fact, weakened by such an oversight in reference to the date of the marriage of Edward's infant son Richard, which, Miss Halsted says, " occurred on the 15th of January, 1477, about a month after the demise of the Lady Isabel, and at the identical period when the inconsiderate Clarence had ascribed her death to sorcery."* The date is correct; but as Miss Halsted's authority uses the *old* computation, whilst she gives the latter fact according to new style, the two incidents were really separated by thirteen months. Miss Halsted's argument, then, would seem to prove that Richard *was* in London just one month before Clarence's murder, and at the time of his trial. There is further evidence that he was present at the opening of Parliament on the 16th of January.

The proofs that Richard had no hand in the impeachment of his brother, that he was not amongst the witnesses called against him, nor instrumental in carrying out the sentence of Parliament are so strong, that his proved presence in London cannot weaken them. On the contrary, at a time when there was no postal communication, and for all practical purposes Middleham was as distant from London as Moscow is to-day, it lends consistency to the statements of contemporaries that Richard opposed the extreme measures to which the King's vindictive character impelled him. It is impossible to doubt that in this he would have the support of his mother, the Lady Cecily, who, on Edward's return from exile, had joined

---

* Miss Halsted's " Richard III.," vol. i., p. 334.

with the only son who had thus far proved himself worthy of her training and of his father's name, in reconciling her two elder sons, who had disappointed all her most cherished hopes, and brought ruin to her house. To such efforts we may reasonably assign the deferred execution of the capital sentence which Edward IV., the sole pleader against Clarence, had secured. The base hypocrisy, with which Shakspeare represents Richard as veiling his hatred and jealousy of Clarence, may be dismissed as clearly unsupported by and inconsistent with ascertained facts.

Sir Thomas More, in the "Life of Richard III.," which is Shakspeare's leading authority,* says, "Some men ween that his drift, covertly conveyed, lacked not in helping forth his brother of Clarence to his death, *which he resisted openly*, howbeit somewhat as men deemed, more faintly than he that were heartily minded to his wealth." And he adds, "But of all this point there is no certainty. And *whoso divineth upon conjectures* may as well shoot too far as too short." Divining upon conjectures, Shakspeare has blackened the character of Richard perhaps beyond the possibility of reclamation. Minds that have been long dominated by vivid impressions become a prey to prejudice, which the best authenticated facts are powerless to remove. The insinuation of More is followed by Shakspeare for the purpose of dramatic effect, and is repeated as a fact by Bacon, who says that Richard was *the contriver* of his brother's death.†

---

* Beauty of style and adaptation to dramatic treatment lend a factitious importance to the work attributed to Sir Thomas More, for a further account of which the reader is referred to the preface.

† Bacon's "Henry VII.," p. 2. The only remark of Rous upon the death of Clarence is "he died in the Tower of London and is buryed at Tuexburye

Sandford improves upon this by making him the actual perpetrator of the murder. "He was drowned," he says, "in a butt of Malmsey, his brother, the Duke of Gloucester, assisting thereat with his own hands." But if More is to be trusted, Richard should at least have the credit of a remonstrance against the death sentence upon his brother. Feeble and halting it may have been, and indeed a protest against the decision of the King involved a responsibility from which the boldest might well shrink. Edward had become arbitrary, suspicious, and cruel, jealous of his prerogative, and performing the duties of his office "with such a high hand that he appeared to be dreaded by all his subjects." * An expression ever on his lips when any one crossed him, "He shall repent it through every vein of his heart," shows the ferocious character of the King, every member of whose family and court was a foe of the Duke of Gloucester.

Unlike his brother Richard, Clarence had never acquiesced in Edward's marriage or tempered his aversion to the Queen. He had been unrelenting in his antagonism to the whole Woodville faction, and to their unrelenting vengeance he was now abandoned. "He was too open-handed for the court, where suspicion looks through a man and discerns his resolutions, though in the dark, and locked up in secrecy. But what was his ruin, he was, whether the House of York or Lancaster prevailed, still second to the Crown. So that his eye, by looking too steadfastly on the beauty of it, became unlawfully enamoured with it, and that being observed by the

the 25th day of February, 1477."—JOHN ROSS, "Historical Account of the Earls of Warwick," p. 239.

   * "Croyland Chronicle," p. 480.

King's jealousy, he suffered as if he actually had sinned." *
"The King," says the same historian, "was certainly wrought
to it by the practice and the misinformation of an envious
faction at court." † The remorseful ejaculation attributed to
Edward IV., "O unfortunate brother, for whose life not one
creature would make intercessions!" has been held to invali-
date the statement of More, that Richard "resisted openly"
the infliction of the death sentence. But, without attaching
any value as an authority to the work attributed to Sir Thomas
More, its testimony is that of one bitterly hostile to Richard;
whilst the lament of the King rests only upon tradition. At
least its slight historical basis has been perverted. Intercession having been made for a criminal, Edward exclaimed:
"How many and urgent applications are made to save a
wretch who ought to die by the laws of his country, but not
one mouth was opened to plead for a brother in distress!" ‡
There is reason in the remark of Buck that these words
were uttered by the King "when his wrath had cooled;" but
that "no man durst move on his (Clarence's) behalf" when
he was regarded as an aspirant to the throne. But in truth
Edward's remorseful lament is the strongest proof of Richard's
innocence. The death of Clarence was a crime of jealousy
and resentment, responsibility for which the King made no
attempt to transfer either to the Duke of Gloucester or any
one else. Nor was it Richard alone, or specially, whom he
reproached for having failed to remonstrate against his own
merciless sentence. Far more likely is it that, in Edward's
mind, Richard alone was excepted in the rebuke addressed to

---

* Habington, p. 475.   † *Ibid.* p. 479.   ‡ Hutton, p. 165.

the whole Council. By the appointment of the Duke of
Buckingham (who was at this time espoused to the Lady
Katharine, the Queen's sister) to the office of High Steward of
England in order that he might not only pass upon Clarence
the judgment of the Peers, but himself superintend its execution, the King had handed his brother over to the vindictive
hatred of the Woodvilles, who probably enough subdued in
his mind those feelings of natural compunction, of which the
fact that judgment was deferred appears to afford some
indication.

The question of motive can never be ignored in a judicial
inquiry of this nature. Assuming that Richard was at this
time entertaining those ambitious and nefarious designs which
More says were attributed to him—a suspicion which Shakspeare represents as a fact—Clarence at liberty presented an
insuperable obstacle to their attainment. Not so, however,
Clarence a prisoner in the Tower. Again, Richard benefited
less directly by Clarence's attainder than the Woodvilles.
Clarence and Rivers were rivals for the hand of Mary of
Burgundy, and upon the latter was conferred the larger
portion of the attainted Duke's estates, whilst the wardship
of his heir—a lucrative and coveted office—was granted to the
Marquis of Dorset. On the other hand, before the Duke's
death, one of his titles was conferred on Richard's infant son,
who became Earl of Salisbury, whilst the moiety of the lordship of Barnard Castle, which Clarence had held in right of
his wife, was afterwards secured to Richard by direct grant
from the Crown. But these and other advantages would have
been equally guaranteed to Richard whilst Clarence was safely
lodged in the Tower. If therefore motives, apart from

BARNARD CASTLE.

evidence, should fasten upon either the guilt of arresting the hand of mercy, it must be assigned to Earl Rivers rather than to the Duke of Gloucester. And this is borne out by the contemporary historians, who attributed the sacrifice of Clarence to the influence of the Queen and her avaricious kindred. Upon the question of Richard's complicity in a fratricidal murder it must be allowed that there is no particle of evidence on which to incriminate him. Not even suspicion attached to him, until the chroniclers, whose interest it was to load his name with the vilest calumnies, fastened upon every act of violence that had occurred in his time, and so manipulated it as to blacken his reputation.

Immediately after the death of Clarence, Richard obtained licences from the King for the foundation of two religious establishments—at Barnard Castle and at Middleham.* By Act of Parliament he was prohibited from alienating any portion of his wife's dowry, which alone, of all his many lordships and estates, was at present a source of income, or available for his purpose. His partiality for Middleham has been already noticed. Whittaker says that for a considerable time he divided his residence " between his castle here and that of Skipton. He bestowed liberally on the monks of Coverham and the parish of Skipton, for the repair of their respective churches. But under the walls of his own castle he meditated greater things." † In January, 1478, he petitioned the King : " In consideration that I, your said suppliant, purpose by the

---

* These licences, as will presently appear, had been applied for at least as early as the first week of January, and *received the sanction of Parliament on the 16th of that month.*

† Whittaker's " History of Richmondshire," vol. i., p. 335.

grace of God to edifie, founde, endowe, and make a collage of a Dene, xii. prests, to sing and pray for the prosperous estate of you, sovereign Lord, the quene, your issue, and my lady moder, the welfare of me, Anne my wyff, and my issue wheel we live in this present world, and for the soules of us when we be departed out of this world; the sowles of my lord my Fader, my brethren and susters, and of all Christen soules," it be ordained that "we have authority to set aside that Act, without any other licence thereof to be had." *

By his marriage with the heiress of the Nevilles, the advowson of the Rectory of Middleham vested in Richard. But the first step towards the new foundation was to procure the consent of the rector in possession, one William Beverley; and as "the whole profits of the living belonged to himself, a mere addition of dignity could ill compensate for the incumbrance of six chaplains and several clerks. To provide for this inconvenience, therefore, a licence of mortmain was granted, empowering the new foundation to acquire lands, etc. to the amount of one hundred marks per annum." †

The consent of the rector, and the terms in which it was conveyed, showed that he, at all events, attributed Richard's endowment to honourable motives of generosity and piety. Recognising that the solemnities of the mass are " deservedly esteemed to be gretful to the Divine mercy," he welcomes the proposal to amplify the parish church of Middleham. "Wherefore from me on behalf of the said most excellent Prince, it was besought that I would consent unto the erection of the

---

* " Rot. Parl.," vol. vi., p. 172.
† Whittaker's " Richmondshire," vol. i., p. 335.

said parish church of Middleham into a collegiate church. Wereupon I, the said William Beverley, being mindful that the proposition of the said most excellent Prince was laudable and meritorious, and being desirous to act consistently with these pious desires to the erection of the said parish church into a collegiate church, I do hereby express consent thereunto." *

In this transaction Mr. Gairdner sees a desire to atone for the perpetration of crime by an act of piety. An assumption so dishonouring to Richard should admit at least of some quasi-justification from facts, or from the recorded judgments of competent observers. It rests, however, simply upon the coincidence of time, a method of deduction which would expose the most upright and high-minded men of his age to similar unnatural and impossible charges. The "native religious sentiment," "never utterly extinguished," which Mr. Gairdner allows to Richard,† would account for an act so entirely in harmony with the customs of the age. When, on the death of his brother Edward, Richard ordered a thousand masses to be said for his soul; or when Hastings, in his will, ordered "a thousand priests to say a thousand masses for his soul," and that "each should have sixpence," they but conformed to the religious sentiment of their times, and without the strong inducements which prompted Richard and Anne Neville to "meditate greater things in connection with the home of their childhood, which both loved so well." The absence of the name of Clarence in Richard's petition to the King, whilst those of his father, of Edward and his Queen, of

---

* Whittaker's "Richmondshire," vol. i., p. 336.
† "Life of Richard III.," by James Gairdner, p. 47.

himself and his wife, as those for the benefit of whose souls masses were to be said continually, divests this offering of piety of all semblance of an act of atonement for the death of one who is only included among his "brothers and sisters." Moreover, Richard's "pious desires" must have been entertained before the death or even the impeachment of Clarence, since, as we have seen, they received *the sanction of Parliament* on the 16th of January, 1478.* The death of Clarence occurred more than a month later. If we must seek an explanation in some particular contemporary event for this act of piety on behalf of Richard and his wife, one wholly congenial with his nature might be conjectured in the birth of his son. The exact date of his birth is indeed uncertain, but as Rous states that he was seven years old when created Prince of Wales, in September, 1483, we may conclude that it was in 1477. Richard's petition, which received the sanction of Parliament on the 16th January, must have been presented to the King in the preceding year, and the argument from the coincidence of dates is fatal to the idea of an act of atonement, and favours that of a thank-offering, which it naturally suggests to the unprejudiced inquirer.

New honours and emoluments were now heaped upon the Duke of Gloucester, who certainly never stood higher in the King's confidence and favour. Probably Edward was conscious that he had himself lost the confidence and esteem of his subjects. The introduction of an elaborate spy system had produced a general sense of insecurity; the use of the rack, and an habitual interference with the purity of justice† had

---

* Whittaker, vol. i., p. 335; and "Rot. Parl.," vi., 172.
† Green's "History of the English People," vol. ii., p. 51.

alienated the peasantry. He put the penal laws into execution, "so that a general fear possessed the people that his after government would be both sharp and heavy."* The Parliamentary Rolls bear witness to the many grievances suffered by the Commons at the hands of a pampered aristocracy. No remonstrances moved a servile Parliament, which existed only to register the King's decisions. Thus the very Parliament which was now in session passed an Act forbidding any other than a lord's son, unless possessed of freehold estate of the yearly value of five marks, from " possessing any mark or game of his own swans." The prohibition pressed heavily upon the population inhabiting the fen districts of Lincolnshire and Cambridgeshire. It was especially oppressive to the people of Croyland, who prayed for exemption. Time out of mind, they say, the people have used to have " great game of swans " in the fens and marshes. These were a source of livelihood to many of the inhabitants of the town, which " stondeth all in marshe and fenne, and noon arable lands ne pasture about it, soo that few or noon other profitts may or can be founde in the precincte of that town to the relief of the inhabitaunts ther." † There was no class of the community that was not oppressed by exactions, restrictions, monopolies, or penalties. The King himself entered into competition with the merchants, and checked that spirit of commercial enterprise which had revived with the cessation of foreign embroilments. For with the King of England it was impossible for private enterprise to compete. His ships were annually freighted " with tin, wool, and cloth, and the merchandise of

---

* Habington, p. 476.   † " Rot. Parl.," vol. vi., p. 260.

the King of England was publicly exposed to sale in the ports of Italy and Greece."* He became enriched at the cost of those who had been the staunchest supporters of his House, and leaving the government of the country to the prudent and now universally popular Duke of Gloucester, he abandoned himself to those dissolute habits but for which his name might have been handed down as that of the greatest of the Plantagenets.

The responsibilities now devolving upon Richard demanded that he should fix his residence in the metropolis. Amongst the confiscated possessions of Clarence, which the King had bestowed on him, was the ancient London mansion of the Nevilles, known as the "Erber." The house was probably no longer suited for the magnificence in which all the family of York delighted, and which was considered necessary for the Great Chamberlain of England. Richard, therefore, purchased in 1476 from Lady Crosby, a neighbouring palace, which is thus felicitously described by Miss Halsted : †

"Erected in a style of princely grandeur, it was completed both within and without with that gorgeous splendour which peculiarly characterised the buildings of the fifteenth century ; and Crosby Place, with its embowered oriels, its superb hall, and matchless roof, so famed as perpetuating in this present day the only specimen now remaining in the metropolis of the domestic architecture of the Middle Ages, is as interesting from its association with the last monarch of the Plantagenet race, as is Barnard Castle, the abode of Richard of Gloucester in early and less troubled times, from the preservation there

---

* Lingard, vol. iv., p. 207.   † "Richard III.," vol. i., p. 363.

of his household cognizance, 'the bristled boar.'"* This almost unique example of domestic Gothic architecture has, after much mutilation, in the last century, been preserved through the public spirit of Miss Haskett. In her efforts for its conservation fifty years ago, she received much discriminating assistance from Mr. W. Williams, of Great St. Helen's, but the public showed little appreciation of her efforts.† Ten years later Crosby Hall became the home of a literary and scientific society, and has since been converted into a restaurant, where, beneath the ancient timber roof, one of the most glorious which England possesses, and in the oriel of the fine old banqueting hall, surrounded by historic paintings and gorgeous windows emblazoned with the Crosby arms, the citizens of London take their mid-day meal.

---

* Crosby House was built in 1466 by Sir John Crosby, alderman. It had a frontage to Bishopsgate Street, of which only one gable now exists. It is described as "the highest and finest house in the city."

† Walford's "Old and New London," vol. ii., p. 158.

CHAPTER V.

EDWARD's inertness was observed both from Scotland and France. In the former country active preparations for war were in progress, whilst Louis XI. ceased to pay the tribute which had provided Edward with the means of gratifying his frivolous tastes. But the King had long since fallen a prey to the lethargy which springs from satiety. Money was again raised by benevolences;* Richard was appointed Lieutenant-General of the kingdom whose destinies were in his uncontrolled power, and, pending negotiations, occupied himself in strengthening the border districts against invasion.

When it was found that Louis XI. was secretly inciting James III. to a rupture with England, war was at once decided on, the entire command of the English army of 25,000 men being entrusted to Richard.† The causes which led to this war, and its results, may be briefly stated. The Princess Cecily, Edward's second daughter, had been betrothed to the

---

* "No one presumed to reject the prayer of the sovereign, and considerable sums were thus procured from the shame, the hopes, or the fears of the donors."
—LINGARD, vol. iv., p. 201.

† "Croyland Chronicle," p. 481.

CROSBY HALL IN 1790.

son of James. Three instalments of her dowry, of one thousand marks a year, had been paid in advance, and James refused either to consummate the marriage or return the money. Matters might have been arranged had not both Kings been exasperated by the perfidy of Alexander, Duke of Albany, King James' brother. The Duke, who had been exiled from Scotland for seditious conduct, had found an asylum at the court of Edward. He claimed the throne of Scotland on the plea of his brother's illegitimacy, and having sworn to restore Berwick to the .English, to terminate the alliance between France and Scotland, and to do homage to England whenever he should obtain his kingdom,* Edward undertook to place him on the throne which he unjustly claimed, and thus avenge his quarrel with James III. The cost of this expedition weighed heavily upon the overburdened tax-payers in England, who would probably have resisted the new exactions, had not their confidence in the honour as well as the ability of the Duke of Gloucester encouraged the belief that the war would be short and successful, as well as permanently advantageous to England. "For," says Sir George Buck, "his wisdom and courage had not then their nicknames as now, but drew the eyes and acknowledgment of the whole kingdom towards him."

In the war which culminated in his triumphal entry into Edinburgh, Richard won new laurels, adding lustre to the great reputation he had already achieved as a successful general, and received the thanks of Parliament. "His services," says Mr. Gairdner, "were of a kind that the whole nation could

---

* Gairdner, p. 49.   " Fœdera," vol. xii., p. 173.   Lingard, vol. iv.

appreciate, and it may well be believed that whatever may have been thought of his character by close observers, no man stood in higher honour at this time throughout the kingdom generally."* These words convey an insinuation which facts do not warrant. We have absolutely no reason to suppose that "close observers" formed a different estimate of Richard's character than that which obtained universally.† He was accompanied by the most renowned English warriors of the day, some of whom, at least, were true to him to the end of life, as they had been in his past vicissitudes. One of these, who appears at this time only to have reached the rank of an esquire of the body, was Robert Brackenbury, a cadet of an ancient family, seated in the immediate neighbourhood of Barnard Castle, and not improbably owing feudal service to its lord. Richard early distinguished Brackenbury by marks of his favour; his honour was unimpeachable, and his fidelity unwavering.

The results of the war were that Berwick, which had been surrendered by Queen Margaret as the price of an asylum, was ceded to England,‡ the money advanced by King Edward

---

* Gairdner's "Richard III.," p. 24.

† It is true that all classes, from the King to the peasant, regretted the large expenditure which this expedition involved, amounting, it is said, to £100,000. But the "close observers" of the Duke of Gloucester could hardly fail to admire both the policy and the magnanimity displayed by him in sparing the opulent city of Edinburgh, which he left untouched.—*Croyland Chronicle*, p. 481.

‡ "He took truce with King James, and returned the right way to Berwick, which, in the mean time, Thomas Lord Stanley had won without loss of many his men."—POLYDORE VERGIL, Book 24. The *town* had been surrendered without opposition, owing probably to the suddenness of the Duke of Gloucester's appearance; but the castle, "the strongest fort then in the north," was defended by the Earl of Bothwell, who, after repeated assaults, surrendered to Lord Stanley.

restored, and the marriage treaty annulled. King James, whose subjects bare him no good will, "was forced by necessity, after truce taken, to digest that displeasure of winning the town."* The Duke of Gloucester appears to have remained in the north. Certainly he did not proceed so far south as York. He was at the head of an army flushed with victory and devoted to him. Had he now entertained those ambitious views with which he has been credited, the prestige attaching to his name and the dissensions which distracted Edward's court, "all rotten with discord and envy," placed the Crown within his grasp. It is one of his most envenomed detractors who tells us that "the difference between him and his brother was that the one possessed, the other deserved the crown." † He was munificently rewarded by Parliament for his services against the Scots. By an Act passed in January, 1483, he received a grant of the city and lordship of Carlisle, a proof that Parliament, who could best appraise his services, did not think that he had been too munificently enriched by the King.

But high and powerful as was Richard's position, he was discontent. Earl Rivers was the Mordecai sitting in the King's gate, and "all this availed him nothing" until he could supersede him. Perhaps this "open question" may account for Richard's remaining in the north. In the divided court of his brother the number of his friends had increased. He seems in fact to have been already regarded as the unacknowledged head of a party, and that party embraced all who were hostile to the Queen, and not simply those to whom the

* Polydore Vergil, Cam. S., Book xxiv., p. 170. Habington, p. 476.
† Habington, p. 477.

Queen was hostile. The distinction is not unimportant; for whilst the latter were " the chiefest both in blood and power,"* amongst the minor barons and knights whom Elizabeth haughtily disdained, were not a few who, attributing to her the death of Clarence, had become bitterly hostile to her faction.

Earl Rivers controlled the household of the young Prince of Wales. Under the title of Governor he had the charge of his person and education, assisted by a Council, in which the Duke of Gloucester held a subordinate position. An accomplished and superior character, Earl Rivers possessed the entire confidence of the King, who had conferred upon him many lucrative offices, the rewards less of service than of favouritism. Richard alone, amongst those to whom the Woodvilles were obnoxious, viewed these marks of the King's favour with equanimity, until Rivers was appointed Governor of the Prince's household. In this he saw an attempt to secure an ascendency of the Woodville influence, which was full of danger to himself and to the State. The constitution of the Prince's household showed that his objection was valid. Sir Thomas Vaughan had been in the Prince's service from his birth, and to his appointment as Chamberlain no objection could be urged. The Bishop of Rochester, the Bishop of St. Davids, and Alcock, Bishop of Worcester, were perhaps the fittest men to conduct the education of the heir to the throne. Sir William Stanley, as Steward, and Sir Richard Crofts, as Treasurer of the Household, strengthened the Woodville faction, whilst the presence of two youths—the

---

* Habington.

Marquis of Dorset and Lord Richard Gray, the Queen's sons—rendered that influence. supreme. In this year the Marquis of Dorset was put in possession of his estates, "without proof of his being of age, an evidence that he had scarcely attained it." Lord Richard Gray was still younger.*

With a view, perhaps, to propitiate the Welsh, the young Prince's residence had been fixed at Ludlow, and here he had for some time pursued his studies under the enlightened direction of his uncle. The Duke of Gloucester was still in the north. By what means he sought to supersede Earl Rivers as Governor of the Prince's household is not known. The coveted office fell to him somewhat unexpectedly. Meanwhile his attention had been diverted to matters of imperial concern, and more worthy of the warrior and the patriot. Louis XI. had thrown off the mask, withheld the tribute, and, cancelling the marriage treaty by which the Princess Elizabeth was contracted to the Dauphin, he wounded Edward where he was most susceptible—in his ambitious views for the aggrandisement of his children. Twice within a few months had his projected matrimonial alliances for his daughters been rejected. Now, before all the world, after his eldest daughter had been recognised for years at the French Court as "Madame la Dauphine," without parley or defence she was set aside in favour of another. The opportunity of recovering to France a portion of the rich province of Burgundy was more to Louis than kingly honour. At the very time that Edward, whose impecuniosity was too well known in France, was illegally extorting money from his subjects to enable him

---

* Sharon Turner, vol. iii., p. 402.

to carry on the Scotch War, the death of Mary of Burgundy, caused by a fall from her horse, placed this within his grasp.* Maximilian, now a widower, in hope of obtaining the hand of Anne of Brittany, assented to the betrothal of his infant daughter Margaret to the Dauphin. Although only two years of age, she was delivered to commissioners appointed by Louis XI. to go through the ceremony of betrothal, and to be educated at the court of her future husband. Sunk as he was in indolence, and debilitated by excess, Edward could not fail bitterly to resent this insult to his daughter. Throwing off the effeminacy which had so long clouded the promise of his early years, all his Plantagenet pride inflamed by the perfidy of Louis, he resolved to humble the French King as he had already humbled James III. of Scotland. The rumours of the perfidy of King Louis were presently confirmed by the arrival of the Lord Howard, who reported that he had seen the Lady Margaret brought with all pomp and ceremony to Ambois, and there married to Charles the Dauphin.† At this intelligence Edward "burst into a paroxism of rage, and thought of nothing else but taking revenge." ‡

Summoning his Council with other members of the nobility, the King thus addressed them: "The injuries I have received are divulged everywhere, and the eye of the world is fixed upon me, to observe with what countenance I suffer. . . . I must neglect the principal office of a Prince if I omit to chastise him. For this ungrateful man . . . . denies not only the marriage of the Dauphin

---

* "Louis, forgetting the Princess Elizabeth, demanded Mary (Margaret?) for the Dauphin."—LINGARD, vol. iv., p. 215.

† Habington, p. 477.　　　　‡ "Public Records."

to our daughter, which would have proved so great an honour to his blood and security to his kingdom, but even the annual tribute of 50,000 crowns. . . . . We seem to have a deputation from heaven to exercise the office of the Supreme Judge in chastising the impious. . . . . I see the clouds of due revenge gathered in your brow, and the lightning of fury break from your eyes; which bodes thunder against our enemy. Let us therefore lose no time, but suddenly and severely scourge this perjured coward." *

With the dauntless feeling of Englishmen, the leading nobility resented the affront which Louis had offered their King and country, with indignation fully as great as their sovereign's. And when Edward further appealed to them "to regain honour to our nation and his kingdom to our crown," the whole court, "nay, the whole kingdom, was loud in calling for war, and requiring instant preparation for invasion." † But above all, the Duke of Gloucester appeared zealous in the quarrel, "expressing aloud his desire that all his estates might be spent, and all his veins emptied in revenge of this injury." ‡

● But Edward's coffers, lately filled with the tribute from France, were exhausted by the Scottish campaign and the costly habits of an indolent and refined voluptuary. Great as was the warlike enthusiasm, he knew that it would be extinguished by an appeal to the Commons for the sinews of war. In these circumstances he addressed himself to the prelates, appealing to them on the ground of the exemption of the clergy from military service, to grant him

---

* Habington, p. 478. † "Public Records." ‡ Habington, p. 478.

the tithes then falling due. His demand was granted, but the comment of the Croyland chronicler reflects the resentment of the clergy. " As though," he exclaims, " when the prelates and clergy once make their appearance in convocation, whatever the King thinks fit to ask that same ought to be done. Oh, deadly destruction to the church, which must arise from such servility ! May God avert it from the minds of all succeeding Kings ever to make a precedent of an act of this nature ! lest perchance evils may chance to befall them, worse than ever can be conceived, and such as shortly afterwards miserably befell this same King and his most illustrious progeny." *

But no King was ever yet diverted from making war by the want of resources for its prosecution ; least of all when his subjects "with a fierce appetite desired to arm." The great feudal lords, hastening to their ancient halls, summoned their vassals and retainers. The tocsin of war was everywhere heard. The enthusiasm of the nobles infected all classes, so that " no language was heard but martial, and all the gallantry was in new armour or other conveniences for service." Whilst the busy preparations were in progress, Edward IV. retired to Windsor, determined to begin the war in the approaching spring. North and south the voice of busy preparation was heard ; from east and west recruits voluntarily joined the royal standard. The time for calling King Louis to a reckoning had arrived ; an army, exceeding the means of transport, was equipped and impatiently awaiting the order to march. "Neighing steeds, exulting clarions,

---

* " Croyland Chronicle," p. 483.

warriors in burnished steel," displaying on their breasts the
badge which visibly proclaimed the liege lord to whose service
they were attached, the shouts of wild applause with which
their leaders were greeted, declared the readiness of the
army and the eagerness with which the King's appearance
at its head was awaited.* But the King came not. It was
Easter—the anniversary of Barnet—but the King's thoughts
were not of war. At the Palace at Westminster, on the bed
of suffering which in a few hours must be the bed of death,
he lay a worn-out voluptuary. On the 9th April, 1483, he
died. In the face of the world France had pointed the finger
of scorn at the debauched yet ambitious King. Vain now
were all those costly preparations, that expenditure of a
nation's energies to humble Louis XI. "He was diverted
on the sudden from calling King Louis to a reckoning for
this crime, and summoned by death to give a strict account
for all his own. Death arrested him, and in the space of not
many hours instructed him in more than all the oratory from
pulpits had done for forty years." †

That the King's death was due directly to a surfeit cannot be questioned. Monstrelet attributes it to drinking too
much of the good wine of Challuan which he had received
as a present from the King of France. ‡ He had long been
the slave of enervating habits, and both mind and body exhibited their deleterious effects. Rejecting the advice of his
physicians, he sought to dispel the gloom and weariness
wrought by satiety, by increased indulgence in the pleasures
of the table. His constitution, long since undermined,

---

* Sharon Turner, vol. iii., p. 392.   † Habington, p. 478.
‡ Monstrelet, vol. iv., p. 424.

possessed no rallying power. Excitement, anger, and perhaps
an attack of ague, may have contributed to his enfeeblement ;
but all authorities agree with Habington that "it was
questionless a surfeit brought this great Prince so suddenly to
his end. For who observes well the scope of his pleasure
finds it to have been placed much in wantonness and riot—the
two mighty destroyers of nature."

More ascribes to Edward IV. in his last hours a long
speech, urging union upon his divided court, family, and
ministers. Knowing as he did the rivalries and jealousies
which divided them, it is likely that he may have expressed
briefly the wishes which, in accordance with an unfortunate
habit of his age, More elaborates into a formal speech.
Nothing is more likely—not to say certain—than that he
urged them, by their united counsels, and by "discarding
those feelings of suspicion which had been the occasion of
discord among persons whose strength lay in union, harmony,
and peace among themselves," to maintain the cause of the
White Rose, and to promote the well-being of his family.
The one important fact to notice is that, after this alleged
attempt to unite his family and court, Edward IV. made his
will, "wherein he constituted his sons his heirs, *whom he
committed to the tuition of Richard his brother, Duke of
Gloucester.*"*

Thus passed away a King whose reign began in brilliant
promise, whom fortune favoured, and whose worst enemy was
himself. He had great qualities ; but the pleasures of the
table, the society of women, the frivolities of dress which

---

* Polydore Vergil, Book xxiv., p. 171.

occupied his mind, when released from the excitement of war, reduced him intellectually and morally to a lower level than that which the humblest of his courtiers might claim. Even when hunting, we are told that it was his custom to have " several tents set up for the ladies whom he entertained in a magnificent manner."* The enervating effects of sensual indulgence had made inroads upon his constitution; the fickleness of his character had begotten envy and intrigues among his courtiers; he knew that his children's infancy would be a bar to their succession; and the would-be founder of an illustrious dynasty of Kings meets death, not indeed impenitent, but stung by remorse and dreading the Nemesis which must attend upon his unkingly deeds. If he reposed confidence in any one it was in his brother Richard, who alone stood aloof from faction or was capable of grappling with the rivalries, the disorders, and the dangers which formed the King's bequest to his country. Hence it was that to his guardianship he committed the young Prince Edward, then in his thirteenth year, and by will declared him to be Protector of the kingdom.

The career thus opened up to Richard was one of difficulty and of distinction. It is impossible to doubt that it was one of his own contrivance. The overthrow of the Woodvilles, and the attachment of the old nobility to his person and his Protectorate, were the objects primarily sought. The great influence of the Duke of Buckingham, himself a Prince of the House of Lancaster, was a guarantee for the union of all the old nobility, whether Yorkist or

---

* De Comines.

Lancastrian, in supporting Richard in his opposition to
the Queen, at whose instigation Edward had curtailed their
dangerous power by the creation of a new aristocracy. The
jealousy of the old feudal lords was justified by a real danger
both to their caste and to the State. The Queen's relatives
were simple esquires and gentlewomen, and the rapacity with
which they sought to monopolise high offices in the State, and
to contract absurd matrimonial alliances with the old nobility,
were legitimate grounds of derision and alarm. Thus, as we
have seen, the Queen's youngest brother John, at the age of
nineteen, married the Dowager Duchess of Norfolk, then in her
eightieth year. The hand of her elder brother, Anthony, Earl
Rivers, was successively offered to two princesses, whilst her
five sisters had all married members of the old aristocracy.
Thus preferred above the oldest and proudest barons of the
land Earl Rivers had become, in spite of much real excellence
of character, an object of distrust. Even men like Hastings
and Stanley found their loyalty strained by the favours heaped
upon obnoxious favourites, and, as Richard had had the sagacity
to foresee, were ready to support him in any plans for their
humiliation that were consistent with their own fealty to the
son and heir of Edward IV.

The fact that the Duke of Gloucester was in the north did
not protect him from the charge of being the instrument of his
brother's death. "The passionate enemies of Richard," says
Habington, "permit not nature at that time to have been
obnoxious to decay, but make the death of every prince an act
of violence or practice, and . . . . condemn him for those
crimes from which he was however actually innocent."* De

* Habington, p. 478.

Comines is the only contemporary writer who hints at Edward's death being one of violence. He died, he says, of a catarrh, " for that is their phrase in France when a man is made away by poison." This idle story sufficed for the Tudor Chroniclers, who could think of no other possible regicide than Richard.

Archbishop Bourchier * excused himself on the plea of old age from officiating at the funeral of the King, which was conducted on a scale of surpassing magnificence. The prominent part in public affairs which he was compelled to take during the three remaining years of his life, renders it necessary briefly to review his great career, in order that we may understand his position of commanding influence.

Thomas Bourchier was the great-grandson of Edward III. The sixth and youngest son of that monarch married Eleanor, eldest daughter of Humphrey Bohun, Earl of Hereford. His eldest daughter, the Lady Ann Plantagenet, married successively two brothers, Earls of Stafford, and William Bourchier. By her last husband, Ann had three sons, of whom Thomas was the youngest, and was born about the year 1404. At an early age he went to Oxford, where his rank brought him into notice, and where, by his own experience, he learnt something of the abuses which closed the universities to all but the wealthy or high-born; abuses which he sought, in later life, to remedy. He was but twenty-three years old when he was appointed to the deanery

---

* This name at various times has been spelt at least twelve different ways. It occurs, as in the text, in the Rolls of Parliament for 1461, and I have accepted this form, in preference to the " Bouchier " of Dean Hook, because I find the " r " preserved in the middle of the word in eleven out of the twelve variations which I have discovered. That the Archbishop himself spelt it " Bourghchier " does not admit of a doubt.

of St. Martin-le-Grand. In 1433 he was nominated to the bishopric of Worcester, and the appointment was sustained in spite of the opposition of the Pope, who had a candidate of his own for the vacant see. Repudiating the Papal nominee, Henry VI. addressed a *congé d'élire* to the convent at Worcester. The permission to make a *free election* was, of course, accompanied with positive instructions as to the object of their choice. "There was, however, in these days," says Dean Hook, "a little more delicacy observed in the nomination; and the King condescended to assign some reasons why the clerk to be elected was chosen." The reasons given were, notwithstanding that the near kinship of the bishop-elect was one of them, honourable both to the King and to Bourchier; his personal qualifications for the sacred office, the will of Parliament, and the advantage to the Church, were enlarged upon.

The ambition of the young prelate, who was but thirty years of age, outran the willingness of the King to sanction it. Within a year he was intriguing to secure his translation to the more opulent see of Ely. Anticipating the royal objection, he obtained the sanction of Eugenius to his desired translation. The Papal Bulls were actually issued; but both Pope and bishop, as well as the Chapter of Ely, who had ventured to ignore the royal letter missive in favour of the Bishop of St. David's, had to submit to the will of the King. In 1443 the see of Ely was again vacant, and with consent of King, Pope, and Chapter, Bourchier realised his ambition. The young prelate was so absorbed in politics that he thought of his sacred office only as a source of income.*

---

* Hook's "Archbishops," vol. v., p. 231.

It is said that during an incumbency at Ely of ten and a half years he only once officiated in his cathedral, and that was on the day of his installation.

Bourchier enjoyed the political advantage of being united by ties of blood to the houses both of York and Lancaster. With the former he had acquired popularity by his outspoken indignation at the surrender of English interests in France, which was attributed to Henry VI.'s marriage with Margaret of Anjou. The King respected " the cunning and virtues that rest in his person," and he had been far too prudent to give any offence to the Queen's party.

In the spring of 1454 three notable events happened. After eight years of childlessness, Henry VI. had become the father of a son—the unfortunate Prince Edward, who fell at Tewkesbury. The continued mental alienation of the King induced the Lords to nominate Richard, Duke of York, Protector of the realm; and, on the 24th March, Cardinal Kemp, Archbishop of Canterbury, died. The House of Commons petitioned for the appointment of Bourchier to the see of Canterbury, and the Duke of York more than willingly acquiesced in their prayer. His installation took place in February, 1455. He had, at the age of fifty, attained the highest position which the Church or Government of England could confer. But his vaulting ambition was yet unsatisfied. Thus far he had shown no sense of the responsibilities of his sacred office, the duties of which he had culpably neglected. And in this he did but reflect the lack of spiritual enthusiasm which characterised his age. The inertness of the Church was a reaction from the fierce religious zeal and relentless persecution which had united the prelates and the monastic orders in an effort to stamp out Lollardism.

Sixty years had passed since Wyclif had said, in reference to this combination of mortal foes for the suppression of religious freedom, "Pontius Pilate and Herod are made friends to-day!" Wealthy and powerful, without faith, condemned to celibacy, without sympathy with the common duties and common pleasures of ordinary life, in which they could have no participation, the clergy had become sunk in corruption, the religious houses the scenes of abominations as revolting as they were notorious. It is only justice to Bourchier to say that, however much he may have shared the practical infidelity of the clergy, there is no evidence that he ever participated in their immoralities. It should also be recorded to his honour that one of the first acts of his primacy was the issue of a pastoral letter denouncing the iniquities and irregularities prevalent amongst the clergy.

Neither as an ecclesiastic, nor as a statesman, was Bourchier characterised by brilliance or originality. His reputation in either department rests rather upon the moderation which distinguished him when his contemporaries in Church or State were swayed by passion, fear, or hatred. Yet as an ecclesiastic he could be severe even to cruelty, bold, arbitrary, and unjust, as in the notorious instance of Pecock. Not content with the abject submission of the haughty prelate, with the burning of his precious books—eleven quarto and three folio volumes of manuscript—in defiance of the Pope, and with doubtful legality, he proceeded to degrade and imprison the ecclesiastic who had dared to enter the lists against him.

But it is from the part which, in the disordered state of

the country, Bourchier was called to take in public affairs,
that he is chiefly conspicuous. Enjoying the confidence of the
leaders of the rival factions, and entitled to that confidence as
the only living statesman who preferred the welfare of his
country to the exigencies of party, his appointment as Lord
Chancellor was regarded as a pledge of peace. Even the
Queen was civil to the young prelate who, perhaps, she
expected to win by her charms from his well-known
sympathies with the Yorkist party. The Archbishop received
the Great Seal on the 7th of March, 1455, * but he was
not destined to retain his high office for more than a few
eventful months.

We have already seen that the Duke of Somerset fell in
the affray at St. Albans in May, 1455. Before the Parliament, which assembled six weeks later, Bourchier courageously
defended the Duke of York from the imputation of disloyalty,
and threw the blame of the skirmish upon Somerset and his
party. The Archbishop thus prevailed upon Parliament to
pass a general amnesty, whilst Margaret had hoped to have
seen York and Warwick attainted. Her plans for revenge
were marred by the King's relapse into a state of imbecility.
But, though her exasperation knew no bounds when the
House of Lords again summoned the Duke of York to
assume the Protectorate, her triumph was at hand. Within
three months the King recovered; York retired from his
high office, and Henry Beaufort, son of the late Duke of
Somerset, with the Duke of Buckingham, were called to the
royal council. The Queen now determined to sacrifice the

---

* " He behaved himself so well in his great station that King Henry made
him his chancellor."—DANIEL's *Life of Henry VI.*, p. 410.

Archbishop. His last official act was to summon a Parliament to meet at Coventry in October. And, that her triumph might not be again abortive, Margaret further plotted the assassination of York and Warwick on their arrival at Coventry. Warned of their danger, the nobles held aloof, and all that Margaret gained by her machinations was the removal of Archbishop Bourchier, who resigned the Great Seal to Waynfleet, Bishop of Winchester.*

But if the Queen, upon whom the functions of royalty really devolved, was relieved of the presence of the two men most obnoxious to her—the Duke of York. and the Lord Chancellor—she had also prepared the way for the latter, with whom the new Chancellor cordially co-operated, to bring about that reconciliation of the two parties which has been already related. This truce was arranged in March, 1458. In the disturbances and conflicts which soon again placed the parties to the act of reconciliation in hostile array, Bourchier alone held to its terms. Neither the Acts of Attainder obtained against the whole family of the Duke of York, nor the strenuous efforts of the Yorkists to prevail upon him to give his sanction to extreme measures, moved him from that attitude of moderation which he had deliberately chosen.

The crimes and follies of the Queen at length completed the alienation of the Archbishop, who recognised the impossibility of their being ever condoned by the House of York. When, therefore, in June, 1460, the Earl of Warwick landed at Sandwich, and marched with "near 40,000 fighting men"

---

* Chandler's " Life of William Waynflete," p. 83.

to London, the Archbishop, with a great retinue and amid the plaudits of the people, received his army, "congratulated their arrival," and pronounced upon it the blessing of the Church.* The triumph of the Yorkists was assured. But this was not the intention of Bourchier. He summoned a convocation of the clergy at St. Paul's, where the Earls of Salisbury and Warwick knelt before him and took the oath of allegiance to King Henry VI. In them the Primate recognised not rebels in arms against their King, but men who, excluded from their rights by the influence of "the foreign woman," came to state their grievances, and assert the rights of the people. The very fact that the Duke of York was still in Ireland proves how little, at this time, a change of dynasty was contemplated.

The King was at Northampton, and was personally disposed to treat with the insurgents as he had done at St. Albans. Not so the Queen, who, denouncing the Yorkists as traitors and rebels, disdained the idea of a reconciliation, perhaps all the more that the Archbishop was marching with the troops. We have already seen the issue of this infatuation. All that concerns us here is the part played by the Primate. That his purpose was to prevent the effusion of blood, and to effect the reconciliation of revolted subjects with their King, is certain. The means by which he proposed to accomplish this end are less clear; but it was probably by placing the King in their hands. "He ought," writes Dean Hook, "to have disconnected himself from all party combinations; and, as Primate of All England, attended by as many of his suffragans as a hasty summons could reach, have ap-

* Daniel's " Henry VI.," in Kennett, vol. i., p. 421.

proached the royalists in a solemn religious procession." *
But it must be remembered that the Primate had detached
himself from the rival factions during the four years which
had elapsed since he resigned the Great Seal; that his final
adhesion to the one had been the result of the insane excesses
of the other; and that, in consequence of that adhesion, it
was at least doubtful whether the sanctity of his person would
be respected by the Queen's party. He sent four missions of
peace to the royalist camp, and, when the battle which he
laboured to prevent was over, he took charge of the King's
person, placed him at the head of the army, and saw him
safely lodged in the palace of the Bishop of London until the
royal palace was ready for his reception.†

The Archbishop appears prominently on the scene only
once more before the coronation of Edward IV., and again his
moderation is apparent. The Duke of York arrived from
Ireland in October, shortly after the opening of Parliament.
The news of the victory at Northampton induced him to assert
that hereditary claim to the throne which was in conflict with
the right of election inherent in the two Houses. Entering the
Painted Chamber when the House was sitting, he boldly
ascended the steps of the throne, anticipating an invitation to
take possession of it. The Lords were silent in dumb amaze-
ment; and when he put his hand on the throne, turning an
inquiring gaze towards them, murmurs of disapproval were
uttered. The Duke stood irresolute. At that moment the
Archbishop, whose suspicions had been aroused, entered the
Chamber. "He made a reverence to the Duke, and, in a tone

---

* "Lives of the Archbishops," vol. v., p. 332.
† Hook, vol. v., p. 335.

which expressed surprise mingled with indignation that he had
not first performed his *devoirs* to his sovereign, he said : " Will
not my Lord of York go and pay his respects to the King ? "*
He complied with reluctance.† The Archbishop had suppressed
a revolution.

On the 4th March, 1461, Edward IV. was proclaimed King
at Westminster. On the 29th of the following June he was
crowned by Archbishop Bourchier. The Primate has been
charged with inconsistency in refusing his consent to the
deposition of Henry VI., in favour of the late Duke of York,
whilst he countenanced it in favour of his son. But consistency in principle is one thing, in action quite another ; and
the latter may often become feasible only by the sacrifice of
the former, owing to the perversity of men or the unfolding of
events which the individual is powerless to regulate. Thus
was it with the Archbishop. His position was one of great
difficulty, which may perhaps explain the long delay of the
coronation. For how could he, the head of the English
Church, give the sanction of that Church to the crowning
of a new King whilst the anointed of the Lord still
lived ? Dean Hook suggests that he would " bring feudal
notions to bear upon the subject." And they would go
far to solve the difficulty which confronted him. If the King
could not, and the Queen would not, protect the interests of
the State, they who made such interests their first concern
were absolved from their allegiance. The question then for

---

* Hook, vol. v., p. 336.

† " The Duke, at this question, was observed to change his colour, and then
answered him in a passion that he knew none in this kingdom to whom he
owed that duty or honour ; but on the contrary all men owed it to him, and
therefore King Henry ought to come to him."—DANIEL, in Kennett, vol. i., 423.

the Archbishop would be whether the terms of compact between sovereign and people had been, were, or were capable of being observed. His residence with the King, and the knowledge recently acquired of the vindictiveness and implacability of the Queen, left him no doubt as to the reply. Moreover, Edward *was* King *de facto,* an arrangement in regard to which the Primate had not been consulted; and Parliament had exercised its undoubted right of deposition. By withholding the sanction of the Church, Bourchier would but inflame the passions of both parties, and inspire with new hopes the supporters of Margaret, who were believed to be for ever extinguished. Such procedure would have been treason against the State to which, in its sore distraction, his moderation brought a respite of nine years, only once interrupted by Margaret's final effort at Hexham.

In no event of his life was the moderation of the Archbishop, his unselfishness, and consideration for the King, more conspicuous than in his allowing an interval of nine years to elapse between the date of his nomination as Cardinal Priest and his reception of the red hat. The new Pope, Paul II., in pursuance of the policy of his predecessors, desired to accustom the English people to the presence of a resident Cardinal. In 1464 he nominated Bourchier a Cardinal Presbyter. That was the year of Edward IV.'s marriage with Elizabeth Woodville. The King was surrounded with difficulties and dangers, and the Archbishop was far too considerate to add to his perplexities in order to secure his own aggrandisement. Had he accepted the Pope's nomination without the royal consent he would have brought upon himself the penalties of a *præmunire.* The personal ambition, and the readiness in its pursuit to·

jeopardise the friendly relations between King and Pope, which we have witnessed in the youthful Bishop of Worcester, have disappeared in the Archbishop of Canterbury, full of years and burdened with responsibilities. In the following year the honour was formally solicited from Rome by Edward IV. But then the Pontiff who had proposed to confer it was dead, and it was not until September, 1462, that Sixtus IV. signified his consent. In May of the following year the red hat was placed on the Cardinal's head with all due solemnity by Waynfleet, Bishop of Winchester.

The Archbishop had ceased to take an active part in public affairs after the battle of Northampton in 1460. In 1463 he availed himself of the assistance of a suffragan, and, feeling the infirmities of age growing upon him, he sought such rest as was consistent with the discharge of his archi-episcopal duties, in retirement at Knowle. The revival of learning, which was now exciting the universal mind of Europe, had awakened sympathetic echoes amongst the clergy and some few of the laity in England. If Bourchier had discouraged literary enterprise and independence in burning the portly tomes of Pecock, he had therein sacrificed his genuine love of literature to episcopal intolerance and priestly jealousy of free thought. Learned men he encouraged, and fortunately he possessed, in an eminent degree, the episcopal virtue of hospitality.* At Knowle he had erected a stately castellated mansion, and learning, or a sympathy with learning, was a pass to its hospitality. Dean Hook indeed suggests that the politics of Fabyan may have prevented him

---

* Dean Hook, vol. v., p. 355.

from being intimate with the Archbishop. If so, we are sure
the fault would be that of the prejudiced, but intelligent and
conscientious alderman. The contemporary chroniclers to
whom we are so much indebted—Fabyan, the busy merchant
and alderman, of London; Dr. Warkworth, Master of St.
Peter's College, Cambridge; perhaps also betimes the Prior of
Croyland were here hospitably entertained, and would for the
first time see on the Archbishop's board "a new kind of fruit,
called *currants*, lately introduced from Zante." Here, too,
the Queen's accomplished brother, Anthony, Earl Rivers;
Tiptoft, Earl of Worcester; Botonor, better known as
William of Wyrcester; and Waynfleet, Bishop of Winchester,
would be honoured guests; whilst the numerous musicians,
astronomers, and clergy to whom the Archbishop extended
his patronage and protection would not be passed over.

But the age was not one in which the prolonged enjoyment
of this Arcadian life was possible. The disastrous events—
which are elsewhere narrated—of the year 1470, again called
the Archbishop to the front—again as a peacemaker. The
unwise marriage of Edward IV. had alienated many of the
old nobility. Warwick had overthrown the monarchy. Returning from exile, Edward, as we have seen, had found
London clamouring for the restoration of Henry VI. The
Primate repaired to Lambeth, and by his prudence and
moderation prevailed upon the City authorities, and through
them upon the populace, to welcome Edward as their King.
Clad in his pontificals, and surrounded by the Dean and
Chapter, and clergy of all ranks, the Cardinal-Archbishop,
who was informed of Edward's plans, awaited his arrival in
St. Paul's. Edward IV., who had expected to find the gates

of London closed against him, was received with enthusiasm.
His march through the City was a triumphal procession. The
dense throng around St. Paul's rent the air with their acclamations, and then relapsed into awe-stricken silence as
they saw their sovereign, on bended knee, receiving the
Archbishop's benediction. A second time Archbishop Bourchier had suppressed a revolution.

Once more, and for the last time in the reign of Edward IV.,
the Archbishop—now Cardinal—at the age of seventy, is
summoned to take part in political affairs. And again he is
the ambassador of peace. After the abortive invasion of
France in 1475, Louis XI. had employed high dignitaries of
the Gallican Church to negotiate the treaty of Picquigny.
For this reason the Cardinal Archbishop was nominated as
one of four arbitrators to whom all differences between the
two Kings were to be submitted.* But he had no responsibility for the ignominious terms of that treaty, which we have
elsewhere discussed. Nor does he appear to have bartered
his conscience, as did Morton and all Edward's generals, with
the single exception of Richard, Duke of Gloucester, by
the acceptance of French gold. On the other hand he
shared with them the encomiums which De Comines passed
upon the English ambassadors for their straightforwardness.
"The English," he says, "do not manage their treaties and
capitulations with so much cunning as the French, let people
say what they will, but proceed with greater freedom in their

---

* Lingard, vol. iv., p. 205. Dean Hook is clearly in error when he says
that Cardinal Bourchier was at the head of the embassy at Picquigny. He
is apparently misled by a solecism of De Comines, who, in naming "the Archbishop," obviously refers to Morton.

affairs; yet a man must be cautious, and have a care not to affront them, for it is dangerous meddling with them." *

In 1480 the infirmities of age compelled Cardinal Bourchier to transfer to a suffragan the arduous duties of the primacy. He was seventy-six years of age when he again retired to the beloved seclusion of Knowle.   He desired to have done with State affairs, and to spend the late evening of his eventful life amid his books and roses, content with such fitful echoes from the outside world as came to him in the occasional visits of his literary friends.   But the world which he had relinquished still had need of him, and his hopes of a well-earned freedom from its cares were not destined to be realised until he had crowned two more English Kings, and himself stood on the brink of the grave.   At least he might claim that future service demanded of him should be on behalf of the living, and he declined to leave his retreat to officiate at the splendid obsequies of Edward IV.

---

* De Comines, Book iv., chap. ix.

CHAPTER VI.

AT the time of his father's death the Prince of Wales was at Ludlow, under the charge of his maternal uncle, Earl Rivers. The Queen, who "had a mighty sway over the King's affections," had so arranged matters that "all her own kindred and relations were placed in the greatest offices about him;" * and the absence of the Duke of Gloucester favoured her purposes. Lord Hastings, who was in London discharging his functions as Lord Chamberlain, sent trusty messengers to certify Richard of his brother's death, "and from himself to signify that the King at his death had committed to him only, wife, children, goods, and all that ever he had, and therefore to exhort him that he would with all convenient speed repair unto Prince Edward into Wales, and come with him to London to undertake the government." †

Immediately after the funeral of Edward IV., which was conducted with great pomp at Windsor, the Prince of Wales was proclaimed King by the title of Edward V.

It has already been observed that Richard was not behind his brother of Clarence in his dislike of the Queen, and his disapproval of the advancement of her numerous relations.

---

* Habington, p. 481.   † Polydore Vergil, Book xxv., p. 173.

But, whilst Clarence was rash and intemperate in the expression of his opinions, and so rushed upon his own destruction, Richard—whose dislike to the Queen was political rather
than personal—affable and courteous,* early learnt the wisdom
of caution in communicating his thoughts.   By his prudence,
and the hold he acquired upon Edward's confidence and
affection, he so far checked the indiscriminate preferment
of the Woodvilles, that he personally " had no competitor
in greatness both of judgment and power." †   How far that
influence availed to check Edward IV.'s great indiscretions
can only be matter of conjecture;   that it was cautiously
so employed we have seen in his protest against the King's
arrangements for the education of the royal Princes.   Now
his reserve was at an end.   He was the natural, as he believed
he was also the legal, guardian of the heir to the throne.
That acquiescence in the will of his royal brother which
had been the part of prudence, would, if extended to the
Queen and her family, have been treason to the State.
The crisis demanded that promptness and energy in which
Richard was never deficient.   The chastisement of Louis XI.
could be deferred, but the question who should acquire the
control of the young King and the direction of public affairs
was one of transcendently greater importance—one, moreover,
which the least delay or vacillation would place beyond his
power to decide.

But Richard's decision was already formed.   He " wrote
the most soothing letters in order to console the Queen, with

* " At Court and in his general deportment of an affable respect and
tractable clearness."—Buck.
† Habington, p. 202.

promises that he would shortly arrive, and assurances of all duty, fealty, and due obedience to his King and lord, Edward the Fifth, the eldest son of the deceased King, his brother, and of the Queen." * At York, where he arrived with a retinue of bowmen, all attired in deep mourning, he performed a solemn funeral service for his brother, "the same being accompanied with plenteous tears," and he constrained the nobles in his retinue to follow his example, and take the oath of fealty to Edward's son.†

Meanwhile, the Queen, anxious above all things to secure the interests of her kindred and to hasten the coronation of her son, was urging her brother to bring the young King to London under an imposing escort. How the Duke of Buckingham, who was in Wales, came to hear of the Queen's order does not appear, but, according to More, he found means to inform the Duke of Gloucester, and to join him and the Lord Hastings in protesting against an unnecessary display of force.‡ Probably no one—not even the Duke of. Buckingham—at this time thought of preventing the coronation of Edward V. But the necessity for fixing a reasonable limit to his escort was obvious, otherwise Rivers who held

* "Croyland Chronicle," p. 486.

† Polydore Vergil, Book xxv. Mr. Nichols ("Grants of Edward V.") questions the fact of Richard's performing this funeral service for his brother at York, on the ground that the "York Records" afford no trace of it. But such negative evidence is of small importance beside the positive statement of the well-informed continuator of the "Croyland Chronicle." Moreover, had the Duke of Gloucester been at Middleham Castle, as Mr. Nichols supposes, the delay in his reaching Northampton would be altogether inexplicable.

‡ "All this might happen, undoubtedly; and yet who will believe that such mysterious and rapid negotiations came to the knowledge of Sir Thomas More twenty-five years afterwards, when he knew nothing of very material and public facts that happened at the same period?"—HORACE WALPOLE. See also "Croyland Chronicle," p. 485.

supreme command in South Wales, might have taken London by storm. He had acquired a commanding influence over the mind and affections of his nephew, and it was to ensure his substitution for the Duke of Gloucester as the future head of the Government that "every one as he was neerest of kinne unto the queene, so was he planted nere about the Prince." *

The Privy Council, from which the Dukes of Gloucester and Buckingham were absent, and in which Earl Rivers and the Marquis of Dorset possessed the first seats, met hurriedly on the 10th of April, and fixed the 4th of May as the date for the young King's coronation. But when Earl Rivers broached the question of the retinue by which he should be accompanied to London, he discovered that there were those at the Council-board who were resolved to appeal to force rather than acquiesce in the Queen's project. Within forty-eight hours of the efforts made by the dying King to silence the rivalries and dissensions which divided his court they were again in full activity! Hastings declared that unless the King advanced to the metropolis with such a retinue as could cause no alarm, he would retire to his government at Calais and there abide the issue.† The objection of Hastings was reasonable, since his head would not have been safe for an hour with Earl Rivers at the head of an imposing force in London. All desired that the Prince should have a suitable escort, and the dispute was finally settled by a compromise limiting the retinue to 2,000 men, which proved large enough so to encumber the royal progress as to defeat the Queen's purpose.

---

* Grafton, p. 761. It need hardly be said that Grafton, who closely follows More, is of little or no value as an independent authority.

† Sharon Turner, vol. iii., p. 423.

The theory was that after his coronation Edward V.
would choose his own advisers, or in other words that the
Queen would choose for him. It was certain that the Duke of
Gloucester would not acquiesce in this arrangement if he
reached London before the King. The Queen's party were
but plotting their own ruin. Richard was not only Lord
Protector by the provisions of the late King's will; but as
the only adult Prince of the House of Plantagenet, the
Regency must, according to all precedent, devolve upon him.
And, in addition, Buckingham, Hastings, Stanley, and the old
nobility generally, who saw in him the protector of their
order, gave their voices in his favour. In that character
Cardinal Bourchier also, shrinking though he did from contact
with the world's affairs, gave him his cordial support. But at
present Edward V. was in the hands of Earl Rivers. The
Marquis of Dorset, who was in command of the Tower, was
busy with the Queen in preparing for his reception. The
Duke of Gloucester was at York. Could the coronation be
accomplished before his arrival? It was a race with time.
In these circumstances the dilatoriness of Richard's movements must be regarded as evidence of his determination to
pursue a strictly constitutional course, and of the absence of
that reckless ambition which has been alleged against him.
His conduct was as honourable and loyal, as it was frank and
decided. Had his purpose at this time been to seize supreme
power, instead of solemnising requiems in every large town in
his route, he would surely have hastened to London and
secured the suffrages of the citizens to whom he was favourably
known; or, with the large disciplined force at his command,
cut off the King's approach to the metropolis. That he did

neither is so far a confirmation of all the evidence which history affords, that up to this time he had no other purpose than to subvert the power of the Woodvilles, and to secure the protectorship during the minority of Edward V. after allowing his peaceful succession to the throne. He was well informed by Hastings, who "shewed great forwardness," * of all that transpired in the Queen's Council, and to this must be assigned his determination, at all hazards, to accept the responsibility imposed upon him by his brother's will. In order to this it was essential that he should obtain possession of the young King.

The numerous retinue by which Edward V. was accompanied impeded his movements. Leaving Ludlow on the 24th of April, five days passed before Northampton was reached. A few hours later Richard arrived at the same town, not at the head of a powerful army such as the Lieutenant-General of the land forces and the Commander-in-Chief of the army raised for the French war might have controlled, but with a modest following of 600 knights. The King meanwhile had been hurried on to Stony Stratford, whence Earl Rivers, his maternal uncle, and Lord Richard Gray, his half-brother, returned to salute the Duke of Gloucester in the King's name; to "do him reverence," and "to submit the conduct of everything to his will and discretion." † They were received "with cheerful and joyous countenance;" but the situation must have been embarrassing. Richard was disappointed at not meeting his nephew; Rivers and Gray must have been conscious of dissimulation in consulting the

---

* More.   † "Croyland Chronicle," p. 486.

Duke of Gloucester upon matters in regard to which a decision adverse to his interests had been already taken. But the three noblemen, with the Duke of Buckingham, who reached Northampton the same day, passed some convivial hours together. "They feasted him (Rivers) that night with all demonstrations of joy and signs of friendship till they parted with him to his lodging." * The Duke had brought with him a retinue of 300 knights and esquires. According to Hall (whose uncorroborated statements should always be received with caution) he had already, by means of a trusted messenger to Richard, insinuated ideas which might well have proved perilous to the virtue of a man less nurtured in ambition than the Duke of Gloucester.

Rivers and Gray, believing their designs to be unsuspected, retired for the night—"because it was late they went to their several abodes." † The two Dukes, with some chosen friends, passed the hours of that night in close and earnest consultation. More professes to give a report of the speech addressed by the Duke of Gloucester "to the lords and gentlemen assembled." In substance it ran thus : It was not reasonable nor tolerable to leave the young King their master in the hands and custody of his mother's kindred, who, to engross an honour to themselves, would exclude the best of the nobility from their attendance on him, though all of them were as ready and willing to perform all the services of a good subject to him as themselves. All the ancient nobility were removed from the King's presence, which was neither honourable to his Majesty nor to them, and must in

---

* "Works of Sir Thomas More," p. 40.   † "Croyland Chronicle."

the issue be both dangerous to the nation in general, and unsafe for the King. If the friendships of some persons had not prevailed more with the King, sometimes, than the suits of his kindred, they had before this brought some of us to ruin, *as they did some of as great degree* as any of us. Was it likely that their old resentments were so completely buried that they would not remember to revenge them upon the least disquiet ? These things considered, it was their greatest wisdom to take the young King out of their enemies' hands.*

If anything were needed to demonstrate the prudence of this counsel, it was supplied by the Duke of Buckingham, who had brought intelligence of an act of violence on the part of the Woodvilles which showed their contempt for the trammels of law. The Marquis of Dorset had seized the royal treasure, and given illegal orders for the equipment of a naval force.† It was not, as More suggests, for necessary and national purposes, but to provide at sea a force under his own command "which the compact of the Queen had, through the vigilance of Hastings and Buckingham, prevented on land."‡ The ambitious designs of the Woodvilles were no longer disguised. The object contemplated in sending the young King forward to Stony Stratford when Richard's arrival at Northampton was hourly expected was now explained, and the decision to secure his person was unanimously approved.§

---

* More's "Edward V.," in Kennett, vol. i., p. 483.
† Buck, in Kennett, vol. i., p. 529.
‡ Sharon Turner, vol. iii., pp. 423, 424.
§ It was no private plotting between Gloucester, Buckingham, and Hastings; for More himself tells us that "the two Dukes, *with a few of their most privy friends*, set them down in council, wherein they spent a great part of the night."—MORE'S *Works*, p. 41. Mr. Sharon Turner, therefore, has the

I am unable to agree with Mr. Gairdner that it was at this meeting that the Duke of Gloucester resolved to supplant his nephew, as the only effectual means of securing his own safety, or of curbing the power and ambition of the Woodvilles. They were discredited; he had recently acquired new distinction both as a warrior and an administrator. They were detested by the old nobility; he was their hope and pride. They had no justification to offer to a suspicious Parliament for securing the custody of the Prince; he had not only been named Protector in the will of Edward IV.,* but it was his office by natural right sanctioned by custom. However conscious of his power and determined to exercise it, we have absolutely no ground for supposing that Richard aimed higher than the Protectorate. He was Protector *de jure* as well as *de facto*, and was not even accountable to Parliament for the legal exercise of the functions of that office. The first and most pressing of these was the duty of controlling the movements of the boy-King.

If Richard's resolutions were quickly formed, they were no less firmly carried into execution. On the morning following the momentous conference at Northampton, the four Lords rode in company and apparent good-fellowship towards Stony Stratford. As they approached the town, the Duke of Gloucester suddenly charged Rivers and Gray with having·

---

sanction of More's authority to his contention that this conference at North-ampton "was a serious discussion of their party on the measures proper to be taken . . . ; whether the Queen's family should exclude or be excluded from the Regency or Government, and whether this should be determined by an appeal to open war, or by their use of the opportunities that lay before them."—SHARON TURNER, vol. iii., p. 427.

* "His brother Richard, whom he left protector and guardian over the young King."—DRAKE'S *Eboracum*, vol. i., p. 124.

alienated from him his nephew's confidence. They denied the charge, and, at a signal from Gloucester or Buckingham, were arrested by the latter Duke's retainers, and immediately conducted into the rear.* They were sent back to Northampton and confined in an inn, of the keys of which the two Dukes obtained possession, allowing the captives no intercourse with their dependants. The road from Stony Stratford was lined with guards charged to suffer no person to enter that town until the Dukes returned. When Rivers learned what was done, "his thoughts were in a great hurry, and what the reasons should be he could not conjecture." His remonstrances were unheeded, and the Dukes rode off to Stony Stratford, where the King and his retinue were impatiently awaiting the arrival of Rivers and Gray. There they found the young King "ready to leap on horseback and depart forward."

Richard and his attendants saluted him upon their knees. Every face expressed apprehension and disgust, which was not mitigated when Buckingham called aloud to the gentlemen and yeomen to march forward.† Gloucester ordered the King's attendants to withdraw from the town, and not to approach any place to which Edward might chance to come, on penalty of death.‡ This was on the 30th of April. It required all the courage and determination of the two Dukes to obtain access to the King's presence, and their violent seizure of his person has been generally condemned. Amongst his contemporaries, Rous was the last man living to palliate any undue exercise of authority on the part of the Duke

---

* More's "Works," p. 41.   Lingard, vol. iv., p. 223.
† More's "Works," p. 42.   ‡ "Croyland Chronicle," p. 487.

of Gloucester; yet he supplies an ample justification of this act of violence. The attempt of Earl Rivers to hasten the young King to London before his uncle Gloucester should see him, was calculated to excite both suspicion and anger in the mind of the latter. The ostensible reason assigned for the removal from Stony Stratford could not deceive the Duke of Gloucester. The town, it was urged, was "too straight for both companies." Perhaps so; but Northampton was not, and the fact that the King was found ready to leap on his horse on the expected arrival of his uncle Rivers, removes all doubt as to the purpose of the precipitate retreat from either town.

The prescience of the Duke of Gloucester defeated a carefully planned scheme, the successful execution of which was of the highest importance to the Woodville faction. It was, indeed, the pivot upon which their entire policy turned. And now ensued that memorable scene in which the boy-King appears struggling impotently against the resistless power of an iron will; his keen sensibility and unsophisticated mind investing it with unutterable pathos. The stern uncle, doubtless supposing his nephew to be a party to the plot, of which, in all probability, he was really ignorant, asserts his legal rights as Protector of the royal person; arrests Sir Thomas Vaughan and his companions, and charges Earl Rivers, the maternal uncle, with Lord Richard Gray and the Marquis of Dorset, half-brothers of the hapless Prince, with treason, in that they designed to seize the Government, in defiance of the will of Edward IV. Alarmed and perplexed, the young King answered with dignity: "What my brother the Marquis may have done, I cannot say, but in truth I dare well answer for my uncle Rivers, and my brother *here*, that they are innocent of such matters, *having been continually with me."* * Richard replied that they were indeed guilty, but had deceived their Prince. "At this dealing," says Sir Thomas More, "he wept and was nothing content, but it booted not." Sir Thomas Vaughan, Richard Hawte (or Hawes),† and others were ordered to withdraw in custody, and sent into Yorkshire "to be done with God wot." ‡ There they remained, to use the pathetic words of Earl Rivers, "somewhat musing and more mourning," until the middle of June; whilst the two Dukes conducted the disconsolate Edward back to Northampton. These measures were precautionary.§ The prisoners were certainly treated with consideration, and, whatever may have been the wishes of Hastings, there is no evidence that the Duke of Gloucester purposed anything beyond a temporary incarceration. He sent Rivers a dish from his own table at Northampton, praying him to be of good cheer, for all should go well.|| If we do not believe that such was his purpose, we must conclude—what no one has had the hardihood to suggest—that he was already "an atrocious and preternatural villain," that the Prince

---

* More is evidently mistaken here, as Rivers and Gray had been already arrested and sent back to Northampton.

† Hawte was an Esquire, not, as almost invariably described, a Knight. He is mentioned by Fabyan, but not by the continuator of the "Croyland Chronicle" or by Rous.

‡ Earl Rivers was confined at Sheriff Hutton, a castle belonging to the Duke of Gloucester, ten miles north of York; Lord Gray at Middleham; Sir Thomas Vaughan and Hawte at Pontefract.—*Grants of Edward V.*

§ "Whom after he had taken, supposing that they *would not assent to his intent and purpose*, he sent back to be kept in ward."—POLYDORE VERGIL.

|| Sharon Turner, vol. iii., p. 429.

who was looked up to as the head of a brave and chivalrous nobility could deliberately act the part of a vulgar mountebank, and make sport of a noble and chivalrous victim.

More fortunate than his friend, the Marquis of Dorset " by some private notice given him," fled from the Tower, of which he had the command, and took sanctuary at Westminster.* Remembering the fate of the Duke of Somerset after the battle of Tewkesbury, he may well have felt insecure even at that sacred shrine, and he accordingly resolved to flee the country before the Duke of Gloucester could reach London. After experiencing " many wonderfull daungers, both aboute London, Ely, and other places whereof to wryte the names and circumstaunce wolde aske a longe and great leysour," he escaped to Flanders.†

Alarmed at the tidings which reached her the Queen also took sanctuary at Westminster, with her younger son and five daughters, " where, being received into the Abbot's lodgings, she and all her children and all her company were immediately registered for sanctuary persons, and so looked upon themselves as in an inviolable fortress against their enemies' power or malice." ‡ An incident now occurred which shows how little even the Queen suspected the Duke of Gloucester of those ambitious designs which the Lancastrian historians have imputed to him. Rotheram, Archbishop of York and Lord Chancellor, on receiving private intelligence of the arrest of Rivers and Gray, repaired to her with the Great Seal, and delivered into her hands this important badge, " for the use and behoof of her son," with a friendly message

---

* Buck, p. 13.   † Fabyan, p. 669.   ‡ More, in Kennett, p. 484.

with which he was charged from Hastings. "A woe worth him," exclaimed the Queen, "for *it is he that goeth about to destroy me and my blood.*" The consolation which the Archbishop offered her was the reverse of reassuring. "Madam," he said, "be of good comfort, and assure you, if they crown any other King than your son whom they now have, we will on the morrow crown his brother whom you have here with you." * Small comfort this to the mother, that if one son was murdered or attainted the other should be crowned in sanctuary, which was virtually a prison !

More important than in these latter days was the question, what will the Lords do ? It was a time for action, not for argument. The Duke of Gloucester immediately communicated to the Privy Council all that had transpired, and, says More, "the Lord Hastings whose trouth towards the King no man doubted, nor needed to doubt, persuaded the lords to believe that the Duke of Gloucester was sure and fastly faithful to his Prince, and the lord Rivers, and lord Richard, with the other knights, were, for matters attempted by them against the Dukes of Gloucester and Buckingham, put under arrest *for their surety*, not for the King's jeopardy." London was thrown into great excitement by conflicting rumours of these events, and of all that they portended. Rotheram, who had had time to recover from the irritation he had manifested on being aroused from his slumbers in the small hours of the morning, and to reflect upon his folly in delivering up the Great Seal, sent to the Queen and saved his head by recovering it.

At the call of the Queen's party many of the citizens rose

---

* More, in Kennett, p. 485. Walpole's "Historic Doubts," p. 28.

in arms—they scarce knew wherefore. Men were these who excited the scorn of Caxton: "fayrer, ne wiser, ne bet bespoken children in theyre youth ben no wher then ther ben in London; but at their full ryping there is no carnel, no good corn founden, but chaffe for the most parte." Explanations offered by Hastings reassured the prominent citizens, whom he hastily called together, as they had already done the Lords of the Council. He advised them to depart to their dwellings, and not pretend to judge or censure the actions of their superiors till they knew the truth of their designs. With these words he pacified them, and order was restored.* The assurance given by Hastings that the arrested Lords were charged with conspiring against the Dukes, both of whom were of the blood royal, changed the current of the popular clamour. One of the consequences of this agitation in London was the selection of the Tower as the temporary residence of the young King, both for his personal security, for the satisfaction of the citizens, and doubtless, for the purpose of bringing him into the Protector's safe keeping. For Richard, with that singular faculty which he possessed of reading men's thoughts, perceived that those who appeared his fastest friends were unreliable. The overthrow of the Woodvilles was an object common to them and to himself. That accomplished, there was too much reason to apprehend that the bond of union would be relaxed, and that personal rivalries and ambitions would interpose new obstacles to the accomplishment of his settled purpose of securing the sanction of Parliament to his Protectorate.

---

* More, in Kennett, p. 485.

Stanley and Hastings by no means acquiesced in Richard's Protectorate, although the latter had been the first to inform him that it was bequeathed to him by Edward IV. They were willing to aid him in the overthrow of the Queen's party, and Hastings especially desired the execution of her brother and son. But the utmost that they were prepared to concede to the Duke of Gloucester was the office of President of a Council of Regency. They miscalculated both their own strength and Richard's force of character, as well as his sagacity in apprehending and profiting by that very popular feeling which they had assisted to create. Of Hastings it has been truly said that few persons so able acted as frequently from impulse. He had now lent the sanction of his great authority to that initial act of Richard's policy which involved all that followed.

On the day which the Woodvilles had fixed for the coronation, Edward V. arrived in London in the charge of his uncle Gloucester, and was joined by an imposing retinue outside the city. The Protector, it is said, "rode barehead behind him, and in passing along said with a loud voice to the peoples, Behold your Prince and Soveraigne."* It must have been an anxious hour for the Duke of Gloucester. The ominous murmurs with which the citizens had at first received the tidings of his recent measures would be known to him, whilst not a few of them were aware of the incompatibility between his views and those of the equally aspiring Hastings. But it soon became apparent that his seizure of the Woodvilles had increased his popularity, and even More admits that "he was on all hands accounted the best, as he was the first subject

---

* Buck, p. 11.

in the kingdom." At the palace of the Bishop of London Edward V. received the fealty of the Lords spiritual and temporal, and of the Mayor and Aldermen of the City of London,* the aged Primate having quitted his retirement at Knowle for this purpose. What would *they* have to say to the high-handed procedure of his uncle of Gloucester in seizing the royal person? The words in which the history attributed to Sir Thomas More describes the tactics of the Queen's party, do not assist us in answering the question. Divers lords, knights, and gentlemen, we read, either for favour of the Queen, or for fear of themselves, assembled companies and went flocking together in harness. But if, as Horace Walpole observes, "we strip this passage of its historic buskins," its meaning is plain, that the Queen's party took up arms.† The nobles were alarmed; the party of the Queen were in rebellion, and the old nobility rallied round the only man capable of preserving order.

Richard had acted as became the Protector of the realm and the custodian of the youthful monarch. The authentic records of history afford not the slightest warrant for the gratuitous assumption of his calumniators that he had any personal designs upon the throne. The friends of the young King were numerous and powerful. Cardinal Bourchier had pledged his word to Edward IV. that he would "take and accept him for true, very true and righteous King of England," and, had the Queen been amenable to reason, the coronation of Edward V. would have taken place with only such delay as was consistent with decency and the convenience

---

* "Croyland Chronicle," p. 487.
† Horace Walpole's "Historic Doubts," p. 32.

of the nobility.   I quote with especial gratification the
following words of the late Dean Hook.   Whilst entertaining
the traditional view of the character of Richard, the fairness,
candour, and moderation which so eminently characterise
the splendid monument to the Dean's industry, are here
conspicuous.

"No one can read attentively this portion of history,
comparing the tradition with the authentic documents, without
seeing that the blame of the quarrel between him and the late
King's family, in the first instance, attaches to the Queen and
her relatives.   Richard was, in all probability, prepared to
treat that weak and wayward woman with respect; to place
her at the head of her son's Court; and to be satisfied for
himself with the substance of authority, without the trappings
of royalty.   But he found that she and her party were plotting
against his authority, his liberty, perhaps his life.   Richard
was not the man to submit patiently to this state of things.
If the Queen's party were not annihilated, nothing less than
the annihilation of Richard would satisfy their ambition or
silence their fears. . . . It is not for us, even in the nineteenth century, to examine too closely into the circumstances
of a *coup d'état.*" *

In spite of his aversion to the Queen, Hastings was every
day committing himself to her policy.   Repenting the assistance he had given the Protector, he now determined to oppose,
to the utmost of his power, the prolongation of the Protectorate after the coronation.   He openly allied himself with the
Queen's friends, calling such of them "as he knew to be

---

* "Lives of the Archbishops," vol. v., p. 367.

right careful for the life, dignity, and estate of Prince Edward," to meet him at St. Paul's Church, to confer with him as to their future proceedings.*

As uncle of the King, it was in accordance with the precedents of the last two minorities that Richard should aspire to the Protectorate, not simply for the few days which must elapse before the coronation, but during the King's minority. Yet he may well have reflected that two Dukes of Gloucester, both uncles to the reigning sovereign, had, in the position to which he aspired, suffered death from the caprice or the weakness of the crown.

> Gloucester's dukedom is too ominous,

are the words of remonstrance with which Shakspeare represents Richard as reluctantly receiving the title after the battle of Towton. He knew the pitfalls which beset him, the irreconcilable aims and ambitions alike of friends and foes, and he knew that those who looked up to him to-day as their patron and head, would to-morrow plot his ruin. It cannot be too much insisted upon that the goal at which he ultimately arrived was not at this time the object of his ambition. "He was surrounded and circumscribed in all his movements," observes that eminent historian who devoted fifty-three years of his life to the study of this period, "by active and able men, and he could not in any of his measures effect what he wished against the general will, nor without the co-operation of the most leading men of the country."† That he was countenanced by men of ability,

---

* Polydore Vergil, Book xxv., p. 175.
† Sharon Turner, vol. iii., p. 407.

reputation, and influence, who gave him "great thanks" for his "discreet guiding,"* must be accepted as proof that he was not regarded by his contemporaries as "that vulgar and Satanic anomaly which party prejudice has represented him to be. He was, like most great men who stride forward and command their contemporaries, the creature and the mirror of his age and its circumstances."†

Attempts have been made to discredit the proofs which Richard furnished of the treasonable designs entertained by the Woodville family. But, resting as they do upon authorities which are habitually appealed to by his detractors, as well as upon those of greater worth, their authenticity is sufficiently established: The baggage of the Woodvilles had been seized, and with it arms and ammunition in very large quantities. Sir Thomas More himself admits the fact, and that when proofs of these treasonable purposes were established the people cried out "that it would be a great charity to the nation to hang them."‡ For the attainment of their treasonable purposes the Marquis of Dorset had availed himself of his control of the Tower, secretly to remove a great quantity of the King's treasure. It was thus that the Woodvilles had been enabled to make "good preparations of Armes, of which some were met by the way as they were conveighed close packed in carts."§ As these tidings rapidly spread, all eyes were turned towards the wise and vigilant Duke of Gloucester, who was hailed as a deliverer, the old nobility especially

---

* " The Rous Roll," published by the late Mr. Pickering, p. 63.
† Sharon Turner. vol. iii., p. 411.
‡ More, in Kennett, p. 486.   § Buck's " Richard III.," p. 13.

applauding him, and offering their services with enthusiasm to the vanquisher of the hated Woodvilles. The memories of the Civil War were yet fresh enough to create a shudder at the thought of their recurrence. The danger, so it seemed, had been nipped in the bud by the resolute courage and sagacious policy of the Duke of Gloucester. His former services to the State were recalled to memory, and many felt that they were eclipsed by the overthrow of the Woodville family.

On the 13th of May liberal grants were bestowed on three of the four most prominent supporters of the Protector. The Duke of Buckingham was appointed to the Chamberlainship of North and South Wales, vacant by the accession of the Prince of Wales to the throne;* Lovell received the office of Chief Butler, formerly held by Earl Rivers; and Lord Howard, in addition to several manors, was made Seneschal of the Duchy of Lancaster. Lord Howard has been censured for abandoning the widow and children of his benefactor, Edward IV. His fidelity to Richard, to the last hour of his life, is the only ground for a charge so entirely unsupported by facts. Edward had removed him from his office of Constable of the Tower, that he might confer it upon the Queen's brother. He had done him more grievous wrong in seeking to divert to the royal family the rich estates of the Duke of Norfolk by marrying his infant son, the Duke of York, to Anne Mowbray, sole daughter and heiress of John, Duke of Norfolk. On the death of Anne Mowbray in 1481, Howard and Berkeley

---

* Nichols' "Grants of Edward V.," p. 36.

became co-heirs of the Norfolk estates. "But there would have been no hopes for their rights of inheritance so long as Edward IV. and his son the Duke of York lived. This circumstance clearly supplies the motive of the Lord Howard's adherence to Richard." *

It is significant that no grants were made to Hastings. He saw Buckingham, Howard, and Lovell rewarded, whilst he, who had contributed more than all to the overthrow of the Woodvilles, whom he had more reason than all to fear, was subordinate to all in the Protector's confidence.† Whether his just claims were disregarded, or postponed as a test of his loyalty, it is impossible to say; but the fact that they were unrecognised may not improbably have suggested to him the possibility and the prudence of effecting a reconciliation with the Queen, and of avenging himself by hurling the Protector from power, and perhaps of supplanting him.

There had been delay in proving the late King's will; a circumstance which claims attention here only for a side glimpse which it incidentally gives us of the Protector's character. A meeting of the executors was held at Baynard's Castle on the 12th of May. Amongst those present the name of Alcock, the Bishop of Worcester, is found. This prelate was one of those who, at Stony Stratford, had been forbidden to approach any place in which the young King might reside. Already, then, Richard had given proof of his conciliatory disposition in restoring to his nephew his valued counsellor and friend.

---

* Nichols' " Grants of Edward V.," p. 27.

† Buckingham and Hastings were old rivals, "not bearing each to other so much love as hatred unto the Queen's party."—MORE'S *Works*, p. 40.

EDWARD V.

It was with the cordial approval of the citizens of London that the Council, "without the least contradiction," confirmed Richard in his office of Protector,* "Because," says Sir Thomas More, "not only as the King's uncle and the next Prince of the blood, and a person fit for that trust as of eminent wit and courage; but as one that was most loyal and loving to the King, and likely to prove the most faithful in that station." † But Richard's position was full of peril. It was at least possible that his Protectorate would end with the coronation. He was not, like his father and grandfather, Regent and Protector; but, with power far more circumscribed, he held by an uncertain tenure an office which simply gave him precedence amongst the Lords of the Council.‡ In order to its prolongation it was necessary that his Protectorate should receive the sanction of Parliament, and for this purpose the Houses were summoned for the 25th of June, the coronation being fixed for the 22nd.

Queen Elizabeth was in sanctuary, and one party in the Council complained that "the Protector did not with a sufficient degree of considerateness take measures for the preservation of her dignity and safety."§ The young King, also, bitterly complained that Rivers and Gray were not released. In this case the Protector's difficulties were complicated by a difference between the dissident members of the Council, Hastings reasonably fearing that if these noblemen were set at liberty they would avenge upon him the injuries which

---

* Mr. Gairdner has, I think, shown conclusively that Richard had been recognised as Protector before he came to London ("Life of Richard III.," p. 69). † More, p. 486.

‡ Sharon Turner, vol. iii., p. 436. "Grants of Edward V.," p. xxi.

§ "Croyland Chronicle," p. 488.

P

they had received, and in consequence of which there had long existed extreme ill-will between them and him.*

Meanwhile a royal residence had to be chosen. The Council gravely discussed the question, and were divided in opinion; but there is reason to believe that the Protector and the Duke of Buckingham had already decided that it should be the Tower.

I do not like the Tower, of any place,

are the words which Shakspeare has put into the mouth of the young King; and, with the knowledge which he doubtless had of the yet recent murder of his uncle Clarence within its walls, we may well believe that he yielded a reluctant consent to an irresistible decision. To modern ears the very name of the Tower is ominous; but it was otherwise in the fifteenth century, when it was a royal palace, the state apartments of which continued to be occupied by the sovereign until the days of Elizabeth. Edward IV. had been lodged there before his coronation, and had frequently kept his Court there with great magnificence. The Tower had been selected because the Prince would there be less accessible to the influences from which it was deemed important to separate him. So far from its being intended to make it a place of captivity, the Croyland Chronicler informs us that "a discussion took place in the Council" ("*in Senatu*," by which, as elsewhere, he doubtless means in *the Council*, and not, as has been invariably represented, *in Parliament*), "about removing the King to some place where *fewer restrictions* would be imposed upon him."† It had long been the custom for the

---

* "Croyland Chronicle," p. 485.   † *Ibid.*, p. 457.

sovereigns to take up their residence at the Tower for a short time previous to their coronation, "and thence they generally proceeded in state through the city to be crowned at Westminster."* All authorities are agreed in representing Richard as acting with the tenderness which his nephew's temperament and circumstances demanded. He is even said to have besought him on his knees to banish fear, to confide in his affection, and rely on the necessity of those summary measures which occasioned him such painful forebodings.† The removal to the Tower seems to have taken place about the 19th of May, and the preparations for the coronation were hurried forward.

In all this we see no trace of that indecent haste for the deposition of his nephew, with which Richard has been charged by writers who forget that history sinks into romance when it dogmatises upon the unrecorded motives of its heroes. Provocation so to terminate a strife, which the Woodvilles had precipitated, Richard had in abundance. He contented himself with supplanting the Queen, whose attempt to wield an unconstitutional authority and to rob her brother-in-law of that which was constitutionally his, probably first suggested to him the necessity of uniting a Regency with a Protectorate. He had, indeed, already attained a position of perilous power which the conspiracies of the Queen and her friends, dark, malignant, pertinacious, and reckless, alone rendered inadequate. Had he used that power unscrupulously, everything was possible to him. Invested with regal prerogatives, the idol of the army, in the command of which the Duke of

---

* Bayley's "History of the Tower," vol. ii., p. 263.
† Miss Halsted's "Richard III.," vol. ii., p. 34.

Buckingham and the Earl of Northumberland divided the
authority formerly shared by Earl Rivers and himself, proved
by experience to be as capable of administering a kingdom as
of commanding an army, and having just added to all his
other claims upon the allegiance of the old nobility his humiliation of the hated Woodvilles, had Richard chosen to
depose his nephew and to claim the throne, no formidable
opposition could have been organised. The country was
wearied with "the insolency of the Queen's kindred, who,"
says Sir George Buck, "stirred up competition and turbulence among the nobles, and became so insolent and public in
their pride and outrages towards the people, that they forced
their murmurs at length to bring forth mutiny against them."[*]
The Duke of Gloucester seized this popular ferment, not for
his own aggrandisement, but to secure the peaceful succession
of his nephew, to deliver him from evil counsellors, and to
win confidence to the throne which he has been charged with
desiring to usurp.

Nothing is more certain than that Richard—who well
knew the dissoluteness of Hastings' private life, his personal
animosities, and his ambition to acquire over the young King
the influence he had wielded in the counsels of his father—
had determined to shield his nephew from so baneful an influence. "Was he fit to be a statesman or counsellor," asks
Cornewaleys, "that not only enticed and accompanied his
master in all sensuality, that in his most unworthy actions was
his accomplice?"[†] It is clear that the opinion which the
Protector had formed of this aspiring nobleman was shared

---

[*] Sir George Buck, Book i., p. 12.
[†] "Encomium of Richard III.," p. 4.

by some of the purest and noblest of his contemporaries. It is
not the less entitled to recognition because Hastings was at
the same time the most strenuous opponent of the prolongation of the Protectorate.

Through the month of May, and certainly up to the
13th of June, the young King was under no confinement,
hardly any restraint. Every member of the Council had
free access to him. Mr. Sharon Turner quotes official documents to show that he was now at the Tower, now at Westminster, and again at the Bishop's Palace. "There are," he
says, "six royal Acts dated from Westminster in the months
of May and June. These imply that Edward went from the
Tower to meet his Council at Westminster as occasion
required." * But, as all these documents are entries from
the Patent Roll, and Letters Patent were not signed by
the King, but sealed by the Lord Chancellor, they fail to
prove a fact in itself very probable. Mr. Nichols has pointed
out that "every grant on the Patent Roll is dated at
Westminster, as proceeding from the Court of Chancery,
and not as implying that the King was personally at that
palace." † But there are other proofs that Edward V. was
not rigidly confined to the Tower. Thus the Royal Grants
show that he was at the Bishop's Palace on the 4th of May,
at the Tower on the 19th, whilst on the 13th of June he
was again at the Bishop's Palace to receive his brother, the
Duke of York.

Throughout the first week of June, amid a political calm,
undisturbed by the secret plottings at Westminster, the

* Sharon Turner, vol. iii., p. 444.
† "Grants of Edward V.," p. xxviii.

arrangements for the coronation and for the meeting of
Parliament were actively prosecuted. On the 5th, official
letters in the King's name were written by the Protector
to forty Esquires, summoning them to receive "the noble
order of knighthood at our coronation, which by God's
grace we intend shall be solemnized on the 22nd day of
this present month at our Palace of Westminster, commanding
you to be here at our Tower of London four days afore
our said coronation." On the same day Richard was so
little preoccupied with thoughts of any violent political
crisis that he found time to address a letter to the Corporation of York in reference to an application made by that
body for a reduction of 'the city fee-farm. In terms of
studied courtesy he assured them of his willing service.
On the 6th of June the writ was presented to the Council
of York, and four citizens were elected to serve in the
Parliament summoned for the 25th of June.*

But under this outward calm, seething rivalries, bitter
hatreds, and desperate resolves were forcing on a crisis.
Both parties were prepared for a trial of strength. In
these circumstances, the Protector determined to surround
himself with a powerful muster of friends from the North.
On the 10th of June, Sir Richard Ratcliffe was entrusted with
urgent missives addressed to Lord Lovell and to the Corporation of York. The former is instructed to "come to me
with what ye may make, defensibly arrayed, in all the haste
that is possible." In a longer letter addressed to the Mayor
of York, the Protector writes : " Right trusty and well beloved
we greet you well. And as you love the weal of us and the

---

* Davies' "York Records," p. 144.

weal and surety of your own self, we heartily pray you to come unto us to London in all diligence ye can possible, after the sight hereof, with as many as ye can make defensibly arrayed, there to aid and assist us against the Queen, her bloody adherents and affinity which have intended and daily do intend to murder and utterly destroy us, and our cousin the Duke of Buckingham, and the old royal blood of this realm, and as it is now openly known by their subtle and damnable ways forecasted the same, and also the final destruction and disheryson of you and all other inheritors and men of honour as well in these parts as other countries that belong to us, as our trusty servant this bearer shall more at large shew you, to whom we pray you give credence, and as ever we may do for you in time coming fail not to haste you to us hither."[*]

These wholesale accusations were undoubtedly exaggerated, but they at least warrant the belief that Richard had information of a plot, the object of which was the subversion of his power and probably the release of Rivers and Gray. Sir Richard Ratcliffe was, as Rous informs us, charged with instructions to the Earl of Northumberland to preside at the trial of Earl Rivers. He also conveyed a warrant for the execution of Gray and Vaughan. Why this sudden decision? The meagre records of the period leave the question unanswered, nor is any light thrown upon it by the guesses and insinuations of Tudor historians. But a couple of lines in Fabyan's "Chronicle," corroborated as they are by private letters,[†] show that more was known than has been recorded

---

[*] Davies' "York Records," pp. 149-50.

[†] "Excerpta Historica," p. 16. In a letter of Stallworth's, dated the 9th day of June, the very day before Ratcliffe was sent to York, reference is

of the conspiracy which determined Richard's procedure. "For fear of the Queen's blood and other which he had in jealousy, he sent for a strength of men out of the North." It is not a little suggestive that on the 5th of June, apparently the day on which Richard's purposes and actions underwent a sudden and violent change, the Duchess of York arrived in London. Bearing in mind her influence over her son, her personal ambition, and her hatred of the Queen, this fact may be regarded as one at least of the immediate causes of the sudden bursting of the storm.

It is evident that some great change, affecting Richard's present or prospective attitude towards the State, and the revolution which he had effected " without shedding so much blood as would have flowed from a cut finger," had taken place during the past month. Whilst it is difficult to get a clear and connected view of the events of that fatal month, we know enough to warrant two conclusions: that Richard actually aspired to the Crown, and that, amongst the motives by which he was actuated, not the least weighty was the factiousness of his Council, which interposed difficulties to the prolongation of his Protectorate until his nephew could assume the reins of a Government with a grasp firm as his own.

The authority with which the Privy Council had invested the Duke of Gloucester was ample, for it conferred "power to order and forbid in every matter, just like another King,

made to a meeting of the Council at Westminster, which probably took place on that or the preceding day. "My Lord Protector, my Lord of Buckingham, *with all other Lords* as well temporal as spiritual were at Westminster at the Council Chambers from ten to two o'clock, but there was none that spoke with the Queen."

and according as the necessity of the case should demand." * But it would terminate with the King's coronation. Richard loved power for its own sake. One of the many groundless charges made against him is that even its symbols were made to minister to his "vain-gloriousness," and we are pointed to the fact that he issued his mandates as Protector under the ostentatious title of "Duke of Gloucester, Brother and Uncle of Kings, Protector and Defender of the Realm, Great Chamberlain, Constable, and Lord High Admiral of England." But in so doing, he adhered strictly to precedent; † the titles used by the uncle of Henry VI. during his Protectorate were even more elaborate. Alike as a patriot, aware of the rancorous hatreds, the conflicting ambitions, and the threatening hostilities which only waited the withdrawal of his strong hand from the helm, to burst forth in unrestrained fury; and as the almost absolute ruler "in everything like another king," to whom a sudden descent into the position of a subject, the compeer of a mushroom nobility, was intolerable, Richard realised the danger of allowing the coronation to take place. He had been cradled in ambition, taught from infancy to regard a crown as the only object worthy of a Plantagenet's desire; he was conscious of his ability to rule the distracted State. The petulant young King was in his power; his interests and the interests of the State were one. If he had resisted thus far those promptings of ambition first insinuated into his mind by Buckingham, it was little wonder that they germinated in such a mind, and gained the ascendency at last.

---

* "Croyland Chronicle," p. 488.
† Davies' "York Records," p. 149, *note.*

Nor is it difficult to trace the causes of Richard's fall from that pure integrity, prudence, and unselfishness of aim by which he had hitherto been distinguished. It was an act of prudence, of necessity indeed, to have formed what may be called a coalition Council, including with his own avowed supporters some of the firmest friends of the family of Edward IV. Amongst these were Morton, Bishop of Ely, Lord Hastings, and Lord Stanley, both of whom had been ministers of the late King. But this arrangement, however necessary, entailed inconvenient consequences. It was the boast of Hastings that "nothing whatever had been done but the transferring of the Government of the kingdom from two of the Queen's blood to two more powerful persons of the King's."* The implied protest against the prolongation of the Protectorate, and the assumption of superior power by the Duke of Gloucester, soon found expression in words. Richard was now residing at Crosby Place, where, according to More, he held private meetings of his friends, whilst those who favoured the young King met in Council at the Tower. This at least shows that whatever restraint was imposed upon Edward V. was with the consent of his own friends in the Council. The continuator of the "Croyland Chronicle" so far confirms Sir Thomas More's statement, that he says: "The Protector, with singular adroitness, divided the Council, so that one part met in the morning at Westminster, and the other at the Tower of London, where the King was."† Whether the dis-

---

* "Croyland Chronicle," p. 488.

† "Croyland Chronicle," p. 488. The Council is represented by various writers as meeting at four different places. The explanation I take to be this. The meetings at Baynard's Castle were those of a *sub-committee*, charged with the arrangements for the coronation; those at Crosby House were of a private character; whilst the formal meetings of the Council were

affected members of the Council met at St. Paul's, at West-minster, or at the Tower, Richard was accurately informed of their proceedings through his agent, William Catesby, whom Hastings was at the same time employing as a spy upon the Protector. Richard's Council employed this unprincipled man, who had forgotten all his former obligations to Hastings,* to propound their designs to that lord, knowing that if they gained him they would gain all the rest, "but with some dis-tance, lest his refusal should betray all." Presuming upon the familiarity to which Hastings admitted him, this incomparable scoundrel insinuated that, if it could be lawfully done, it would be better that an experienced person and a brave commander should rule than a child. With his habitual impulsiveness and an implicit faith in the loyalty of Catesby, Hastings denounced the idea, and "engaged himself, his uttermost powers and abilities against it," declaring that "he would rather see the death and destruction of the Protector and the Duke of Buckingham than the young King deprived of the crown." This reply the minion conveyed to Richard, as More observes, "not with the mollifying terms of a friend." The Protector received it with much trouble and regret, "not for the disappointment only, but because he had a great love for him who had always been his friend." By subtlety and hypocrisy, Catesby, who was ready to seek advancement by his patron's downfall, elicited the compromising words from Hastings,† and represented him as so irreconcilable to the

---

held, as circumstances determined, at Westminster or at the Tower. Private meetings of Hastings and the Queen's friends were also held at St. Paul's.

    * "No man was so much beholden to Hastings as was this Catesby."—MORE, p. 68.

    † "And of truth the Lord Chamberlain showed unto Catesby the distrust that others began to have in the matter."—HOLINSHED, p. 379.

Protector's proceedings that he "changed his love into hatred to him, and made him lay hold upon any slight pretences to take away his life, without which he saw that he must meet with a great impediment in the road of his ambition." *

The Protector had, in reality, little to fear from the conspirators; and he knew it. The Cardinal Archbishop alone amongst the spiritual peers favoured his pretensions. Of the civil lords, Hastings and Buckingham were the most powerful and active. Whilst the former, though hating and fearing the Queen, had now openly allied himself with her party, the latter was believed to be faltering in his allegiance to Richard. " He was warned," says More, " by such as were then craft-masters in the handling of such wicked devices," that he had gone too far; that the King was offended with him for his kinsfolks' sakes, and if possible would revenge them; that if Rivers and Gray escaped they would not forget their imprisonment, or if they were put to death it would but inflame the anger of the King. If, then, Richard felt secure amid false friends and open enemies, it was because of his conscious superiority to all, of his ability to bend other wills to his own, and of his knowledge of what was essential to the security, the peace, and the prosperity of the country. But he was now contemplating an act of cruel tyranny which would justify the plots of his enemies, and win the populace to their side, unless he was able to control them by an imposing force against which resistance would be useless. This, I think, is the true explanation of his hurrying to London trusted troops from the North, where the memory

---

* More, pp. 492–3. Buck, p. 13.

of his exploits in Scotland was untarnished, and his character unsullied by the sinister rumours which his enemies had circulated in London.

No man had contributed more than Hastings to the overthrow of the Woodvilles; yet no man less commended himself to the Protector as an accomplice in the revolution they had jointly brought about. If it be true, as alleged by many historians, that he was urgently pressing for the execution of Rivers and Gray, Richard well understood his motives. He had made a mortal enemy of Earl Rivers by his successful rivalry in regard to the Lordship of Calais, described by De Comines as "the best preferment in Christendom." This may account for Richard's hesitation in disposing of his noble prisoners, and, as Mr. Sharon Turner has observed, such delay would naturally induce in the mind of Hastings mistrust of the Duke of Gloucester's future intentions. The character which Sir Thomas More has drawn of Lord Hastings may be accepted as substantially true. He was, he says, "a loving man, and passing well beloved; very faithful and trusty enough; trusting too much." It was his double boast that he had effected a revolution without bloodshed, and that the end of the revolution was simply the transfer of the Government from the family of the Queen to that of the late King. For, when his aversion to the Queen Dowager and her family had been most intense, Hastings was loyal to the young Princes. Nor was he the only one who was rendered uneasy by the postponement of the coronation. Cardinal Bourchier shared his anxiety, whilst the common people began to murmur. Lord Stanley, also, prognosticated evil from the separate Councils. According to More—who, however, here as elsewhere, draws largely upon his imagination—Stanley complained to Hastings that "he much disliked these doings," and could not believe that two different Councils could produce any good effects. "We are," he said, "conscious of the loyalty and integrity of our actions; but who knows what the cabal at Crosby's Place talk and contrive? I fear what we are building they are plucking down, and unless we could unite or know their councils ours will be in vain."

"Peace, my Lord," said the Lord Hastings; "never fear or misdoubt anything. I durst assure you upon my life all's well, or at least nothing ill is intended against us. For, *while one man is there*, who is never thence, never can there be thing propounded which should sound amiss toward me, but it should be in mine ears ere it were well out of their mouths." *

If we suppose, as seems probable, that the Protector was already aspiring to the crown, it is obvious that the removal of Hastings must be his first step. Their interests were irreconcilable. The one essential thing for Richard was the formation of a strong homogeneous party favourable to the prolongation of the Protectorate, and powerful enough to quell all opposition. To this Hastings was the only impediment. And upon the removal of Hastings—whether we call it an act of tyranny or of policy — Richard had already decided.† There are degrees of guilt—even in a political murder. The character of Richard is unjustly blackened by our great dramatist, and it is well-nigh impossible to rid the mind of the impression produced by his art. Justice, however, demands the recognition of the fact that Shakspeare's drama is based

---

* More's Works, p. 53.   † Polydore Vergil, Book xxv., p. 179.

upon a portraiture of Richard drawn by his implacable foes. If this expression is inapplicable to Sir Thomas More, the evidence against his authorship of the history is so far strengthened. It has been plausibly suggested that he was too conscientious to complete a history which his better judgment condemned as slanderous and sophistical. "It should seeme he founde the work so melancholy and uncharitable, as dul'd his disposition to it, for he began it 1513 . . . . and had the intermission of twenty-two years to finish it before he died, which was in 1535, but did not."* But, as I have endeavoured to show elsewhere,† More is responsible only for the "classical varnish" of a work written by a hand which designedly propagated deliberate falsehood. However honest may have been More's intentions, the history which bears his name, and upon which, unhappily for historical truth, Shakspeare has so largely drawn, is at the best the strongly-coloured narrative of a partisan.‡ It does not surprise us, therefore, that More, and after him Shakspeare, are silent upon the subject of Hastings' overtures to the Queen Dowager, and of his influence over the young King, who desired nothing more than the restoration to power of his maternal relatives, to which the nation as one man was opposed. Yet these are well-attested facts, and it was Hastings alone who, by his complicity, invested with any importance the conspiracies which were the ostensible reason assigned by Richard for surrounding himself with a large body of troops.

The story that Hastings had been opposed to the deposi-

---

* Buck. † See Preface.
‡ "Mr. Gairdner considers it a translation of a work of Morton."—*Letters of Richard III.*, vol. ii., p. xviii., no'e.

tion of Henry VI. rests upon nothing more substantial than
an inference of Sir Thomas More. Hastings owed his
advancement to Edward IV., and was sincerely attached to
the family of York. More himself acknowledges that Richard
"undoubtedly loved him well, and loth he was to have him
lost." But he could not close his eyes to the fact that an
alliance between Hastings and the Queen's friends must
deprive him of power, perhaps of liberty and life. He had a
warning before him in the fate of that Duke of Gloucester
who, although the uncle of Richard II., was destroyed by
him, owing to political oppositions; and in the last Duke of
Gloucester who, sustaining the same relationship to Henry VI.,
and his presumptive heir, had been treacherously murdered at
Bury St. Edmunds. There is reason in Horace Walpole's
remark that Hastings was really plotting to defeat the new
settlement, contrary to the intention of the three estates; and
that his execution was an act of self-defence, justified by
"that wicked code of State necessity," rather than "a wanton,
unnecessary, and disgusting cruelty." *

The time had now arrived for the execution of Richard's
tragic purpose. Parliament was about to meet for the purpose
of taking into consideration the prolongation of the Protec·
torate during the minority of Edward V. Hastings was
probably powerful enough to defeat this purpose. If Richard
cherished ulterior designs upon the throne, so much the
greater was the necessity to be rid of the only man who
could offer effectual opposition. On Friday, the 13th of
June, 1483, two days after Richard had written to the

---

* "Historic Doubts," p. 47.

Corporation of York, "many lords assembled in Council at the Tower to conclude upon all that was necessary for the coronation."* Every schoolboy knows the sequel. Richard joined the Council at nine o'clock, his bearing gracious even to pleasantry. "My Lord," he said, addressing Morton, Bishop of Ely, as one whose mind was disengaged from sinister thoughts, "you have very good strawberries in your garden at Holborn, I pray you let us have a mess of them." The Bishop, who was proud of his horticulture, gladly complied. Begging the Council not to suspend their deliberations, the Protector withdrew, accompanied by the Duke of Buckingham. The remaining members of the Council exchanged significant glances of congratulation at the Protector's auspicious bearing. It is in matters of detail communicated, if not written, by Morton, that Shakspeare, following More, harmonises the creations of his imagination with historical facts. Let him describe this scene:

Ely. Where is my lord Protector? I have sent for those
        strawberries.
Hastings. His grace looks cheerfully and smooth this morning;
        There's some conceit or other likes him well,
        When he doth bid good-morrow with high spirit.
        I think there's ne'er a man in Christendom
        Can lesser hide his love or hate than he:
        For by his face straight shall you know his heart.
Stanley. What of his heart perceive you in his face,
        By any likelihood he shewed to-day?
Hastings. Marry, that with no man here he is offended;
        For were he, he had shewn it in his looks.

The colloquy was interrupted by the entrance of the Protector and Buckingham. It was at once apparent that

* More's Works, p. 53.

something had occurred displeasing to Richard, who, with
"a wonderful sour angry countenance, frowning and fretting,"
and biting his lower lip, as was his habit when agitated or
in a meditative mood, silently took his seat.* Suddenly he
sprang to his feet. Like Milton's Satan,

> with stern
> Aspect he rose, and in his rising seem'd
> A pillar of state; deep on his front engraven
> Deliberation sat, and public care;
> And princely counsel in his face yet shone,
> Majestic, though in ruin; sage he stood,
> .   .   .   .   .   his look
> Drew audience and attention still as night
> Or summer's noontide air, while thus he spake:

"What punishment deserve they who have conspired
against the life of one so nearly related to the King as
myself, who am, besides, entrusted with the government
of this realm?"

It is Hastings, the man of sudden impulse, and the
paramour of Jane Shore, who breaks the awful silence by
declaring that they merited the punishment due to all
traitors. We are now clearly in the region of romance, and
the story of this scene, as related by More, is full of improba-
bilities, from which it is impossible to separate fact and
fiction. When he relates that, plucking up his doublet sleeve
to the elbow of the left arm, he showed "a werish, withered
arm, and small," we recall the fact that not only is there no
authority for the tradition, but that so distinguished a warrior,
clad in ponderous armour and bearing the gigantic weapons
used in his day, could not have encountered Warwick at

* More's Works, p. 54.

Barnet, and afterwards unhorsed Sir Hugh Brandon on Bosworth Field, with that "werish, withered arm, and small." But More continues that the Protector exclaimed : "That sorceress, my brother's wife, *and others with her*, see how they have wasted my body by their sorcery and witchcraft." None would have dared, perhaps none would have cared to resent even so frivolous a charge as this against the Queen-mother. But who were the "others with her"? They were not long left to speculate. Jane Shore, the late paramour of Edward IV., the present mistress of Hastings, was named by the irate Protector as the accomplice of the Queen, and he demanded what were her deserts ?

The object of this romance was clearly to bring obloquy upon Richard for having, by a cruel artifice, designed to entrap Hastings, and to be rid of a dangerous woman whose relations with the Lord Chamberlain and the Queen had made her obnoxious. The suggestion that Richard's object was to obtain possession of her property, estimated at 2,000 marks, is one of the absurd fabrications of the chroniclers which requires no refutation. She had been employed as a political agent, and possibly by her influence the reconciliation of Hastings to the Queen had been effected. It is Hastings again who replies to the Protector's angry inquiry, " If they have done so heinously they are worthy of heinous punishment." By the employment of that " if," he probably intended to convey his conviction that the accusation was false.

"What!" exclaimed Richard, "dost thou serve me with ifs and with ands? I tell thee, traitor, they have done it, and thou in this villainy hast joined with them. Yea, and by Holy Paul I swear that dine I will not till thy head is brought to me."

The Protector is said to have placed privily in a chamber adjoining that in which the Council sat, "a sort right ready to do a mischief, giving them in charge that when he should give a sign, they should suddenly rush out, and, compassing about them who should sit with him, lay hands specially upon William Lord Hastings, and kill him forthwith." * But this was not Richard's method. The death of Hastings would have lost all its significance had it occurred in a tumultuous *mêlée*. More's story is here the more probable. The Protector, he says, when he uttered this oath, clapped his fist down hard upon the board, at which sign several men in arms rushed into the room, crying "Treason!" With his stern glance still fixed upon Hastings, the Protector exclaimed: "I arrest thee, traitor!" "What! me, my lord?" protested Hastings indignantly, as he was roughly handled by the guards. Stanley, Morton, and Rotheram were also arrested, and in the sudden tumult, Stanley seems to have been struck with a poleaxe.† It was afterwards affirmed by the Tudor historians that Richard ordered one of the ruffians to despatch Stanley with his battle-axe, as if by mistake, as he sat at the Council Board, and that he escaped destruction by sinking under the table. But this story, like so many others, is apocryphal. Within an hour, the unfortunate Hastings was "brought forth unto the green beside the chapel within the Tower," and beheaded "upon the end of

---

* Polydore Vergil. In *The True Tragedy of Richard III.*, a play anterior to Shakspeare's drama, these words are uttered by the page: "My lord hath willed me to get half-a-dozen ruffians in readiness, and when he knocks with his fist upon the board they to rush in and cry 'Treason,' and to lay hands upon the Lord Hastings and the Lord Stanley."—P. 33.

† More's Works, pp. 53-54.

a long and great timber log, which there lay with other for the repairing of the Tower." *

The execution of Hastings must be pronounced a crime which leaves a deadly blot upon the character of Richard III. All that can be said in its extenuation is that he was a fatal obstacle to that freedom of activity and resolve which the Protector regarded as needful to the effectual employment of his great powers for the protection of the Commonwealth. But, in truth, it was not so much one definite cause, however influential that may have been, which led to the perpetration of this crime. It was rather the confusion and collision of purposes long formed, of good and evil thoughts long cherished, suddenly blazing into action, inspired by sentiments of expediency, uncontrolled by the moral sense. Sir George Buck argues that Richard had more conscience or less cruelty than has been attributed to him, inasmuch as he did not execute the Earl of Pembroke, the Earl of Richmond, or Bishop Morton. Whilst condemning the execution of Hastings, he contends that the criminality " is not so cleare but that there may be some State mystery suspected in it." And he adds: " Let us leave it upon that accompt," which reminds us of the old commentator who expounds a difficult passage of Scripture in some such words as these: " Let us look this difficulty in the face, and—pass on ! "

It is no palliation of the Protector's guilt to affirm that, in the very hour of his arrest, Hastings was rejoicing in the execution of his old foes Rivers and Gray, which he believed to have taken place that very morning at Pontefract. That such was the case, however, is beyond question. The Protector

* More, p. 54. Fabyan, p. 668.

was formidable to him whilst they lived. Now that he believed them dead the question was whether he or Richard should follow them to the block, and in this game of death the weaker man paid the penalty of his unscrupulous ambition and of accomplished and projected crimes. "So the lord Hastings learnt by his own loss at the last that the law of nature whereof the Gospel speaketh, 'whatsoever ye will that men do unto you, do you so also unto them,' cannot be broken without punishment. He was one of the smiters of Prince Edward, Henry VI.'s son, who was finally quit with like manner of death." *

That Hastings was forewarned of the danger awaiting him on that fatal day is an authenticated fact; it is impossible, however, to say how much of fiction is woven into the curious story told by Holinshed. "A marvellous case is it," he says, "to hear either the warnings of that he should have voided, or the tokens of that he could not void. For the self night next before his death the lord Stanley sent a trusty messenger unto him at midnight in haste, requiring him to rise and ride away with him." The messenger was charged to report that his master had had a disturbing dream, in which he thought that "a boar with his tusks† so rased them both by their heads, that the blood ran about both their shoulders." He informed Hastings that he had horses ready if he would flee with him. It can hardly be doubted that *under colour of a dream* Stanley thus warned Hastings of approaching danger, and that the knowledge of the Protector's purpose was shared by other lords. Hastings is said to have replied: "Leaneth

---

* Polydore Vergil, Book xxv., p. 181.
† The allusion is of course to Richard's cognizance.

my lord your master so much to such trifles, and hath such
faith in dreams? Tell him it is plain witchcraft." He declined to flee, alleging that if their flight were intercepted
the boar would deal with them "as folke that fled for some
falsehood." The peril was rather in flying; he would not
show a faint heart. "Go to thy master," he added, "pray him
to be merry and have no fear. I am as sure of the man that
he woteth of as I am of mine own hand."

"In riding towards the Tower," continues Holinshed, "the
same morning in which he was beheaded, his horse twice or
thrice stumbled with him." Hastings was uninfluenced by
the gross superstition of his age, which led the historian to see
in this a token "notably foregoing some great misfortune."
Other premonitions are cited which he equally disregarded.
He pursued his ride beside the bush-grown banks of the
Thames, until "upon the very Tower wharfe so near the place
where his head was cut off soon after, there met he with one
Hastings, a pursuivant of his own name. And at their meeting in that place he was put in remembrance of another time
in which it had happened them before to meet in like manner
at the same place." He had then been accused to Edward IV.
by Earl Rivers, had "far fallen into the King's indignation,"
and, an object of distrust to the Queen, "had stood in great
fear of himself." Now meeting this man in the hour of his
triumph, it gave him pleasure to gossip with him as he had
done when last they met on that spot.

"Art thou remembered," he asked, "that I met thee here
once with a heavy heart?"

"Yea, my lord, well; and thanked be God they got no
good nor you no harm thereby."

"Thou would'st say so if thou knewest so much as I know, which few know else as yet, but more shall hereafter.* In faith, man, I was never so sorry, nor never stood in so great dread in my life as I did when thou and I met here. And lo! how the world is turned. Now stand mine enemies in the danger, and I never in my life so merry, nor never in so great surety."

"O, good God!" exclaims More, "the blindness of our mortal nature; when he most feared he was in good surety, when he reckoned himself surest he lost his life, and that within two hours after." †

The execution being accomplished, the Protector sent for the Mayor and chief citizens to the Tower, and charged Hastings with conspiracy with the Queen's party to overthrow the Government and to take his life. More says that he and Buckingham put on old rusty armour, which lay neglected in the Tower, for the purpose of suggesting that their sudden danger had caused them to take anything that lay at hand for their defence. "They all answered fair," all allowed that

> Justice had done her unrelenting part,
> If she indeed be Justice who drives on,
> Bloody and blind, the chariot wheels of death.

Hastings was popular with the people, and the ferment which the news of his sudden arrest and execution had created could only be appeased by convincing them of its

---

* Mr. Sharon Turner sees in this remark a confirmation of Richard's statements about a counter conspiracy, and evidence that Hastings had intended that day to perpetrate upon the Protector the violence he was himself about to suffer ("History," vol. iii., p. 456). But with the deference which is due to so accomplished and conscientious an historian, who devoted fifty-three years of his life to the study of this period, I think the inference is unwarranted. To me it appears obvious that the reference is to the death of Rivers and Gray, who at the time to which he refers had sought his disgrace, and whose execution he believed to have taken place at Pontefract at that very hour.   † Sir Thomas More's Works, p. 55.

juṣtice. To this end a proclamation was issued, reciting "that the lord Hastings with divers others, wicked conspirators, had traitorously contrived the same day to have slain the Protector and the Duke of Buckingham sitting in council, with a purpose and design to take upon him the government of the King and kingdom." It further explained that his execution had been swift "lest any delay might have encouraged other mischievous persons who were engaged in the conspiracy with him to make an insurrection for his deliverance." The proclamation, which was very well indited, "as was thought by Catesby, who was a chief actor in this tragedy," did very little good. It was received with ominous silence, and there were not wanting those who saw in the neatness of its execution a glaring inconsistence with the assumed haste and panic which had produced it, and thence concluded that Hastings' ruin being determined on, it was composed and written before his death.* Its history is probably given with substantial accuracy by Shakspeare in words which he puts into the mouth of a scrivener :

> Here is the indictment of the good Lord Hastings;
> Which in a set hand fairly is engrossed,
> That it may be to-day read o'er in Paul's.
> And mark how well the sequel hangs together;
> Eleven hours I have spent to write it over ;
> For yesternight by Catesby was it sent me :
> The precedent was full as long a dooing :
> And yet within these five hours Hastings lived,
> Untainted, unexamined, free, at liberty.
> Here's a good world the while !   Who is so gross
> That cannot see this palpable device ?
> Yet who so bold but says he sees it not ?
> Bad is the world ; and all will come to nought
> When such bad dealing must be seen in thought.

---

* More, in Kennett, p. 495.

The prevailing opinion was that Hastings had been sacrificed to panic. Of his actual guilt there was no means of forming a judgment. But his fate would be a warning to other malcontents, and after the first shock of disgust which it called forth had subsided, it seemed to have increased rather than lessened the public confidence in the Protector. The resentments between him and Hastings had been a source of public danger. By their removal it was felt that a sanguinary civil war had been prevented.

CHAPTER VII.

SHAKSPEARE, as usual following More, has familiarised us
with the belief that Earl Rivers and Lord Richard Gray
suffered at Pontefract on the same day that Hastings was
beheaded in the Tower.* There is, however, the clearest
evidence that More was mistaken. Polydore Vergil writes :
" *When these things were done*, Richard, knowing for certain
that there was no cause why he should any further dissemble
the matter, sent his letters of warrant to the Keeper of
Pomfret Castle to behead Anthony Lord Rivers, Richard
Gray, and Thomas Vaughan, which was done soon after." †
Again, the will of Earl Rivers is dated *Sheriff Hutton, the*
23*rd of June,* or ten days after the death of Hastings. He
was subsequently removed to Pontefract, where he was tried
before the Earl of Northumberland on the charge of conspiring against the Protector's life. It is, therefore, probable
that his execution took place on the 25th of June. All
authorities are agreed that it was carried out under the Earl

---

* So also Stow says that all " suffered in one day."—STOW's *Chronicle
Abridged*, p. 190. Following these authorities Holinshed not only adopts their
error, but, with characteristic inaccuracy, adds yet another fiction, and says
that " about the self-same hour" that Hastings suffered " was there beheaded
at Pontefract . . . the lords *and knights* that were taken from the King at
Northampton."—Vol. iii., p. 285.

† Polydore Vergil, Book xxv., p. 182.

of Northumberland, and it is now ascertained that that nobleman was at York on the 13th.* It is probable that Gray, and possibly Vaughan, suffered a few days earlier than Rivers, at the end of whose will, after the names of witnesses, these words occur : "My will is *now* to be buried before an image of our blessed lady Mary *with my lord Richard* in Pomfret." This appears to indicate a quite recent change of purpose consequent on the fact that Gray had been already executed and buried at Pontefract.

Cruel as was the execution of these noblemen, it was not, as More repeatedly asserts, without any trial or form of justice.† If in any respect it was not consonant with the manners of that age of violence, it was just in this fact, that a form of trial was observed. Its issue may not have been uncertain, but neither was the fact of their treasonable conduct doubtful, and there is no reason to suppose that Richard's Letters of Warrant for their execution were issued before the result of the trial had officially reached him.

It has been reasonably urged that the execution of Rivers may be regarded as a just retribution for the murder of Clarence. According to the spirit of those times, Richard's revenge would be justifiable, as prompted by a laudable resentment.‡ This also is certain, that Richard was not at that time accounted, even by his victims, that human monster which history has depicted. In his will, Earl Rivers makes an appeal to his generosity to see it executed: "I humbly beseech my lord of Gloucester in the worship of Christ's

---

* Davies' "York Records," p. 145.
† See Gairdner's "Richard III.," p. 91.
‡ "History of Great Britain," by Dr. Henry, vol. xii., p. 414.

passion, and for the merit and weal of his soul, to comfort, help, and assist as supervisor (for very trust) of this testament, that mine executors may, with his pleasure, fulfil this my last will." Rous has also preserved a ballad, composed by the Earl after his trial, in which he expresses "content" with his lot:

> Bounden am I
> And that greatly
> To be content.

Words which are inconsistent with any strong sense of the injustice of his sentence. The humanity of the Protector is further illustrated in the fact that he secured to the son of Lord Gray an annuity of 100 marks out of "the honour and lordship of Pomfret." *

The Queen, with her younger son, the Duke of York, and her five daughters, were in sanctuary at Westminster. Had Richard been the cruel monster depicted by the Tudor chroniclers, it is inconceivable that he should have permitted Elizabeth thus to escape his power. Nothing was easier than to have prevented it; † whilst, in sanctuary, she could not fail to prove at least a source of serious embarrassment. It soon became evident that she would be more than this; the sanctuary had become a cave of Adullam, and the Queen's intercourse with her relatives and her partisans in the Council had been a source of perennial strife. Her control, moreover, of the heir presumptive to the throne was unconstitutional,

---

* Harl. MSS., No. 433 f., 23 b.

† Stow, in his narrative of Rotheram's visit to the Queen on the day upon which she entered sanctuary, writes : "He returned home in the dawning of the day, by which time he might in his chamber window see *all the Thames full of boats of the Duke of Gloucester's servants.*"—*Chronicle*, p. 439.

and full of danger to the state. It is perfectly clear from More's narrative of Archbishop Rotheram's visit to the Queen, that she had made preparations for a long resistance. "The Archbishop," he writes, "came yet before day unto the Queen, about whom he found much heaviness, rumble, haste, and business; carriage and conveyance of her stuff into sanctuary, chests, coffers, packs, fardells, trusses, all on men's backs; no man unoccupied, some lading, some going, some discharging, some coming for more, some breaking down the walls to bring in the next way, etc." All this Richard had connived at—both from considerations of prudence and that chivalrous tenderness towards women which he always evinced—so long as anarchy prevailed or was apprehended in the city. To remain there when order had been restored, the Protectorate confirmed by the Council, and the date of the coronation fixed, was "an insult to the King, the Protector, and the Council." * Richard acted with characteristic caution. It was obviously impossible that he should leave the Duke of York in the custody of his enemies. If the coronation took place at the date fixed, it was desirable that he should figure in the pageant; but a reason more likely to weigh with the Council was the probability that he would be conveyed out of the country, thus endangering the succession.

The ex-Chancellor Rotheram, Archbishop of York, had been released shortly after the arrest of Hastings. Richard sent a messenger to assure him that there was no sort of danger to either of the Princes, that his intentions were fair, and his only purpose in demanding the Duke of York was

---

* More erroneously places Richard's order to the Queen to leave sanctuary *before* the death of Hastings.

that he might keep the King his brother company, and walk at his coronation. But Rotheram was firm even to defiance. "Be it as well as it will," he replied, "I assure him it will never be as well as we have seen it."* The Queen also resisted all importunities and threats. By what means the Protector eventually overcame the obduracy of Archbishop Rotheram does not appear. But his knowledge of human nature, and his unique power of bending other minds to his own, were equal to every emergency. Rotheram had committed a grave misdemeanor in delivering the Great Seal to the Queen, and it is possible that Richard was thus enabled to work upon his fears. He accomplished two purposes where, so far as men knew, he was pursuing only one. The Chancellor's opposition to the surrender of the Duke of York was withdrawn, and Lord Campbell writes: "Rotheram appears soon after to have surrendered the Great Seal into the hands of the Protector." This is but a euphonious way of saying that he was disgraced. His successor in the Chancellorship was Russell, Bishop of Lincoln, "a wise man and a good," says More, "and one of the best learned men undoubtedly that England had in his time." Summoning Archbishop Bourchier and the other Lords of the Council, Richard thus addressed them:

"I pray God that I never live if I be not careful for the commodytie of my nephews whose calamity I know well must need redound likewise to the commonwealth and myself also. Therefore seeing that my brother Edward our King did upon his death-bed constitute and appoint me Protector of the

---

* Lord Campbell's "Lives of the Chancellors," vol. i., pp. 343–4.

Realm, I had more regard to nothing than to repair hither, and bring with me Prince Edward his eldest son, that in time convenient all things might be done by the advice of the Council; for *I am determined to do nothing without your authority*, whom I am willing to have mine associates, aiders, and partakers in all dealings, that you thereby may well bear witness whatsoever I shall henceforth do as touching the government of this realm, the same wholly to be employed faithfully and without fraud for the utility of the commonwealth and the commodity of Prince Edward, the charge and government of whom I suppose you know sufficiently that his father committed to me for that only cause. But Anthony Rivers attempted of late to hinder me that I should not according to my duty take on hand that charge, whom therefore we have been compelled to commit with others who also made resistance therein, that by their examples other men might learn not to have our commandments in contempt. But what shall we say to the evil counsel which they who most malign and hate me have given to Queen Elizabeth who, without any just cause, counterfeating fear so foolishly hath enterprised to carry in all haste the King's children as wicked, wretched, and desperate naughty persons into sanctuary?"* It dishonours him, he says, will mar the coronation spectacle, and, after other objections assigned, continues: "It is therefore my opinion, these reasons and considerations being well weighed, that some honourable and

---

* "A heavy cause when princes fly for aid where cutthroats, rebels, and bankrupts should be." These words, attributed to Cardinal Bourchier, show that Richard justly described the character of "sanctuary persons," amongst whom he reasonably objected to allow his brother's children to remain. See *The True Tragedy of Richard III.*, p. 31.

trusty person who cannot be doubted to tender the King's wealth, and reputation of the Council, and is in credit with the Queen, be sent to her to demand the release of the Duke of York, and for this office I think no person better qualified than the most reverend Father my lord Cardinal the Archbishop of Canterbury if he pleases to take the trouble upon him, which of his great goodness I do believe that he will not refuse for the King's sake and our's, and the wealth of the young Duke himself." If, however, the Queen is obdurate, he concludes : "Then 'tis my opinion that we fetch the Duke of York out of that prison by force, and bring him into the King's company and presence, in which we will take such care of him and give him such honourable treatment that all the world shall perceive to our honour and her reproach that it was nothing but her frowardness and groundless suspicion that first carried and then kept him there. This is my judgment in this affair, but if any of you, my lords, are of contrary sentiments and find me mistaken, *I never was, nor by God's grace ever shall be, so wedded to my own opinion but I shall be ready to change it upon better reasons and grounds."*

The two Archbishops protested against the threatened sacrilege. No King of England had ever dared to violate that Church which, five hundred years gone by, St. Peter came down from heaven to consecrate, "accompanied with many angels by night to do it," and which "many popes and kings had adorned with the privilege of a sanctuary, and therefore as no bishop ever dare attempt to consecrate that Church, so no prince had ever yet been so fierce and indevout

---

* Polydore Vergil, Book xxv., p. 178. More, p. 487.

as to violate the privileges of it." * But though the Archbishops threatened the vengeance of heaven against any
who should commit such sacrilege, they trusted to accomplish
the Protector's purpose, of which they acknowledged the
justice, by moral suasion. The Cardinal Archbishop, as
became his office, defended the rights of sanctuary, especially
as belonging to Westminster Abbey, "among the treasuries
of which Church was the very cope in which St. Peter had
officiated." He uttered not a word in defence of the Queen,
to whom he undertook to convey the decision of the Council,
in which she had no longer any partisans, promising so to
perform his part that they " should be convinced there wanted
no good will or endeavour in himself, but the Queen's dread,
and womanly fear was the only cause " of failure.

At these words the Duke of Buckingham, who had
listened with impatience to the aged prelate, sprang to
his feet and exclaimed with an oath : " ' Womanish fear,' say
you, my lord ? Nay, womanish frowardness, for I dare take
it upon my soul that she knows she has no just reason to
fear any danger to her son or to herself." † The Duke
proceeded to denounce the Queen as then engaged with her
family in plotting against the Government. He applauded
the Protector's purpose of employing force for the removal
of the Duke of York, maintained that it was contrary to law
to extend the privilege of sanctuary to an infant who had
committed no offence, and was too young to apply for it of
his own free will; and, finally, he censured the clergy for
encouraging those abuses of the right of sanctuary which

---

* Habington, p. 487.   † *Ibid.*, p. 488.

were notorious. The Council were visibly impressed. The Protector rose, and argued the case with calmness and irresistible force. The Archbishops were silent : they concurred in the unanimous resolve that the Queen should be desired to resign the custody of her son to the Duke of Gloucester.* Many thought that the summons would not be obeyed, and it was further resolved that force should be employed if persuasion failed.

A deputation, headed by the venerable Cardinal, proceeded to Westminster, whilst the other members of the Council repaired to the Star Chamber to await their report. The Queen knew the conciliatory character of the Archbishop, whom she received with courtesy. But she absolutely refused to surrender the Prince, or to accept for herself the place of dignity in her son's Court which the Protector offered her. Had she done so, Edward V. would in all probability have enjoyed a tranquil reign, and the name of Richard, Duke of Gloucester, been handed down to posterity as that of a stainless patriot, an illustrious general, a sagacious administrator, and a model Prince Regent, the idol of his age and country.† Her attitude of defiance had already been the cause of Hastings' death; it had also sent the young King to the Tower, where alone he could be considered safe.

The graciousness with which the Queen received the

---

* The continuator of the " Croyland Chronicle " says that force was used to secure the co-operation of Cardinal Bourchier.

† Grafton confesses that if Richard had remained Lord Protector and suffered his nephew to reign the realm would have prospered, and he would have been as much praised and beloved as he became abhorred and despised. But this is an admission that Richard did possess merits inconsistent with that abuse. Had he been prosperous his errors would have been lost in oblivion by sycophants who, like Rous, have shown us the kind of portrait they would have handed down to posterity.

Archbishop instantly gave place to passionate indignation
when he announced that " he was, with those other lords,
sent by the Protector and the Privy Council to her Majesty to
let her know how much her detaining of the Duke of York
in that place was scandalous to the public and disliked by the
King his brother . . . . that the King himself was much
grieved at it, and the Council offended because it looked as
if one brother was in danger from the other and could not
be preserved by the other's life; that it would be a very
great comfort to his Majesty to have his brother with him,
nor would it be of less advantage to the young duke himself. . . . So he could not but earnestly entreat her to
comply with a thing so very reasonable and every way convenient." *

The Queen pleaded that the child was ill, and needed a
mother's care. In vain the Primate urged that no one wished
to deprive her of the solace of nursing him; all that was
desired was that it should be done in the proper place. In
vain he convicted her of the insincerity of this and other
pretexts for defying the Government of the Protector. In
vain he announced the decision of the Council to remove the
child by force, and explained that the right of sanctuary
could not be claimed for him. The Queen's anger was
aroused. "I do not intend to depart out of this place,"
she exclaimed, "and as for my son the Duke of York, I
purpose to keep him with me. The more some men wanted
to get him into their hands without any substantial cause,
the more determined I am not to part with him."

---

* More's Works, p. 49.

"And the more suspicious you are, madam," replied the Archbishop with equal firmness, "the more jealous are others of you, lest, under a causeless pretence of danger, you should convey him out of the nation. . . . And I assure you, madam, that the Prince, who bears a most tender love to his nephews, and the Council, who have an equal care and respect for your children, will certainly set him at liberty unless you resign him to us, lest you should send him away." *

It is impossible to doubt that the Queen was influenced by genuine maternal anxiety for the safety of her son. So far she claims our sympathy. But she was a weak and wayward, a designing, unscrupulous, and ambitious woman. Her position was entirely illogical. Instead of giving up one son, she was invited to become, in her proper station, the natural protectress of both in King Edward's Court. She chose to defy the Protector, angrily declaring that she had entertained no thought of sending her son out of the country, and expressing distrust of his uncle, to whom, she said, it would be unsafe to trust the heir presumptive, since he ignored the claims of her daughters, and asserted that, next to the Princes he was the rightful heir to the throne.

"I know," she said, "the Protector and the Council have power enough, if they have will, to take him and me from this place; but whosoever he be that shall dare to do it, I pray God send him shortly need of a sanctuary, and no possibility to come to it."

The Cardinal, seeing the Queen wax more and more passionate, thought it time to break off the discussion, and

---

* Dean Hook's "Lives of the Archbishops," vol. v., p. 371. More, in Kennett, p. 490.

replied : " Madam, I will not dispute the matter longer with
you. It is equal to me whether you deliver him or no."

The Cardinal felt that his mission had failed. In his
secret soul he recoiled from that resort to violence upon which
he knew that the Council were determined. He had brought
to the Queen an opportunity of conciliating those whom her
perversity must convert into irreconcilable enemies. He
would make one more effort to induce her voluntarily to
release her child. " If you resign your son to us," he said,
" I will pawn my soul and body for his safety; if you refuse,
I shall have done my part, and shall depart with the full
determination never again to interfere in this matter. You
evidently consider both me and the other members of the
Council deficient either in wisdom or in honesty; in wisdom,
for that, not perceiving the evil designs of the Protector, we
are mere tools in his hands; or in honesty, for that, knowing
his wickedness and craft, we have endeavoured to place your
son in his hands for the child's destruction; an execrable
treason which, as we ourselves abhor it, so we dare boldly say,
that it never entered into the Protector's thoughts."

Further resistance was useless. The Cardinal waited for a
reply. The Queen seemed suddenly to realise her position.
Hoping that things might not prove so bad as she had feared,
she recovered her calmness. And, says Dean Hook, " with
that graciousness for which she was distinguished, she recalled
the words uttered under feelings of excitement."* Taking the
Duke of York by the hand she led him to the Cardinal.

" My Lord," she said, addressing the Archbishop, " and all

---

* " Lives of the Archbishops," vol. v., p. 374.

my lords now present, I am not so opinionated of myself, or ill-advised concerning you, as to mistrust either your wisdom or fidelity, as I shall prove to you by reposing such trust in you as, if either of them be wanting in you, shall redound to my inexpressible grief, the damage of the whole realm, and your eternal shame and disgrace. For lo! here is my son, the person whom you desire, and though I doubt not but that I could keep him safe in this sanctuary from all violence, yet here I resign him into your hands. I am sensible that I run great hazards in so doing . . . . but notwithstanding this I do here deliver him, and his brother with him, to your keeping; of whom I shall ask him again at all times before God and the world, and I am confident of your fidelity."*

More never loses an opportunity of throwing pathos into his narrative; and in this address of the Queen and the scene which followed it, there is doubtless more of historiographical art than of strict historical truth. Holding her boy by the hand, he tells us that she thus addressed him: "'Farewell, my own sweet son. The Almighty be thy Protector. Let me kiss thee once more before we part, for God knows when we shall kiss again.' . . . And then having kissed him, she blessed him, and turned from him and wept, and so went her way, leaving the child with the lords weeping also for her departure."

At the Star Chamber the Protector received his nephew with expressions of affection. "Now welcome, my lord," he said, "with all my heart." And without attributing sinister designs to Richard, we may well believe that his satisfaction

---

* More's Works, p. 51.

in receiving the Duke was unfeigned. He carried him to the Bishop of London's palace at St. Paul's. There the brothers met, and More says, the Protector "left them a few days together, and because all things were in a great forwardness for the coronation which he was zealous to promote, he caused the King and the Duke his brother to be removed to the Tower, the usual place from which the solemnity began." * The pathos which More throws into his story has here a certain value, inasmuch as the minute details which he records reveal the character of the young King as void of energy and moral courage, sentimental, and "of a weak and sickly disposition." † "After which time," he says, "the Prince never tied his points, nor aught wrought himself, but with that young babe his brother lingered in thought and heaviness." It must be remembered that Edward was no mere child, but a youth trained in accordance with the current practices of chivalry in those heroic times, and verging upon the recognised estate of manhood. Ill fitted was one so effeminate to resist the intrigues of unworthy favourites, or to control a factious nobility. Hence the general satisfaction that the Protector's claim to the Regency during the minority of his nephew had now no formidable opponent, and hence also his reason for asserting that claim and aspiring to a yet higher dignity.

Three days only had elapsed since the death of Hastings. The Council had met on the morning of Monday, the 16th of June. On the afternoon of that day the Queen had surrendered the Duke of York, and before night the Protector had issued orders (writs of *supersedeas*) to prevent the assembling of

---

* More, in Kennett, p. 491.   † Buck.

Parliament, which had been fixed for the 25th.* This display
of energy, and of the possession of natural powers of the
highest order, created a favourable impression, and strengthened the hands of the Protector, by winning the adhesion of
some who had been his opponents, and notably of Lord Lisle,
the brother of the Queen's first husband.

In anticipation of the meeting of Parliament on the 25th
of June, the Chancellor had prepared an elaborate speech for
that day.† It is preserved in the Cottonian MSS., and has
been reprinted by Mr. Nichols, occupying twenty-three pages
of his "Grants of Edward V.," and is worth consulting as a
literary monument of the time. The Lord Chancellor was
always a prelate of the Church, and the speech naturally
assumed a religious complexion, being based upon a text
of Scripture: "Listen, O isles, unto me, and hearken, ye
people from afar: the Lord hath called me from the womb."
The lords spiritual and temporal were indicated by "the isles"
of the text; the Commons by "the people from afar." The

---

* The writ of *supersedeas* was received by the Sheriffs at York on the 21st,
which completes the evidence that it was issued on the 16th.—DAVIES' *York
Records*, p. 155.

† Mr. Sharon Turner is certainly mistaken in assuming that this speech
was delivered by Edward V. on the 19th of May. For, in the first place, no
Parliament met during the young King's reign; and the ingenious reasoning
by which Mr. Turner fixes the date is now shown to be delusive. He founds
his argument on the Chancellor's citing a text "such as I found in the divine
service of yesterday's feast." The word *yesterday* he thinks implies that the
speech was made on a Monday, and as the first grant of Edward V. from the
Tower is on the 19th of May, which was a Monday, he infers that on that day
the speech was delivered. But *feast-days* are more frequent than Sundays,
and Dr. Lingard has shown the particular feast to which the Chancellor's text
refers, and has thus cleared up an historical puzzle. The feast is that of the
Nativity of St. John the Baptist, which is observed on the 24th of June. This
confirms the testimony of the "York Records" and of the Croyland Chronicler
that Parliament was summoned for the 25th of June. See Nichols' "Grants
of Edward V."

young Prince was the Lord's Anointed, called to rule over them. The simile was dwelt upon with a play upon words which would readily catch the ears of his audience : " Hyt be undoubted that alle the habitacion of man be eyther in loud or in water. Then yf there be any suerte or permenesse here yn thys worlde, such as may be fownde oute of hevyn hyt ys rathyr in Isles and londes enirounde with water than in the see *or in eny grete Ryvers.*" * The King's youth and inexperience rendered it necessary that, during his minority, the authority of the Protector should be confirmed : " Well is this young Prince our sovereign lord here present between two brethren, that one his father, that other his uncle ; the rule of the first is determined by the over hasty course of nature. The second is ordeigned as next in perfect age of the blood royal to be his tutor and protector."

It would be straining the significance of an official document, in the preparation of which Edward V. could have had no hand, to attribute the censure of the Woodvilles to his personal convictions ; but the following significant words undoubtedly expressed the sense of the Council, if not of the King, of the unique position of the Duke of Gloucester as the only man to whose wisdom and prudence the defence of the realm could be entrusted : " The power and authority of my lord Protector is so behofull and of reason to be asserted and established by the authority of this hygh court, that among all the causes of the assemblyng of the parliament in thys tyme of the year, thys is the greatest and most necessary to be affirmed." †

---

* "Grants of Edward V.," p. 40.
† "Croyland Chronicle," p. 486.

The speech was not delivered. For, however accurately it may have reflected Richard's sentiments up to the 5th of June, before Parliament met he had planned other business for it than the recognition of "our glorious Prince and King Edward V." There can be no doubt that the Protector had now determined that his nephew should not be crowned. Yet it was necessary to allow the preparations for the coronation to go forward. The citizens were preparing to regale themselves with the spectacle; the very viands for the banquet in Westminster Hall had been actually purchased; and the people would grumble at the heavy expenditure incurred if, after all, the coronation was abandoned. On the other hand, the meeting of Parliament, which was to have extended the Protectorate or conferred a Regency, was postponed. By law and precedent the Protectorship would cease when the anointed King ascended the throne. The work of the revolution would be undone, and if the Protector escaped the block, he must descend to his former station as a subject.* For this he was not prepared. The dazzling lustre of a crown had corrupted his moral sense. Yielding to the temptation to seize an inheritance not rightfully his, "he cast from him the glory of being held up to the admiration of posterity as an example of rigid virtue and self-denial, instead of being chronicled as an usurper and the slave of his ungovernable ambition." †

---

* After the coronation of Henry VI. a motion was made in the House of Lords to the effect that since the King (a child nine years old) had taken upon himself, by his coronation, the protectorate and defence of the realm, the name and power of Protector granted to the Dukes of Bedford and Gloucester had ceased, and the two royal Dukes were henceforth to be contented with the title of Principal Counsellors.

† Miss Halsted's "Richard III.," vol. ii., p. 88.

The perplexities of the Protector's position were enhanced by the fact that his expected troops from the north had not arrived. But his decision was taken. The coronation, which was fixed for the 22nd of June, was postponed to the 2nd of November, and this was understood to point to further postponement, or possibly to a change in the succession. If the citizens murmured, it is evident that Richard himself had no lack of confidence in the popularity, if not in the justice, of his cause. The necessity of the hour was a strong government. The legitimate sovereign was a boy of thirteen, already trained to intrigue, and respecting whose legitimacy disquieting rumours were afloat. This latter fact was doubtless one of the strongest incentives to Richard to listen to what he afterwards termed the "diabolical temptation" to seize the crown whilst he could do so with some appearance of justice.

The Duke of Gloucester was almost universally regarded as a wise and capable Prince, in whose hands the peace and prosperity of the country were safe. He had proved himself a successful general and an able administrator, whilst the old nobility and many of the clergy regarded him as the champion of their privileges, and 20,000 men were within a few days' march of London to reinforce an army devoted to him. Such at least was the report industriously circulated to overawe the citizens. Whether, therefore, he demanded a prolonged Protectorate or the crown itself, either alternative was preferable to the weakness and the danger of a long minority, or to the return of the Woodvilles to power.

The story which later historians have repeated after Sir Thomas More, that Richard now opened to the Duke of

Buckingham his design of superseding his nephew, is simply incredible.* It carries its own refutation. But it may have originated in the fact that he now decided upon the open assertion of his right to the crown, and may have communicated to the Duke the ground upon which he elected to base his claim. This was the illegitimacy of his brother's children, attested by the civil lawyers. The faithful services of the Duke demanded his confidence equally with material rewards. We have More's unsubstantiated statement that Richard desired a family alliance and proposed that his son should betroth Buckingham's daughter, whilst he promised to allow the Duke a large share of King Edward's treasure, and so much of the wardrobe as should furnish his house. But when More adds that he offered to give him the Earldom of Hereford with all its appurtenances, and to settle upon him and his posterity the office of High Constable of England,† he is demonstrably in error. The Earldom of Hereford continued, as we shall see, to be a bone of contention after Richard had become King, and the office of High Constable of England had been hereditary in the Duke's family for many generations.

It was no unusual thing in a great national crisis for a Court divine to preach a political sermon at St. Paul's Cross. Not many years had passed since the chaplain of the Earl of Warwick had from that pulpit declared Edward IV. to be a usurper. Yet the citizens of London were hardly prepared

---

* Hume says, "The Protector then assailed the fidelity of Buckingham," representing that the only method of preventing mischief was by putting the sceptre in the hands of a man of whose friendship the Duke might be assured. Vol. iii., p. 273.

† More, in Kennett, p. 402.

for what happened on the very Sunday that was to have witnessed the young King's coronation. The Lord Mayor, Sir Edmund Shaw, had been already won over to Richard's cause. He was a munificent and much-respected citizen, probably a native of Stockport, where he founded and endowed a free school. His brother, a preacher of much repute, was engaged to preach a sermon at Paul's Cross, designed to prepare the citizens for that *coup d'état* upon which it is certain that Richard had now decided. The fact that he had the countenance both of the clergy and of the City magistracy indicates a recognition of the validity of his claim to the crown on the part of the most conservative and the best-informed section of the community. The incident possesses an importance which has not been recognised, in the evidence it affords that Richard did not, and had no reason to entertain the sanguinary purposes with which history and the drama have charged him. The murder of the Princes would have been the grossest of political blunders whilst he had, or believed that he had, evidence of their illegitimacy, which in the present temper of the public mind would have been hailed with a sense of relief. Dr. Shaw took for his text a passage from the Wisdom of Solomon (chap. iv., v. 3): "The multiplying brood of the ungodly shall not thrive, nor take deep rooting from bastard slips, nor lay any fast foundations." The Duke of Gloucester, the Duke of Buckingham, and other lords are said to have been present. The preacher directed the attention of his audience to the dissolute life of the late King, and more especially to the fact of the illegitimacy of all his children owing to their father's former marriage, of which abundant evidence existed. The main object of this discourse was to set forth the Protector's title to the crown as the only legitimate representative of the House of York.

So far all were agreed. But in that spirit of romance which pervades the work attributed to Sir Thomas More, we are told that the Lord Protector consented to act the part of a clown in a contemptible farce, by suddenly appearing on the scene as the preacher directed attention to him as the legitimate King. "Now was it before devised that in the speaking of these words the Protector should have come in among the people to the sermon, to the end that these words, *meeting with his presence,* might have been taken among the hearers as though the Holy Ghost had put them in the preacher's mouth, and should have moved the people even there to cry 'King Richard!' 'King Richard!' that it might have been after said that he was specially chosen by God, and in manner by miracle." The device failed, as More insinuates, either owing to the rapidity of the preacher, or the dilatoriness of the Protector, who appeared on the scene at the wrong moment! "The priest was entered on some other matter when the Duke appeared, which, however, he left, and repeated again abruptly, 'The Lord Protector, that very noble Prince, the pattern of all heroic deeds, represents the very face and mind of the great Duke, his father! his features are the same, and the plain express likeness of that noble Duke.'"* But, he adds, "The populace were so far from shouting, 'King Richard!' that they were rather as though turned to stone by what followed."

Various reports of the sermon have come down to us.

---

* More's Works, p. 617. Hall, p. 308.

Writing in the reign of Henry VIII., More and Polydore Vergil represent the preacher as having outraged the feelings of the citizens by aspersing the chastity of the Duchess of York, and that by the direct authority of her son the Protector. There is independent evidence that Dr. Shaw did, probably from an officious and ill-advised desire to curry favour at Court, adopt the outrageous calumny originally uttered by the Duke of Clarence,* since Fabyan, who may well have heard the sermon, asserts that he durst never show his face afterwards.

Polydore Vergil writes : " The Protector declared that he esteemed it more mete to neglect his mother's honour and honesty than to suffer so noble a realm to be polluted with such a race of Kings." † He adds that when the people heard the outrageous imputations, " they were wondrous vehemently troubled in mind therewith." This Italian cleric has so clear an insight into the workings of Providence, and is always prepared to name the particular sin in an enemy, or virtue in a friend, which is punished or rewarded, that we naturally look for the record of retribution in Dr. Shaw's case. Nor do we so look in vain. Not long after, we read, he acknowledged his error, and " so sore repented the doing thereof that, dying shortly for very sorrow, he suffered worthy punishment for his lewdness." ‡

If this story, in which Polydoro Vergil reflects the temper

---

* In the attainder of George, Duke of Clarence, it was alleged against him, "that to advance himself in the kingdom, and for ever to disable the King and his posterity from inheriting the crown, he had contrary to truth, nature, and religion, viper-like destroying her who gave him life, published that King Edward was a bastard and in no way capable to reign."—MORE, in Kennett, p. 482.

† Book xxv., 183.   ‡ *Ibid.,* 184.

of his age, were true, it constitutes one of the foulest blots on Richard's character. So revolting a scandal would probably never have commanded the credence of historians, were it not for the fact that it derived a quasi-confirmation from the well-authenticated fact that the citizens were roused to indignation by the assertions and insinuations of Dr. Shaw's sermon. But Richard shared that indignation! Nay, he, more than all, resented Dr. Shaw's insinuations as both a blunder and a crime. This may be gathered from every contemporary writer, not excepting More, who says that Dr. Shaw admitted that *he had done wrong to the Protector,* " who was ever known to bear a reverend and filial love unto her " (his mother). The Duke of Buckingham, also, in his speech to the Lord Mayor, affirmed " that Dr. Shaw had incurred the great displeasure of the Protector for speaking so dishonourably of the Duchess, his mother, a princess of so spotless character." * It is both idle, and opposed to all the evidence we possess, to affirm, as the detractors of Richard have done, that this was an after-thought of Gloucester and Buckingham, when they found that the populace resented the imputation cast upon the Duchess. It is simply incredible that Richard, conspicuous throughout life for his filial devotion, whose public acts at this very time were prompted and shaped in no small degree by his proud and ambitious mother,† and who was then residing under her roof at Baynard's Castle, could have originated or sanctioned so monstrous a calumny.

Any missile is good enough to fling at the object of personal aversion. This scandal was, as we have seen, first

---

* Buck, p. 82. † See p. 216, *ante.*

invented by the Duke of Clarence in his envious hatred of his brother, and it formed one of the articles of his attainder. Dr. Shaw's blunder afforded the Lancastrians an opportunity of disingenuously transferring it to Richard, only *when neither he nor his mother were alive to confute the audacious slander.* But were there no evidence to guide us, the question of Richard's turpitude in this matter might well be decided by the balance of probability. He knew the temper of the citizens, and he was far too astute a man to stand forth as the unblushing defamer of his mother's virtue; whilst an alternative and less revolting means of establishing his claim to the crown was not only open to him, but fully matured. A man so cautious and calculating was unlikely thus to overreach himself. " It is rather likely," says a valuable contemporary writer, " that Shaw, being more ambitious than his calling required, . . . was bold to publish his [sermon (?)] in hope of preferment." We should expect, he adds, that if the Protector had set him this work, " he would likewise have paid him his hire; but it is not proved that ever after he favoured or preferred him." *

We may, then, regard this unnatural and most odious accusation as wholly unfounded. The silence of the Croyland Chronicler alone would warrant this inference; but we are on firmer ground in following the contemporary chronicler Fabyan, the highest authority for all matters occurring in London, and who, as one of the civic authorities, was in all probability present on the occasion. His narrative points to the conclusion that Dr. Shaw's part in the nefarious

---

* " The Encomium of Richard III.," by W. Cornewaleys, p. 5.

business has been greatly exaggerated, and wholly exonerates the Protector. He tells us that Dr. Shaw disputed the validity of Edward IV.'s marriage with Elizabeth Woodville; "he shewed openly that the children of Edward IV. were not legitimate nor rightful inheritors of the crown; with many dislanderous words in preferring of the title of the said Lord Protector, and in disannulling of the other to the great abusion of all the audience except such as favoured the matter, who were few in number."* The children of Clarence were cut off from the succession by their father's attainder, and Richard was thus left the sole lawful heir. The case was perfectly met by this argument, which, though it offended many, was less exasperating to the citizens, though artfully designed to inflame their hostility to the Woodville marriage. It harmonises also with the eloquent harangue, which, on the following Tuesday, the Duke of Buckingham addressed to the Lord Mayor and citizens at the Guildhall. He appealed to the popular prejudices by pointing out the evils of the late King's reign; the oppressive taxation; the insecurity of life, honour, and property; the King's immoral habits; the unworthiness of Elizabeth Woodville's family of the honour of elevation to the throne of England. He affirmed that the marriage had been fraught with evil to the country; that it was illegal, the King having a wife alive at the time that it was contracted; the children were therefore bastards, and the Protector enjoyed the only hereditary rihgt to the rown. "Wherefore we have much reason to bless God, that the

---

* Fabyan, p. 669.

prince whose right it is to reign over us is of so ripe age,
so great wisdom and experience; who, though he is unwilling
to take the government upon himself, yet the petition of
the lords and gentlemen will meet with the more favourable
acceptance if you, the worshipful citizens of the metropolis
of the kingdom will join with us in our request, which for
your own welfare we doubt not but that ye will. However
I heartily entreat you to do it for the common good of the
people of England whom you will oblige by choosing them
so good a king, and his majesty by showing early your
ready disposition to his election. In which my most dear
friends I require you in the name of myself and these lords
to shew us plainly your minds and intentions."

At this point the Duke is said to have paused, expecting
his audience to have cried out, "God save King Richard!"
But, if we may believe More, his eloquent advocacy was
unsuccessful; the cries of "King Richard!" by which it was
greeted being drowned by the sobs and murmurs of the assembled citizens. To some extent this testimony is supported
by Fabyan, who says that at his "so sugred words of exortacion
and accordynge sentence, many a wise man that day marvelled
and commended him for the good order of his words, but not
for the intent and purpose." *

The Duke's proposal undoubtedly took his audience by
surprise, and whilst some shouted applause, more were hushed
and silent, "at which," continues More, "the Duke was
extremely surprised; and, taking aside the Mayor . . . asked,
'How comes it the people are so still?' 'Sir,' said the Mayor,
'it may be they don't understand you well.' The Duke, to

---

* Fabyan, p. 669.

help the matter, repeated his speech with a little variation, and with such grace and eloquence, that never so ill a subject was handled with so much oratory." But the assembly remained silent. The Mayor suggested that the citizens might like to receive the proposal through their Recorder, and that functionary was constrained to address them. " Yet he managed his speech so well as to be understood to speak the Duke's sense, and not his own. The people being still as before, the Duke muttered to the Lord Mayor, saying, ' they are wonderfully obstinate in their silence,' and, turning to the assembly : ' Dear friends, we came to acquaint you with a thing which we needed not have done, had it not been for the affection we bear you. The Lords and Commons could have determined the matter without you, but would gladly have you join with us. . . . We require you therefore to give your answer one way or other—whether you are willing, as the lords are, to have the most excellent prince the Lord Protector to be your king or not.' The assembly then began to murmur, and at last some of the Protector's and the Duke's servants, some of the city apprentices, and the rabble that had crowded into the hall cried out, ' King Richard ! King Richard !' The Duke perceived easily enough who they were that made the noise ; yet, as if the acclamations had been general, he exclaimed : ''Tis a goodly and joyful cry to hear every man with one voice agree to it, and nobody say no. Since, therefore, dear friends, we see you are all as one man inclined to have this noble prince to be your king, we shall report the matter so effectually to him, that we doubt not it will be much for your advantage.' " *

* More, in Kennett, p. 499.

The next day Buckingham, accompanied by the Lord Mayor, the aldermen, and the chief of the Common Council, resorted to Baynard's Castle. The Duke set forth eloquently and pathetically the grievances of the people, and prayed the Protector to redress them by assuming the sovereign authority which of right belonged to him, and which the whole kingdom, he declared, with unusual unanimity desired he would take to himself. The Protector replied that, though he knew the things alleged to be true, yet he loved King Edward and his children above any crown whatsoever, and therefore could not grant their request. When, however, the Duke assured him in the name of the Council that they were all agreed not to recognise any of King Edward's line as sovereign, and that if he would not accept the crown they must look out some worthy person who would, the Protector replied :

" Since we perceive that the whole realm is bent upon it not to have King Edward's children to govern them, of which we are sorry, and knowing that the crown can belong to no man so justly as to ourself, the right heir, lawfully begotten of the body of our most dear father Richard, late Duke of York ; to which title is now joined your election, the nobles and commons of this realm, which we, of all titles possible, take for the most effectual ; we are content and agree favourably to receive your petition and request, and according to the same take upon us the royal estate, pre-eminence, and kingdoms of the two noble realms, England and France ; the one from this day forward by us and our heirs to rule, govern, and defend ; the other, by God's grace and your good help, to get again, subdue, and establish for ever in due obedience unto this realm of England; and we ask of God to live no longer than we intend to procure its advancement." *

At the close of this speech there was a great shout of "God save King Richard!" The Lords gathered round their chosen King, and the people departed, every man talking for or against the revolution as he was inclined by humour or interest.†

It did not suit the purpose of the Tudor historians to give prominence to the fact that Richard based his claim to the crown upon the invalidity of Edward's marriage. The atrocious imputation of his having sanctioned reflections upon his mother's chastity, betrays an anxiety to divert the public mind from the one fact upon which he relied as conferring a title to the Crown, and which rendered his nephews harmless pretenders, with whom a man of his strong sense and sagacity was not likely to deal harshly. Their silence did not proceed from ignorance. For although men might be terrorised into silence by the King who had hung the grocer for a foolish jest, no sooner was Edward IV. dead than "the silence broke into a general muttering against his marriage, then into loud and public inveighing against it." All tongues were at liberty to discuss the validity of the unpopular marriage, "the general and common opinion being quite against it and the children." ‡

A greater man than Dr. Shaw had used the pulpit to create a public opinion adverse to the children of the late King. The name of Thomas Penketh, an Augustine friar of

Warrington and a scholar of European reputation, has been linked to immortality by Shakspeare in the lines,

> Go, Lovel, with all speed to Dr. Shaw,
> Go thou to Friar Penker, etc.

Penketh had been educated at Oxford, where "his progress in the sciences and particularly in philosophy and theology was so great that he attained the highest honours usually bestowed by that University on her best divines."[*] His acuteness in scholastic disputation acquired by the study and imitation of John Scotus was such that it has been said that, if the writings of that philosopher had entirely perished, he would have been able to reproduce them from memory. Inducements were offered him to visit Padua, where he taught theology for some years. Returning to England he espoused the cause of the Protector; but he took little part in public affairs save in assisting Richard in proving the illegitimacy of Edward's children, and in this his renown as a scholar and a theologian were of great service.

The question of the previous marriage of Edward IV. is involved in some obscurity. The force of Richard's contention can only be fully realised if we bear in mind that before the Reformation—as subsequently in Scotland—a contract of marriage was valid, without further ceremony, whether ecclesiastical or secular.[†] Consent constituted the essence, and was recognised by the canon law as equally binding as the rites of marriage. Any length of time after their accomplishment marriages could be annulled on the ground of an earlier contract or betrothal, which could only be canonically

---

[*] Chetham Society's Publications, vol. xvii., p. xl.
[†] See Gibson's "Codex."

set aside by a dispensation from Rome.* This, it will be remembered, was the ground upon which Henry VIII. claimed his divorce from Anne Boleyn, and the Ecclesiastical Courts furnished earlier precedents.

The evidence of the pre-contract, which was alleged to have invalidated Edward's marriage with Elizabeth Woodville, was at best unsatisfactory. It rested, indeed, upon the uncorroborated statement of Dr. Stillington, Bishop of Bath and Wells, a member of Edward's Privy Council. But there is no reason to discredit his story. He had been much in the confidence of the King,† and he declared that he himself performed the marriage ceremony between Edward IV. and the lady whose virtue was unassailable. He was the only witness, and to this fact he attributed the jealousy and relentless persecution he afterwards experienced. Eleanor Talbot, daughter of John Lord Talbot, Earl of Shrewsbury, was the widow of Lord Butler, Baron of Sudeley.‡ Sir George Buck writes: "Her beauty and sweetness of disposition drew the King's desire so vehemently and with such

---

* In *Measure for Measure* every reader will remember that the Duke relies upon the pre-contract in substituting Mariana for Isabella in Angelo's bower :

> " Nor, gentle daughter, fear you not at all ;
> *He is your husband on a pre-contráct :*
> To bring you thus together 'tis no sin,
> Sith that the justice of your life to him
> Doth flourish the deceit."

And so Mariana :

> " *My husband bids me ;* now I will unmask."

† When the Duke of Brittany refused to give up the Earls of Pembroke and Richmond, Stillington was employed by Edward IV. to allure them into his power.—GRAFTON, p. 737.

‡ Hence she is sometimes called Lady Eleanor Butler, sometimes Lady Eleanor Talbot.

respect that he was suddenly contracted, and after married
by Dr. Thomas Stillington, Bishop of Bath. . . . . This is
witnessed by our English writers, and veritable Philip de
Comines, in these words : ' The Bishop of Bath and Privy
Councellor of King Edward said that the King had plighted
his faith to marry a lady of England, whom the bishop named
the Lady Eleanor Talbot, and that this contract was made in
the hands of the bishop, who said that afterwards he married
them, no persons being present but they twain and he, the
King charging him strictly not to reveal it.' " *

Several circumstances lend probability to this story of
Bishop Stillington's. Prompted by jealousy and apprehension,
the King, with his vacillating temper, alternately bribed and
persecuted the custodian of his dangerous secret. The brother
of the Earl of Warwick was put out of the Chancellorship that
it might be conferred on Stillington. Subsequently he was
imprisoned, and the arbitrary sentence of the King was only
commuted on payment of a heavy fine. And again, in the
reign of Henry VII., it was proposed to summon him to the
bar of Parliament, to give evidence upon an inquiry into all
the circumstances of the alleged marriage; but he obtained a
"pardon," and the inquiry was abandoned. It is difficult to
believe that the secret was confined to himself and the Protector after the death of Clarence. It was almost certainly
known to the Earl and Countess of Shrewsbury, and the suggestion that the Duke of Clarence's participation in it was a
ground of Edward's consent to his death, is so far probable,

---

* Buck, in Kennett, p. 562. The testimony of Buck in this matter may be
of little value, but he further says of the Lady Eleanor : " the King contracted,
married, and had a child by her."

that it constituted him heir apparent to the throne. That the
Duchess of York was aware of the marriage or contract is
evident, for she urges it as one of several grounds of objection
to her son's marriage with Elizabeth Woodville: "It must
needs stick as a foul disparagement of the sacred majestie of
a Prince . . . to be defiled with bigamy in his first
marriage." * Sir Thomas More gives the name of the lady
with whom the pre-contract had been made as Elizabeth Lucy,
and so Shakspeare:

> *Gloucester*. Touched you the bastardy of Edward's children?
> *Buckingham*. I did; with his contráct with Lady Lucy.

It is not difficult to account for the discrepancy. More's
blunder,† in substituting the name of a person of low birth,
one of Edward's mistresses, for that of the Lady Eleanor is
explained by the care that was taken, after the accession of
Henry VII., to suppress or to pervert the facts, in consequence
of which, says Buck, "historians have much and foully erred."‡
Mr. Gairdner sees in this, evidence of the truth of Stillington's
story. It may be so; but at least the readiness of More and
Shakspeare to take up a perverted story should put us on our
guard against credulously following them in graver matters,
where their information is demonstrably drawn from poisoned
channels. The testimony of Philip de Comines, of Dr. Warkworth, and of the continuator of the Croy land Chronicle,

---

* Buck, p. 120.

† "I am unwilling to charge that great man with wilful falsehood."—HORACE
WALPOLE.

‡ Thus Habington represents the Duchess of York as objecting to Edward's
marriage on the ground of a pre-contract, not with the Lady Eleanor, but with
this Lady Lucy who, he says (as also Holinshed), herself acquitted the King,
on laying to his charge the guilt of a most winning courtship which she hoped
would end in marriage (p. 437).

might suffice to establish the fact of the marriage. But More must have been acquainted with the record on the Rolls of Parliament, which for two centuries after his day were inaccessible to the historian. And it is there recorded that "King Edward was and stood married and troth plight to one dame Eleanor Butler, daughter of the Earl of Shrewsbury, with whom the said King Edward had made a pre-contract of matrimony, long before he made his pretended marriage with Elizabeth Gray." The evidence which satisfied Parliament amply justified Richard in regarding himself as his brother's rightful heir, and his nephew as a harmless pretender to the crown.

The writs of *supersedeas* issued by the Protector did not prevent the assembling of Parliament. They had failed to reach some boroughs and had been disregarded in others. If we consider the physical difficulties of communicating with distant places, the absence of roads, the trackless forests, the impassable morasses, we need not go further for an explanation of the assembly in London of a considerable number of both Lords and Commons. It appears, moreover, from the number of Lords spiritual and temporal, as well as Knights, who were present at the funeral of Edward IV.,* that no inconsiderable proportion of the two Houses would be in London at this time. In spite, therefore, of the writs of *supersedeas* it was inevitable that they would meet, albeit as informally convened. It is also upon record that, on the 26th of June, when, as we shall see, Richard was petitioned to assume the crown, he was accompanied in the procession to

---

* "Letters, etc., of Richard III.," vol. i., pp. 6–9.

Westminster "by welle nere alle the lordes spirituelle and temporelle of this royaume." *

Whether Parliament had been summoned with or (as some have held) without Richard's approval, his reason for issuing writs of *supersedeas* is intelligible, without assuming any antagonism on his part towards the Parliament. It had been summoned for the avowed purpose of extending the Protectorate "till ripeness of years and personal rule be, as by God's grace they must once be, concurrent together." † It has been contended that a Parliament, summoned in the name of a King whose legitimacy was disputed, was not one whose sanction to the assumption of the crown by the Protector could confer a good title. Its subserviency might be relied upon; but this was of no avail if its authority were invalid. There is no suggestion that it was a packed or venal Parliament; as little reason is there to believe that the attempt to prevent its meeting was the work of Richard's enemies. In any case, Parliament actually assembled on Wednesday, the 25th of June, the day for which it had been summoned, Richard himself sitting among them in the marble chair still preserved in St. Edward's Chapel. Attenuated in numbers, it was doubly incompetent to discharge its proper functions; yet seldom has any constitutional Parliament assumed responsibility so grave and so far-reaching in its effects, as was now accepted with hardly an indication of dissent or hesitation.

The prevalent disorders, the intrigues inseparable from a long minority, the prejudices of the old nobility against the Woodville family, were all skilfully seized upon by the Pro-

---

* "Letters, etc., of Richard III.," vol. i., p. 12.
† Chancellor Russell's Speech.

tector and Buckingham, to inflame the fears and the passions
of men who were as ready as their descendants, four centuries
later, to inscribe " Peace with Honour " upon a settlement
fraught with injustice and dishonour, unless influenced by a
knowledge of the fact of Edward's marriage with the Lady
Eleanor Talbot. The members of both Houses of this informal
Parliament, summoned to extend the Protectorate, were already
prepared to confer the crown. Importuning the Duke of
Buckingham to become their speaker, they secured an audience
in the great chamber in Baynard's Castle, then known as York
House. Here Buckingham recapitulated the arguments
which, at the Guildhall, he had addressed to the Lord Mayor
and aldermen, who now supported him in petitioning the Lord
Protector to assume the crown. He concluded his address in
these words :

" And the Mayor, Aldermen, and Commons of this city
of London have all allowed, and gladly embraced, this
general choice of your Grace; and are come hither to beseech
you to accept their just election, of which they have chosen
me their unworthy advocate and speaker. I must therefore
again crave leave, in the behalf of all, to desire your Grace
will be pleased, in your noble and gracious zeal to the good of
this realm, to cast your eyes upon the growing distresses and
decay of our estate, and to set your happy hand to the redress
thereof; for which we can conceive no other remedy than by
your undertaking the crown and government, which we doubt
not shall accrue to the laud of God, the profit of this land,
and your Grace's happiness."

To this address the Protector replied :

" My most noble lords, and my most loving friends, and

dear countrymen, albeit I must confess your request most
respective and favourable, and the points and necessities
alleged and urged true and certain, yet for the entire love and
reverent respect I owe to my brother deceased, and to his
children, my princely cousins, you must give me leave more to
regard mine honour and fame in other realms; for where the
truth and certain proceedings herein are not known, it may be
thought an ambition in me to seek what you voluntarily proffer,
which would charge so deep a reproach and stain upon my
honour and sincerity that I would not bear for the world's
diadem." He then proceeds to declare that the crown was
never his aim, that he will serve his nephew faithfully, and
counsel him for the good of the kingdom, whose "hereditary
right in France" he would seek to recover. The Protector
paused, either by design or accident, when Buckingham interposed with a declaration that the barons and people were
immovably resolved that the children of Edward IV. should
not reign over them. "But," he added, "if neither the
general good, the earnest petitions of the nobility and
commonalty can move you, we most humbly desire your
answer, and leave to elect some other that may be worthy of
the imperial charges; in which (we hope) we shall not incur
your displeasure, considering the desperate necessity of our
welfare and kingdom urges it. And this is our last suit and
petition to your Grace."

Whether the Protector's reluctance was simulated or
genuine, this declaration that another than Edward's son—
and possibly the Earl of Richmond himself—would be raised
to the throne, was the pretext for allowing himself to be
persuaded. It is noteworthy that Sir Thomas More himself

expresses the opinion that on no other ground would he have
inclined to their suit.   He replied :

" My most noble good Lords, and most loving and faithful
friends, the better sense of your loves and most eminent
inconveniences insinuated by your noble speaker, hath made
me more serious to apprehend the benefit of your proffer
and election.   And I must confess, in the meditation thereof,.
I find an alteration in myself, not without some distraction,
when I consider all the realm so bent against the sons of
King Edward.   And therefore being certain there is no man
to whom the crown by just title can be so due as to ourself,
the rightful son and heir of our most dear and princely father,
Richard, Duke of York; to which title of blood and nature
your favours have joined this of election, wherein we hold
ourself to be most strong and safe; and, having the lawful
power of both, why should I endure my professed enemy to
usurp my right, and become a vassal to my envious subject ?
The necessity of these causes, as admitting no other remedy,
urges me to accept your offer; and according to your request
and our own right, we here assume the regal pre-eminence
of the two kingdoms, England and France, from this day
forward by us and our heirs to govern and defend the one.
and by God's grace and your good aids to recover and
establish the other to the ancient allegiance of England;
desiring of God to live no longer than we intend and endeavour the advancement and flourishing estate of this
kingdom." *

Shouts of "God save King Richard!" completed this

---

* Sir George Buck, pp. 20-23.

singular election. The cry was taken up by the multitude outside; and if some gravely asked, what would be the fate of Edward's children? the pervading feeling was one of satisfaction that the perils of a long minority were removed, and not a voice was raised in their behalf. It is noteworthy that this meeting took place at Baynard's Castle, the residence of the Duchess of York. She had become a Benedictine nun in 1480, but, as we have seen, had returned to London on the 5th of June, leaving her religious retirement at Berkhampstead, as we can hardly doubt, from the singular coincidence of dates, to fire the ambition and mould the policy of her son who, "letting I dare not, wait upon I would," had already suffered a dangerous conspiracy to consolidate itself. But whether she recognised Richard's claims or not, it is inconceivable that she could thus have opened her house to a son who had but yesterday proclaimed her an adulteress.

CHAPTER VIII.

SCANT justice has been done to Richard III. in the indiscriminate censures which historians have passed upon his "hypocrisy" and "duplicity" in affecting to decline the offer of the crown. Discarding the romance which Shakspeare has woven into the scene, there is no doubt that Richard did assume an indisposition to respond to the prayer of Parliament which was foreign to his real purpose; and that his consent was withheld until assured that refusal would not secure the succession to the heirs of Edward IV. But there was more of craft than of hypocrisy in the hesitancy which Richard feigned. The former might be surmised; the latter was transparent, but it was part of a consummate scheme. He knew the fickleness of popular favour. The Duke of Buckingham professed to speak in the names of the nobility and commons of England; the Lord Mayor for the citizens of London. Upon these, and upon the people who raised the shout of "King Richard!", now rested the responsibility for that usurpation which, possibly foreseeing that the time would come when it would be charged upon him as a crime, he seems to have shrunk from taking upon himself.

On the 4th of July the Protector was proclaimed King. After the ceremony had been performed he proceeded in great pomp to Westminster, and from the coronation stone* addressed a charge to the judges. Leaving Westminster Hall, he was met at the door of the Abbey by a procession of monks, and the abbot delivered into his hands the sceptre of St. Edward. Whilst the monks sang Te Deum he presented an offering at the shrine, after which he repaired to St. Paul's, and thence, amid the exulting plaudits of the people, to his mother's mansion of Baynard's Castle.

It seems probable that from this time the Princes were closely confined. The chroniclers tell us that when Prince Edward was informed that his uncle had been chosen King, "he was sore abashed, sighed, and said, ' Alas, I would my uncle would let me have my life although I lose my kingdom.' Then he that told him the tale used him with good words, and put him to the best comfort that he could; but forthwith he and his brother were both shut up, and all removed from them, one called Will or William Slaughter only except, which were set to serve them, and four others to see them sure." †

After placing the royal youths in the palace of the Tower, Archbishop Bourchier had sought retirement at Knowle, until

---

* This Stone of Scone, which has been traced by credulous archæologists up to the Pharaohs—which formed the pillow of Jacob and of St. Columba— which was brought out of Palestine into Ireland, and thence carried into Scotland by King Keneth, and afterwards miraculously translated to the city of Scone and used as the coronation chair of the kings of Scotland for eight hundred years before Edward I. carried it to Westminster, when subjected to a geological test can be traced neither to Palestine, nor to Egypt, nor to Iona. Science has ruthlessly torn to shreds every picturesque legend with which the piety of Celt, and Scot, and Saxon have embalmed it, and shown it to be but a piece of sandstone partly prepared for building purposes and cast aside. See Stanley's " Westminster Abbey," pp. 492–500.

† Grafton, p. 804.

he should be summoned to officiate at the deferred coronation of Edward V. When the summons came, it was not to crown the royal youth whom he had sworn to "take and accept for true, very and righteous King of England," but the Protector. His ready acquiescence must be taken as evidence that he was satisfied with the proofs afforded of Edward IV.'s alleged bigamy. Otherwise it is certain that the Duke of Gloucester would have found in him an uncompromising opponent of a shameless usurpation. If the children of Edward IV. were illegitimate, through their father's earlier marriage with the Lady Eleanor Butler, he was free from his oath, and Richard was the rightful heir to the throne. The Archbishop would recall many circumstances which lent colour to the Protector's alleged discovery of the former marriage. Why was Edward's marriage with Elizabeth Woodville clandestine?* Why should he have extorted from Bourchier the oath of fealty to his son if his legitimacy was not doubtful? This precaution may not have been without precedent, but at least it was suspicious. The Duchess of York was now residing at Baynard's Castle, and it is probable that the Archbishop would receive from her lips that confirmation of the bastardy of Edward's children, of which we have seen that she was aware. His belief of the story is not evidence of its truth, but it exonerates him from the charge of infidelity to his oath. We may also well believe that he would see in this setting aside of their pretensions to the throne a security for their safety. Not even faction would rally round an illegitimate scion of the House of York.

---

* Dr. Warkworth writes (p. 3) : "The weddynge was privily in a secrete place, the first day of May."

If the Archbishop had any misgiving as to the security of the royal children, Richard's acts of clemency would reassure him. For these extended to the Queen's most steadfast friends. On the 5th, Lord Stanley was restored to liberty, and made Steward of the Household, an act of generosity rather than of prudence.* Many honours were conferred as rewards for attachment to the Protector's person, and in token of his forgiveness of past injuries. Francis Lord Lovell was created a viscount of the same name. Thomas Rotheram, Chancellor and Archbishop of York, who had been imprisoned for delivering the Great Seal to Queen Elizabeth, had already been released; he was now received back into favour. The ancient Order of the Bath was revived, and seventeen gentlemen received the honour of knighthood. At the same time Richard proclaimed a general amnesty for all offences against himself, and, in proof of his sincerity, sent for Sir John Fogge from a neighbouring sanctuary and publicly extended to him the hand of friendship. More calls this a "deceitful" clemency, and naturally fails to point out that Richard's sincerity was attested by a license issued in January following, conferring liberty upon another member of his family, and by the substantial favours which *eight months after- wards* he conferred upon Sir John himself.† His subsequent severities had no reference to the past, but were occasioned and justified by Fogge's disloyalty.

The motive of his leniency has been assigned to fear as well as to duplicity. "It was neither," observes a reliable

---

* Fabyan sees in this an act of *policy*. "The Earl of Derby, for fear of his son the Lord Strange, lest he should have arrayed Cheshire and Lancashire against him, was set at large."—P. 669.

† Harl. MSS., cod. 433, art. 1662.

contemporary writer. "No; it was a worthy, a kingly humility that would rather abate his greatness than gain it stained with the blood of so mean a vassal, for a crime committed against himself." *

The sagacity displayed in this futile attempt to win a friend was equally conspicuous in the effort, equally unsuccessful, to conciliate Morton, Bishop of Ely. He was released from the Tower and committed to the charge of the Duke of Buckingham, by whom he was conveyed to Breck-nock Castle, to be kept in honourable captivity until he should give some assurance that he would recognise the established order of things.

It was important to keep the public in good humour, during the hours that must precede the coronation. To this end pageants and processions were organised, the most noticeable feature of which was the liberal support accorded alike by the Yorkist and Lancastrian barons, and the entire absence of any attempt at a counter demonstration. The dislike of the Queen's party was shared by many of the Lancastrian nobles, whilst those Yorkists whom it had estranged from Edward IV. now returned to their allegiance to his house.† And there were not a few barons who shared the indifference of the mercantile classes to the Red or the White Rose, desiring only a just and stable government. Thus all parties regarded the new settlement with hope, if not with favour; and the tried firmness, wisdom, and moderation of the Duke of Gloucester commanded the admiration of men

---

* The Cornwallis MS. in the possession of the Duke of Devonshire, p. 9.

† Amongst these William Lord Berkeley, who afterwards joined the Lancastrian party; he was created Earl of Nottingham.

like De Comines, and, through him, of the sovereigns of Europe.

Richard loved pomp and display. Inclination, therefore, and policy combined to induce him to surround his coronation with all possible splendour and impressiveness. On the 5th he made a right royal progress through the City. In his train, we are told, were three Dukes—all that England could boast—nine Earls, twenty-two Lords, and eighty Knights, with an innumerable company of gentlemen. Had Parliament been in regular session these numbers would not have been surprising; but remembering that the majority of members of both Houses had not come to London, and that half the nation was ignorant of what had there occurred, it is evident that the coronation of Richard III., of which this scene was the prelude, had the practically unanimous approval of the Lords and Knights then in London.* And it is, *pro tanto,* evidence that they were satisfied of the illegitimacy of Edward's children. More says that on this occasion Richard created his son—then ten years of age—Prince of Wales. This is inconsistent with the statement of the Croyland chronicler; and the Prince was certainly then residing at Middleham, since it is recorded in the minutes of the Corporation of York, that, on the 12th of July, the Lord Mayor and Aldermen rode to Middleham with a present to the Prince as a mark of their respect and loyalty, immediately upon hearing of his parent's coronation.†

---

* The number of the Lords summoned to the Parliaments of Edward IV. and Henry VII. did not exceed thirty-six, and no less than thirty-four appear to have attended the coronation of Richard III.—Dr. Henry, vol. xii., p. 416, *note.*

† The two narratives may be reconciled by the assumption that the Prince was now created Prince of Wales by Letters Patent, and two months later was invested with the dignity of his hereditary office, at York.

The Duke of Buckingham is said to have outshone the whole company in that day's pageant, in the splendour of his attire. "His horse and himself were dressed in a suit of blue velvet, embroidered with gold in imitation of fire, which seemed even to kindle and flame in the sun. The rich trappings hung to the ground and, being furnished with gold tassels, were supported like a pall by footmen in the most costly dresses. His horse, in this gaudy procession, was taught to be as proud as its rider." * The proud spirit of the Duke revelled in this extravagant parade. The office of High Constable of England was one of great dignity. His place at the approaching coronation was immediately in advance of the King, his duty to carry the sword of state in a rich scabbard. And this office, so congenial to the spirit of the Duke, was his by hereditary right.

The coronation took place on the 6th of July, and in magnificence surpassed anything that had been heretofore witnessed. The fact that the ceremony was performed by the venerable Archbishop of Canterbury, the sacredness of whose office would protect him from all constraint, and sanctioned, as we shall see, by the entire hierarchy of the Church, the Judges, and numerous Barons and Knights, completes the circle of evidence that Richard ascended the throne, not as an usurper, but with the free consent of the nation. *Veli regno cujus rex puer est.* More himself quotes with approval words which had sunk deep into the heart of every reflecting man, of whatever order or party. In this case the warning they conveyed was emphasised by the fact

---

* Buck, p. 526.

of a defective title, and the inevitable calamities which must thence ensue.

The preparations for the coronation had necessarily been hasty. The pages of Richard III. appeared dressed in the apparel which had been prepared for those of Edward V.; the gilt spurs, the blue velvet saddle-housings, which set off the figures of those noblemen who had conspired to deprive that unfortunate Prince of his Crown, had been designed for Hastings, Rivers, and Gray.* Richard chose this opportunity for compelling the proud Duke, who was already claiming the guerdon of his great services, to feel his power. Thomas Howard, eldest son of the newly-created Duke of Norfolk, was created Earl of Surrey, Knight of the Garter, and, *for the day of the coronation only*, High Constable of England. Buckingham was appointed, also for that day only, High Steward of England, involving the less dignified duty of carrying the royal train and occupying a subordinate place in the ceremonial. It was an indignity which he could neither forget nor forgive, and to it his subsequent revolt has been attributed. His *rôle* was to make and

---

* The account of Peter Courteys, Keeper of the Great Wardrobe, contains an entry of long and short gowns of cloth of gold, lined with black velvet and green damask, with other apparel provided for Prince Edward's attire. From this Horace Walpole draws the inferences that the Prince not only walked in the coronation procession, but that Richard intended by that fact to convey his purpose of restoring the Crown to Edward V. when he should have attained full age. But although Morton doubtless informed Buckingham that such was the Protector's original intention, this "amazing entry," as Walpole calls it, does not warrant his no less amazing inference. There is no reason to suppose that preparations for the coronation of Prince Edward were suspended before the meeting of Parliament on the 25th of June. Richard's coronation took place eleven days later, and this entry obviously refers to the magnificent apparel which, though ordered for the boy-King, he was never destined to wear. This view is confirmed by the absence of all reference to the Duke of

unmake Kings at his pleasure, like the great Earl of Warwick. He alone had rendered it possible for Richard to seize the crown, and for this service he thought no reward too great.

The Bishop of Rochester, bearing the Cross, led the van of the procession from the Tower to Westminster. Cardinal Bourchier, bending beneath the weight of his pontificals, and the Earl of Huntington, with the gilt spurs, followed. Next came the Earl of Bedford, with St. Edward's staff, the Earl of Northumberland bearing the pointless sword—emblem of mercy—Lord Stanley with the mace, the Earl of Kent and Lord Lovell each bearing a sharply-pointed sword—emblem of justice—and the Duke of Suffolk with the sceptre. Then, occupying the most coveted posts, came the Duke of Norfolk and his son the Earl of Surrey bearing respectively the crown and the sword of state. Immediately following these favoured Lords, and between the Bishops of Bath and Durham, came the King, richly attired, under a silken canopy carried by the Lords of the Cinque Ports,* the Duke of Buckingham bearing the royal train. But yesterday the Duke had been

---

York, who, being then in sanctuary, was not expected to grace the procession. On the other hand, there is a charge for "8000 boars, made and wrought upon fustian at 20s. per thousand." It is impossible to doubt that the order for this extraordinary display of the cognisance of Richard would be given *after* the surrender of the Duke of York; why then are no robes provided for him? The supposition that he may have been too ill to walk in the procession is inadmissible since we find the following entry, so in harmony with Richard's considerateness: "To the Lady Bridget, one of the daughters of King Edward IV., *being sick,* two long pillows of fustian stuffed with down." The only explanation of the absence of the Duke of York's name in the Wardrobe Accounts is that he may have died shortly after his confinement in the Tower, and the fact concealed in order not to throw a gloom over the coronation festival. See "Archæologia," vol. i., pp. 366–70.

* Adam Oxenbury, Thomas Bayeu, Mayor of Rye, and Robert Croshe who "after the said coronation on the same day claimed in the right of the town of Rye, the canopy, etc."—*Corporation of Rye Manuscripts.*

described as "the glory of the day." No mention is made of his dress on the coronation day, "a further evidence," says Hutton, "that rancour, from disappointment, entered his heart the preceding day." The King was followed by the Queen, wearing a coronet set with diamonds, her brother-in-law, Viscount Lisle, carrying the dove-crowned rod and the Earl of Wiltshire her crown. She was surrounded and followed by a brilliant company of attendants; and it was a curious coincidence—if it was nothing more—that *her* train-bearer was one in whose heart rancour, no less bitter than that which swelled the heart of Buckingham, must have found a place. For she was no other than Margaret Bourchier, Countess of Richmond. The proud mother of the Prince whom she regarded as England's rightful King, might take what comfort she could in the fact that precedence over the Duchesses of Norfolk and of Suffolk was accorded her.

The procession entered the west door of the Abbey, and the choir chanted a royal service prepared for the occasion; the King and Queen being seated in chairs of state. Their Majesties then approached the high altar, doffed their gorgeous robes, and put on others slit open in various places to facilitate the ordeal of anointing. This idle ceremony performed, they again changed their robes for cloth of gold, and returned to their seats. Cardinal Bourchier then approached them, accompanied by the Duke of Suffolk bearing the sceptre, and the Earl of Lincoln the globe, which the Cardinal transferred to the King's hands, and then placed the crown upon his head. The Queen's sceptre was placed in her right hand, and the rod with the dove in her left. As the Archbishop completed the ceremony by blessing the royal pair, the soft strains of the organ reverberated like the echoes of a heavenly choir. A grand Te Deum was then sung by the priests and clergy, after which the Cardinal sang mass and gave the blessing, the Earl of Surrey standing before the King with his sword of state. The Dukes of Norfolk and Buckingham took up their positions on either side of the King, the Duchess of Suffolk and the Countess of Richmond of the Queen, behind whom knelt the Duchess of Norfolk and other ladies whilst mass was being said. The King and Queen jointly received the sacrament kneeling at the high altar, after which the King returned to St. Edward's shrine, and offered up his crown, which originally belonged to the Saint, with other relics. Another crown was placed on his head and the procession returned, in the same order in which it had come, to Westminster Hall. Shortly afterwards the Duke of Norfolk, superbly mounted and covered with cloth of gold to the ground, appeared, to disperse the crowd in the Hall, where the banquet commenced at four o'clock in the afternoon.

At the King's table the Queen, attended by two Countesses, occupied a place on his left, whilst Cardinal Bourchier sat on his right. At three other tables were seated the ladies, the Lord Chancellor with the nobles, and the Lord Mayor and Aldermen. Knights and other gentlemen had separate tables allotted to them. To serve at such a banquet was an honour more coveted than to sit at meat. The lesser honour was accorded to Buckingham, whilst the Earl of Surrey in his temporary office of High Constable, his father the Duke of Norfolk as Earl Marshal, Lord Stanley, Sir W. Hopton, and Sir Thomas Percy served the King's table with dishes of gold.

The Queen was served in gilt, and Cardinal Bourchier in silver vessels. In the middle of the second course Sir Robert Dymock, the King's Champion, rode into the Hall wearing a cumbrous helmet, and caparisoned with all the ornaments of his office. This functionary was a creation of William the Conqueror. The office was first conferred upon Marmion, a powerful baron who held, amongst other manors, that of Scrivleby, in Leicestershire, which bound him and his heirs as royal champions at every coronation to give a challenge at the King's table, and fight any man who should deny his title. On the extinction of the male line one of the co-heirs married a Dymock, who inherited the manors with the office. Advancing to the King's table Sir Robert proclaimed in a loud voice, whoever should say King Richard III. was not lawfully King, he would fight him at all hazards. As he threw down his gauntlet the Hall resounded to the cry, "King Richard!" "God save King Richard!" The challenge was thrice repeated, and louder and louder grew the hoarse hurrahs, when an officer of the cellar brought a gilded cup filled with wine which he drank, and then appropriated the vessel as his traditional fee. The heralds then approached, and after thrice shouting the word "Largesse!" departed with the fees appointed to their office.

The night was now far advanced, when the Lord Mayor, as Lord Chief Butler of England, served the King and Queen with sweet wines, and the banquet was at an end.* "The day

* Stow says that after dinner the Mayor offered the King wine in a gold cup, with a golden vessel full of water. "After that the wine was taken by the lord the King, the mayor retained the said cup and viol of gold to his own proper use." Similar offerings were made to the Queen, who also "gave the cup with the viol to the mayor, according to the privileges, liberties, and

began to give way to the night, and the King and Queen departed to their lodgings."* This, in the words of Sir George Buck, "is a briefe and true Relation of his Coronation, testified by all the best Writers and Chroniclers of our Stories, publicke and allowed, which may comforte the boldnesse of that slander that sayes he was not rightfully and Authentically crowned, but obscurely and indirectly crept in at the Window."†

A ceremony which in magnificence surpassed any upon record was over. Richard III. was the anointed King of England; his title and his person invested with a sanctity which none could gainsay. It is surely amazing that in the face of facts such as these—the assumption of the crown at the request of Parliament; a coronation at the hands of the Cardinal Archbishop, who had formerly been Lord Chancellor; attended at his coronation (and subsequently at his visit to the University of Cambridge) by numerous Bishops, four of whom had also held the office of Lord Chancellor; crowned again, as many writers aver, at York, by Archbishop Rotheram, also an ex-Lord Chancellor, and eulogised by Lord Campbell as the greatest equity lawyer of the age—it is, I say, amazing that Hume should have the audacity to say that Richard's title "was never acknowledged by any national assembly, scarcely even by the lowest of the populace to whom he appealed, and it had become prevalent merely for the want of some person of distinction who might stand forth against him." ‡

News travelled slowly in the year of grace 1483. Had it

---

customs of the city of London in such cases used."—*Survey of London,* Book v., p. 154.

   * More, Hall, Holinshed, Buck, and Hutton.

   † Buck, in Kennett, p. 27.   ‡ Hume's History, vol. iii., p. 284.

been known in London that, whilst the mob at Baynard's Castle rent the air with shouts of "King Richard!", Earl Rivers and Lord Richard Gray were suffering judicial murder at Pontefract, and that the army of 20,000 men, daily expected in London, was, in fact, a company of raw recruits "evil apparelled and worse harnessed," hardly numbering 5,000, the counsels of the Duke of Buckingham might not have seemed the best solution of the distractions of the state.* But the sagacity of the Duke of Gloucester had provided against any such miscarriage, and timed events, undisturbed by apprehensions of discomfiture through the agency of that yet undreamt-of curb to despotism and crime, the electric telegraph. If he had been

> Cheated of feature by dissembling Nature,

he at least enjoyed the compensation of superior strength of mind. Before his coronation took place, every personal or political foe had been either put to death, driven into exile, or imprisoned.

Richard's assumption of the crown has with a universal consensus been called a usurpation. It was so regarded in his own day. The Croyland chronicler distinctly says that he "intruded" himself into the marble chair at Westminster. Yet we must not forget that the country acquiesced in a usurpation in which the sword had no place. And further, as Mr. Gairdner has observed, a declaration of his inherent right to the crown was made, first by the

---

* Fabyan's description (p. 869) of this force, which he must have seen in Moorfields, differs widely from that of Hall and Grafton; but it leaves the impression that the words quoted from Hall in the text describe with substantial accuracy both their appearance and the impression they produced upon spectators.

Council of the realm, then by the City, and last of all by
Parliament, " proceedings much more regular and punctilious
than had been observed in the case of Edward IV."* A
usurpation sanctioned by the Lords spiritual and temporal,
by the Commons, and by a large majority of the people, was
not a political misdemeanour so flagrant as to justify the
censures which history has passed upon it, and which rather
belong to the Parliament which conferred his crown. That
Parliament deposed Edward V. on a side issue. Equally
with Richard it was unfaithful to its oath of allegiance, and
on the same ground, viz., that it had been sworn in ignorance
of his defective title. That being proved to the satisfaction
of the three estates of the realm, the throne became *ipso facto*
vacant. That Richard was the next heir after Edward's
children, is unquestioned.† When, therefore, the Parliament which excluded them on the ground of illegitimacy,
offered the crown to Richard, it was not as a usurper but
as rightful heir that he ascended the throne, and history
is bound to recognise in him England's legitimate sovereign.
" Instead of a violent usurpation we discover an accession,
irregular according to modern usage, but established without
violence on a legal title. The crimes imputed to his youth
disappear ; and in the execution of Rivers, Gray, and
Hastings, if the ultimate object was to secure his succession,
some intermediate mysterious cause will be suspected by those
whose inquiries have taught them to peruse our ancient
historians with extreme mistrust." ‡ The suppression by

---

* Gairdner's " Richard III.," p. 121.
† The attainder of Clarence had disposed of the prior claim of Edward, the
young Earl of Warwick.
‡ Laing's " Appendix " to Henry, vol. xii., p. 414.

Henry VII. of the Act which recited the disqualification of Edward V., is one of the strongest proofs of the validity of Richard's title; otherwise, examination and exposure, rather than obliteration, would have commended itself to Henry's counsellors. It was not even allowed to be read to the House which sanctioned its destruction; a proposal that it should be read, for the purpose of fastening upon Bishop Stillington responsibility for its falsehood, being overruled and stifled by the King's immediate declaration of pardon.*

The lawlessness of the times had called Richard to the throne. A civil war, a descent upon the English coasts by the allies of the ambitious and restless Margaret Beaufort, were imminent dangers. They called for a ruler of tried vigour and ability. These traits, all were agreed, were found in the Prince whom Parliament, however irregularly constituted, had declared to be the sole rightful heir of Edward IV. As yet his public acts had been either condoned or approved by that popular sentiment which condemned Hastings as the agent of Edward's despotism, and the abettor of the Queen's obstinacy and treasonable designs. And if dissimulation and crime had been employed for the furtherance of his ambition, a grateful people called to mind that he had averted all the horrors of a threatening civil war, and that, whatever the defects of his double title to the throne, they were more than covered by the solemn recognition of Parliament.

One of Richard's first objects was to avert a danger which the influence of Hastings had created at Calais and Guisnes. The garrisons of both these towns had sworn fealty to

---

* Miss Halsted's " Richard III.," vol. ii., p. 113, *note.*

Edward V., and they might well become a centre of perilous intrigue. On the 28th of June Richard wrote to Lord Mountjoy, who was in command at Calais, to persuade the troops that they might lawfully violate an oath taken in ignorance, and these two important fortresses were secured. It is not easy to discover the casuistry in this transaction with which Richard has been charged. If he, and the Parliament which offered him the crown, believed that they might lawfully violate *their* oaths of allegiance, because taken in ignorance of the illegitimacy of Edward's children, surely the troops were not bound by an oath taken in like ignorance, and to a pretender already deposed by Parliament.

Lord Dynham was Governor of Calais, and the Articles of Instruction addressed to him by the hand of Lord Mountjoy are found in the Harleian Manuscripts. The Governor is reminded that, notwithstanding the oath of allegiance to Edward V., made "not onely at Calais but also in diverse places in England by many gret estates and personages, being then ignorant of this verraye sure and true title which oure soverayn lord that now is, King Richard the iijde, hath and had the same tyme to the Coroune of England; that othe notwithstanding now every good true Englissheman is bounde upon knowledge had of the said verray true title to depart from the first othe so ignorantly gyven to whom it apperteyned not, and thereupon to make his outhe of newe and owe his service and fidelite to him that good laws, reason, and the concorde assent of the lordes and comons of the royaume have ordeigned to reine upon the people, which is oure said soverayne lord, King Richard the iijde." *

* "Letters and Papers of Richard III.," vol. i., p. 14.

By the same instrument Lord Dynham is confirmed in the Governorship of Calais, Lord Mountjoy appointed to that of Guisnes, and James Blunt to that of Hammes. The circumstances which we have now to relate very early demonstrated the prudence of Richard III., in thus depriving of a safe retreat the only formidable rival not in his power.

When Owen Glendower was defeated by Henry IV. at Shrewsbury, he numbered amongst his followers one Theodore Tudor or Teador, a brewer of Beaumaris who, having committed homicide whilst filling the humble office of shield-bearer to the Bishop of Bangor, had found it convenient to fly to the mountains. This man was the founder of the Tudor dynasty. His son Owen accompanied Henry V. to France, and so distinguished himself at the battle of Agincourt that the King made him one of his esquires of the body. Queen Katherine, who was a daughter of Charles VI. of France, was attracted by the accomplishments and "goodly gifts both of nature and grace" of the young Welshman. On the death of her Consort, she retained his services as esquire of the body to her infant son, King Henry VI. The son of the Beaumaris brewer and military adventurer continued to grow in favour with the royal widow, and ere long they were secretly married.* "Being young in years," says Poly-dore Vergil, "and thereby of less discretion to judge what was decent for her estate she married one Owen Tudor, a gentleman of Wales."

Four children were the issue of this marriage. The eldest son, Edmund, afterwards married Margaret Beaufort; whilst

---

* For which offence Owen Tudor was imprisoned in Newgate and at Wallingford Castle.—RYMER.

the second son, Jasper, was created Earl of Pembroke. Of the many vicissitudes of fortune presented in the annals of the fifteenth century, none is more remarkable than that of the family of the brewer of Beaumaris—the shield-bearer of the Bishop of Bangor.*

The family of Henry IV. in the direct line was now extinct; but that of John of Gaunt had still a representative in his great-granddaughter, Margaret Beaufort, the progenitrix of all subsequent sovereigns of England. Margaret was the only daughter and heiress of John de Beaufort, first Duke of Somerset, who fell at St. Alban's in 1455, and of Margaret, daughter of Sir John, afterwards Lord Beauchamp, whose wealth and large domains she also inherited. The custody of the lands of minors was an important part of the royal prerogative,† and four days after her father's death the wardship of Margaret was granted to William de la Pole. Her education, judging from her accomplishments, was carefully conducted for an age in which writing was deemed an extraordinary acquirement for a female. ‡ She understood French, was skilled in needlework, and, says Bishop Fisher, "right studious she was in books, which she had in great number both in English and in French." The vast wealth of the young heiress, and her remarkable accomplishments, to which Erasmus bears witness, brought her many suitors from noble houses. William de la Pole, now Duke of Suffolk, enjoyed the legal right of disposing of his ward in marriage.

---

* "Appendix C."

† In 1455 the Commons presented a petition to the King complaining that the grants of wards to needy suitors or powerful favourites diminished the royal revenue.

‡ "Memoir of Margaret, Countess of Richmond," by C. H. Cooper, p. 4.

He naturally favoured the suit of his son, whilst Henry VI. desired her hand for his half-brother, Edmund Tudor, Earl of Richmond. In her perplexity, says Bishop Fisher, the maiden not yet nine years of age, asked counsel of an old gentlewoman whom she much loved and trusted. By her she was directed to seek counsel of St. Nicholas, "patron and helper of all true maidens." As she lay in prayer, one arrayed like a bishop appeared, and, naming Edmund, bade her take him. The vision probably indicates that her choice accorded with the wish of her sovereign. But Suffolk stood upon his rights, and contracted his ward to his son, John de la Pole, "for she was held by many to be next heir to the crown." The marriage was, however treated as a nullity when by his attainder all the Duke's rights were forfeited; and at the age of fourteen, Margaret was united to her chosen husband, Edmund ap Meredith ap Tudor, the King's uterine brother.*

Within a year the youthful Margaret was a widow. On the 28th of January, 1457, at Pembroke Castle, she gave birth to her only son Henry. Though afterwards married to Henry Stafford, younger son of Humphrey Duke of Buckingham, and to Thomas, second Lord Stanley, yet, says Polydore Vergil, "she never had any more children, as thinking it sufficient for her to have brought into the world one only—and such a son."

The story of his youth is full of pathos. Born three months after his father's death, from his infancy it was his lot to experience misfortune, captivity, and exile. When

---

* "Life of the Countess of Richmond and Derby," by C. H. Cooper.

only four years of age, Jasper Tudor, his uncle and natural
guardian, was driven into exile, on the accession of Edward IV.,
and his possessions, including the lordship of Pembroke, were
conferred upon Sir William Herbert, a staunch Yorkist, to
whose custody the widowed Countess and her son were
confided. Thus the character of the fatherless boy was
moulded by a mother who, if we accept the eulogies pronounced upon her in a funeral oration by the Bishop · of
Rochester, was possessed of every virtue, but who, judged
by the harsh facts of history, was as unscrupulous as she was
ambitious. It was her first and constant purpose to educate
her son to the belief that England looked to him, as the
representative of the House of Lancaster, to overthrow the
Yorkists ; and through life his character exhibited the
impress of her training.

A side-light is thus cast upon the domestic history both
of the Earl of Richmond and of his more famous son, Henry
VIII. Both equally regarded family ties simply as means
for the accomplishment of an ulterior purpose—a trait which
Lord Bacon may have had in view when, echoing the
panegyrics of his contemporaries, he called Henry VII. " the
Solomon of England." At the age of fifteen the Earl was
attainted, and shared the misfortunes of his uncle Jasper,
until the flight of Edward IV., when the Earl of Warwick
brought Henry VI. from the Tower, once more to play the
part of King, and Margaret Beaufort and her son were
restored to their rights. Jasper Tudor had returned with the
Earl of Warwick. On repairing to his castle in Wales he
found his young nephew a prisoner, but " honourably brought
up " by the widow of William Herbert, who, after creating

him Earl of Pembroke, Edward IV. had afterwards beheaded. Jasper conveyed his nephew to London and introduced him to the Court of the restored monarch. "When the King saw the child, beholding within himself without speech a pretty space the haughty disposition thereof, he is reported to have said to the noblemen there present : ' This truly, this is he unto whom both we and our adversaries must yield to give over the dominion.' Thus the holy man shewed it which came to pass, that Henry should in time enjoy the kingdom."* If this prophecy was really uttered it was unlikely to escape the memory of Margaret Beaufort.

But, as we have seen, the triumph of the Lancastrians was brief. They were finally crushed at Tewkesbury, when the unfortunate Henry with his uncle Jasper, escaped with difficulty. Intending to seek an asylum in France, they were driven on the shores of Brittany and were detained by the Duke on the plea that Henry had usurped the title and estates of Richmond, belonging to the ancient Dukes of Brittany, and of which he demanded restitution.† This being beyond his power, the Earl of Richmond remained the prisoner rather than the guest of the Duke of Brittany for twelve years. His mother had meanwhile contracted a second marriage, probably foreseeing contingencies even less remote than she may have supposed. It is difficult to believe that during these years of separation from her son she led the ascetic life indicated by the panegyrics of the Bishop of Rochester.‡ Sir Henry Stafford died in 1481, and in the following year the Countess contracted her third marriage, with Lord Stanley. Such a

---

* Polydore Vergil, Book xxiv., p. 135.
† Buck, in Kennett, p. 545.   ‡ See Funeral Sermon, p. 11.

union, with the supposed pillar of the House of York, suggests rather a morbid craving for the pageantry and pleasures
of Court life than the love of seclusion, and the practice of
piety and self-mortification which the Bishop extols. For it
cannot be supposed that at this period she entertained the idea
of uniting the Houses of York and Lancaster by the marriage
of her son and the Princess Elizabeth.

A redeeming feature in the character of Margaret Beaufort was her strong maternal affection. In her letters to her
son we constantly meet with such expressions as "my own
dearest and only desired joy in this world," and they reflect
the intensity of affection which finds expression in well-nigh
every action of her life; undue praise has, however, been
awarded to her piety and charity. That she was diligent in
her attention to the forms of religion is undoubtedly true, but
her life was that of an intriguing, ambitious woman. It was
only in her old age, when her son was safely seated upon the
throne—to which his title was certainly inferior to that of
Richard the "Usurper"—and all her ambition was realised,
that she applied a portion of that vast wealth for the enjoyment of which she was indebted to the clemency of Richard,
to the foundation of schools and colleges, for which she has
received more than her meed of praise, as, where her bio-
grapher describes her as the brightest example of the strong
devotional feeling and active charity of the age in which she
lived.*

Louis XI. and Richard III. both claimed the surrender of
the Earl of Richmond, as Edward IV., with better right, had

---

* "Memoir of Margaret, Countess of Richmond," by C. H. Cooper.

done; but all alike in vain. Richard was unwilling to embroil himself with France; neither could he afford to quarrel with the Duke. Hitherto his remonstrances against the protection given to Sir Edward Woodville, and other confederates of the Earl of Richmond, had been disregarded. But in August, the Duke of Brittany despatched George de Mainbier to England, charged to acquaint the King of his desire—"for the great love and affection he bears to the said King and his kingdom"—to send ambassadors "about the feast of All Saints," to treat upon this and other matters. Happily the instructions furnished to De Mainbier have been preserved.* Remembering that Louis XI., of whom the Duke professes to stand in such great awe, was actually dead at the time they were written, and that within two months of that time the Earl of Richmond made his futile attempt at invasion, for which 10,000 crowns of gold were provided by the Duke,† they are of a very compromising nature.

Mainbier is instructed to complain of the plundering of the Duke's subjects by Richard's fleet, and to demand its prohibition under heavy penalties. He is then to represent the great pressure which has been brought to bear upon him by Louis XI. to surrender the Earl of Richmond : that "the Duke has given him no inducement, fearing that the said King Louis would thereby create annoyance and injury to some of the friends and well-wishers of the Duke. In consequence of which the said King Louis gives great menaces to the Duke of making war upon him, and the appearances of it are great." The power of the French King in "men of war,

* See "Letters, etc., of Richard III.," vol. i., pp. 37–43.
† *Ibid.*, xxiv., p. 54.

artillery, and finances," and the necessity, as a result of the
threatened attack upon Brittany, that the Duke would "be
compelled to deliver to the said King Louis the said Lord of
Richmond, and to do other things which he would be very loth
for the injury which he knows the said King Louis would or
might inflict upon the said King or Kingdom of England,"
are to be urged to induce Richard to succour him with men
and money. Four thousand archers and their pay for six
months, with two thousand more, if required, at the pay of the
Duke, is the modest demand not for surrendering the Earl to
Richard, but for refusing to surrender him to Louis. By
compliance the King is to be assured that "he will gain the
Duke and Duchy to himself for ever, and oblige them to
desire and procure, according to their power, his weal, surety,
and prosperity by every means to them possible."

What was Richard's answer we do not know. But in the
following spring he sent one thousand archers to Brittany.
Before their arrival, however, the Breton nobles had risen
against their Duke, and Henry Tudor had made good his
escape.

Meanwhile Richard III. was firmly seated upon the throne
of England; firmly, but not so securely that he could ignore
the fact that the stability of his throne must rest in the love
and confidence of his subjects. Without that basis, the
statue of bronze would have no more stable pedestal than
clay. There were pretenders to that throne, all of whom
commanded a certain following in the country. The mighty
Duke, who had been so largely instrumental in placing the
crown upon Richard's head, was the representative of the
youngest son of Edward III., and was believed—certainly by

Margaret, and probably by others—to have designs upon the throne. Already he was pressing his claims for promised guerdon in a way that was offensive to the King, and threatening to create mutual and inauspicious distrust. Then there was Margaret Beaufort, the Duke's sister-in-law, and now the wife of Lord Stanley, ever scheming for the advancement of her son, with many adherents in England, Scotland, Wales, and France. Again the sentiment of the nation was enlisted in behalf of the powerful claims of the young Princes, before whose eyes the crown had been dangled, as if in derision, whilst they were consigned to the perilous custody of that stern uncle, feared by all, loved by none—if we may believe Sir Thomas More not even by his own mother. Finally there was Elizabeth, their sister, who, after them, was heiress of Edward IV. and of the Woodville family, in whose favour a reaction had set in consequent upon the executions at Pontefract.

Confronted with these and other dangers, Richard resolved to pursue a policy at once firm and conciliatory at home, peaceful but prepared for war abroad. He had formed a noble conception of kingship, and for his rule of government he fell back upon the constitution wrung from the Edwards. To his genius for administration he united vigilance, energy, and caution, with a greatness of soul which ungrudgingly conceded civil and political rights in advance of the demands of his subjects. His aim was now to paralyse the power of factions by the preservation of order, the blotting out of grievances, and the obliteration from men's minds of the very remembrance of the bloodshed in which his reign had commenced.

Early in July a proclamation was issued for the preservation of the peace in London, of which the following are the most material passages :

"Richard, by the grace of God, King of England and of France and Lord of Ireland, straitly chargeth and commandeth, under peyn of deth, that noo manere of personne, of what estate, degre or condicion soever he bee, for old or new quarel, rancor, or malice, make any chalenge or affray, nor robbe or dispoile any personne, nor breke any saintuaries, wherthurg his peax shalbee broken, or any sedicion or distourbance of his said peax shall happene within this his citie of London, or any place thereunto adjoynyng. And in case, peradventure that any mysrewled or mysadvised personne attempte to do the contrary, our said souverain lord chargeth that noon othre personne for familiaritie, affeccion, or othre cause, give help or assistance to the personne soo offending ; but that every personne being present at the place and tyme of such offense doon, put hym in his utermost devoir that the personne soo offending bee broughte and delivered to the maire of the said citie of London for his franchise . . ."

Provision is then made for the protection of the lives and property of aliens, and for the regulation of lodgings, which are to be allotted by the King's harbingers, and the proclamation concludes :

"And to thentent that peax and transquillite amonges his people may be rathre kept and had, and thoccasion of breche of the same duely remoeved, our said souverain lord straitly chargeth and commaundeth that every man bee in his loging by X of the clok in the nyght, and that noo personne othre than such that his highnesse hath licensed or shal licence within the franchise of the said citie or in places therunto nygh adjoynyng, bero any manere of wepon such as has been underwritten; that is to say, glayves, billes, long debeofes, long or short swerdes and buklers, under peyn of forfaitur and losyng of the same and imprisonment of hym or thaym that soo offendeth, to endure at the kinges pleasure." *

Richard did not deceive himself. None knew so well as he that, in the mouths of many, obsequious expressions of loyalty covered hatred or suspicion, or expressed no more than the gratitude prompted by the hope of new favours. There is a curious passage in Hall's description of the banquet on the night following the coronation which suggests that the King entertained considerable doubt of the fidelity of Lord Stanley. "When this feast was finished," he says, "the King sent home all the Lords into their counties that would depart, except the Lord Stanley, whom he retained till he heard what the Lord Strange went about."† "He might," says a contemporary writer, "justly have suspected him (Stanley) and would not have wanted colour to have beheaded him, as being father-in-law to his adversary; yet he only detained his son as a pledge. . . . An evidence effective enough to testify that he desired rather to settle than to overthrow the quiet of this land. What Prince would have done less, nay what King would not have done more?"‡

Richard desired to reign in the hearts of his subjects, his

---

* "Letters and Papers of Richard III.," vol. i., pp. 16, 17.
† Hall, in Kennett, p. 376.
‡ MS. by William Cornewaleys in the Duke of Devonshire's Collection, p. 12.

enemies themselves being witness. Of this he gave many indubitable proofs. By enjoining upon the judges the duty of a firm and impartial administration of justice he went to the root of the discontent which had prevailed during the later years of the reign of Edward IV. He himself took his seat in the Court of King's Bench, because, he said, he "considered it was the chiefest duty of the King to administer the laws." He sent home the 5,000 troops that had been brought from York for the protection of the metropolis. In dismissing the Barons and Knights who had called him to the throne, he admonished them to employ their influence for the "security and defence of the King and of his realm, and for the conservation of the peace."* A message of peace was also sent to Ireland, his son Edward being appointed Lord Lieutenant, with the Earl of Kildare as his deputy. "The King," so ran his commission, "after the establishing of this his realm of England, principally afore other things intendeth for the weal of this land of Ireland." Ten days later, he gave evidence of the sincerity of this declaration by raising the value of the Irish coinage in which great abuses had prevailed.† To this desire of winning the hearts of his people, and to his belief in the possibility of its realisation, must also be attributed that royal progress through the midland and northern counties, upon which Richard and his Queen set out a fortnight after the coronation. Fabyan indeed says that its object was the pacification of the North Country, in which some local and unimportant riots had taken place. But the direction which Richard took, and all the incidents

---

* Fabyan.　　　† See "Miss Halsted," vol. ii., p. 142.

of his journey show that this was one of those guesses in which Fabyan was wont to indulge when writing of events outside the range of his personal observation. As plainly do they suggest that the King's motive was to make all classes of his subjects acquainted with himself, and to win their attachment by his courteous and gracious deportment.

Pausing at Greenwich, and again at Windsor, the royal train went by Reading to Oxford, where the King was entertained by the fellows of Magdalen College; "the Muses," says Buck, "crowned their brows with fragrant wreaths for his entertainment." The King gave expression to his respect for the seat of learning by remitting the fee due to a sovereign on his accession. This was but the first of many favours shown by Richard to the two universities. Resuming his journey towards Gloucester, he rested at Woodstock, where he disforested the Chase of Whichwood, the enclosure of which by Edward IV. had occasioned a standing grievance with the people of Woodstock; everywhere dispensing favours, redressing wrongs, making princely gifts, and winning popularity. Gloucester, whence he took his dukedom, had been true to his brother Edward when besieged by Queen Margaret. The city now received many marks of his grateful remembrance of its loyalty. Passing thence to Tewkesbury, the scene of his great victory, he bestowed a liberal gift upon the abbey, and proceeded to Worcester where he was again received with loyalty and enthusiasm. Warwick was the birthplace of his Queen who here joined the King with a numerous retinue. The young Earl of Warwick, son of the Duke of Clarence, the Duke of Albany, brother of the King of Scotland, with numerous bishops, barons, knights, and ladies, also awaited

the arrival of the King, who held his court for some days at
Warwick Castle, the princely mansion of his wife's father.
Here also he received the ambassadors of Spain, France, and
Burgundy, from which circumstances we must conclude that
Louis XI. had acknowledged his title.* Accompanied by this
numerous and brilliant retinue, the King continued his journey
by Coventry, Leicester, and Nottingham to York "the scope
and goale of his progresse."

The cities of London, Gloucester, and Worcester had
loyally offered their sovereign a benevolence to defray the
expenses of his progress. In each case he gracefully declined
the proffered bounty, saying that he desired the hearts and
not the money of his subjects. At York, Richard was at
home; not unwilling that the southern lords who accompanied him should witness the exuberant loyalty with which
the citizens received him; or that those who had known him
as a fellow subject should salute him as their sovereign.

That the men of York were ready to stand upon their
rights, and to assert a sturdy independence, inconsistent with
that slavish subjection to the Duke of Gloucester which has
been imputed to them, is apparent from an incident which
occurred at the election of mayor in this very year. It had
been reported in the gossip of an ale-house that the Duke
desired the election of one Wrangwysh, who had been useful
to him. The burgesses instantly asserted their freedom of
choice, and though a charge of disloyalty was preferred

---

* Richard had sent an embassy to Louis XI. shortly before his death to
conclude a truce, trusting also to obtain payment of the lapsed tribute. But
this model of morality, who lived only for the gratification of his passions, "so
abhorred him and his cruelty that he would neither see nor hear his ambassadors, and so in vain they returned."—HALL, p. 377.

WARWICK CASTLE.

against the malcontents, it remains upon record that the voice of protest was raised. It was asserted that "the mayor must be chosen by the commonalty, and not by no lord;" that "if my Lord of Gloucester would have Maister Wrangwysh mayor, that then he shall not be."* That the objection of the men of York was to the supposed dictation of the Duke of Gloucester, and not to the individual, is shown by the fact that, a few months later, Wrangwysh was elected to represent the city in Parliament, and in the following February was chosen mayor.† The loyalty of such subjects was not likely to be evanescent, and its exhibition could not fail to be gratifying to the King.

Richard had issued proclamations from Nottingham summoning the nobility and gentry of the north to meet him at York and take the oath of allegiance. His estimate of his exalted position would not have been depreciated by the homage so recently paid to him at Warwick, and as the Spanish Envoy accompanied him northwards he probably designed to impress him with a display of that enthusiasm on the part of his subjects upon which he could nowhere more confidently reckon than at the seat and centre of that virtually separate kingdom which he had so long and successfully administered. Accordingly in conveying the King's directions to the Mayor of York, "to stir up a zeal in the citizens towards his reception there," his private secretary, John Kendall,‡

---

* Davies' "York Records," p. 141.   † *Ibid.,* p. 185.

‡ John Kendall, from the nature of the office he filled, perhaps knew Richard more intimately than any of his friends or confederates, and was steadfast in his loyal attachment. He fell at the Battle of Bosworth Field. The letter referred to in the text is dated the 23rd of August. See Davies' "York Records," pp. 163, 164.

advises that the streets should be hung with " cloth of arras, tapestry-work, and other; for that there come many southern lords, and men of worship with them, which will mark greatly your receiving their graces."*   Miss Halsted shows by a reference to King Richard's Household Book of Costs at Middleham,† that Prince Edward left Middleham for York on the 22nd of August, the very day that the notification was sent to that city of the King's purpose of making a triumphant entry, and there repeating the gorgeous scene which had marked his coronation at Westminster.

The corporation of York were aware of the King's intention to visit the city as early as the 31st of July, from which day there are numerous records indicating their expectation of the "Kyng's cumyng." On the 4th of August it was agreed that he should be met at St. James' Church ‡ by the Lord Mayor and Aldermen in scarlet, the Chamberlain, and all who had been chamberlains, "in reid gownys," the burgomaster, and all who had been burgomasters, with "all other onest men of the cite," in red, and all other persons of every occupation in blue velvet. Heavy penalties were ordered to be levied from such as should fail to comply with these regulations.§ On the 28th it was decided to offer gifts in cups of gold to the King and Queen on their entry into the city, which must have taken place a day or two later. There was no need to propitiate their former governor, who now

---

* Drake's " Eboracum," vol. i., p. 126.

† "Richard III.," vol. ii., p. 157.

‡ On the east side of the mount without Micklegate Bar; its ruins were removed in 1736 in making the present carriage way.

§ Davies' " York Records," p. 161.

returned to them as their sovereign; but the fact that eighteen members of the council headed a voluntary contribution with £437—equivalent to £5000 of modern money—is evidence of the loyalty of York.

There can be no doubt that the citizens would have joyfully welcomed their King without a stimulus, which they were nothing lothe to receive, such as John Kendall's letter conveyed. Yet it must be confessed that the extraordinary enthusiasm, and the emulation which led the citizens to excel all other places in the costliness and splendour of their entertainment, loses something of its significance when we learn that the King had promised to do for them beyond what "all the Kings that ever reigned bestowed upon you, did they never so much." This letter, says Drake, "was wrote in such style as to produce an extraordinary emulation in our citizens to outvie other places, and even one another, in the pomp and ceremony of the King's reception." *

If there is one incident in the life of Richard III. in relation to which all modern historians are agreed, it is that of his second coronation at York on the 8th of September. Yet this alleged fact rests upon no credible authority, is not affirmed by any contemporary writer, and is almost certainly apocryphal. It is one of the innumerable illustrations of the uncritical spirit in which historians have approached this period of our country's annals, and indiscriminately seized upon every unauthenticated story that reflects upon the

* Drake's "Eboracum," vol. i., p. 126.

character of our unpopular King. The sole authority for the story in question is Buck, who apparently relied upon the following equivocal passage in the Chronicle of Croyland. "Here (at York), on a day appointed for repeating his coronation in the Metropolitan Church, he also presented his only son Edward, whom on the same day he had elevated to the rank of Prince of Wales, with the insignia of the golden wand and the wreath upon the head." * It is perfectly obvious that the Croyland chronicler, in this brief passage, summarises popular reports without regard to their authenticity and chronology. Richard's son, as we have already seen, had been created Prince of Wales immediately after his father's coronation. He was then at Middleham, and now, on the occasion of his father's visit to York, he was invested with the insignia of his high rank as Prince of Wales and Earl of Chester. A copy of the Letters Patent by which he was created Prince of Wales is preserved in the Harleian MSS. "Unfortunately," observes Mr. Davies, "the date is not added ; but it is included among numerous transcripts having the general heading, Grants dated 28th of June, *anno primo.*" †

Richard III. was always careful to observe the Church festivals, and he expressly appointed the 8th of September, the day of the Nativity of the Blessed Virgin, for his son's admission to the honourable degree of knighthood. This is attested by the Letters Patent conferring the same honour upon the Spanish envoy, which, it records, was on the same

---

* "Croyland Chronicle," p. 490.   † "York Records," p. 281.

day as the creation of Prince Edward, the festival of the Blessed Virgin, and this was the 8th of September.* Hall is therefore in error as to the date when he says that Richard, indulging in his love of pomp and pageantry, desired to show himself to his northern subjects " in habit royal, with sceptre in hand and diadem on his head, made proclamation that all persons should resort to York *on the day of the ascension of our Lord,* where all men should both behold and see him, his Queen, and Prince in their high estates and degrees." † But not even Hall hints at a second coronation.

When More, Fabyan, Rous, and Polydore Vergil are silent upon an event which must have called forth much animadversion, we can hardly escape the conviction that the inference which Buck has drawn from the words of the Croyland chronicler, and which has been implicitly adopted by nearly every writer, is erroneous. Moreover, the continuator of the Croyland Chronicle speaks only of a day *appointed* for the coronation, but is silent as to the actual performance of the ceremony or the instrumentality of Archbishop Rotheram. These are accretions of later centuries whose only foundation, like many others, are the portentously developed imaginative faculties of writers untrammelled by the testimony of historic records. The alleged fact can only be disproved by negative evidence; but such evidence is absolutely conclusive. No fact respecting the royal visit was too commonplace to find a

---

* *Ibid.*, p. 286. The young Earl of Warwick was knighted on the same day. " Edward, son of George, Duke of Clarence, was made knight at York by King Richard III. with Prince Edward his son and heir, the first year of his reign." —*The Rous Roll*, published by the late Mr. Pickering, section 60.

† Hall's " Chronicle," p. 380.

record in the minutes of the corporation of the loyal borough.
Yet its archives contain not the most ambiguous allusion to
a coronation. The archiepiscopal registry contains records of
all the official acts of Archbishop Rotheram "in a state of
perfect preservation;" these have been inspected, "and
nothing whatever has been discovered in them bearing the
slightest reference to the act of coronation which that prelate
is reported to have performed in York Minster." * The only
objective fact to which historians appeal in support of this
more than doubtful story, is that the King and Queen paraded
the streets of York with crowns on their heads, the Queen
leading by the hand her young son, who also wore the diadem
of the heir apparent of England.†

The splendid apparel in which Richard was arrayed on this,
as on all State occasions, has been the subject of disparaging
comment. To say that it was extravagant is simply to affirm
that it was in conformity with the spirit of the age in which
he lived. If, however, his practice is compared with that of
Edward IV., instead of exposing him to the charge of
excessive vanity, it entitles him to the credit of moderation in
the adornment of his person. The order to the keeper of the
wardrobe at Middleham proves, however, that on few, if any,
occasions, was there more extravagant ostentation than at
the splendid *fête* at York. The reason is obvious. It was
designed to impress the representatives of foreign courts,

---

* Davies' " York Records," p. 287.

† Grafton says that to please both himself and the citizens of York Richard
appeared among them in his royal robes, with the sceptre in his hand and the
crown on his head. The surrounding gentry were invited to York on a specified
day, " *but it was to receive his thanks for their good-will.*"

where splendour of apparel was carried to greater excess. The mandate to Piers Curteis, the keeper of the wardrobe, has been often printed. Whilst it suggests greater magnificence in personal decoration than perhaps any English sovereign has since displayed, a careful and judicious writer has observed that " an examination of the warrant will show that the articles specified in it, though suitable to the processional ceremony which they were intended to adorn, were by no means adapted to the more important and elaborate ceremonies of a coronation." *

On the same day, the 8th of September, the King knighted many country gentlemen, and also his illegitimate son, Lord John Plantagenet, whom he made Captain of Calais, " which increased more grudge to him-ward." † The foreign envoys were then dismissed, and, as Drake records, valuable privileges were bestowed upon the city " without any petition or asking." For a fortnight longer the citizens continued their rejoicings, " tilts, tournaments, stage-plays, and banquets, with feasting to the utmost prodigality." ‡ About the middle of September, Richard left York for Pontefract, carrying with him the good-will of the citizens, whose loyalty—alone of all towns in the kingdom—never slackened; being testified in their city records even when fortune had forsaken him, and when Lancastrian jealousy rendered its avowal dangerous. " The memory of King Richard," says Lord Bacon, " was so strong in the north, that it lay, like lees, in the bottom of men's hearts, and if the

---

* Davies' "York Records," p. 288.   "Archæol.," vol. i., p. 363.
† Fabyan, p. 670.   ‡ Drake's "Eboracum," vol. i., p. 127.

vessel was but stirred, it would come up." * When, therefore, his detractors speak of the slavish subjection of these
sturdy Yorkshiremen, and charge Richard with dangerous
innovation in going through the ceremony of a second coronation, and with exceeding his prerogative in a vain-glorious
display of his newly-acquired authority, doubts are reasonably
suggested of the relevancy of other charges which it may be
less easy to confute.

Richard desired to reign in the hearts of his subjects.
Will he do so? Let us hear the words of an eye-witness of
his progress to the north, written with all the unreserve
of a private letter, whilst the King was still at York.

" He contents the people where he goes best that ever did
prince; for many a poor man that hath suffered wrong many
days have been relieved and helped by him and his commands
in his progress. And in many great cities and towns were
great sums of money given him which he hath refused. On
my truth, I never liked the conditions of any prince so
well as his. God hath sent him to us for the weal of
us all." †

Edward IV., in his mad sensuality, had violated public de-
corum; Richard was punctilious in his regard for morality and
the observances of religion. Edward had been affable in
order to win popularity, Richard was so from the depths
of his nature. Edward had amused some, whilst he scan-
dalised others by a boisterous and undignified hilarity. The
grave, sad face of Richard seemed more in harmony with

* Bacon's " Henry VII."
† Sheppard's " Christchurch Letters," p. 46. Quoted by Mr. Gairdner.

the distracted state of the country and the responsibilities of royalty. And though Edward had been "the handsomest man in the country," who could assume a proud bearing, and look "every inch a king," with the common people the comparison drawn was everywhere in Richard's favour.

Again, let us listen to the words of a contemporary; words that refer not to the people under the glamour of royal condescension and munificence, but to those nobles by whose aid Richard had mounted the throne. "It followed anon that as this man had taken upon him, he fell in great hatred of the more part of the nobles of his realm, insomuch that such as before loved and praised him, and would have jeopardised life and goods with him if he had remained still as Protector, now murmured and grudged against him, in such wise that few or none favoured his party, except it were for dread or for the great gifts that they received of him ; by means whereof he won divers to follow his mind, the which after deceived him." *
Nor were there wanting other symptoms of personal and political enmity indicating that Richard was not to enjoy a reign of uninterrupted tranquillity. Rumours of "great divisions and dissentions" at Northampton had reached him on his journey towards York; but his active measures had prevented any formidable outbreak. It is probable, however, as we shall see in the next chapter, that his tranquillity was rather assumed than real, and that thus early he was informed, though imperfectly, of events occurring in the west which it was politic on his part not to disclose.

---

* Fabyan, p. 670.

Richard went southwards to suppress a revolution, leaving his queen to bear her meek sorrows and virtuous distress. With their young son she retired to Middleham; the gentle mother, in her ardent, genuine love of husband and child, contrasting with the equally devoted but stern, and already storm-battered father, as the placid moon shines over the convulsions of an earthquake.

END OF VOL. I.

WARD & DOWNEY'S NEW BOOKS.

ROYALTY RESTORED; or, London under Charles II. By J. FITZ-GERALD MOLLOY, Author of "Court Life Below Stairs," &c. 2 vols. Large crown 8vo. With Illustrations.

THE UNPOPULAR KING: The Life and Times of Richard III. By ALFRED O. LEGGE, Author of "The Life of Pius IX.," &c. 2 vols. Demy 8vo. With Illustrations.

VICTOR HUGO: His Life and Work. By G. BARNETT SMITH. With an engraved Portrait of Victor Hugo. Crown 8vo. 6s.

RUSSIA UNDER THE TZARS. By STEPNIAK, Author of "Underground Russia," &c. Translated by WILLIAM WESTALL. Second Edition. 2 vols. Crown 8vo. 18s.

PHILOSOPHY IN THE KITCHEN: General Hints on Foods and Drinks. By "THE OLD BOHEMIAN." Crown 8vo. 3s. 6d.

AN APOLOGY FOR THE LIFE OF MR. GLADSTONE; or, The New Politics. Crown 8vo. 7s. 6d.

SONGS FROM THE NOVELISTS. Edited, and with Introduction and Notes, by W. DAVENPORT ADAMS. Foolscap 4to. Printed in coloured ink on hand-made paper. Bound in illuminated parchment, gilt top, rough edges. 12s. 6d.

COURT LIFE BELOW STAIRS; or, London under the Four Georges. By J. FITZGERALD MOLLOY. New Edition. 2 vols. Crown 8vo. 12s.

LEAVES FROM THE LIFE OF A SPECIAL CORRESPONDENT. With a Portrait of the Author. By JOHN AUGUSTUS O'SHEA. 2 vols. Crown 8vo. 21s.

THE NEW NOVELS.

IN SIGHT OF LAND. By LADY DUFFUS HARDY, Author of "Beryl Fortescue," &c. 3 vols. 31s. 6d.

LORD VANECOURT'S DAUGHTER. By MABEL COLLINS, Author of "The Prettiest Woman in Warsaw," &c. 3 vols. 31s. 6d.

AS IN A LOOKING GLASS. By F. C. PHILIPS. 2 vols. 21s.

THE SACRED NUGGET. Second Edition. By B. L. FARJEON, Author of "Great Porter Square," &c. 3 vols. 31s. 6d.

A PRINCE OF DARKNESS. By FLORENCE WARDEN, Author of "The House in the Marsh," &c. 3 vols. 31s. 6d.

O

* 9 7 8 3 7 4 4 6 7 5 2 9 1 *